Tommy Adams was on duty with the Denmark Hill ARP when his brother Sammy, on standby, was called out amid the thunder of bombers heading for the City. Sammy arrived at the post just before a wayward bomb hit and destroyed one house and damaged the properties on either side. The family trapped inside were friends and neighbours of Tommy and Sammy, and they plunged into the rubble alongside firemen to help to dig the family out. It took a tortuous thirty minutes to release them, and every minute was hideous with the sound of bombers passing overhead. Tommy thought the City must be suffering a far worse night than any so far.

The news the next morning was of widespread destruction, and for Sammy, his inclination to sleep late was broken by a phone call at eight-thirty. On the line was Mr Eli Greenberg, the well-known rag and bone merchant of South London, and a long-standing friend to Sammy and other members of the Adams family. His call brought Sammy out of bed and out of the house at once.

Fire Over London

Mary Jane Staples

CORGI BOOKS

FIRE OVER LONDON
A CORGI BOOK : 0 552 14606 4

First publication in Great Britain

PRINTING HISTORY
Corgi edition published 1998

Set in 11/12pt New Baskerville by
Phoenix Typesetting, Ilkley, West Yorkshire.

Corgi Books are published by Transworld Publishers Ltd,
61–63 Uxbridge Road, London W5 5SA,
in Australia by Transworld Publishers (Australia) Pty Ltd,
15–25 Helles Avenue, Moorebank, NSW 2170
and in New Zealand by Transworld Publishers (NZ) Ltd,
3 William Pickering Drive, Albany, Auckland.

Reproduced, printed and bound in Great Britain by
Cox & Wyman Ltd, Reading, Berks.

Fire Over London

THE ADAMS FAMILY

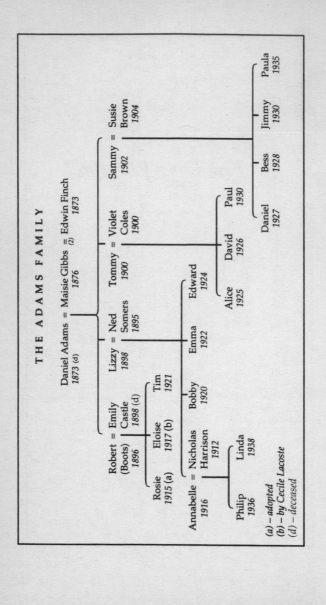

Daniel Adams = Maisie Gibbs = Edwin Finch
1873 (d)   (2) 1876   1873

Robert = Emily Castle   Lizzy = Ned Somers   Tommy = Violet Coles   Sammy = Susie Brown
(Boots)   1898 (d)   1898   1895   1900   1900   1902   1904
1896

Rosie   Eloise   Tim
1915 (a) 1917 (b) 1921

Annabelle = Nicholas Harrison
1916   1912

Bobby   Emma   Edward
1920   1922   1924

Philip   Linda
1936   1938

Alice   David   Paul
1925   1926   1930

Daniel   Bess   Jimmy   Paula
1927   1928   1930   1935

(a) – adopted
(b) – by Cecile Lacoste
(d) – deceased

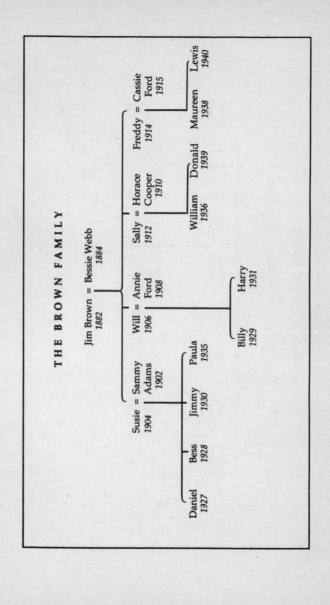

THE BROWN FAMILY

Jim Brown = Bessie Webb
1882   1884

Susie = Sammy Adams
1904   1902

Will = Annie Ford
1906   1908

Sally = Horace Cooper
1912   1910

Freddy = Cassie Ford
1914   1915

Daniel 1927
Bess 1928
Jimmy 1930
Paula 1935

Billy 1929
Harry 1931

William 1936
Donald 1939

Maureen 1938
Lewis 1940

Chapter One

The first Great Fire of London occurred in 1666, by accident. The second happened on the night of December 29, 1940, by design. It began in the late evening, when an initial wave of German bombers, unchecked by the flak of anti-aircraft batteries, flew in over the City and dropped hundreds of incendiary and explosive bombs on the targets below. Hundreds became thousands as other formations followed at intervals in a progressively horrendous attempt by the *Luftwaffe* to annihilate the heart of London and the riverside docks.

Many of Sir Christopher Wren's world-famous churches were reduced to smouldering shells. Miraculously, St Paul's Cathedral escaped the onslaught, although buildings were ablaze all around it, and there was the awesome sight of the great dome silhouetted against a background of leaping flame. Just as awesome was the impression, created by blazing buildings in the docklands, that the Thames itself was on fire.

Hundreds of shops and office buildings were destroyed, and so were a large number of houses and other dwellings on the perimeters of the City. Three hospitals were hit, but casualties there were mercifully minimal. All through the terrifying night, people in public shelters or down in the depths of underground railway stations, felt that inner London was vibrating and shuddering under the shock of high explosives. From the fiery onset until smoking dawn and beyond, the police, the ambulance services, the fire brigades and the men and women of Civil Defence stayed on duty.

The bombs and incendiaries, aiming for the docks north and south of the river, reached out beyond and hit Finsbury, Bethnal Green, Stepney, Limehouse, Wapping, Bermondsey, Lambeth and Walworth. In Walworth, the Elephant and Castle area was flattened, the great Spurgeon's Tabernacle destroyed.

Some bombs were dropped haphazardly well outside Central London. Tommy Adams was on duty with the Denmark Hill ARP, and his brother Sammy, on standby, was called out amid the thunder of bombers heading for the City. Sammy arrived at the post just before a wayward bomb hit and destroyed one house and damaged the properties on either side. As if struck by the hand of a fiendish giant, the house turned into a colossal heap of brick, stone, glass, tiles and wrecked timbers, above which hung clouds of dust. Nothing caught fire, but after a few minutes there was a smell of escaping gas. In the garden, a mound of shattered tiles and torn brickwork formed a barrier in front of the Anderson shelter, trapping the occupants.

Firemen, policemen, and ARP wardens reached the scene. Almost at once the shouts of firemen rent the night, shouts of warning concerning the escaping gas. But the trapped family were friends and neighbours of Tommy and Sammy, and they plunged into the rubble alongside firemen to help dig the family out. Meanwhile, a policeman, using the nearest public phone box, sent an SOS to the local branch of the Gas Board.

Tommy, Sammy and the firemen, all wearing gas masks, dug into the rubble, Sammy muttering ferocious damnation to Hitler. He felt the swine had never been born of woman but had crawled out of rotted woodwork somewhere.

It took a tortuous thirty minutes to release the trapped family, and every minute was hideous with the sound of Heinkel and Dornier bombers passing overhead. Tommy thought the City must be suffering a far worse night than any so far, and said so to Sammy.

'If you'll excuse me, Tommy mate,' said Sammy, heaving at bricks, 'I'm not in the mood for talkin'.'

'Who the hell is?' said Tommy.

The released family, shaken and shocked, were taken care of, by which time a couple of experienced old stagers, arriving from the gasworks, had managed to clear the gas main and turn it off.

It wasn't until the all-clear sounded at about four in the morning that Tommy and Sammy returned home, faces grimy, clothes dusty and eyes rimmed. Vi, out of the garden shelter, took one look at Tommy and ran the bath for him. Susie was momentarily shocked when she saw Sammy's state, but quickly recovered herself and made a pot of scalding tea. While she shared it with him, Sammy gave her details of the incident. Susie said she had

11

a feeling that thousands of incidents must have happened in the City alone. In the shelter with little Paula she had listened to the sounds of German raiders that never seemed to stop coming and going.

'Jesus,' said Sammy, 'everyone could see the City was well and truly on fire. The ruddy sky itself was alight, and you can believe that, Susie. Goering's bombers must have turned the City into hell. Tommy was worried no end, and God knows if our Shoreditch factories are still standing.'

'Tommy will just grit his teeth, Sammy,' said Susie, 'and so will everyone else. So will Mr Churchill. He'll hate what's happening night after night, but he won't give in, even if he's terribly shocked about the way Hitler is killing women and children. He'll pay Germany back in kind one day, he'll use our own bombers as soon as we have enough. Sammy, I believe Hitler and his Nazis are going to suffer a terrible revenge, because I'm sure that one day Mr Churchill is going to roar like a raging lion. And I can't help saying serve the Germans right.'

'You're talkin' like a bit of a lion yourself, Susie.'

'I'm a tiger, Sammy, with claws,' said Susie. 'Now, it's back to bed for you, and you can sleep a bit late.'

'I might just do that, Susie, I'm flaked,' said Sammy, and up he went to bed.

In Berlin, Goering advised his omnipotent Fuehrer that the capital of the British Empire was now, as promised, little more than a heap of rubble, and that Churchill, the warmonger, would be on his knees begging for mercy in a day or so. His

Fuehrer believed him, thus proving himself to be as mad as the March hare. Anyone, however omnipotent, who believed gasbag Goering to that extent had to be insane.

Indeed, Winston Churchill at this particular time was a growling bear of a man, and the last thing he had in mind was surrender to Hitler and his Nazis, whom he saw as a collective abomination. His prevailing moods were all aggressive, his inclinations all directed towards retaliatory bombing raids, the destruction of the Italian Army threatening British bases in Egypt, and ways and means of harassing the Germans in northern France, primarily by newly formed British Commando groups.

The news that morning brought of widespread destruction appalled him but did not lessen his determination to hang on.

Far from it.

As for Sammy, his inclination to sleep late was broken by a phone call at eight-thirty.

On the line was Mr Eli Greenberg, the well-known rag and bone merchant of South London, a long-standing friend to Sammy and other members of the Adams family.

His call brought Sammy out of bed and out of the house.

Chapter Two

At daylight, thousands of Londoners emerged from their shelters to face up to the sight of smouldering ruins. Prime Minister Churchill set out to survey the devastation and to show his bulldog self to bombed-out citizens. He had a message to give them, a promise that Germany would be repaid threefold.

Just after nine-thirty, Sammy was picking his way through the rubble of Lower Marsh, off Waterloo Road. In the grey light, smoke curled and drifted over the riverside, and south of Blackfriars Bridge and Waterloo Bridge, factories were down and houses had collapsed inwards. The police, the fire services, ARP wardens and medical teams were still on duty. Gangs of civilian volunteers were at work in every affected street, searching bombed homes for any signs of people who might be buried beneath mounds of brick, mortar, tiles and timber.

Beside Sammy plodded Mr Eli Greenberg. He was dark, brooding and unforgiving. His yard off Blackfriars Road had been destroyed, the yard that had been his second home and his comfort.

'My life, Sammy, my death, vhat has our happy vorld come to? It's the devil's vorld, ain't it?'

'It's bloody horrendous, Eli, and that's putting it

mildly,' said Sammy. A great flood of residents had swept into public shelters at the first sound of the sirens last night, reappearing at daylight to hurry and scurry back to their houses in the hope of finding them unscathed. There were many that weren't, and people discovering themselves homeless were gazing in shock at their bombed dwelling-places. However, help was being offered by ARP wardens, who were informing them where they could be temporarily accommodated before being rehoused. Church halls and Salvation Army hostels were among the places that could accommodate them and provide them with food and clothing. Fortunately, most children of school age had been evacuated, but a number of very young ones were still in the care of parents.

Mr Greenberg's phone call to Sammy had informed him of the destruction of the rag and bone man's yard, and of the fact that Lower Marsh had suffered badly. Rachel Goodman, a treasured friend of the Adams family, lived with her husband and father in a large flat above shops in Lower Marsh. Sammy arranged to meet Mr Greenberg at once, but before setting out he phoned Rachel. The number, however, proved unobtainable.

Subsequently, he kept his appointment with Mr Greenberg, meeting him at the entrance to Lower Marsh. From there they made their way to the site of Rachel's flat.

The prevailing sense of shock hit Sammy hard then. The flat had been bombed out of existence. It was now simply a pile of rubble along with the collapsed shops below. Smoke issued, lazy and ugly.

Somewhere, a fire engine clanged, and somewhere else the bell of a rushing ambulance sounded.

'Sammy, it's murder, ain't it?' grieved Mr Greenberg.

'Worse, if Rachel and her family are under that lot,' said Sammy, eyes fierce. 'No, wait, they can't be. Rachel's daughters are in the country, and Rachel would have gone to a shelter. Benjamin would have insisted. He's the local chief warden, isn't he?'

'So I believe, Sammy, so I believe,' said Mr Greenberg, his grey-flecked beard stiff, the dust-coated brim of his round black hat casting its dark shadow over his brooding eyes. 'Vhere has mercy gone, Sammy, vhen var like this is made on vomen and children?'

'You tell me,' said Sammy, looking around. People were wandering about, bewildered. A gang of men were at the desperate work of clearing collapsed brick and timber from what was left of a ruined house. A woman in a coat and Wellingtons, a green scarf covering her head, was helping the gang. 'There she is, Eli, there's Rachel.' Sammy made quick strides over the littered street, Mr Greenberg following.

Mrs Rachel Goodman turned as Sammy reached her.

'Rachel?'

She blinked at him. She was covered with brick dust, and her velvety brown eyes seemed to peer through a film of it.

'Sammy?'

'You've had a hell of a night,' said Sammy.

'What's goin' on here, are you trying to dig someone out?'

'Sammy, oh, my God,' breathed Rachel, 'it's Benjamin and another warden. They're under here somewhere, so I was told ten minutes ago. They went in to bring a woman out after the house was partly wrecked. It collapsed on them while they were inside. But they've been heard. They're still alive. Sammy, help me.'

Sammy saw a haunted expression on her dust-stained face. He took off his coat and tossed it to Mr Greenberg. He joined Rachel and the straining, striving men. There was an instinctive urge to work quickly, but it had to be controlled. Care and caution had to govern the removal of every brick, every large piece of plaster, and every shattered timber. Further collapse might prove fatal. Not many hours since, Sammy had helped to clear rubble trapping a family in their shelter on Denmark Hill. That had been a simple if muscle-straining exercise. Here, in Lower Marsh, the clearance had to be far more deliberate, the lifted rubble passing from hand to hand. Rachel, feverish in her need to have Benjamin emerge alive, was white beneath her mask of dust, and Sammy knew why she had a haunted look. She was blaming herself for what had happened to Benjamin. He had wanted to take her and their daughters as immigrants to America. Rachel was against the move, and asked Sammy and Boots to help her. They gave her some reassurance, but refrained from any positive act that would mean interfering in the affairs of a husband and wife. In the event,

Benjamin's application was turned down, but Rachel thought her plea to Sammy and Boots had borne fruit. Benjamin had taken the disappointment like a man, and when war came he volunteered immediately for service with the ARP.

Rachel had spent last night in a public air raid shelter, and of all her family only Benjamin, on ARP duty, had been in danger. Her daughters, Rebecca and Leah, were safe in the West Country. Her father, the esteemed Isaac Moses, was in the Middle East with a deputation of international Jewry seeking permission from Mussolini to enter Italy for an audience with the Pope. The intention was to try to persuade the Pope to intercede with Germany on behalf of persecuted Jews.

'It's my fault Benjamin's under here, Sammy,' Rachel breathed distraughtly, as Sammy helped her to lift a large joist that had been carefully uncovered.

'Rachel, no,' said Sammy. 'There's no blame on anyone. Boots couldn't really do anything, nor me. The application was turned down because the American Embassy was being overwhelmed, wasn't it? Wasn't that what they said? Yes, of course it was, you quoted their letter to me.' Sammy was taking brick after brick from her as she took them from the man in front of her. He threw each brick aside.

'Sammy, I still feel it's my fault.'

'Well, it's not, so stop fretting,' said Sammy. 'Things like this are always waitin' to happen. Life's like that, Rachel, there's always happenings we don't bargain for and can't prevent, like Em'ly's death. I talked to Benjamin a couple of times about

18

the war, about what we could expect from Hitler and his mob, and it struck me each time that Benjamin wanted to see the war through here, not in America, that he'd made up his mind it was what he ought to do.'

'You believe that, Sammy, you really believe it?' said Rachel, bending to the work.

'All the way,' said Sammy. The neighbourhood was alive with activity, gangs of men specially recruited by the Government at work in other streets, and the collective sound was gravelly, grating and harsh. 'Put any blame out of your mind, Rachel. You've got more than enough to worry about. It's costing us, this war, but it's not goin' to cost you Benjamin. We'll get him out.'

'Sammy, thank you for coming—'

'Hold up, hold up!' It was a husky shout from the foremost man, up to his waist in a cavity. 'Don't move, anyone, don't touch anything. I think we've reached 'em. I'm 'earing something. For Christ's sake, tread careful and stay quiet.' He stooped low. 'You there, mate? You there?'

A faint voice reached straining ears.

'Yes – yes – all three of us.'

'Good on yer, mate. Alive and well, are yer?'

'I am meself.' The voice was dry and cracked. 'But Benjy Goodman and the woman are under a beam. They're alive, but can't move. One end of the beam's buried under bricks and plaster.' The trapped man coughed. 'If you could clear it, I could 'elp you lift the beam. I'm Warden Brooks, Dave Brooks.' Another cough. 'Could you let me wife know?'

'I'm 'ere, Dave, I'm 'ere!' shouted a middle-aged woman.

Warden Dave Brooks made an effort. His cracked voice rose from the depths.

'That's me girl. Go 'ome and put the kettle on.'

His wife emitted a short, slightly hysterical laugh.

The man in the cavity, still stooping, his eyes searching the dusty depths, said, 'You 'old on now, Mr Brooks, we'll get you all out. Don't move, just leave it all to us. Like a mug of water?'

'I bloody would,' said Warden Brooks, 'for Benjy and the lady.'

The water was brought from a standing pail while the gang sized up the situation around the cavity, Rachel tense and hollow-eyed, Sammy looking on and waiting. The enamel mug was handed down to Warden Brooks. Then the men set about the task of clearing more rubble with extreme care, Sammy and Rachel helping with the disposal of the bricks and mortar. Mr Greenberg also lent a hand.

It took a great deal of time to widen the cavity and to permit the lifting of the large joist that was pinning down Benjamin and the woman. That was done with everyone holding their breath, but once accomplished things were easier. Warden Brooks was brought out first, his face and body bruised and racked, but no bones broken. Ambulance men and women were on the spot by then, and the release of Benjamin and the woman was effected with professional care. They were smothered in dust. Benjamin, just conscious, was quietly moaning, the woman in a similar state. Rachel and Sammy watched as they were stretchered into an ambulance to be taken to King's College Hospital. Nearer hospitals were all overwhelmed with casualties. Rachel asked if Benjamin was seriously hurt.

'Can't say, lady, not until he's been examined.' The ambulance man could have said he knew both legs were broken, but refrained. 'Don't you worry now, he'll be okay.'

It distressed Rachel that there was no room for her in the ambulance, for she naturally wanted to go with Benjamin. Further, she now had to face the fact that with her home destroyed, she had nothing except her handbag and the clothes she was wearing. But her immediate need, she said, was to get to the hospital in the wake of her husband.

'I'll get you there,' said Sammy. 'Look, things could be worse.'

'Just now,' said Rachel, 'tell me what's worse than a badly injured husband and no home.'

'Not a good question, Rachel,' said Sammy gently.

'Rachel, I have a home,' said Mr Greenberg, 'and room alvays for a friend.'

'Every Adams family's got a home and plenty of room,' said Sammy. 'I'd be happy to—' He broke off and paused. The three of them were all drinking hot tea, supplied by the emergency services. Sammy knew he and Susie could easily accommodate Rachel. All their children were in the country, except for little Paula, their youngest. But should he offer to have Rachel? Would it work, Susie and Rachel together under the same roof? Because of the circumstances, Susie would supply any amount of kindness and help, but undercurrents would develop for certain. A happier thought occurred to him. There was one person who'd give Rachel a very warm welcome. 'Rachel, you need a roof, a bed and comfortin' company, and I know where you'd get all that and more. With my dear old Ma. She's short of company, with all the family away in the Army except me stepdad, and she'll fall over herself at havin' you around.'

'That's a kindness, Rachel, ain't it?' said Mr Greenberg.

'Sammy,' said Rachel, her still lustrous looks drained of their richness, 'how can I—'

'I don't have to remind you, do I, Rachel, how long you've been a friend of the fam'ly?' said Sammy.

'My life, Sammy, such a reminder would shame me,' said Rachel. 'There's no-one I would more gladly turn to than your mother, but shouldn't you ask her first?'

'If my old Ma thought I'd do that, ask her first, she'd make my ears ring,' said Sammy. 'She's the Good Samaritan's first cousin. And might I point out you'll be fairly close to King's College Hospital? You'll be able to drop in on Benjamin daily if you cross Matron's hand with a good luck charm. I know it's not good, his condition, but they'll get him on his feet again, and meanwhile you can put the flags out on account of him provin' himself a bit of a hero. All right now? Come on, then, I'll drive you to the hospital first, then to the number one fam'ly home, my dear old Ma's castle.'

'Sammy, bless you,' said Rachel huskily. 'One can

be left with nothing and then discover one has everything.'

'In the vay of treasured friendship?' said Mr Greenberg. 'For sure, Rachel, ain't it, my dear?'

'Eli, I'll come and see you in a day or so,' said Sammy, 'and we'll see what can be done about gettin' you a new yard.'

'Sammy, I can get a hundred new yards,' sighed Mr Greenberg, 'but who vants yards on vhich bombs will drop?'

'You need a yard well away from the City,' said Sammy. 'You push off home now and cheer up your missus.' He cast another look around and shook his head. 'Jesus, what a mess. Come on, Rachel, so long, Eli.'

'So long, Sammy,' said Mr Greenberg. 'Ve ain't down and out yet, eh? Vell, Benjamin might be down a bit just now, Rachel, but my life, a hero, ain't he?'

'Goodbye, Eli, thank you so much for being here,' said Rachel.

Smoke, ash and dust clouds drifted above the City of London as Sammy and Rachel parted from Mr Greenberg.

Chapter Three

There was a happening elsewhere that morning.

'Oh, no!' gasped Sergeant Eloise Adams of the ATS. She was on the crown of the road, the bend too unexpectedly sharp, the oncoming car too far over, she thought. Fender made aggressive contact with fender, and there was a frightful sound of metal cracking and mangling. Both cars stopped.

'That's done it,' said Sergeant Fowler, instructor. 'Did you have to pick Major Lucas's chariot, Sergeant Adams?'

Bombardier Wright, Major Lucas's driver of the moment, glared at Eloise through his windscreen. In the back sat Major Lucas himself, with his adjutant, Captain Pearson. Bombardier Wright made a move to get out. The Major spoke to him and got out himself, closing the door with what Eloise thought was ominous deliberation. An Anglo-French young lady of twenty-three, she remained sitting at the wheel with her teeth clenched, determined not to admit she'd been at fault. In the Army, never admit anything that would put you at a disadvantage. Her English father had given her that piece of advice.

'The Major wants us out,' said Sergeant Fowler.

'I hope he's not going to play God,' said Eloise,

and she and her instructor alighted. Major Lucas, tall, broad-shouldered and as rugged as a heavyweight boxer, was inspecting the damaged fender. The country lane, winding, was strewn with the leaves of winter on this damp and cloudy day in late December.

'Damn me,' said Major Lucas, blue eyes piercing, cane in his gloved hand and an expression verging on the ferocious. Along with other battery commanders and the regiment's CO, he had not enjoyed a very good time yesterday at Brigade Headquarters. He didn't like Brigadier Bottomley, for a start, and nor did he like his theories on how to get re-formed artillery regiments trained to cope with German panzers. The man was an idiot. 'Is this piece of mayhem your doing, Sergeant Adams?'

'Sir, I refuse absolutely to take the blame,' said Eloise, and Sergeant Fowler blinked.

'As your instructor, it's Sergeant Fowler's fault, is it?' growled Major Lucas.

'Certainly not, sir,' said Eloise, never a young lady who could be made to feel inferior. 'I accuse your driver of being too far over, sir.'

Sergeant Fowler swallowed. Major Lucas regarded Eloise menacingly.

'Would you like to repeat that, Sergeant Adams?'

'Yes, sir. I accuse your driver of being too far over.'

'Damn my boots, you've said it twice. Sergeant Fowler, what's your explanation?'

'Very sharp bend, sir, very unfortunate,' said Sergeant Fowler.

'So are you,' said the Major. 'You've been guilty

of dereliction of duty while in charge of a learner-driver. Report to the BSM and let him know that. Sergeant Adams, as soon as you've managed to drive this mangled heap back to the workshop, report to me.'

'Very good, sir,' said Eloise.

'Now back off,' said Major Lucas.

'I'll do that,' said Sergeant Fowler to Eloise.

'You won't,' said Major Lucas, 'you'll instruct your pupil, and God help you both if you allow her to back the car into the ditch.'

Really, what an uncivilized brute, thought Eloise, I'll begin to wish I'd never agreed to be posted to his battery. But she and Sergeant Fowler got back into the car.

'Reverse gear, Sergeant Adams,' he said, 'and steady as you go.'

'I'll show him,' said Eloise, and under the glowering gaze of Major Lucas she performed a reverse movement that untangled the cars, although with a wrenching sound.

'Bit noisy,' commented Sergeant Fowler, 'but don't worry.'

'Who is worrying? I am not,' said Eloise, slowly continuing the movement.

'We'll only get a caution, that's all,' said Sergeant Fowler. 'And a few swear words. That's it, stop now and let them pass.'

Major Lucas re-entered his car, a Morris. His driver started up, and the car swept by. Eloise then did a three-point turn and followed the Morris back to the camp. There, she reported the happening to her immediate superior, Subaltern Rosemary

26

Forbes, an attractive woman with a sense of humour, who laughed.

'Excuse me, ma'am, it's no joke,' said Eloise.

'Bashing the Major's car? It's made my day,' said Subaltern Forbes. 'Wait till I tell Captain Miller.' Captain Helen Miller was the senior officer of the attached ATS unit. 'It'll make her day too.'

'Then I'm pleased for both of you, ma'am,' said Eloise, who scorned Captain Miller, a large-boned county type almost six feet tall with a way of talking through enlarged tonsils.

'No sauce,' said Subaltern Forbes. Sergeant Adams was very much an individualist, with quite a tongue on her, as well as an air of being above all the fussy rules and regulations of military life. 'All right, go and report to Major Lucas, but don't say anything that'll make him throw the book at you.'

Eloise made her way to his office, thinking it might be like reporting to a clap of thunder. She had met him at Ramsgate at the beginning of June when he landed from one of the little ships during the evacuation of Dunkirk. He was a growling bear of a man, disgusted by the defeat of the BEF and its misuse of tanks. But he was impressed by the help she gave him, and she felt stimulated by his aggressive determination to let the brass-hats know what he thought of the BEF's mistaken tactics. He told her he was going to get her posted for admin. duties to his battery, and had done so in August, when he told her she would become his official driver. The extensive camp, quartering the regiment of three gun batteries, was in the Peak District, the terrain as rugged as he was. The regiment at that time was still in the process of being reorganized and made up to strength following the army's defeat in France. It was also awaiting delivery of new guns and new equipment and the admin. work involved was such that not until three weeks ago had Eloise begun intermittent driving lessons. By that time she'd become fretful at the amount of hours she spent at a desk, especially as Major Lucas did not seem to realize she was an exceptional young woman compared to the rest of the ATS personnel. Of course, there were occasions when he did compliment her on her efficiency as a member of the admin. staff, but that only made her feel she could be anybody. Well, everyone in admin. was efficient. They had to be, or he'd have sent them packing.

She knocked.

'Come.'

She entered. Major Lucas was sitting at his desk, scribbling on a pad. He looked up. She advanced and saluted, her peaked cap slightly tilted, which was against the regulations. She knew that, and so did he, but there it was, slightly tilted and giving her a bit of French dash. Her oval features were set in a classical mould, dark lashes framing grey eyes with a hint of blue, eyes that could be either haughty or beguiling. She had known several handsome admirers, but without ever feeling she wished to commit herself to any of them.

'Sir?' she said, chin up, expression close to being defiant. It brought a glint to his blue eyes. He had a small jagged scar just above his right eyebrow, the result of a wound taken during the retreat to Dunkirk.

'Yes, Sergeant Adams?'

'I'm reporting, sir, as ordered.'

'With your nose in the air, I see,' he said.

'Sir?' she said aloofly.

'As usual,' he said. That was for her impertinent air. He couldn't have cared less about her cap.

'I cannot comment, sir,' she said.

'You would if you thought I'd let you get away with it,' he said.

Really, what a difficult man he was, thought Eloise, always producing arguments that she couldn't take up because of his rank.

'I cannot comment on that, either, sir,' she said.

'Why not?' he asked.

'I don't wish to be executed by a firing squad, sir.'

Major Lucas sat back. Only with a struggle did he keep his face straight.

'I see,' he said, 'you've got hard words to say about me, have you, Sergeant Adams? What are they?'

'About the accident, sir. I deny—'

'Never mind that, I accept your instructor was at fault,' he said.

'I deny it, sir,' said Eloise. 'If I may be allowed to say so, it was neither his fault nor mine, and really, with bombs dropping on London every night and killing people and putting my relatives at terrible risk, I'm surprised at so much fuss, especially as I'm now already a very good driver. You will see that for yourself when I become your regular driver in place

29

of Bombardier Wright, who seems to have careless moments.'

'Ye gods,' said Major Lucas, 'I can't believe my ears. How would you like me to report you to Captain Miller, with a recommendation to reduce you to the ranks for impertinence?'

'I should hope, sir, that you would remember you asked me to say what I thought.'

'I didn't ask you to give me a lecture, Sergeant Adams. Damn me if you don't take the biscuit.' A helpless little grin touched the Major's mouth. What a Tartar she was, afraid neither of Mars nor his gruesome war machines, and intimidated neither by sergeant-majors nor demanding officers. 'Are there any others like you in your family?'

'Of course not,' said Eloise, 'I am the only one who is myself.'

'Just as well, I'd say,' said Major Lucas. He conceded, however, that she had good reason to worry about the air raids, for her stepmother had been among the fatal victims of a daylight raid. She had been upset for many days after attending the funeral. 'No, forget I said that, Sergeant Adams.'

'Very well, sir,' she said. 'But I would like you to know I take after my English father. We are both very agreeable people.'

'What can I say to that?' asked Major Lucas. He knew her father was on the staff of General Sir Henry Simms. She hadn't failed to let him know that. 'Well, I will say that as soon as you receive your certificate, you'll become my official driver.'

'I'm confident, sir, of being an improvement on Bombardier Wright,' said Eloise.

'Competence, Sergeant Adams, is all I ask for,' he said. He had talked with Captain Miller about her, and they both agreed she was officer material. Captain Miller, however, insisted she would not recommend Sergeant Adams until she had acquired a proper regard for the King's Regulations. Major Lucas made no comment on that, since he knew that under certain circumstances he himself was inclined to dump the more pettifogging rules and regulations. 'Hitler's Germans are cursedly competent, and we've got to match them.'

'Very well, sir,' said Eloise, 'I shall be as cursedly competent as I can.'

'You will, will you?'

'Sir, I only—'

'Repeated what I said? I know that, I heard you.' Major Lucas had a distinct feeling she often got the better of him. It didn't upset him. He was more inclined to laugh. 'Sometimes, Sergeant Adams, I'm not sure what to do with you.'

'Really, sir, I know what my duty is, to do the best I can for my father's country and my mother's country,' said Eloise, who had volunteered for the ATS at the expense of her job with the French Embassy.

'I believe you,' he said. He knew she was quick, efficient and unflappable. She simply had an over-done air of self-importance. From what she had said on some occasions this seemed to stem from her belief that as the daughter of a French mother and an English father she was exceptional. She had more than once said her English father was very exceptional, and that she took after him. There were no half-measures about Sergeant Eloise Adams's belief in herself. 'However, don't always say what you think to your officers or mine. I'm less touchy myself.'

'I cannot comment, sir.'

'Not much you can't,' he said.

'Really, sir, you make it most awkward for me to say anything at all.'

'Damned if I've noticed it,' he said.

'Am I allowed to ask you not to swear at me, sir?' she said.

'Swear? Who's swearing? I'm the soul of moderation. However, conduct yourself blamelessly, and perhaps sometime in the future you'll be recommended for a commission. It's entirely up to you.'

Eloise, who naturally thought herself worth a commission, said, 'I always conduct myself blamelessly.'

Major Lucas let the ghost of a smile touch his mouth.

'If Captain Miller comes to be convinced of that,' he said, 'you'll get your recommendation, and I'll back it up. It might mean we'll lose you, but it wouldn't be fair to stand in your way.'

'Sir, what do you mean, the battery will lose me?' asked Eloise, feeling alarmed.

'If the selection board finds in your favour, it's very unlikely you'll return to us. It's not the usual thing to post a newly-commissioned ATS officer back to her previous unit.'

'Well, I object to that silly rule very much,' said Eloise, 'and won't obey it.'

'Great balls of fire,' said Major Lucas, 'have I got a French prima donna dancing a fandango in front of my eyes?'

'I'm Anglo-French, sir, with a British passport,' said Eloise, 'and I won't accept a commission unless I'm allowed to return to this battery.'

'Did you say you won't, Sergeant Adams?'

'Yes, sir, I did,' said Eloise.

'Jesus give me strength,' he said.

'Amen,' said Eloise.

Major Lucas strangled a cough and looked for a moment as if he was going to give up. Then he said, 'It could be arranged.'

'Then really, sir, I don't know why you're arguing,' said Eloise.

'I thought all the arguments were coming from you, Sergeant Adams,' he said.

'I'm sure you are mistaken,' said Eloise, her English always precise, but very fluent.

'I'll pass that over,' said Major Lucas. 'That's all. Dismiss, Sergeant Adams.'

'Thank you, sir,' said Eloise. She saluted and left. Major Lucas smiled. His temper had cooled. Sergeant Eloise Adams was always a star turn.

He smiled again, then picked up his cane and left his office. He had an appointment with his gunnery officers and their gun crews on the firing range in the bleakest area of the moors. He was likely to instil the fear of God into any gunner not putting one hundred and one per cent into his training programme. He was also likely to do some swearing about the fact that new heavy artillery had still not arrived, although he knew the British Army in Egypt had prior claim at the moment.

Chapter Four

At home, Chinese Lady wasn't quite sure whether
to go out and do some shopping or to stay and
listen to the wireless. Not that she was attached to
the wireless. Far from it. In her opinion, nothing
good had come out of it since her husband Edwin
bought it some years ago. Right from its inception,
it acquired the habit of delivering the kind of news
that upset her, more particularly when it began to
refer almost daily to that loud shouting German,
Adolf Hitler, the most aggravating man Chinese
Lady had ever imagined. She felt from the start that
he'd cause trouble, and she said so, repeatedly. But
no-one took any notice of her, of course, and now
look, the country was at war with Germany again
and the blessed wireless was more upsetting than
ever, especially about these air raids.

In Chinese Lady's opinion, it had only twice
given out welcome news since the beginning of the
war, first about the amazing Dunkirk evacuation,
and then when it announced details of a daring
escape from France by a British soldier. The soldier
was her grandson Bobby, and he'd made his escape
with the help of a young Frenchwoman. They had
actually spoken on the wireless, and Chinese Lady
could hardly believe what she was hearing. It was as

if the contraption had turned over a new leaf.

It hadn't. It soon went back to its dismal ways. This morning, for instance, it was going on and on about how shocking last night's air raid had been. It was almost mesmerizing her with its gloominess. She and her husband Edwin had been in their Anderson shelter nearly all night, which she heartily disliked. No-one had the right to deliberately drop bombs on innocent civilians and make others spend their nights in uncomfortable shelters. Trust Hitler to act like a heathen. He was as much responsible for the death of her daughter-in-law Emily, during a daylight air raid in August, as the Germans who dropped the fatal bomb. The Lord would find Hitler out one day.

Chinese Lady, now sixty-four but with very few tints of grey in her brown hair, still had a decidedly Victorian approach to life. But although she could be old-fashioned and admonishing, she had never expressed hate for anyone, being inclined to put the worst faults of people down to unfortunate upbringings. She had, however, found exceptions in Hitler and his clique of German warmongers. She not only hated them, she seriously questioned the Lord's judgement in allowing them to be born. I never ever believed the Almighty could make that kind of mistake, she had said to her eldest son Boots just before his last home leave ended. Well, perhaps even the Almighty sleeps at times, perhaps some mistakes creep past Him when He's tucked down and dreaming of His favourite angels, said Boots. I hope you're not being irreverent, said Chinese Lady. No, just finding an excuse for our

Maker, said Boots. Well, something must have gone wrong when He made that German lot, said Chinese Lady, they're downright evil and ought to be put where they could only be evil to each other. Say in a lifeboat without food and water? suggested Boots. Chinese Lady asked if that would finish them off. Yes, said Boots, that lot are the kind who'd happily eat each other, and they'd dine on Goering, the fat one, first.

Hitler and his warmongers were responsible for so many of her family being in uniform. There was Boots to start with, and both his daughters, Rosie and Eloise. And his son Tim. Then there was Lizzy's eldest son Bobby, her son-in-law Nick Harrison, and her daughter Emma's fiancé, Jonathan Hardy. As if that wasn't enough, Susie's brother Freddy and her brother-in-law Horace Cooper were also serving.

As for these nightly air raids, people weren't safe anywhere in London, not even in the Denmark Hill area or places like Norbury and Streatham. She and her husband Edwin were still grievously upset about Emily's death. But life had to go on, and they were doing all they could to come to terms with the loss, like the rest of the family. It was a kind of consolation knowing that Lizzy's younger daughter Emma, eighteen, was to marry that very upstanding Sussex-born young man, Jonathan Hardy. The wedding would take place as soon as Jonathan could get seven days leave, although that might not be too soon because the Army was undergoing a lot of very serious training. It seemed that after Dunkirk, Prime Minister Churchill wanted every officer and every soldier to be given a new kind of training, one that would make every man a lot more competent and a lot tougher. Leave was being granted to only a few until they were all turned into efficient men of iron. Well, that was what Jonathan kept telling Emma in his letters. Emma said she didn't know how she was going to cope with Jonathan as a man of iron, that she preferred him as a happy-go-lucky bloke.

Emma was doing her bit for the country in an unexpected way. She had thought about following Rosie and Eloise into the ATS, but after a successful interview for a shorthand-typist's job at the War Office in September, she was now working there. It was Chinese Lady's husband, Edwin Finch, who had secured the interview for Emma. Emma had told her grandparents she wasn't really all that keen on joining the Army.

'Well, I'm pleased to hear you say so, Emma,' said Chinese Lady at the time. 'It's unnatural for young ladies to be soldiers, and it's been a grief to me that Rosie and Eloise actually went and volunteered.'

'Oh, Rosie had to, Grandma,' said Emma, 'she was never going to let Uncle Boots fight the war without her.'

'Rosie's old enough to have left that sort of thing behind her ages ago,' said Chinese Lady.

'What sort of thing?' asked Mr Finch.

'She shouldn't still be hero-worshippin' Boots,' said Chinese Lady. 'That was all right when she was a schoolgirl, but not now she's a grown woman that ought to be married. I've never heard before of any grown-up daughter going off to war with her father.'

'I've always seen Rosie and Boots as inseparable,' said Mr Finch.

'More so now that poor Aunt Emily has gone,' said Emma, 'and I don't think Rosie will actually have to fire any guns, Grandma.'

'I should hope not,' said Chinese Lady. 'If it ever happened, Edwin, I'd want you to speak to the Government about it. As it is, I'm only thankful Rosie was such a help and comfort to Boots when he lost Emily. I don't know how he'd have managed without her.'

'Exactly, Maisie,' said Mr Finch.

'Yes, exactly, Grandma,' said Emma.

'Exactly what?' asked Chinese Lady.

'Rosie and Boots harmonize,' said Mr Finch.

'That's no excuse for Rosie goin' off to fight the war with him,' said Chinese Lady a little peevishly. 'And I was shocked when Eloise joined the Army too. I must say it's a relief you don't want to, Emma.'

'I may have to one day, Grandma,' said Emma, 'or I'll find myself being directed into war factory work.'

'Emma, I think I may be able to help,' said Mr Finch, and was as good as his word. For over two months now, Emma, classified as a temporary Civil Servant, had been working at the War Office surrounded by sandbags.

There was yet one more thing occupying Chinese Lady's ever-active mind. Boots's intentions regarding Polly Simms. She had spoken to him after he'd had a meeting with Polly in Ruskin Park during his leave.

She met him in the hall when he returned. No-one else was there. Rosie, also on leave, was out with her Aunt Lizzy, and Edwin was in London, still working for a Government department, despite wanting to retire.

'You're back, I see, Boots,' she said.

'Hello, old lady,' he said, smiling.

'I don't know how many times I've told you not to call me old lady,' she complained.

'Bad habit of mine,' said Boots. Curiosity uppermost, she examined him with a searching eye. The eldest of her sons, she conceded he had more of his father's looks than Tommy or Sammy. His father, her first husband, Daniel Adams, had been an Army corporal in the Royal West Kent Regiment, and a very arresting man to look at. Tall, firm of body and muscle, with fine and clear grey eyes. Boots was all that himself, except that his left eye was impaired, a result of the 1914–18 War.

'Miss Simms called,' she said.

'Yes, I know,' he said, placing his hat on the hall-stand.

'She wanted to see you, so I told her you'd gone to the park. She found you there, did she, Boots?' Chinese Lady put the question quite gently.

'Let's talk in the kitchen,' said Boots.

'I'll put the kettle on for a cup of tea,' she said. Boots smiled as he followed her into the kitchen. A thousand family discussions, in good times and bad, had taken place over his mother's never-failing teapot. While she was preparing one more pot, he •

40

stood at the kitchen window, looking out over the garden, which on that particular day in November was showing quite green under some welcome if unseasonable sunshine. He thought of Emily and Polly, Emily now gone and Polly vital with life. Would it be unfair to the dead to take up with the living? He did not positively think so, but it was on his mind. They had talked in the park, he and Polly, and he had made a promise to her. His mother broke into his reflections. 'Sit down, Boots.'

He sat down with her at the kitchen table and she poured the hot golden tea.

'You want to know about Polly,' he said.

'I want to know about both of you,' said Chinese Lady.

'Well, how would you feel if I married her?' asked Boots.

'It wouldn't surprise me, but I'd feel shocked if you married her tomorrow,' said Chinese Lady.

'So would everyone else, I daresay,' said Boots. 'But you're not against the idea of Polly as a new daughter-in-law?'

'No, Boots, I'm not against it,' said Chinese Lady, 'but I'm blessed if I know what the fam'ly's goin' to think about a son of mine marrying the daughter of Sir Henry and Lady Simms. It's a mystery to me, I'm sure, how it's come about that Miss Simms, who's aristocratic and looks it, is willing. Still, as long as it's not tomorrow or next week, I don't see that anyone can object serious, except Lizzy might. Lizzy might say you're not showing respect for Em'ly's memory unless you wait a decent while, which I'm sure you will.'

41

'Sometime in March, say?' suggested Boots.

'Well, you're both not young any more, Boots, so no-one would expect a long wait, especially as there's this war and all the bombing.' Chinese Lady was conducting her part in the discussion with unusual quietness. 'But I can't help reminding you that Polly's upper class.'

'That means nothing to Polly,' said Boots.

'Well, I will say she's never come among us with her nose in the air,' said Chinese Lady. 'All the same, I don't know if she'll fit in, she's not like Vi or Susie.'

'That's the only thing worrying you?' said Boots.

'She's fitted in as a fam'ly friend,' said Chinese Lady, 'but will it be easy for her fittin' in as my new daughter-in-law?'

'Well,' smiled Boots, 'I can tell you she won't call you Mum, as Vi and Susie do, she'll call you Maisie.'

'Now, Boots, this isn't the time for any of your airy-fairy remarks.'

'Nothing airy-fairy about that, old lady. Polly asked me to ask you if you'll mind. She thinks she's too old and you're too young at heart for her to call you Mum.'

'And I don't suppose Polly's kind ever say Mum to their mothers,' said Chinese Lady. 'Still, it's like her to be compliment'ry to me. I must say she's always been that way, and I did tell her I understood about her feelings for you, I did understand that with Emily gone she would want to know about your feelings for her. And I couldn't see you staying a widower for the rest of your life. Boots, is marrying her what you want?'

'It's what we both want, old lady,' said Boots, 'and what we also want is your blessing.'

'Well, I think Em'ly would like you to be happy,' said Chinese Lady, even if she also thought Emily's ghost might wince a bit that he'd chosen Polly. 'So you've got my blessing, Boots.' She reached across the table to lightly pat his hand. 'Now you'll have to tell the rest of the fam'ly and get their blessing too.'

Well, of course, as she and Boots both suspected, that was easier said than done. Lizzy was shocked. It was out of all respect for Emily's memory, she said to her husband Ned, and nor was it even decent. Ned, however, said it was very decent, Boots fixing to marry Polly instead of merely jumping into bed with her. And March would mean there'd be a respectful interval between the funeral and the wedding. Lizzy said only seven months wouldn't be respectful by a long chalk. More like disrespectful, she said. There's a war on, said Ned, and lovers can't wait too long. It's not right or proper, said Lizzy, not when Emily's probably still warm in her grave. You'll come round, said Ned. Trust you to be on Boots's side, said Lizzy.

Tommy, discussing the unexpected with Vi, said Boots must be a lot deeper than any of the family had thought. Well, I mean, he said, how long has it been going on? I ask you, Vi. I don't think anything's been going on, not actually going on, said Vi. Tommy said not a bit of adultery now and again? Tommy, I don't know how you can think about Boots like that, said Vi. You're right. I can't, said Tommy, he's me respected older brother, but

43

I can ask a question. I'm asking now, d'you think Polly's had him in her bed occasional? I think Polly would have liked him there, said Vi, but I don't think Boots would ever have let Emily down like that. Of course, she said, it is a bit startling, him and Polly actually getting married, but at least it's not until next year, so I hope we don't have any family rows about it. Chinese Lady won't stand for any rows, said Tommy, and if she's in favour, well, who's going to get on the wrong side of her? Yes, who, I'd like to know, said Vi.

Susie for one wasn't going to. She was very pro-Boots.

'What a lovely happening, Sammy. I'm delighted, aren't you?'

'I'm wondering, Susie, how long it's goin' to be before our fact'ries are flattened,' said Sammy, brow darkening at the thought of Army and RAF contracts being mucked up. 'I can't get me seamstresses to move out of London, not even though I've got an option on an empty fact'ry in Luton, which won't stay empty for long.'

'They might move to Luton if you found livin' accommodation for them and their families,' said Susie.

'I know their kids have been evacuated, Susie,' said Sammy, 'but they still don't fancy movin' to Luton. Gertie Roper says it'll be like living with foreigners. So I don't know what you're delighted about.'

'Sammy love, I said I was delighted about Boots and Polly.'

'Susie, don't say things like that out loud,' said

Sammy, 'it might make Emily rise up from her grave and do something shockingly injurious to Polly.'

'Oh, I know Em'ly didn't see Polly as her favourite person,' said Susie, 'but I'm sure she wouldn't do any rising up. I'm sure she'd rather rest in peace. She deserves to, considering she hardly ever stayed still all her life. There were a lot of family tears wept for our Em'ly, but she's gone and we've all got to get used to that. She had a good marriage with Boots, and she wouldn't object to him making a new life for himself.'

'With Polly?' Sammy chewed on that. 'I'm not so sure.'

'Sammy, with Em'ly gone, it was bound to happen,' said Susie. 'Boots was bound to turn to Polly, and Polly was never going to step aside for someone else. She adores Boots. She always has. You do know that, don't you?'

'Should I know?' asked Sammy. 'I haven't had it in writing.'

'Oh, dear, what a shame, Sammy love. Never mind, you can take my word for it. Boots is going to make a very happy woman of Polly, and she's going to be his shining light.'

'Shining light?' said Sammy. 'Leave off, Susie, they're not a couple of dizzy young lovers, they're both past forty. Further, Mrs Adams, kindly don't hurt my fam'ly feelings by talkin' as if Em'ly's already a back number. I know she's gone, but nobody's forgotten her yet.'

'No, of course not, Sammy love,' said Susie, a very knowing and perceptive woman at thirty-six, 'it's

45

just that life has to go on for Boots and the rest of us.'

'There's a lot of life perishing every night,' said Sammy, 'and a lot of London fact'ries bein' blown to tiny bits, and people's homes as well. It's my frank opinion, Susie, that we'll get things out of proportion if we spend all our time discussing Polly and Boots. Now, I've brought home some new weatherproof groundsheets for the air raid shelter, because I've got a feeling our present ones will give our bed blankets chronic problems of rising damp now that winter's comin'. D'you get me, Susie?'

'Yes, Sammy, and that's what I mean,' said Susie. 'The war's horrendous, it's blowing London to pieces, and because of that we ought to give Boots and Polly our blessing.'

'Well, all right, I won't say no to that, Susie.'

'That's my Sammy. Did you know you bring warm feet to bed with you? Warm feet, Sammy, go with a warm heart.'

'Might I point out, Susie, that when I kip down in our air raid shelter, I wear me Wellington boots?'

'I suppose I've got to thank the Duke of Wellington for that,' said Susie.

'Well, we had to thank him for finishing off Napoleon,' said Sammy. 'Did I mention about Em'ly rising up from her grave? No, let her rest in peace. What we need is for Wellington to do the rising up to finish off Hitler.'

Chinese Lady had heard none of these discussions, but she did get to know that Lizzy simply didn't think it right or proper for Boots and Polly

46

to marry until next August at least, that Ned thought March reasonable, that Tommy was unsure about the whole thing, and that Vi was ypically unwilling to be contentious. Susie was wholly in favour and Sammy of the opinion that if Boots wanted to make Polly his shining light, the family couldn't seriously object to that, seeing what she'd done for the troops in the '14–18 war. He confided to Chinese Lady over the phone that he was going along with Susie's instincts that Boots and Polly deserved each other. Somehow, he said, Susie's instincts make her a bit of an oracle. Chinese Lady asked what an oracle was. Search me, said Sammy, it's something Boots called her once, but it's still all Greek to me. Well, I want to know, said Chinese Lady, so see if it's in the dictionary.

Sammy looked it up, then went back to the phone.

'I don't believe it,' he said.

'What's it mean, then?' asked Chinese Lady.

'It means Susie's a medium of divine revelation,' said Sammy.

'She's what?' said Chinese Lady in shock.

'It also says here she speaks the word of God,' said Sammy. 'Well, good as.'

'Sammy Adams, don't you talk like that over the phone to me,' said Chinese Lady. 'It's blasphemy. I don't know where you got that dictionary from, but you'd better put it on the fire and burn it. D'you hear me?'

'Yes, Ma.'

'Don't call me Ma, it's common.'

'No, Ma. Burn the dictionary, right.'

'And I don't want to hear any more about Susie speakin' the word of God.'

'Well, I hope she won't,' said Sammy, 'I don't know I could live with it for more than five minutes. Holy Joe, Ma, she could end up as Saint Susie.'

Chinese Lady's prolonged reflections on so many matters concerning her kith and kin were broken by a little smile at that point. That Sammy, he still talked sometimes as if he'd never grow out of being a saucebox.

Well, there it was, Boots and Polly were going to get married in March. They were both back with the Army now. So was Rosie. Rosie, of course, had favoured Boots in his intention to marry Polly. Rosie would never go against him.

The doorbell rang, breaking into Chinese Lady's reflections. She turned off the blessed wireless and answered the summons. On the step stood Sammy, and beside him was Rachel Goodman.

'Hello, Ma, glad you're home,' said Sammy.

Chinese Lady stared at Rachel, who had been able to clean herself up at the hospital, but looked far from her usual lustrous and well-dressed self.

'Rachel?' said Chinese Lady.

'Unfortunately, Ma,' said Sammy, 'Rachel's been bombed out, and Benjamin's a casualty. Can we come in and talk to you?'

'Bombed out?' said Chinese Lady, quivering with shock. 'Lord Above, that's dreadful. There's a house on Denmark Hill been bombed, I heard, and I thought that was bad enough. Come in, come in, come and sit round the kitchen fire. Rachel,

I never saw you lookin' more tired. And you don't look too good, Sammy.'

'I'm all right,' said Sammy, keeping quiet about the bombed house and his hours on duty.

'Rachel, come and tell me all about what happened,' said Chinese Lady.

In the warm kitchen, she received detailed accounts. Sammy was unusually sober, and Rachel close to letting emotions spill over. Chinese Lady thought no wonder, it must have been terrible knowing her husband was buried under a collapsed house. Rachel had always been a pleasure to know, first as a lovely, open-hearted girl and then as a very warm and friendly woman. She didn't deserve to lose her home and to have her husband in hospital. However, he wasn't in a really serious condition, apparently, even though both his legs were broken and he was suffering concussion. According to what Rachel had been told, he would be on the mend in a week or so. Chinese Lady said she was relieved to hear it, and that if there was anything she could help with, Rachel only had to say. Sammy referred to the necessity of finding Rachel a temporary home.

'Could you help with that, Ma?' he asked.

'You don't have to ask, Sammy,' said Chinese Lady. 'Rachel is here, and here she can stay for as long as she likes. I couldn't be more pleased you've brought her. You go off to your office and leave her with me, and when you've finished your work I'll expect you to come here again and bring whatever clothes Rachel needs from one of your shops.'

'I'll do that,' said Sammy, 'I'll bring some essential

49

stuff, includin' a change of – er – well, I'll bring the basics. Then if Rachel can come to the office tomorrow, I'll see about gettin' her a new wardrobe. We don't have factories and shops for nothing.'

'There's times, Sammy, when I feel there's quite a lot of good in you,' said Chinese Lady.

'Inherited, Ma,' said Sammy.

'Don't keep calling me Ma, specially not in front of Rachel,' said Chinese Lady. 'Off you go now, I'll see to her. I'll put the kettle on first.'

However, she allowed Rachel to go to the door with Sammy.

'Sammy, you're a love,' said Rachel.

'Dark days, Rachel, and bloody dark nights,' said Sammy. 'You'd have been better off in America, after all.'

'I'd still rather be here, facing up to Hitler,' said Rachel, 'I've never wanted to run away. Sammy, how does a man with two broken legs learn to walk again?'

'With the help of crutches, Rachel, and the arm and support of his wife and friends,' said Sammy. 'If I know Benjy, he'll be up and about by daffodil time. Early spring, let's say, and I'll bet on it.'

'If you will, then so will I,' said Rachel, 'and if you can manage to bring a change of – er – you know, I'd like pink, just to give myself a lift. My life, lovey, everything I'm wearing at the moment feels dust-laden and grey.'

'Pink, you said?' Sammy smiled. 'Right, understood.'

'Sammy, you always understand,' said Rachel softly.

'Well, in times of worrying setbacks, Rachel, a little of what you fancy, like pink, ought to do some good,' said Sammy. 'But I won't select anything myself, of course, on account of suchlike being highly personal. I'll just get the manageress of our Brixton shop to make a choice.'

'Just what you should do as a respectable married husband for another man's respectable married wife,' said Rachel with a slightly wan smile. She knew Benjamin suspected she had always been in love with Sammy, and the last thing he'd want to know would be that Sammy had supplied her with underwear selected by himself.

By evening, Sammy's understanding and a visit to his Brixton shop had brought forth a costume, a blouse, a jumper, a winter coat and a set of lingerie that delighted Rachel.

Everything fitted so well that had Susie been present, she would almost certainly have said that Sammy's understanding was of a suspiciously knowing kind.

Sammy, of course, simply had a fine rag-trade eye for a lady's figure, an eye that was as accurate as a measuring tape, and which not even the most devastating air raid on London could put out of focus.

Chapter Five

'You're doing what?' said Susie to Sammy at breakfast the next morning, and after another, if less
pulverizing, raid on inner London.

'Takin' Rachel to our Brixton shop so she can fit
herself out with a new wardrobe,' said Sammy.

'Don't say things like that in front of Paula,' said
Susie.

'What's Daddy saying, Mummy?' asked little
Paula.

'Something suspicious,' said Susie.

'Is that naughty?' asked Paula.

'More like me Christian duty,' said Sammy.

'Oh, yes?' said Susie. 'Does your Christian duty
include helping Rachel to try things on?'

'I'll just be standing by,' said Sammy.

'Sammy Adams, you'll just be working in your
office, as usual,' said Susie. 'I'll go with Rachel to
Brixton. I'll come to the office after taking Paula
to her nursery school, and meet Rachel there.'

'Susie, you don't need to do that,' said Sammy.

'Yes, I do, it's my Christian duty more than yours,
Sammy love,' said Susie. 'It's my duty as a woman
who can feel for another woman who's just lost her
home and everything in it.' It was also her right as
a wife to make sure her husband didn't offer his

comforting shoulder too much to the woman who had once been his only girlfriend.

'Well, Susie, if you'd rather do it yourself—'

'Yes, I think so, Sammy, it's a woman's work and Benjamin would think so too,' said Susie.

'Fair enough,' said Sammy. 'But tell the manageress to charge it all up to the firm.'

'Of course,' said Susie, 'it's the least we can do for Rachel.'

'Plum Pudding,' said Sammy to Paula, 'take a note that your mum's got a warm and sympathetic jam tart.'

'I like jam tart, and Mummy makes nice porridge as well,' said Paula.

'Well, I've never associated her with lumpy porridge,' said Sammy.

'Thank you, Sammy,' said Susie, 'I've waited all my life to be compared favourably to lumpy porridge.'

At twenty minutes to ten, Chinese Lady left her house in company with Rachel. Rachel was meeting Susie at Sammy's offices in Camberwell Green, and from there Susie was taking her to the firm's Brixton shop. Susie had been on the phone about it, and Rachel was more than happy at this friendly gesture. She had always wanted Susie to know she had no designs on Sammy, and she felt the gesture was a reassuring one. She had no idea it was motivated by Susie's determination not to allow Sammy to get too close to his old girlfriend during these days of Rachel's emotional stress.

Chinese Lady parted from Rachel outside the

offices, and then went shopping. She was frowning a little. Last night had been another noisy one, and there'd been moments during these recent air raids when she was sure Denmark Hill itself was trembling from the impact of bombs dropping on the City of London.

In the open air of bustling Camberwell Green, Chinese Lady wondered if she could actually smell the smoke which that blessed wireless had said was still rising from fire-bombed buildings on the south side of the Thames. The smoke might be quite a distance from Camberwell, but she was sure she could detect faint whiffs.

On her way to Kennedy's cooked meats shop, where she hoped to get some of their famous sausages, she met an old friend and neighbour from Walworth, Mrs Enid Pullen.

'Well, fancy seeing you, Mrs Pullen.'

Mrs Pullen blinked a little, stared a little, then came up with a slightly glassy smile.

'Well, I never, it's you, Mrs Adams,' she said.

'I'm Mrs Finch now, I've been married to Mr Finch for some years,' said Chinese Lady.

'Bless me, yes, so you 'ave,' said Mrs Pullen, 'me and me old man come to yer weddin', I remember. What an 'appy occasion, who'd 'ave thought then that there'd be another war, and all these bombs? It's enough to make me and Mr Pullen wonder at times if we're ever goin' to get any sleep. Mind, we 'aven't 'ad our 'ouse blown up yet, or I wouldn't be 'ere talkin' to you now, even if me 'ead don't feel right and me voice is a bit off colour, like.'

'Did it give you a headache, last night's raid?'

asked Chinese Lady sympathetically.

'Well, I was that lucky, Mrs Adams—'

'Mrs Finch.'

'Yes, me old man shared 'is sleeping draught with me and we both slept sound all night, like there was no tomorrow,' said Mrs Pullen. 'Didn't 'ear a thing down in the public shelter.'

'Is Mr Pullen takin' sleeping draughts these days?' asked Chinese Lady. 'Mind, I wouldn't be surprised if we all had to take them.'

'What he took last night was just what the doctor ordered,' said Mrs Pullen. 'He 'appened to come across a quart bottle of stout, and we 'ad half each. It's what me old man believes in. Mind, I'm not sure I don't still feel a bit tiddly. Well, we finished up a bit of gin first, and me voice don't seem to be me own this mornin'. Still, I've made an effort to come out and I'm on me way to Kennedy's. I thought a tram ride to Camberwell would clear me 'ead. Is me hat on straight?'

'Well, Mrs Pullen, to tell the truth—'

'It ain't on straight?' said Mrs Pullen, looking a bit alarmed.

'You're not wearing any hat,' said Chinese Lady gently. Lor', she thought, has Mrs Pullen taken to drink?

'There, I knew it, I'm not properly recovered yet from me stout and gin.' Mrs Pullen became flustered. 'Lor', me comin' out without me hat on? Would yer mind kindly excusin' me, Mrs Lynch, while I go back for it?'

'But you're here now, and only a little way from Kennedy's,' said Chinese Lady.

'Oh, I couldn't go in the shop, not without no hat on, I'd look undressed,' said Mrs Pullen.

'I shouldn't worry about that,' said Chinese Lady. 'I'm goin' to Kennedy's myself, and what with the war and the air raids, I don't suppose anybody will make any loud remarks about you leavin' your hat off.'

'Well, that's nice of yer to say so,' said Mrs Pullen, 'you always was a kindly neighbour. If I could 'ave the pleasure of yer company while we're queueing, we could pass a bit of time together before I do some more shoppin', then p'raps treat meself to a small glass of stout at the pub. Well, me old man always says an 'air of the dog can do wonders for what 'appened the night before, like.'

She latched onto Chinese Lady, joining the queue at Kennedy's with her, and regaling her with all the latest news about old neighbours. After twenty minutes in the queue, and when they'd each managed to be served with a pound of sausages and some brawn, Mrs Pullen went her separate way in slightly bleary fashion, leaving Chinese Lady with the impression that what she had heard pointed to the possibility that all her old neighbours had taken to drink, even if only at night in air raid shelters. Which, in Chinese Lady's opinion, was something else Hitler could be blamed for, driving respectable people to cuddling bottles of drink at night. Well, if that gloomy wireless set at home started talking about it, she'd get Edwin to take it back to the shop and buy a different one, one that might be a bit more cheerful.

Still, it wouldn't do to be too complaining about

a wireless set, not when there were so many people who had far more real worries than that.

Chinese Lady decided there and then not to take to drink herself.

That night bombs kept raining down on London. Hermann Goering had promised Hitler to raze the capital to the ground and bring Winston Churchill to his knees, begging for peace. Provincial cities, such as Coventry, Southampton and Plymouth, had also been attacked from the air. Hitler, however, suspected Goering's *Luftwaffe* was going to fail him again. It had failed earlier in not eradicating the RAF and its fighter stations. 1940 having given way to 1941, Germany's Fuehrer began to lose interest in Britain and he turned his attention to the necessity of making plans for the conquest of the Soviet Union. Goering, however, hopefully continued to launch his bombers, although not in the numbers that had attacked London on the 29th of December.

January became surprisingly fine.

Sammy sat in his office one morning, thinking that the challenges and excitements of business had gone for a long walk into the sunset, like Charlie Chaplin at the end of one of his films. And the business itself might soon follow. The destruction of his East End factories was almost inevitable if the German bombing raids didn't stop. He knew it and so did his workers, his good old reliable seamstresses and machinists, who were having to take to the shelters from dusk till dawn nearly every ruddy night. Some had gone to join their evacuated kids in the country. The rest, however, rarely failed to turn up for work every day, including those who had been bombed out and been rehoused elsewhere. They lamented their shattered homes, even if they had been only rented dwellings of which their landlords should be ashamed. Sammy hated landlords who had greedy grasping paws and no feelings. That gave him an idea. He had money, he had capital, and so did the firm, which was making a good steady profit from the manufacture of uniforms for the Army, the ATS, the RAF and the WAAF. Underwear too. Got it, Sammy me lad, Adams Enterprises can go into property after the war, buy up rows of those East End slum dwellings and build solid terraces of houses that'll be nearly as good as palaces for the workers, workers like my seamstresses. Start buying as soon as the end of the war's in sight. Point is, though, can we win the ruddy war? And what's going to happen if the factories do get bombed and I've got to relinquish contracts for uniforms? That's the meat of the business at the moment. There's nothing much going into the firm's retail dress shops except wartime rubbish – square-shouldered styles that gave feminine females an awkward military look. There was so little for his fashion designer Lilian to do that she'd retired into the country with her husband Bill, an ex-milk roundsman and a Gentile. True, she'd promised to come back as soon as the war was over, but when would it be over? When could he start enjoying work again?

The staff in his offices had been reduced to a handful. There was no longer a hum of activity. His niece Emma had gone, wisely taking on a wartime occupation in Whitehall. He missed her and he missed Boots as general manager. Boots had always been a great sounding-board for suggestions and ideas, and a dead clever bloke at finding solutions to problems of all kinds. Emily had taken his place as general manager, and had fitted into the job overnight. Gone now, poor old Em. The family owed Hitler a thunderbolt for that bitter blow.

He hadn't bothered to replace her. Wartime restrictions on the production of civilian garments, and the routine nature of manufacturing uniforms, had reduced office work considerably. All the girls eligible for call-up into the Services or war work had left. He had an assistant, Myra Symonds, an unmarried female of forty-one. Efficient enough, and quite a handsome female, but about as lively as the office broom when it was standing in its cupboard. He'd committed the mistake once of asking her if she'd care to make him a cup of tea after he'd got back from a visit to the factories.

'I'm not here, Mr Adams, to make cups of tea,' she informed him frowningly, 'I'm an experienced shorthand-typist, having spent fifteen years with a City firm and five years as the typists' pool supervisor, and I hope you won't regard me as an office boy.'

'Sorry I spoke,' said Sammy. Sorry I took you on, he thought.

His reflections wandered. That was the curse of things these days. There wasn't a lot to hold his attention, except for his new idea of buying up slum property. The real challenges existed in factories turning out engines of war, and in the Forces.

He thought of one bright light.

Susie, the ever-present beacon in his life. Susie, who was all for Boots and Polly, and didn't mind who knew it. She'd had an argument with Lizzy over it, and stuck to her guns all the way. She'd left Lizzy feeling uncertain about her own attitude, one of disapproval.

Restless, Sammy came to his feet and put himself clear of the old desk at which he'd happily sat up to his eyes in work for many years.

At home, the phone rang. Susie picked it up.

'Hello, yes, who's that?' she asked.

'Good morning, Susie.'

'Bless me, is that Boots?' said Susie.

'How are you, Mrs Sammy?' asked Boots, on the line from Corps Headquarters in Dorset.

'Fed-up with German bombers but ever so happy to talk with you,' said Susie. After Sammy, Boots was her favourite man. And she liked Polly, very much. She mourned Emily, as all the family did, but thought Polly would make Boots the kind of wife who'd be a delight to him because she was witty, funny, engaging and vivacious. Boots responded to all that. 'Why are you phoning me, Boots? Has the war stopped for you?'

'Not yet,' said Boots. 'I wanted to talk to Sammy, but he's not in his office. Are the factories still standing?'

'Only by the grace of the One Above,' said Susie, 'but we feel it'll be any night now. The fires, oh

Lordy, we can see the sky alight over the City from here.'

'I'm afraid there'll be a lot more to come, Susie. The Fat One's set on using his bombers to flatten London in the hope of making Churchill sue for peace.'

'Mr Churchill won't do that,' said Susie, 'he's a friend of mine, he wrote me a letter once.'

'Well, no friend of yours will go down on his knees to Hitler and Fatty Goering,' said Boots. 'Listen, I've a young lieutenant in Ops here. His father, Sir Bernard Cunningham, owns an engineering company that turns out machine tools. He's just moved the workforce and jigs to Hereford, and left his present factory vacant, and I know Sammy's been looking for an alternative. It's a large factory with two floors and offices, about a hundred yards up from Belsize Park tube station, well away from Central London. The seamstresses can get there easily enough on the tube from the Angel station. The business itself is only one of several run by Sir Bernard, but this particular factory is owned by his wife, Lady Cunningham.'

'Help,' said Susie, 'what with Sir Henry and Lady Simms, and now Sir Bernard and Lady Cunningham, you're moving in high society, aren't you, Boots?'

'I'm prepared to fight that, Susie,' said Boots. 'Tell Sammy I'm able to take time off tomorrow to call on Lady Cunningham, who's living near a village called Rockbourne in Hampshire. It's not too far from here. On the recommendation of Lady

Cunningham's son, Lieutenant Cunningham, I'm proposing on behalf of Adams Enterprises to offer her two thousand pounds for the freehold. I'm told the factory's in good shape, built only ten years ago. Sammy can write the cheque if I can persuade the lady to sell. The firm can't afford to wait until the Shoreditch factories are blown sky-high. God knows how they've escaped so far. Have you got all that, Susie?'

'Yes, all of it,' said Susie. 'Boots, you love, doing all this for Sammy when you must be up to your eyes with Army nuts and bolts and things.'

'Only on paper,' said Boots.

'Yes, I meant on paper, like blueprints,' said Susie.

'Logistics,' said Boots.

'Now I'm ignorant,' said Susie.

'I'll eat my socks if you are,' said Boots, 'and nobody else would, except with a pint of hot custard.'

'Boots, a factory away from Central London, away from the bombing, it'll do wonders for Sammy's headache and for the Shoreditch staff,' said Susie. 'Oh, I could kiss you all over.'

'You'd be better off eating my socks,' said Boots.

'Oh, help, I didn't mean quite all over,' said Susie. 'Can I ask how Polly is?'

'I haven't seen her lately,' said Boots, 'she's at 17th Infantry Division Headquarters, miles away. But I think she's still herself, with a laugh or two up her khaki sleeve.'

'Boots, I'm so pleased for the two of you, I really am,' said Susie.

'That's a sensitive subject with the family,' said Boots.

'Oh, I suppose so, I suppose some of the family think it's a bit soon,' said Susie, 'but I think this rotten old war makes a difference. You can plan for tomorrow but not for next year.'

'Londoners can't even plan for tomorrow, Susie. Keep your heads down, give little Paula a tickle for me, and don't leave your shelter too often at night to look at London's fireworks. Love to you, regards to Sammy, and tell him I'll be in touch after I've seen Lady Cunningham.'

'Boots, thanks ever so much for phoning.'

'Pleasure to talk to you, Susie. Goodbye now, take care.'

'Goodbye, Boots lovey,' said Susie, and as she put the phone down Sammy entered the house. She went into the hall, and there he was, and it was only ten-thirty. 'Sammy?'

'Hello, Susie, what a treat to see you,' said Sammy.

'I do live here,' said Susie.

'Yes, and I'm tickled you do, believe me,' said Sammy. 'Strike a light, suppose it was Miss Symonds? I wouldn't come home at all.'

'Sammy Adams, why are you here at this time of the day?' asked Susie.

'I'd like to take you out,' said Sammy.

'Well, bless me, this is very sudden, Mr Adams,' said Susie, and thought of the factory at Belsize Park. 'You're all right, are you? You're not ill or something? I mean, I can't ever remember you leaving your work in the middle of a morning.

Your work's always been my closest rival.'

Sammy said he wanted to chuck work for the day and sample some of this very early spring weather. Susie said she'd never heard him talk like that before. Sammy said the air raids were giving him a headache, that Miss Symonds made his teeth grate, and that business was getting so routine he felt about as useful as a bent farthing. Let's go out for the day, he said. Susie asked if he really meant that.

'Cross my heart,' said Sammy.

'Sammy, you love,' said Susie, 'but we'll have to be back by three-thirty to pick Paula up from nursery school.'

'Right,' said Sammy, 'we can't let Plum Pudding the Second walk home by herself.' Plum Pudding the First was his elder daughter Bess, presently living in the safety of Devon with her brothers Daniel and Jimmy and hundreds of other evacuees.

'We'll drive to the Oval, and take the tube from there to Belsize Park,' said Susie.

'Eh?' said Sammy.

'Belsize Park,' said Susie.

'I know Belsize Park,' said Sammy, 'but what's there except some shops and the tube station?'

'A vacant factory,' said Susie, and gave him the details of her conversation with Boots. Sammy received the information with an unusual lack of response. In fact, he stood there in front of her saying nothing, a wry look on his face. 'Sammy?'

'I miss Boots as me business partner, Susie,' he said. 'Come to that, I miss seeing any of his fam'ly whenever we call on Chinese Lady and me stepdad.

There's none of them at home. Boots, Tim, Rosie and Eloise, they're all out of sight doing their bit with the Army, and so is Lizzy's Bobby. I'm around, but all I'm doing is helping to make uniforms.'

'Sammy, are you down in the dumps?' asked Susie.

'It's all ordinary stuff in the office, Susie. Anyone with only half a brainbox could do my job.'

'Anyone with only half a brainbox couldn't have got all those Army and RAF contracts that you have,' said Susie. 'Sammy, someone has to keep the firm going, someone has to keep our shops running and our factories working, and I bet Boots would be the first to agree.'

Sammy found a bit of a smile then. He said that what he liked best about Boots was his family-mindedness which could jump about and fizz even in the middle of a war that was turning very nasty. It always made up for him being the family's Lord-I-Am.

'If you see what I mean, Susie.'

'Sammy, someone has got to be the Lord-I-Am of the Adamses,' said Susie, 'and Boots is best at it. And he does it without hardly trying, so that no-one actually notices. There've been times, Sammy, when the family might have fallen apart if Boots hadn't been around, but there's been all the other times as well, when the prosperity of the business has owed everything to you. Boots is a love for the way he's thinking of the business and finding time to do something about a new factory, but he's not doing it for the firm and the family alone.'

'Well, of course, he needs the business to come

65

home to when the war's over,' said Sammy. 'That bit of foresight on his part doesn't escape me.'

'Yes, but don't you see, Sammy, he needs the business to be prosperous to come home to, he can't afford to see the Germans blow it to pieces. He'll be married to Polly, and you know and I know Polly's never lacked for anything. Boots will want to keep her in the style she's enjoyed all her life, and in their own house. He's never wanted a fortune, but after the war he'll want enough to be able to give Polly her own bank account. Polly adores him, I'm sure, and she probably thinks she won't mind if they're well off or not, but Boots won't see it like that. Sammy, let's go and look at this factory, let's see what Boots is going to make an offer for.'

'We'll do that,' said Sammy.

'And if the war goes on and Paula gets old enough to go and join her sister and brothers in the country,' said Susie, 'I'll come and work for the firm again.'

'In which case,' said Sammy, 'I wonder if I could off-load Miss Symonds onto the Marines? Just for now, though, let's give thanks to Boots for puttin' us in the market for an empty factory that's out of the way of bombs.'

'Yes, write him a letter of gratitude, Sammy, but not now,' said Susie. 'Let's drive to the Oval tube station first.'

'Right,' said Sammy. 'Susie, you're a thinking wife to come home to.'

'Well, write me a letter of gratitude too,' said Susie, 'and send it with red roses.'

Captain Polly Simms, officer commanding a contingent of ATS admin. personnel at 17th Division Headquarters in Dorset, answered her desk phone.

'Hello?'

'Call for you, ma'am,' said the ATS lance-corporal on switchboard duty.

'Who is it?'

'Major Adams of Corps Headquarters, ma'am.'

'Put him through,' said Polly, and a second later Boots was on the line.

'Captain Simms?' he enquired.

Very softly, Polly said, 'Hello, darling.'

'How are you, Polly?'

'In the pink, old love, and dotty about you. To what do I owe the rapturous pleasure of having you ring me?'

'There'll be a message coming through to Division from Corps,' said Boots. 'It'll be asking for Captain Simms to present herself at Corps Headquarters at ten-thirty tomorrow morning. I'll be waiting to drive you to Rockbourne in Hampshire.'

'I'll be tickled, old thing,' said Polly, 'but what's the reason for the get-together? An exciting one?'

'I need your help,' said Boots.

'Darling, ask and you shall receive all that I have to give,' said Polly. 'And even more,' she added.

'I'll tell you all about it on the way to Rockbourne,' said Boots.

'Is it going to be a day out with you?' asked Polly.

'You could say so,' said Boots.

'I can hardly wait,' said Polly.

'So long, Polly.'

'So long, old darling. You'll recognize me when I arrive, I'll be wearing my best regulation stockings.'

'Now I can hardly wait myself,' said Boots.

Chapter Six

Sammy owned a fair supply of petrol coupons as the managing director of a firm with military contracts, and he and Susie motored north to Kennington. The day was bright, the sky clear, and in the sunshine, with battle-scarred Central London not visible, the restless clouds of war departed temporarily from the mind. People walking pavements seemed to have taken on a jaunty step, and traffic was neither dour nor impatient. Buses trundled without coughing or grumbling, trams clanged musically, and other vehicles behaved tolerantly. The night and its droning Dorniers and Heinkels were hours away, and after all, on a day like this, one could feel optimistic enough to think that for once the bombers wouldn't come. From some buildings, the Union Jack flew in bright defiance of the *Luftwaffe*.

Susie and Sammy talked about their absent children, Daniel, Bess and Jimmy, and when they would next go to see them. They visited them once a month, travelling there on a Saturday with Tommy and Vi, whose children were also in Devon. They always stayed overnight at a country inn, and returned on Sunday. Sammy said a split family wasn't natural, that it was one of the reasons why he was losing his touch. Susie said he wasn't losing his touch as far as she was concerned, and that if she hadn't been married to him she'd have had to scream for a policeman on some occasions.

'Now, Susie, is it my fault you've still got all you've got in the way of—'

'Don't you dare say it, Sammy, not out here in public,' said Susie. They were in Camberwell New Road.

'I dispute we're in public, Susie.'

'Well, we are,' said Susie. 'I don't mind all I've got getting a mention in the bedroom, but not when we're car-riding with the hood down. Anyone might hear. A point duty policeman might hear, and you'd get arrested on the spot.'

Sammy laughed. The challenge was back because there was an empty factory waiting to be looked at, a factory well away from the suffering City of London, and because Susie was always a bit of a challenge herself, a teasing provoking feminine female.

There wasn't the slightest hint of mist or fog, and not a single plane of war disturbed the clear sky. But as they reached Kennington Park Road, they saw evidence of what some off-target bombs had done last night in the form of houses reduced to rubble. A gang of men, one of many specially recruited for such work, moved busily about. Theirs was the job of rendering the ruins safe, which often meant pulling down any standing walls liable to collapse, and to retrieve anything of value on behalf of the bombed-out occupants.

Susie winced at the scene of destruction,

picturing what the Adams factories in Shoreditch would look like when they were caught by raining bombs, as they surely would be soon or late. But she said nothing, and neither did Sammy. His mouth was set tight as he drove across the main road into Harleyford Street and parked the car adjacent the Oval cricket ground. From there they walked to the Oval tube station. The underground railway was a better bet than trying to drive through the congestion of bombed London.

Sammy wondered if he and Tommy had their priorities right. He was thirty-eight, Tommy forty, they were both fit and healthy, but there they were, doing Civvy Street work. The business in its present form could have been administered from the Camberwell offices by a retired bloke with enough up top and only too pleased to have the job. Tommy, of course, had a more active and demanding role as manager of the main factory, but all the same, was he happy about it?

Boots, the oldest brother at forty-four, was the only one in uniform, the only one who'd volunteered to face up to shot and shell. He'd been in uniform from the beginning, he'd been at Dunkirk, and on top of that he'd served in the Great War. He was a veteran of France and Flanders, with medals tucked away somewhere. His present uniform sported various ribbons relating to France and Flanders. The wearing of same was compulsory for officers, apparently.

I've got a feeling, thought Sammy, that making uniforms ain't exactly the best thing an Adams ought to be doing in a war against Hitler, who's first cousin to Satan. Kaiser Bill was a cherub compared to Hitler. I think I'll have to talk to Tommy, but I won't say anything to Susie yet.

With her, he travelled by underground all the way to Belsize Park, changing only once, at Camden Town. They emerged from the station into the open air of the Belsize Park neighbourhood. The sun said hello to them again, and brightened the facades of shops and buildings.

'Sammy, this is an awful lot better than Shoreditch,' said Susie.

'I'll say this much, there's a lot more fresh air to spare,' said Sammy. 'Nothing awful about that.'

'Is that a funny joke?' said Susie. 'It's not one of your best. Come along, then,' she added, linking arms with him, 'let's find the factory and not stand about gossiping.'

They walked the sunny road for about a hundred yards and, as Boots had said, there it was, the factory, standing well back and enclosed by a high wire perimeter.

'Look, Sammy,' said Susie.

Sammy looked. Right in front of him was a two-storey factory of clean modern design. A large frontal nameboard advertised, 'CUNNINGHAM & COMPANY LTD, Manufacturers of Machine Tools.'

The place was quiet, and sunlight danced on blank windows. An open gate in the wire surround beckoned them and they walked through. At once, an unseen dog emitted a ferocious bark, and the next moment it was visible, a large Alsatian, rushing at them in snarling hostility.

'Ruddy hell,' breathed Sammy, and put himself

in front of blanching Susie. The Alsatian, snarls and teeth fearsome, leapt. Its jaws closed around the sleeve of Sammy's jacket, its bite scraping his covered arm just above his wrist.

'Oh, my God,' gasped Susie.

The main door of the factory opened and someone emitted a piercing whistle. The Alsatian man-eater immediately relaxed its jaws, let go of Sammy's sleeve, drew back and crouched, red tongue dripping saliva.

'Much obliged,' said Sammy, shaken but grateful.

Out from the factory came an elderly broad-shouldered man in a Home Guard uniform. Up he came to speak to the dog.

'Good boy, 'Ercules,' he said, 'but sit now, sit.' The Alsatian sat, thumping its tail. 'All the same,' said the Home Guard to Sammy and Susie, 'don't move just in case 'e bites yer legs orf. 'E's 'ad one or two legs lately.'

'He nearly had my arm,' said Sammy.

'Arms or legs, mister, 'e ain't pertic'ler,' said the elderly Home Guard. 'What's yer business, if I might ask?'

'It's nothing to do with getting eaten by your dog,' said Susie.

'Ah, well, lady,' said the Home Guard, 'trespassers is liable to get prosecuted or eaten. It's the way of things 'ere, yer know, in case trespassers turn out to be German parachutists lookin' for a place to hide in, like this 'ere vacant fact'ry.'

'Well,' said Susie crossly, 'you ought to keep the gate shut and there ought to be a notice telling parachutists to beware of the dog.'

'Blow me,' said the Home Guard admiringly, 'you're a lively talker, lady, that you are.'

'Is this factory for sale?' asked Sammy.

'It was,' said the Home Guard, face leathery and knobbly. 'Now it's spoke for. I'm the daytime caretaker and I've just been visited by Mr Palmer.'

'Palmer?' said Sammy, admiring the dog's teeth in a reluctant way.

'Agent. 'E's only just left, which is why the gate's still open. Well, 'e came and went on four wheels.'

'Who's spoken for the place?' asked Susie, glad that the dog was no longer hostile. Her legs were still precious to her, and to Sammy as well.

'Name of Adams, accordin' to Mr Palmer's informant over the phone, such informant bein' an officer gent and son of the owner,' said the Home Guard. 'I just been told that this other gent name of Adams 'as got an option on it, which only needs to be confirmed and agreed, like.'

'I'm Adams,' said Sammy.

'Well, yer don't say, mister. Turned up quick, that you 'ave. Might I see yer credentials?'

Susie's are better-looking than mine, thought Sammy with an inward grin, but she won't stand for showing them in public. He produced his business card, and the knobbly Home Guard examined it.

'All right?' said Sammy.

'Pleased to meet you and yer secretary, Mister Adams.'

'Wife,' said Susie, proud of her long-established place in the Adams hierarchy.

'In that case,' said the elderly but well-preserved

caretaker, 'I take the liberty of complimentin' you, Mister Adams.'

'Who wouldn't?' said Susie. 'There aren't many like me.'

'Granted,' said Sammy.

'I'm 'Enry Wade,' said the bloke, now an admirer of Susie. 'Retired dustman for Camden Council, now daytime caretaker for this 'ere fact'ry and a private in the 16th Middlesex 'Ome Guard. Like to look around the building, would yer?'

'Not while Hercules is standing by,' said Sammy.

'Listen 'ere, 'Ercules,' said Private Wade to the tail-thumping Alsatian, 'make friends.' He patted the guard dog, which pushed its nose into Sammy's hand. It sniffed, then licked his fingers.

'I think he's still hungry,' said Sammy.

'Course 'e ain't, Mister Adams, 'e likes yer now, and 'e's yer friend for life,' said Private Wade. 'Come on, I'll conduct yer round, and Mrs Adams likewise.'

Susie allowed the dog to be introduced to her as well. Hercules seemed to like her even more than Sammy. Help, she thought, if it turns nasty I'll be the first to get eaten.

'Good boy,' she said, and patted it.

Hercules went all soppy.

An hour later, Sammy and Susie were in a quaint old inn, once a posthouse for horse-drawn carriage traffic, eating a quite palatable wartime lunch. A wartime lunch meant no more than two courses at a maximum cost of five shillings, and its palatability depended on whether a wartime restaurant chef or cafe cook cared or not. Some cafe cooks didn't care at all, not when the standard fare was something like suspect sausages with tinned tomatoes or baked beans. However, the chef of the Horse and Hounds near Rosslyn Park still cared, so Sammy and Susie were dining on a chicken casserole that was very flavoursome, even if there weren't too many chicken pieces coming to light. Sammy was enjoying a light ale with his meal, Susie a ginger beer shandy.

They were happy about the factory, its two substantial floors, its offices, its amenities and its light and airy spaciousness. Sammy reckoned it could easily accommodate over a hundred machinists and seamstresses. During the tour, Private Wade had become good-old-Henry to Sammy. Good-old-Henry had ventured to hope Sammy would keep him on as caretaker, especially as he wouldn't ask for more than two-pounds-ten a week, with Hercules thrown in on night duty to discourage black market spivs from breaking in and making off with valuable sewing-machines and whatever stocks of material were in store. Sammy said he appreciated the offer, and would take good-old-Henry on as night watchman if Adams Enterprises were allowed to buy the freehold.

Discussing that with Sammy over lunch, Susie said, 'Boots won't fail, not when he's dealing with a lady owner.'

'There's always going to be one lady who'll say no to him,' said Sammy. 'All the same, let's have faith, eh, Susie?'

'My faith can't be shaken,' said Susie.

'I've got to admit the place is just what we want,' said Sammy, 'and if the lady won't sell, I suppose there'd be a way of movin' our workforce in and then claimin' occupation is nine points of the law.'

'You'd have to shoot Hercules first,' said Susie.

'And then bribe good-old-Henry,' said Sammy. 'You game, Susie?'

'Beg your pardon?' said Susie.

'Well, it's a thought,' said Sammy, taking a careful look at other diners, all of whom seemed to be minding their own business, except for two Army officers who wore an air of sharp-nosed authority. He lowered his voice. 'You'd be in favour, wouldn't you, Susie?'

'No,' said Susie.

'Now, Susie—'

'If you want to get arrested, Sammy, you're on your own,' said Susie.

'Here, leave off,' said Sammy, 'you're forgetting we're both for better or worse, especially when there's a war on.'

'Not if you break into a factory and take up unlawful occupation,' said Susie.

'Blow me,' breathed Sammy, 'you said that without hardly movin' your lips.'

'Forget about breaking in, Sammy love.'

'Well, it was only like a thought passin' in the night,' said Sammy. 'Anyway, I feel better now than I did this morning. I like this place and, as you well know, Susie, I like you. I'm gettin' certain ideas. Wonder if they've got a room goin' spare? We'd only want it for half an hour, but I suppose we'd have to pay full whack. Still, blow the expense if the bed's aired—ouch!' Susie had delivered a kick under the table.

Diners looked, the Army officers pointed their sharp noses, and the waiter came hurrying up.

'Anything wrong, sir?' he asked Sammy.

'Yes,' said Sammy, 'I think I've just broken my leg, but I'll pay the bill before I hop off to a hospital.'

They were on their way back to the Oval by tube a little later.

'Does your leg still hurt, Sammy?' asked Susie.

'All over,' said Sammy.

'Serve you right for propositioning me in public,' said Susie.

'That's the last time I'm goin' to buy you a shandy,' said Sammy. 'It's too strong for you.'

Susie smiled. She was thirty-six, and married for fourteen years, but Sammy was still her lover.

Chapter Seven

When Sammy got back to the offices, Miss Symonds at once cornered him to complain that during his absence she had had to deal with two phone calls from a very officious person employed by the Air Ministry.

'Sorry about that,' said Sammy. 'What was his name?'

'Blenkinsop,' sniffed Miss Symonds.

'Oh, I've had some of him myself,' said Sammy. 'It's the war, y'know, it gives some people a feeling they're important, especially Blenkinsop. What was he complaining about?'

Miss Symonds consulted her notebook.

'That you hadn't completed and returned Air Ministry Supply Form AMS 41A. He had the impertinence to phone twice about it, and the further impertinence the second time to suggest your continued absence was very inconvenient.'

'Dear oh lor',' said Sammy, 'Blenkinsop's gettin' saucy. All right, I'll attend to it.'

'Yes, I think you should, Mr Adams,' said Miss Symonds. 'Restrictions and forms make things difficult enough for us. I object to officious persons making them even more difficult. If you like, I'll fill the form in myself and send it off.'

'Well, much obliged,' said Sammy. He found the form among a heap of papers in his tray and handed it to her.

'Thank you,' said Miss Symonds, and made her way to the door, where she turned. 'Shall I ask young Julie to make you a cup of tea, Mr Adams?'

'I could do with that,' said Sammy.

'Very good, Mr Adams.'

Sammy showed a smile as she disappeared. She was human, after all.

He phoned brother Tommy, manager of the main Shoreditch factory and informed him of events. Tommy asked how Boots had managed to put in a good piece of work for the firm in the middle of his Army duties. Sammy said it was his family-mindedness, and Tommy said just the job if it meant they could keep going and come out on a prosperous level when the war was over. They all needed a fair slice of prosperity post-war, Boots included.

'He's airy-fairy about oof,' said Tommy.

'He won't be when he's got an upper-class wife like Polly to keep in style,' said Sammy.

'See what you mean,' said Tommy, 'but I still don't think he'll lose much sleep. Anyway, he'll be in touch after he's seen the fact'ry owner, this Lady Whatsername?'

'So Susie said.'

'Well, take it from me, Sammy,' said Tommy, 'both our present fact'ries are goin' to end up as piles of smokin' bricks all too ruddy soon if these raids keep on. And that's aside from the damage bein' done to people's homes. Hitler's declared war on women, Sammy.'

'There'll come a day when Berlin gets bombed,' said Sammy, 'and he'll foam at the mouth, the bleeder. Hope it's fatal. Keep goin', you and Bert.'

Bert Roper managed the second factory.

'For your information, old cock,' said Tommy, 'Bert's been foamin' at the mouth since the raids started. He's ravin' mad about what the bombers are doin' to the East End.'

'So am I,' said Sammy, 'and so is Boots, I daresay. He's in the Army all right, they've got him where they want him, with his thinking brainbox, but he's still keeping an eye on the family and the firm. Susie and me, and you and Vi, we all miss our kids, but I'm ruddy relieved they're out of the way.'

'I'm on ARP duty again tonight,' said Tommy, 'and I'm wondering if Hitler's bombers are ever goin' to stop comin', the cowsons.'

'I share your worries,' said Sammy, 'I'm off duty myself tonight, unless the "Loftwallers" raid Denmark Hill.'

'The whatter?' said Tommy.

'Yes, that's what I said, Tommy, the "Loftwallers." Listen, keep your fingers crossed that Boots can make Lady Whatsername's boz flutter a bit tomorrow. By the way, I'd like to mention you and me are still civilians.'

'What's that mean?' asked Tommy. 'That we ought to be sailors?'

'Well, it's occurred to me, Tommy, that later on when your Alice asks you what you did in the war, Daddy, and my Bess asks me the same question, what do we tell 'em? That we made uniforms for the Army and the RAF?'

81

'Give over, you're upsettin' me,' said Tommy.

'I suppose we could always join the Home Guard,' said Sammy.

'There's a Denmark Hill platoon,' said Tommy.

'Well, that's what they call food for thought,' said Sammy. 'Anyway, I'll let you know how Boots gets on tomorrow. He's goin' to phone.'

'I've got my fingers crossed here and now,' said Tommy.

'Mister Tommy, you wanted to see me?' said Gertie Roper, entering his office a little later.

'So I did, Gertie,' asked Tommy, thinking his loyal chargehand, now in her late forties, had developed into a handsome matron, nicely fulsome of figure. If she had the typically pale complexion of East End women, she also had their kind of brilliant eyes. That, he always thought, came of growing up hungry and using their eyes in a perpetual search for food.

'What about? You ain't goin' to close the fact'ries down, are yer?' said Gertie.

'That was what I wanted to see you about,' said Tommy, and Gertie looked dismayed.

'Mister Tommy, I never thought you and Mister Sammy would let 'Itler close you down while the fact'ries are still standin' up,' she said. 'I'd 'ave bet me life you wouldn't.'

'You can still bet on that,' said Tommy. 'No, the fact is there's a good chance we can transfer the work to Belsize Park.'

'Belsize Park?' said Gertie. 'Blimey, that's nearly in the country, it's nearly at 'Appy 'Ampstead.'

'And easy to get to by the tube,' said Tommy. 'What d'you think, Gertie, wouldn't you and all the girls like to work where there's more fresh air, and away from all the bomb damage? The fact'ry there is big enough to take everyone from both of ours here.'

'Crikey, near to 'Appy 'Ampstead ev'ry day?' said Gertie.

'The firm 'ud pay your tube fares,' said Tommy. 'Do us all good, wouldn't it, Gertie, to be workin' away from Shoreditch every day? I'm not saying it's fixed yet, but me respected elder brother Boots is in charge of negotiations, and he ain't noted for failing the firm.'

'But ain't 'e in the Army?' said Gertie.

'He's takin' a bit of time off to help us move away from Shoreditch,' said Tommy. 'He ain't in favour of us 'aving nowhere to go if the ruddy Jerries blow us up one night.'

'Which they will do, not 'alf they won't,' said Gertie. 'We been lucky so far, Mister Tommy, both fact'ries still standin', but Bert's been saying for I don't know 'ow long that our turn's goin' to come. I'll talk to the girls 'ere, and you could phone Bert and tell 'im to talk to the girls there, and it's a pound to a bunch of carrots they'll all like workin' near to 'Appy 'Ampstead. Mister Tommy, we can pay our own fares, and be glad to.'

'No, let's debit the firm, Gertie,' said Tommy. 'I'll square that with Sammy when I phone him to let him know if you and the girls are all in favour.'

'Well, if yer brother Boots can get it all fixed up,' said Gertie, 'there ain't goin' to be any of the girls that'll let you down. You ain't ever let us down in all these years, not you, nor yer brothers, and we owe yer for that.'

'Good on yer, Gertie girl,' said Tommy.

'Well, we ain't goin' to get done down by bleedin' 'Itler, Mister Tommy, if you'll excuse me French.'

'You're bleedin' right, Gertie, if you'll excuse mine,' said Tommy.

When he phoned Sammy later, he was able to tell him the workforce was all in favour, and that the firm would stand the cost of their tube fares.

'Eh?' said Sammy.

'That's right,' said Tommy, 'we couldn't do less.'

'The expense of that over a year could cause me a bit of pain,' said Sammy, 'but under the circs I'll grin and bear it. Now all we need is for Boots to go to work on Lady Whatsername and roll her over.'

'Pardon?' said Tommy.

'Only in a manner of speakin',' said Sammy.

'You're snatching at the clutch,' said Sergeant Fowler, driving instructor.

'I am not,' said Eloise.

'Believe me, you—'

'You're mistaken,' said Eloise. They were away from the camp and on a moorland road, heading towards the gun ranges. The weather was crisp and clear, the sun touching the landscapes with colour. 'I am in perfect control.'

'You won't be if you crash the gears,' said Sergeant Fowler.

Approaching a tight bend, Eloise made an excellent change-down.

'There, you see?' she said.

'Better,' said Sergeant Fowler. Eloise took the bend with a suggestion of confident expertise. Her nearside wheels touched the grass verge, however. 'Told you,' said Sergeant Fowler, 'told you ten minutes ago to stay on the road.'

'You fuss,' said Eloise. 'Fuss, fuss, that's not what a man should be like.'

Sergeant Fowler grinned. Everyone knew Sergeant Eloise Adams was a card. Even Lord Beaverbrook, the no-nonsense Minister in charge of getting things done, would have trouble in getting Sergeant Adams to operate in the exact way he demanded.

'What say we pull up for a bit?' he suggested.

'A bit of what?' said Eloise.

'All right, what,' he said. 'Good idea. It's quiet out here.'

Eloise flashed him a pitying glance. Really, what an unimpressive specimen. He belonged to the very ordinary kind of men, even if he did have three stripes.

'You're married, aren't you?' she said, driving with a cautious awareness of the verge.

'Well, yes,' said Sergeant Fowler, 'but the wife don't happen to be here just now, and I'm beginning to fancy you.'

'You're disgusting,' said Eloise.

'Wouldn't you like a ten-minute stop, you dolly-bird?'

'If I stopped, it would only be to smack your face,'

said Eloise. 'You are supposed to be helping me to pass my test, and you had better do that, or I shall ask Major Lucas to find me another instructor. Do you understand, Sergeant Fowler?'

'Yes, I think I've got the picture, you cheeky monkey. All right, go up that hill in the right gear or I'll talk to Major Lucas meself. About you being a bit hopeless.'

Eloise took the hill in the correct gear, although she faltered a bit on the clutch when making the change. The gears grated.

'Everything on this car is rusty,' she said, 'and you aren't much better.'

'All right, cut the funny stuff,' said Sergeant Fowler. He wasn't upset. He had tried his luck, but she wouldn't play. Fair enough.

Eloise, having put him in his place, which was fairly close to the bottom of her subconscious list, settled down to drive smoothly except for an occasional little quarrel with the clutch. Sergeant Fowler said she was coming along pretty well, but if she'd give up being toffee-nosed and take his advice on how to improve her gear changes, she'd do herself a favour.

'You dreadful person,' she said, 'how dare you call me toffee-nosed? I'm not in the least like that. However, I'll accept your advice.'

Which she did, even if his silly grin was harder to put up with. They arrived at the specified range without the gears grating too often, and at the sentry-guarded entrance to the bleak wastes stood Major Lucas himself, talking to a couple of his officers. He at once strode over to the car.

'You're late,' he said.

'Excuse me, sir, I wasn't told a time was speci-fied,' said Eloise.

'This battery,' growled the Major, 'is up to its eyebrows in errors and omissions.'

'Permit me to say, sir, that that isn't my fault,' said Eloise, and Sergeant Fowler gaped at her words. She was telling the battery commander, good as, that he himself was responsible. Sergeant Fowler thought the Major would roar at her, but he didn't, not a bit of it.

He just said, and even with a bit of a grin, 'Don't give my ears a hard time, Sergeant Adams. Drive me back to headquarters.'

'Very good, sir,' said Eloise, pleased to have an opportunity to show him how promising she was at the wheel.

He sat on the back seat during the drive, and spoke only twice during the journey of forty minutes.

On the first occasion, he asked, 'Is something wrong with the gears of this car, Sergeant Fowler?'

'Not as I know of, sir,' said Sergeant Fowler, while Eloise gritted her teeth.

On the second occasion, when they were only a few minutes away from headquarters, the Major said, 'Sergeant Fowler, do something to improve your pupil's clutch work.'

'Yes, sir, I've already got that in mind,' said Sergeant Fowler.

Eloise fumed. Worse than criticism of her gear changes was to speak of her as a pupil. Pupil? Oh, tail of a donkey, pupils were adolescents, unlike grown-up students, such as Rosie had been before the war. Would anyone have called Rosie a pupil, whatever she was learning?

She brought the car to a halt outside the admin. block. Major Lucas got out. He gave her a brief word of thanks and made for the office of Colonel Waters, CO of the regiment. Eloise followed, still fuming. He turned at the main door, quizzing her.

'Excuse me, sir,' she said.

'Well?' he said.

'My gear changes are very good, sir, considering the gears need oiling—'

'They need what?'

'Oiling, sir.'

'You're sure about that, Sergeant Adams?' he said, a glint in his eyes.

'Anyone could tell, sir, from the noise they make sometimes,' said Eloise. 'Also, may I be permitted to say I'm a learner-driver and not a pupil at an infants' school?'

'I can't permit you to say anything so impertinent, Sergeant Adams, but you have said it, so what do I do now, I wonder?'

'I cannot comment, sir.'

'You're positive you can't?' said Major Lucas, his height, his muscular frame and the threat in his eyes collectively formidable.

'Yes, positive, sir,' said Eloise.

'Well, damn me,' said Major Lucas.

'Really, sir—'

'Now I've got some comments of my own to make concerning the inadequate state of our present artillery, but not to you. Dismiss, Sergeant Adams.'

'If you say so, sir,' said Eloise. She saluted. He returned it and disappeared. She knew to whom he was going to deliver his comments. Colonel Waters. And he wouldn't mince words either. Really, what a terribly aggressive man.

Still, one could never say he was as uninteresting as Sergeant Fowler, even if he had no charm. One simply had to stand up to him, that was all.

Chapter Eight

Tim Adams, Boots's son, trudged wearily off the parade ground. He hurt in every limb, and he was sure every limb was black with bruises. Daylight was waning, the misty sun low in the sky over Scotland, flooding the hills of Ayrshire with light and shadow, and flushing the Firth of Clyde with shimmers of pink. Along with other men of No 4 Commando, he had just completed an assault course designed for the specific purpose of pulverizing the healthy and eliminating the fragile. Not that any of the men were fragile. The slightest physical weaknesses would have disqualified any volunteer from entry into a Commando group. Tim had volunteered for a transfer two months ago, in company with ten others from his artillery regiment. Of the eleven men, only five were found to be entirely suitable, Tim among them. It was not enough to be fit and willing. Something else was required, something that smacked of the roving buccaneers of the Spanish Main or the roaring rowdies of the Yukon, or death-defying assassins, or land-grabbing pioneers of the Old West. The really complete Commando was a man who, at any given moment, could ride a motorbike, drive any kind of vehicle, sail a boat, paddle a canoe, scale a cliff, ride a horse, knock off a German sentry with a single blow, and survive a night on a mountain. Tim's part in the fighting retreat to Dunkirk, his adventurous nature and his tendency to chuck rules away in certain circumstances, allied with his physical toughness, qualified him for training as a Commando, although the nature of that training might still find him and others finally wanting.

In his fatigues, he pointed his aching frame in the direction of his billet in the seaport. There were no barracks. Every man was billeted, all three hundred of No 4 Commando, and there were few who were not going to remember with affection the motherly hospitality of their landladies. These warm-hearted Scottish ladies cooked for them, often at irregular hours, got them out of their beds on mornings when they might otherwise have slept the clock round, laundered their shirts and underwear, put their bed linen into the wash with conscientious regularity, supplied them with steaming baths in which to soak racked bodies, and even saw to the cleaning of their military equipment whenever this did not satisfy their watchful eye.

An ATS officer came out of the building housing the orderly room. Tim lifted a weary arm and saluted her. Subaltern Felicity Jessop returned it, airily.

'What-ho, Tim,' she said. Felicity Jessop, twenty, was a jolly hockey sticks type, and also a jolly good sport. One of two ATS officers on the admin. staff, she had the same kind of carefree disregard for regulations as the Commandos, all of whom considered red tape got in the way of blood-and-thunder aggression. The only important regulations were those that required unquestioning obedience to commands during every aspect of training and when action against the enemy took place. 'What was today's assault course like?' asked Subaltern Jessop.

'The usual,' said Tim. 'That is, there are bodies lying about all over Scotland.'

'Oh, well, what's a few bodies?'

'Untidy,' said Tim.

Felicity laughed. She liked Tim. Tall, extrovert and with a welcome sense of humour, he stood out among the roughnecks. Tim, for the most part, was as even-tempered as his father and just as whimsical, but he did have a vein of steel in his make-up, just as Boots did. Physically too, he was very much like Boots had been at twenty, with his dark brown hair, grey eyes, firm mouth and fine features. At this stage in his life, he was without an inch of surplus flesh, a young man of whipcord whose experience of war and tortuous training had completely toughened him. It had also put a few years on him.

'How do you feel yourself?' asked Felicity, an old Croydon High School girl.

'Dead,' said Tim.

'Again? You poor old sod. Well, here's some mail for you. I saw you tottering up from the parade ground and brought it out.' She gave him two letters.

'Thanks,' said Tim, 'you're a good old sport, ma'am.' A bloke could talk to Subaltern Jessop like that.

92

'You're welcome,' she said. She and Tim were noted for their friendly rapport. 'Listen, when you get commissioned, come up and see me sometime. I can't invite you while you're still a corporal. It's one regulation I couldn't break without getting chucked out.'

'I didn't know you fancied me,' said Tim.

She laughed and returned to the orderly room. Tim resumed his trudging walk to his billet. His landlady was Mrs Margaret Andrews, a homely and hospitable woman of forty-two. Her husband, employed before the war on the ferry that served the Isle of Arran, was now in the Merchant Navy. Her son was serving with the RAF, and her daughter was in Edinburgh, training for the nursing profession.

Entering the stone-built house simply by turning the handle of the front door, Tim heard the good lady call from her kitchen.

'Who's that?'

'Me,' said Tim, and out came Mrs Andrews, known as Maggie to her friends and neighbours, to see whether he was fairly intact or needed some serious bandaging. One could never tell how any of these men would arrive back at their billets after a day spent trying to jump over the moon. A buxom Scottish lady, Maggie Andrews alternated between good-natured humour and scolding reproach. She was scolding now.

'Och, aye, I thought so,' she said, 'a fine sight you are, laddie.'

'Fine sight?' said Tim. 'I'm lucky to be still alive. My boots are killing my feet.'

'Whisht, it's to the dustbin wi' you, and your boots,' said Mrs Andrews, apron over her blouse and skirt, dark auburn hair gathered in a large bun. 'I dinna ken I ever saw boots like that in my hoose before.'

'Wait till Saturday, they'll be worse,' said Tim. Every Saturday the Commandos, officers as well as other ranks, had to undergo a forced march into the wilds of the countryside, every man laden with full kit and rifle. The exhausting exercise was carried out at speed, the total distance there and back not far short of twenty miles. It crippled the feet, it turned boots into redhot pincers, it racked body and bones, and it made the men ask themselves, in raw Anglo-Saxon style, why they had ever volunteered. 'Saturdays,' said Tim, 'are the days when our feet and boots die a painful death.'

'Will you no' be serious?' said Mrs Andrews, and her smile came out like the sun over the Firth on a bright spring day. 'Into the kitchen wi' you, and off wi' those boots and their mud.'

In he went. Her kitchen, warm from the range fire, was a storehouse of pots, pans and everything else a domesticated woman required for the process of cooking and baking on a generous level. There, she made Tim remove his boots. She also made a pot of tea and served him a scalding cup, and while he was drinking it she went up to run the bath for him. Down she came to tell him to put himself into the hot water.

'I'll do that if I can find the strength to climb the stairs,' said Tim. 'But thanks for being as good as a mother to me, Maggie.' A little inward wince made itself felt, as it often did when he was reminded that his own mother was dead.

'Maggie, you say?' His landlady was scolding again. 'Is that no' an impudence, calling me Maggie?'

'I've got a weight on my mind,' said Tim. 'It's my head. By the way, if I'm not out of the bath in an hour, send for an ambulance to collect a stiff.'

'Awa' wi' you, McAdams,' said Maggie, and drove him out with her broom. That was what she had taken to calling him, and how she referred to him when talking to her friends and neighbours. McAdams. She did so out of a sense of broad Scottish humour, and because she felt he might have made a presentable Scot.

Tim put himself thankfully and blissfully into the hot bath, as did other aching Commandos in other billets.

While soaking, he read his letters, although they went a little limp in the steam. One was from his sister Rosie, an affectionate and chatty missive that put him up-to-date with happenings at her end, including details of her current relationship with Polly, who was not only her immediate superior but her future stepmother. Was Tim still in favour of the marriage? Tim was, despite his feelings for his late mother. As Chinese Lady said, his dad wasn't cut out to be a widower.

Chinese Lady's letter was all about the family, of course. Everyone was bearing up under the air raids, one of which had left poor Rachel Goodman homeless and put her husband in hospital with both legs broken. Rachel was living with her now, but still in a state of shock, having lost everything. Lizzy and Ned were fine, and so was Emma, a godsend to her parents with her cheerfulness. Tommy and Vi missed their children, but they'd done the best thing in sending them to live in the country, just like Sammy and Susie had with their three eldest. Vi's dad had a touch of lumbago that was keeping him housebound, which was just as well for him at his age, as it wouldn't do to take his lumbago out with him in the winter. Mind, he wasn't actually old, only sixty-seven, but it was still the sort of age when a body could catch the complaint. She hadn't caught it herself, and didn't think she would, she was always too busy to pick up complaints. Grandad was fine considering he was still working for the Government. Rosie phoned regularly, so did Eloise. They were both good girls, though what made them become soldiers, she'd never know. They both ought to be married by now and helping to do up Red Cross parcels. She'd had a very nice letter from Polly, who often wrote, which was pleasing coming from a future new daughter-in-law. The family mustn't have any hard feelings about the marriage, as she was sure Polly and Boots would always have fond and respectful memories of Emily. She hoped Tim wasn't getting any bombs up in Scotland, and was taking care of himself, like Bobby and his lady friend, that young Frenchwoman.

Tim let the letter drop on the bathroom mat, sank back and relaxed in the hot soapy water.

Just the job.

*   *   *

Nearing six o'clock, with daylight gone and the Clyde a dark flow beneath a canopy of star-encrusted ink, Maggie heard a knock on her front door. With a supper of nourishing stew simmering in its iron pot on the range hob, she answered the door and found a soldier there, a private.

'Evening, missus. Is Corporal Adams in?'

'Aye, he's in,' said Maggie.

'I've got a message for him.'

'Step in, laddie,' said Maggie, and Private Clark stepped in. Maggie closed the door. She knew Tim was long out of his bath and called up to him.

'McAdams, will you no' come down now? You've a visitor.'

Tim, refreshed and rested, came down from his room, and Maggie went back to her kitchen.

'You're wanted,' said Private Clark, big and burly.

'Who by?' asked Tim.

'A lady,' said Clark.

'Eh?'

'Subaltern Jessop. Orderly room. And she don't want to be kept waitin'. Good luck, Corp. Can't stop, got a date meself after me supper.'

Out went Private Clark. Tim, intrigued, went back up to his room, put his cap and greatcoat on, came down again, asked Maggie very nicely to keep supper hot for him, and made his way through the darkness to the building near the parade ground. The night and the blackout rendered the building almost invisible, but he found the main door. As he reached it, the door opened and a face beneath an ATS peaked cap appeared.

'Hello, darling, give us a kiss, eh?' said a falsetto voice.

That brought a roar of laughter from skulking men.

'Bloody funny, I don't think,' said Tim.

'Oh, come on, sweetie-pie, give us a smacker,' said falsetto voice.

'Well, you asked for it,' said Tim, and smacked falsetto voice in the gob. Down went the comedian, and that brought more roars of laughter.

'He didna like your style, my bonnie,' said a Scots Commando to the floored joker.

Tim left, and hoots of mirth followed him. However, Maggie served up her nourishing Scottish stew and they sat down to it in her warm kitchen. Tim said it was a stew fit for putting on the table at Edinburgh Castle, and Maggie's sunny smile beamed at him.

Chapter Nine

Just before ten the following morning, Rosie Adams, now a lieutenant with two pips up, equivalent to first subaltern, was talking to Polly outside the headquarters of the 17th Infantry Division, part of Sir Henry Simms's 7 Corps.

'What a swizz,' she said, 'you off for the day with Boots.'

'Yes, leaving you in charge of our detachment, ducky,' said Polly.

Rose, as striking as ever at twenty-five, with her fair hair, blue eyes and quite exceptional looks, regarded Polly critically. But she could see no hint of lines. Although Polly was forty-four, she could pass all too easily for being under forty. She's really going to do it, thought Rosie, she's really going to marry my adoptive father.

'Polly, I'm not going to call you mother, you know.'

'The fiends forbid,' said Polly. 'After all, I'm not going to call your grandma mother. Just Maisie or ducky. Will she stand for ducky? Must go now. Keep those death-defying girls in order. Put 'em all on a charge, if you have to.'

'If there's anything I must do,' said Rosie, 'it's

99

finding time to pick up my car from Chapman's Garage.'

'Make time,' said Polly. 'Fiddle it, dear girl, in the best traditions of the Army. God, if I don't push off now, I'll be late. Boots will skin me alive.'

'Give him my love,' said Rosie. She watched as Polly slid into a staff car, and was driven away by a corporal.

Polly arrived at Corps Headquarters a few minutes after ten-thirty. The car pulled up on the forecourt of a country mansion taken over by the Army for the purpose of housing General Sir Henry Simms and his staff of officers, NCO's and admin. personnel. The place was also the living quarters for the General and his officers.

Out came Boots. He opened the passenger door of the car, and out slid Polly in the circumspect fashion of the ATS officer in uniform. Boots smiled.

'Good morning, Captain Simms.'

'Good morning, sir,' said Captain Simms. 'What time is my driver to pick me up this afternoon?'

'I'll drive you back myself,' said Boots.

'Oh, you darling,' murmured Polly, and spoke to Corporal Jennings in the staff car. 'Shan't need you this afternoon, Corporal. Off you go, and thanks.'

'Pleasure, mum,' said Corporal Jennings and began his drive back to Division. That left Polly alone with Boots. People coming and going from the mansion didn't count as far as she was concerned.

'Like me?' she said lightly. She was uniformed to perfection, her peaked cap sitting as attractively on her head as any of her smart hats.

'Delighted to see you, Captain Simms,' said Boots. 'This way.' He led her to his own car, his Riley, which he kept at Headquarters and not at home.

'Listen, you beast,' said Polly, 'if you call me Captain Simms just once on our journey to wherever and whatever, I won't be responsible for what I'll do to you.'

'Sounds like another war,' said Boots. He opened the passenger door and Polly got in. He closed the door, walked round and eased himself into the driving seat.

'Starry skies,' murmured Polly, 'here we are, just you and me, old love.'

'Not painful, is it?' smiled Boots. He started the car.

'Where's Sir Henry?' asked Polly, referring to her father.

'Working like the very devil on how to persuade our High Command that the Corps's need for more tanks should be given top priority,' said Boots, 'but he's excused me for the day and sends you his love.'

'And Rosie sends you hers,' said Polly.

'How is she?' asked Boots.

'Devoted,' said Polly. Boots smiled and drove off, taking the long drive down to the main gate, where a duty guard saluted him then lifted the barrier. Boots took the car onto the road, turning right to head east for the A31 and Hampshire on this crisp January day. 'Now tell me why I'm here, and don't leave out anything to do with my irresistible appeal as a woman of twenty-five. You can pretend I'm that age, can't you, old sport?'

'Easily,' said Boots. 'You're still as much of a Bright Young Thing as you were in the Twenties, when you were all legs and knees. Very delectable, I remember.'

'I'm happy to say they still are,' said Polly. 'Would you like me to prove it?'

'Isn't that against the regulations for an officer and a lady while in uniform?' smiled Boots.

'For you, old sport, I'd break every regulation,' said Polly, delighted to be with him. He really was the one and only man for her. With a slightly brittle smile that hid her deeper feelings, she said, 'When do I get kissed? I know that makes me sound like a schoolgirl with a crush, but I have to ask.'

'There must be an answer,' said Boots, and edged the car into a lay-by as a huge Army tank-carrier bulldozed its way towards them on the winding road. He stopped and let it grind noisily by.

'The Army's moving mountains,' said Polly.

'If we ever get back to France,' said Boots, 'it'll be a war between our machine mountains and theirs. Titanic. Now, to answer your question, Polly.' He turned, put his left arm around her and delivered a telling kiss on her ready lips. Exhilarated, Polly responded. She hadn't seen him for weeks, and she came alive. He had an extra-ordinary effect on her, the effect of making her feel twenty-one again, with every nerve electric and every pulse racing. It was absurd, they were both past forty, but there it was, the magical revival of the body, the feeling that her best years had not all been spent. She drew her skirt back, took his hand and placed it on her knees, and put her own hand on his left thigh and squeezed.

'Hello, old sport,' she said with simulated lightness. Her love for him had not only survived a thousand moments of bitterness and frustration, it had become an unshakeable permanency. She had fought it, but it had always refused to detach itself. She often thought the reason why she wanted him so much was simply because she had never had him. She kissed him with demonstrable wanting.

Boots thought for a moment of Emily, cruelly and tragically done to death by a German bomb five months ago. He still felt in debt to her for being his steadfast guide and mainstay during his years of blindness following the first battle of the Somme. That kind of devotion could never be fully repaid. But here was Polly, as alive and vital as ever, a woman who hid her most endearing characteristics beneath a brittle exterior, and who had taken a deep hold of his affections. His hand glided upwards over her stockings in caressing movements, and his fingers encountered the little buttress of a suspender clip.

'And what have we here, Captain Simms?' he murmured.

'Nothing that you don't know about, old sport,' she said. 'Are you going to make love to me at last?'

'What a temptation,' said Boots. 'You do have irresistible appeal, Polly, but unfortunately there's an impediment.'

'Impediment? What impediment?'

'The steering-wheel,' said Boots, removing his hand, 'damned if I could get my leg over a steering-wheel and you as well.'

Polly had hysterics.

'Oh, you clown!'

'Not a valid excuse?' said Boots.

'I'll give you valid,' said Polly, 'I'll give you a thick ear. There's a car coming. Drive on to somewhere else.'

'Yes, I think we should, and to Rockbourne,' said Boots, 'we're due to keep a twelve o'clock appointment.' He left the lay-by to make for the A31, and on the way he told Polly the reason for the journey. She suffered feelings of outrage.

'I don't believe it,' she said. 'This is all for the benefit of the family firm? It's nothing to do with taking me out for the day so that you can make love to me somewhere, you stinker?'

Boots, entering the A31, drove a little faster. The rolling greens of Dorset glided away on either side of the road, and the bovine inhabitants of pastures gazed soulfully at the passing car. Dorset, lacking industrial towns, offered a wealth of land to live-stock. It also offered unlimited training ground to various units of the British Army.

'The fact is, Polly, we need a new factory before the present ones get blown sky-high,' he said. 'If production stops, the Army and RAF contracts will be transferred to other manufacturers. Sammy and Tommy can't risk that happening. Neither can I. I get my real income from the firm. It's our future bread and butter.'

'Ours?' said Polly.

'Yours and mine,' said Boots. 'With some iced cake now and again, and a place of our own.'

'You're thinking of me?' said Polly.

'I often think of you,' said Boots. 'A man does about the woman he's going to marry. I care for you, Polly, I care about the way you dress, the way you look and the way you go through life. I want to make sure you can shop for new clothes whenever you need to.'

'Boots?' Polly stared at him. He turned his head for a moment, and his whimsical smile surfaced.

'I'm not thinking you'll shop down Petticoat Lane, Polly,' he said.

'Boots, you don't believe I worry about whether or not you can keep me in furs and diamonds, do you? I want to marry you, ye gods, you know I do, but not for your bank balance. Darling, never. In any case, I have money of my own, you know, left to me by my mother.'

'I do know. You've told me before. It's yours, Polly.'

'Only until we're married, then it's ours,' she said.

'It's yours, Polly,' said Boots. 'Believe me, I need the firm and what it can do for us.'

'Yes, of course. We have to live, and you've got old-fashioned ideas that it's not going to be on my money. Well, old love, I like your devotion to good old proud husbandry. Drive on like merry hell, then, to Lady Cunningham's. But wait a moment, why do you need my help?'

'Because you're irresistible,' said Boots.

'Thank you, ducky.'

'With your own kind of charm,' said Boots.

'A delightful kind?'

'Exquisite,' said Boots, 'with a touch of upper class swank.'

'That's a filthy lie,' said Polly.

'My faith in you is absolute,' said Boots.

'Something's cooking,' said Polly.

'"Something" includes the fact that you're the daughter of Sir Henry Simms.'

'You want me to use my exquisite charm, my upper class swank, and the influence of my parentage on the lady?' said Polly. 'To persuade her to let Sammy buy her factory in Belsize Park?'

'It's a question of class,' said Boots. 'I'm allowing for that being important to her.'

'You devious old dog,' said Polly.

'Ah, well,' said Boots.

'I'll do it,' said Polly.

'Will you?' said Boots, as they approached Wimborne Minster.

'Anything, dear heart, for you,' said Polly, 'but I don't think you'll really need me. Not you. Heavens, you dope, as an Army major you've all the class you need, and a lot more besides. If you don't send poor old Lady Cunningham weak at the knees, I'll eat my best regulation stockings and my suspenders as well.'

'In front of my eyes?' asked Boots.

'On the back seat out of the way of the steering-wheel,' said Polly.

'Well?' said Boots, much later that morning, and a bit of the devil lurking in his eyes. He and Polly were in a wayside pub near the village of Rockbourne, and the proprietor's wife, taken with Boots and his uniform, had offered to make an omelette lunch with eggs from her own chickens.

In regard to Lady Cunningham, however, Boots had failed to impress. He had been right, Polly wrong. Lady Cunningham, fifty, was large, formidable, eccentric, rude, horsy and county. She had consented to receive an Army officer by the name of Adams because of a request by her son, Lieutenant Cunningham. But she received him in the landscaped garden of her magnificent manor house, where she was using secateurs to prune dead bits from her rose bushes. She was wearing a smock over a thick woollen jumper and serge skirt, and an old Army tin hat, 1914–18 vintage, sat on her head. She explained, brusquely, that she couldn't trust the bloody Huns and their bloody flying machines. Understood, said Boots.

She said she couldn't give him more than ten minutes, all her damned roses were going rotten. What exactly did he want? The factory at Belsize Park, said Boots. She said her family used to have a weekend cottage and stables there in Queen Victoria's time, and only God knew why her grandfather had built a factory on the site. Bloody old fool, she said. Ten years ago, she said, her father pulled the place down and built the present factory, then dropped dead, poor bugger. Still, it was all part of extensive family property up and down the country. Boots said Adams Enterprises would be happy to take the Belsize Park property off her hands now that it was no longer being used.

What the hell was Adams Enterprises? Family firm, said Boots. Never heard of it, said Lady Cunningham, snorting. Wouldn't trust it with a chicken house. Let's see, she said, you're the Adams my son mentioned, aren't you? Boots said yes. That boy's a bloody fool as well, she said. Runs after tarts. She then asked Boots what the devil he was up to, trying to buy some family property from her when he ought to be dropping bombs on German property. A hell of a lot of German bombs were dropping on her string of nags at Epsom, she said. Boots said his family firm was manufacturing Service uniforms, that the work was essential. Piffle, said Lady Cunningham, what good were uniforms? Suits of armour, they're the thing, she said. She had one herself to put on if the bloody Prussians invaded. Where'd you come from, she asked, who's your family? Boots said he was from South London and that his family were all serving in the Army, except for his mother, who had a link with royalty in that she'd attended Queen Victoria's funeral.

Polly, standing by, nearly killed herself at that.

It didn't work, however.

Sounds like bloody poppycock to me, said Lady Cunningham. Never heard of any Adams family, she said, and savaged a rose bush. She didn't want to sell the factory, she said, to someone whose family she didn't know. That's all, she said. Hold on, she said, is this woman an Adams too? She'd ignored Polly up to that point. Boots said no, she was Captain Polly Simms, as he'd mentioned when they arrived. She was the daughter of General Sir Henry Simms, whose country seat was in Dulwich

Village. Lady Cunningham took definite notice of Polly then, and Polly went to work on her, using the voice and the language of the upper classes to claim friendship with a duchess who had danced several nights away with the ex-Prince of Wales, while she herself gave the classic upper class elbow to Mrs Simpson. Lady Cunningham went ga-ga, and Polly finished her off by knocking her for six with an absolutely match-winning fairy story of how, as a debutante, she was presented at court and subsequently invited to Sunday tea by King George and Queen Mary. Anyone would have believed her description of what the royal cucumber sandwiches were like.

Lady Cunningham almost took her to her capacious bosom, then gave Boots permission to deposit the cheque for two thousand pounds with the agents in Belsize Park. She followed this up by inviting him and Polly to stay for lunch. Polly whispered to Boots that she'd kill him if he accepted, that lunch with the old haybag was out, out.

Boots declined the invitation on the grounds that he had to return Polly to her father at Sir Henry's headquarters, and they left after handshakes that nearly paralysed their fingers.

Now, at a table in the country pub, Boots was referring obliquely to Polly's promise to eat her best regulation stockings. Polly chose not to understand.

'Who'd have thought you'd have failed with that woman?' she asked.

'Her son cautioned me she was awkward, eccentric and title-loving,' said Boots, 'but all the same, I might have succeeded if I'd told her I once danced with the Prince of Wales.'

'Very funny, old love, but nothing to brag about,' said Polly. 'What a crummy let-down that man was. A fool as well. What he saw in—' She broke off as the proprietor's hospitable wife arrived with the omelettes, fluffy and golden. 'I say, they look absolutely delicious.'

The plates were put in front of them, and a cruet appeared.

'Best eaten directly at once, while they're hot,' said the cheerful landlady. 'Usually, we only do bread and cheese, but for the Army, well, omelettes aren't no trouble.'

'Thanks,' said Boots, and the good lady returned to her bar.

'I feel I'm having quite a happy day,' said Polly.

'Well, you've earned your medal, Polly, in toppling Lady Cunningham,' said Boots.

'What kind of medal did you have in mind?' asked Polly.

'The kind specially struck for the brave, witty and beautiful,' said Boots.

'Heavens,' said Polly to her omelette, 'he must love me. Beautiful, he said? To quote Sammy, me at my age?'

•

Chapter Ten

Rosie, after a quick lunch, secured a lift to Chapman's Garage, which was situated a little way from the peaceful village of Bere Regis. She had bought a 1936 Hillman Minx only a month ago, claiming a petrol allowance on the grounds of using it as an alternative to limited Army transport. It began to suffer starting troubles, and was also inclined to fail her in low gear. The engine simply cut out. The divisional workshop wouldn't look at a privately owned car, so she drove it to Chapman's Garage, where a mechanic booked it in, promised to right the trouble, and asked her to call back in a couple of days.

Chapman's Garage (Prop: Matthew Chapman) specialized in servicing farm tractors and farm machinery, as well as private cars. Rosie, entering the forecourt, noted a tractor, two cars and an ancient open lorry that exuded a faint odour of damp farmyard. And there was her Hillman Minx, parked just outside the workshop, from which issued the noise of men at work.

'Hello in there, anyone at home?' she called.

Out came the mechanic whom she had seen before, a wiry and grizzled native of Dorset.

'Afternoon, miss, it's a fine day and all,' he said.

He turned and hollered. 'Matt, here's the Hillman lady.'

The noise stopped and the owner emerged from the depths of the workshop. A tall and sinewy-looking man in brown overalls, he walked with a pronounced limp. His hair, as dark as a gypsy's, was in need of a trim and a brush. His weathered face showed the hint of a ready smile as he came up to Rosie. He noted her two pips.

'Lieutenant Adams?' he said, stripping off stained thick leather gloves.

'That's me,' smiled Rosie, thinking he had the deep brown country voice of a farmer rather than a garage proprietor.

He regarded her more directly, seeing a decidedly striking young woman in tailored khaki, her peaked cap shading fine blue eyes.

'I'm Matthew Chapman,' he said, 'I was out at the Harpers' farm when you called two days ago. You spoke to Ben, one of my mechanics, about your Hillman.'

'Yes, is it all right now?' asked Rosie.

'Well, it's all in one piece, Lieutenant, with a new set of plugs fitted,' said Matt, 'but the overall condition of its engine means it'll be no better than a heap of old iron in another month or so, blow my hat off if it won't.'

'Steady, you're not wearing a hat,' said Rosie, 'and you're speaking of something I already cherish, even if it has had hiccups.'

'You're lucky it's only had hiccups and not died a death,' said Matt, and his hint of a smile came into being, reminding Rosie of how Boots's smile, always lurking, surfaced so easily. 'Could I ask when you last had it serviced?'

'I only bought it a month ago from Turners the second-hand car dealers near Wareham,' said Rosie.

'Turners?' said Matt. 'No comment,' he added. 'Well, frankly, Lieutenant, I doubt if the previous owner ever had it serviced. Criminal. The oil's filthy, petrol feed pipe bunged up. That model, the 1936 Minx, deserves looking after. It could have belonged to a farmer. Some farmers only nurse their tractors and let their cars look after themselves, those who've got cars. As sure as there was never any cow that could jump over the moon, being short of lift-off power, so I'm sure your Minx has never had a service.'

'You're breaking my heart,' said Rosie.

'Your engine came close to breaking Ben's heart as soon as he unfolded the bonnet,' said Matt. The Minx's bonnet was centrally hinged. 'And it was a sad sight to me when I took a look myself. It'll start now with the new plugs, and the feed pipe clear, but I wouldn't trust it not to fall dangerously ill inside a week.'

'Can you doctor it, Mr Chapman?' asked Rosie.

'We can take the engine out and put it in a bath of cleansing fluid,' said Matt, 'and then give everything a full service. It'll take a few days. Any necessary new parts could be a problem on account of the war, but I know a place that specializes in spares lifted from cars on a scrapheap. But I daresay it'll cost you more than a bit.'

'Well, I really don't want a car that's dangerously ill,' said Rosie.

'I think we could make sure it'll recover before it gets worse,' said Matt. 'D'you want an estimate?'

'Would you have some idea now?' asked Rosie.

'Thirty quid upwards,' said Matt.

'How far upwards?'

'Come back later this week and I'll tell you, Lieutenant.'

Rosie, never short of funds because of her pay and her permanent allowance from Boots, was inclined to say she'd trust Mr Chapman to do everything that was necessary and play fair with her on the cost.

'Well,' she said, 'I—'

'Or you could phone, of course,' said Matt.

'No, I'll call in again sometime,' she said decisively.

'I could show you what your engine looks like after its bath,' said Matt.

'I don't think I'll look at it as it is now,' she said. 'I'm a duffer when it comes to being on close terms with car engines that need a bath.'

He laughed.

'I doubt if you're a duffer in what you're doing for the Army,' he said.

'Well, if we do win the war,' said Rosie, 'I hope my little bit will have helped. Goodbye now, Mr Chapman, I really must get back to headquarters.'

'I'll drive you there, Lieutenant, if you'd like,' offered Matt.

'If it's not going to take up too much of your time,' said Rosie, 'I won't say no.' It was all of two miles, and she had anticipated driving back in her Hillman.

'All part of the service,' said Matt, 'and I need to drop something in at my cottage. It's on the way. We'll use my Morris.'

'Which isn't in a failing condition?' smiled Rosie.

'I'll have egg all over my face if it is,' he said, and Rosie walked with him to one of the cars, to a well-kept Morris parked outside his little office. He limped into the office and came out again, carrying a straw basket. 'Fish,' he said, his smile breaking out again. 'It's fresh and coupon-free.' He placed it on the back seat of the car, then opened the passenger door for Rosie. She got in. He put himself in the driving-seat, called to Ben to let him know he'd be away for fifteen minutes or so, then started the engine. Rosie noted that his lame leg seemed no problem to him, his movements had all been relatively agile.

The Morris hummed a song as he drove, a happy murmurous song, quite unlike that of her own car, which had muttered, coughed and burped.

'Does the war affect your business, Mr Chapman?' she asked, as the countryside rolled greenly by.

'It's affected the repair and maintenance of private cars,' he said, 'there's not a great deal of that, with so many of them off the road. But it's increased work on farming machines. Repair of tractors and the like is a priority, since the Government needs every farm to increase output, and can't afford for any farmer to be stuck with tractors and harvesters that won't work. I'm fortunate that we're on the approved list of repairers. I need the work. I'm also able to teach Land Army girls how to handle a tractor. Some farmers are too busy to spare time for that, so they shout for help and get me.'

'And what's the result, efficient Land Army girls on tractors?' said Rosie.

'Well, they're ready and willing to learn, and game for anything,' said Matt.

'Anything?' said Rosie.

'Correction,' said Matt, and smiled. 'Not anything. I've come across the occasional farm-hand with a black eye.'

'Understood,' said Rosie, liking him. Approaching Bere Regis, he began to slow down. He brought the car to a stop outside a very attractive stone-built cottage with a delightful front garden. Faded honeysuckle tendrils drooped in the dry-stone hedge that was split by a gate.

'Won't be a moment, Lieutenant,' said Matt, and got out. He retrieved the straw basket from the back seat, opened the gate and limped up the path to the front door. The door opened before he reached it, and a pretty plump lady showed herself. He said something to her as he gave her the basket, and her round face beamed. She looked at the car, spotted its passenger, an ATS officer, and said something to Matt. He smiled, shook his head, and limped back along the path. The plump lady stood watching him. Reaching the car, he slipped into his seat and closed the door. The car moved off seconds later.

'That was your wife?' said Rosie.

'My widowed sister,' said Matt. 'She's been

keeping house for me since her husband, a merchant seaman, went down with his ship when it was torpedoed a year ago in the Atlantic.' He became sober. 'It's a deadly war for all merchant seamen.'

'I always feel they're so helpless out there in the Atlantic,' said Rosie, 'and I feel for the people of London too. The air raids must be shattering them.' She bit her lip, thinking how shattered she herself had been by the death of Emily, her adoptive mother, in a daylight bombing raid. If her love for her adoptive father had always been pre-eminent, her love for her adoptive mother had been no small thing. It still hurt to know she had gone.

'It's a filthy old war for London and all its people,' said Matt, as he turned right into the village of Bere Regis. The Morris hummed past the handsome church. 'And it's not too good for the people of Plymouth and Southampton. It's a damned old war all round, but all I've got to complain about is the shortage of what's necessary to keep my garage running. I'm lucky, and you can believe that, for bombs don't whistle down in Dorset and my leg keeps me out of the Army or Navy.' He smiled wryly. 'Never thought the blamed thing would make me lucky, but there you are, Lieutenant, I'm more likely to crack my thumb with a spanner than be torpedoed at sea.'

Rosie felt he was trying to apologize for not being in uniform. What was it like for a disabled man who was otherwise in the prime of health, to be considered unfit for call-up? Did Mr Chapman really count himself lucky, and did he need to apologize?

'What happened to your leg, Mr Chapman?' she asked.

'I broke my ankle badly at the age of ten,' he said. 'Falling out of a tree. I was up there, scrumping Dorset pippins, and my sister was catching them in a basket. Buttercup was a helpful playmate.'

'Buttercup?' said Rosie.

'Right enough,' said Matt. 'Had a smile like a sunbeam, so everyone called her Buttercup. Her real name's Maisie.'

Maisie. Rosie smiled. Maisie was Grandma Finch's name.

'But your ankle was set, wasn't it, Mr Chapman?'

'Not too well, apparently,' said Matt. He was not far from the divisional headquarters now. 'It was re-set twice, but turned cantankerous and stayed that way, and I've had to carry it about with me like damaged goods ever since. All the same, I can manage to get through a barn dance with Mary Hubble.'

'Who's Mary Hubble?' smiled Rosie.

'Our local wartime postwoman,' said Matt. 'Lovely lady.'

'Well, in addition to a barn dance, you can also manage to knock bent cars back into shape and cure their ailments,' said Rosie. 'My car needs your talents. So do the farmers' tractors.'

'It's something that keeps the garage going,' said Matt, and brought the car to a halt at the gates of the perimeter bounding the property presently commandeered by the Army. 'Here we are.' He alighted, went round the car and opened the passenger door for Rosie. She slipped out with an easy movement of her legs, although her skirt slid a little. Matt gallantly turned his eyes elsewhere. Rosie smiled.

'Thanks for the lift, Mr Chapman,' she said, 'and thanks in advance for doing what you can to take my car off the danger list.'

'I'll see to it myself,' said Matt. 'Pleasure to have met you, Lieutenant. Goodbye for now.'

He got back into his car, and while doing a reverse turn he watched her, trim and slender in her khaki, as she walked through the open gate. He saw her return the salute of the sentry.

There, he thought, goes a young lady of grace with not an ounce of side.

I'd like one like her, he said to himself as he drove away, a smile on his face. At his age, thirty, a man was entitled to dream a little. There was more to come by in a dream than in wishes.

Rosie was thinking what a very refreshing man, a man of Dorset.

'Hello, hello?' said Sammy from his office desk, receiver to his ear.

'One hello's enough, Sammy.'

'I think that's you, Boots old soldier. Glad you called. Well, I will be if the news is good.'

'Sammy, deposit a cheque from the firm's property account with the agents for the Belsize Park factory, then get our solicitors to do the rest.'

'That's good news all right,' said Sammy. 'As an incidental comment, why couldn't we have made the purchase through the agents instead of you havin' to see the owner, Lady Whatever?'

'Because her son, Lieutenant Cunningham, said she wouldn't sell to anyone she hadn't personally vetted. She's a cranky old bird. What Lieutenant Cunningham was able to do for us was to phone the agents, tell them that we had first option and to discourage any other interested parties.'

'Well, I don't suppose even a cranky old bird gave you a lot of trouble, Boots,' said Sammy.

'She gave me ten minutes and then told me to push off,' said Boots. 'So Polly stepped in and rolled her over.'

'You took Polly with you?' said Sammy.

Boots said he'd felt Polly was necessary. Lieutenant Cunningham had informed him his mother was an awkward character who had inflated ideas about her standing, and might be a bit diffi-cult, just for the hell of it. Polly put on a sizzling upper class act, which included convincing her stupefied audience that she'd been on dancing terms with the Duke of Windsor before he went off his princely chump over Mrs Simpson. Lady Cunningham then fell over herself in conceding the factory to Adams Enterprises.

'Give Polly my compliments,' said Sammy, 'tell her she's one of the family.'

'She will be in March,' said Boots.

'Right now, as far as I'm concerned, she's already made it,' said Sammy.

'Get that cheque deposited,' said Boots, 'and try to persuade the agents to let you fit the factory up on exchange of contracts. So long, Sammy.'

'Wait a tick,' said Sammy. 'Could the Army use me, would you say?'

'Pardon?' said Boots.

'Well, you know the Army, and you know a bit about what I could offer it.'

'Are you unwell, Sammy?'

'Fortunately,' said Sammy, 'I don't suffer from being unwell, havin' been brought up by Chinese Lady to eat me greens and avoid dubious females. No, I've been thinking the business is just a routine job these days. Anyone with a bit of common could run it. I spoke to our stepdad yesterday evening, and he said with my partic'lar talents I'm a natural for a quartermaster's department store.'

'Did he say department store, Sammy?' asked Boots.

'Something like that,' said Sammy. 'How's yours, Boots, how's your quartermaster's department? Could it do with me organizing abilities? I don't mind startin' as a sergeant and workin' my way up to being a general.'

'The Quartermaster-General of the British Army, Sammy, is next to God.'

'Suits me,' said Sammy, 'I don't mind being next to God. And I don't think Susie would mind, either.'

'Have you spoken to Susie about this brainstorm of yours?' asked Boots.

'Well, no, not yet,' said Sammy. 'If I don't catch her in the right mood, she might catch me with a saucepan.'

'I think you'd better risk that and speak to her,'

said Boots. 'Or take an Aspro and sleep it off. Then get on with running the business. It needs you, Sammy. So long now, love to Susie.' He rang off, a smile on his face. He thanked the proprietor of the pub for the use of his phone and offered to pay for the call.

'On the house, sir,' said the proprietor.

'I'm obliged,' said Boots, and returned to the private bar, where Polly was still at the table, waiting for him. He sat down.

'All arranged?' said Polly, who'd taken the opportunity to powder her nose.

'Yes, Sammy's organized,' said Boots.

'Shall we go, then?' asked Polly, and they left the hospitable pub. The sharp sun of January had its own quality. It was far less enervating than that of high summer. Its light was an invigorating element, not a hot blow. Its pure clarity and the quietness of the country scene could not be related to the obscene warfare being waged by Germany's apparently inexhaustible squadrons of bombers. Polly was introspective as they reached the car.

'Penny for them' said Boots.

'I've got weaknesses I didn't know about,' she said.

'And problems?' said Boots.

'No. Yes,' she said. 'Stupidly, I want to be twenty-one again. All these years, all gone, and all spent on the sidelines, waiting for something to happen between you and me. And now what? Boots old dear, you're marrying a middle-aged has-been. Isn't that ludicrous?'

'Let's get this straight,' said Boots. 'For a start,

you're not a has-been and I don't see you as middle-aged, not with your aptitude for life and living. You're unique, Polly, and I can't think of anything I'd like better than having you around for the rest of my time. Not every man gets a unique woman washing his socks for him.'

'I've never washed anyone's socks in my life,' she said shakily.

'I'll show you the ropes,' said Boots. 'And how are you on ironing shirts?'

'Hopeless.'

'Knitting?' said Boots.

'What?'

'Darning?' said Boots.

'Darning?'

'Putting the cat out at night?'

'Oh, ye gods, we're not going to keep cats, are we?'

'You can turn a mangle, I suppose?' said Boots.

'You idiot,' said Polly.

'How about cooking, can you cook?' asked Boots.

'Does boiling an egg count?'

'Here's the final one,' said Boots. 'Can you wear a see-through black nightie without blushing?' That sent Polly over the top. In the sunshine, beside the car, she had hysterics again, hysterics that sent her doubts and weaknesses flying into limbo. 'Take your time,' said Boots, 'it's not an easy question to answer.'

'Spare me more,' she gasped.

'Is it painful, then?' asked Boots.

'It's painful that there's a war on, that it means we shan't be able to live together even when we are married, that we'll have to wait God knows how long before we can really enjoy what years we've got left to us,' said Polly. 'Listen, old thing, do you think Emily would mind about us marrying?'

'That worries you, Polly?'

'Well, you know, of course, that she never really liked me.'

'The dead have no grievances except about being dead,' said Boots.

'Did you get that epigram from an inferior imitation of Oscar Wilde?' asked Polly.

'No, from a tombstone in a country churchyard,' said Boots. 'Now, how about if we meander back to Wimborne Minster to see if we can find an old-fashioned teashop that doesn't know there's a war on?'

She touched his hand.

'Anywhere with you, old love,' she said.

Chapter Eleven

Twilight preceding frosty January dusk had taken the shine off the surface of the Firth of Clyde when the Troon Commandos were dismissed for the day. Little time was wasted during the hours of daylight, but once the rigours were over and no night exercise scheduled, officers and other ranks were free to hit the pubs or to entertain local talent. Fraternization with the girls of Troon had reached a mutually happy level.

Tim made tracks for his billet in company with Sergeant George Watts.

'Corporal Bloody Adams, I'm expectin' you to wet my whistle this evening,' said Sergeant Watts.

'I'm in favour of wetting my own whistle,' said Tim. 'Why should I wet yours?'

'Because you knocked me off t' bloody hill this morning,' said Sergeant Watts, 'and in front of Sergeant-Major Jarvis, by 'eck. Told you it would cost you summat. Couple of pints. For showin' off, got me?'

'You lost your bearings,' said Tim, 'and I'm learning fast that when the enemy loses his bearings, you knock him off, wherever he's standing, on the Forth Bridge or the side of a hill.'

'Listen here, gormless,' said Watts, mostly made

up of solid beef, 'you ask questions before you knock a sergeant arse-over-elbow.'

'Not in this outfit, and not in these kind of exercises,' said Tim. 'You don't ask questions before or after. You knock 'em off, sergeants, officers and even a sergeant-major if they're the enemy or, like you, acting as the enemy.'

'Happen you're a saucy bugger,' said Watts.

'And afterwards you just say one thing. "You're dead, mate." Still,' said Tim, 'I'll wet your whistle, I'll stand the first round.'

'Your shout, any road,' said Watts, and turned in at his billet.

Tim strolled leisurely on, yesterday's crippling exercise just another memory now. He felt as fit as a hard-riding cowpuncher. Commando training was like that. You felt flogged to death one day, and like spring-heeled Jack the next. One night, there'd be real action. He had to be ready for that, mentally and physically.

At that point, he heard quick footsteps behind him. Well able to believe someone had been sent to test him, he reacted swiftly. He whipped round to face whoever was on his tail.

'Steady, soldier,' said Subaltern Felicity Jessop.

'Thought you were going to jump me,' said Tim.

'That's not my line,' she said. Tim resumed his stroll, and she fell into step with him. 'I'm on my way to my billet.'

'We'll get talked about,' said Tim, remembering last night's incident. Some comics were already thinking things about him and this breezy ATS officer.

'Well, Lieutenant Cary won't like that, of course,' said Felicity. Lieutenant Pauline Cary was her superior. 'Listen, I heard there was some kind of joke played on you last night. What was it about?'

'Oh, just some berks horsing about,' said Tim.

'Some people never grow up,' said Felicity. She laughed. 'Should you be walking me to my billet?'

'Not while I'm only a corporal,' said Tim. 'Can you manage on your own?'

'I usually do,' she said.

'Shout for Captain Coombes if you need an escort,' said Tim, who knew rough and tough Captain Coombes had a keen eye for Subaltern Jessop.

'Not likely,' said Felicity, 'I've had some of that hairy tiger. I know you're all training to be uncivilized, but even so, wouldn't you think an Army captain would show some respect for my uniform?'

'I would think so, yes,' said Tim, 'but with a hundred per cent respect, I've got to say that when an ATS subaltern's sex appeal drives a bloke mad, even a captain, she's got to expect to fight off a tiger here and a tiger there.'

Felicity pealed with laughter, and the sound danced about in the twilight of Troon.

'Funny man,' she said. 'Are you a tiger?'

'I could be,' said Tim.

'I think I'd better push on, then,' said Felicity.

'Here's my billet, anyway,' said Tim, coming to a stop.

'So it is,' said Felicity. 'So long, soldier.' She was laughing again as she went on. What a sport, thought Tim, no wonder I like her.

He entered the house, went into the kitchen and said hello to Maggie.

'Off wi' your boots,' she said, as always.

Tim sat down, removed his webbing gaiters and unlaced his caked boots.

'D'you know Subaltern Jessop, one of the ATS officers?' he asked.

'Aye,' said Maggie, preparing fish for supper.

'You've seen her about?'

'Aye.'

'I think I'd like a photograph of her in a pin-up sweater,' said Tim.

'Och, aye?' said Maggie drily.

'Would you have a Brownie camera somewhere in the house?' asked Tim.

'There's one belonging to my husband,' said Maggie.

'I'll borrow it one day, if you'll lend it,' said Tim.

'Will the officer no' give you a flea in your ear?' said Maggie.

'Probably,' said Tim, 'but it's worth a try.'

Maggie smiled.

'Clean your boots, McAdams,' she said.

Tim simply thought the idea was another way of helping to take his mind off the loss of his mother. The arduous Commando training was a help, the murderous footslogging, the climbing of dizzy heights, the simulated in-fighting which was as near to the real thing as instructors could make it, the lectures on the known characteristics and strengths of the typical German soldier, the ways and means, mostly foul, of disposing of him, and the riding of rough water in a boat converted as a landing-craft, yes, all that helped. So did evenings in a pub, and so did time spent with a landlady like Maggie. And so would an attempt to get jolly, joking Subaltern Jessop to pose for a few snapshots.

He had to fight the moments when he was achingly sad about his late mother. The whole family had to fight their own moments. His dad had Polly Simms to help him. Tim didn't object. Polly was good old Polly. He saw her togetherness with his dad as a natural development. He didn't think it meant his dad had already forgotten his mother. No-one in the family would ever forget her.

A telephone conversation took place that evening between Helene Aarlberg, a young lady of France, and Bobby Somers, the elder son of Lizzy and Ned Somers. Helene and Bobby had escaped to England together a few weeks after the evacuation of Dunkirk, and had done so under the noses of the occupying Germans. Bobby was now in his first week at the Nottingham OCTU, and Helene had just begun training in Bucks with a unit of the First Aid Nursing Yeomanry (FANY), a highly select band of intelligent and resourceful women who could adapt themselves to either the humdrum nature of chauffeuring brasshats or the risk factors of the dangerous. These postings had come about through a recommendation from a certain Colonel Ross.

Helene, very French and accordingly not given to English reserve, was making her feelings known.

'It's disgusting. Everyone here is an imbecile.'

Shades of cousin Eloise, thought Bobby. She could talk just like that.

'Everyone?' he said.

'Yes. They keep awarding me only half the marks I deserve. How cross I am.'

'With anyone in particular?' asked Bobby.

'Yes, you.' Helene was very cross. Having gone overboard for him, in a manner of speaking, his present absence from her life was hard to bear. 'You haven't come to see me for months.'

'We had a weekend together at home in November,' said Bobby.

'That is as good as months. Ah, you English and your stiff upper lids.'

'Lips,' said Bobby, who was grinning at his end. He knew his young French lady very well.

'It makes no difference,' said Helene, 'it means you have no real feelings.'

'I've got my share,' said Bobby, 'and you'd know it if you were here and not there.'

'Then why don't you come to see me?'

'You know very well I can't get any leave until my three months here are up,' said Bobby.

'I am to be left alone for all that time? Ah, do you have an English girl up there? Is that why you don't come to see me?'

'What do I want an English girl for when I've got a French one?' asked Bobby.

'I am the only one you want?'

'Believe me,' said Bobby.

'Bobby, you would like to love me, yes? You would like me to undress for you?'

'Not now,' said Bobby.

'Of course not now, you lunatic. What good would that be, when you aren't here to see me?'

'Just as well,' said Bobby, 'falling eyeballs is a serious complaint in a bloke trying to earn a commission.'

'Excuse me? Falling eyeballs?'

'Yes, you can understand that, can't you?' said Bobby.

'How should I know what your silly English means? No, no, tell me what you would do if I undressed for you.'

'Collapse,' said Bobby.

'Collapse?'

'On the spot,' said Bobby. 'I come from an old-fashioned family. We undress in the dark.'

He heard her laugh, the sound travelling at a higher tonal pitch over the line, very much like an involuntary little shriek. Well, she was a game girl who'd eventually let a sense of humour break down her smouldering resentments about the BEF's performance in France.

'Bobby, you crazy man, you are so comical. Here, everything is very serious and intense.'

'You were like that when we first met,' said Bobby.

'Never! That is a lie!'

'Not to worry, I understood,' said Bobby.

'Bobby, you are not to think about me like that.'

'I don't,' said Bobby, 'I think about you sailing your little dinghy across the Channel in the darkness and telling me French jokes.'

'But I don't know any French jokes.'

'Well, try to think of some next time we meet,' said Bobby. 'Listen, has Colonel Ross been to see you?'

Colonel Ross was the man who had spoken to them months ago about operating in France in collaboration with members of a resistance movement, a movement encouraged by the British Government.

'No, I haven't seen him, no,' said Helene, 'only horsy women who watch me when I am doing First Aid or other things, but say nothing to me. I think, yes, I think they talk only with horses. But has Colonel Ross seen you, Bobby?'

'Just to ask how I'm getting on,' said Bobby, 'and to check my credentials again.'

'Ah, I know. To see if you are still willing. Bobby, do you think we'll be sent to France one day?'

'You're not supposed to mention that over the phone,' said Bobby. 'What extension are you using?'

'The one in the rest room, but no-one is here at the moment, no-one.'

'Fair enough if you trust whoever's manning the switchboard,' said Bobby, 'but all the same, keep to things like cricket.'

'Cricket? Cricket?'

'Yes, all good clean fun,' said Bobby, 'like undressing and so on.'

'I have a very fine body, you know.'

'Well, keep it dark,' said Bobby, 'I blush easily. Didn't I make that clear?'

Helene laughed again.

'Oh, what a funny idiot you are,' she said. Then she wondered again if she and Bobby really would be sent to France, and if so, would she have the chance to see her parents. She raised the possibility with Bobby by saying, 'Perhaps sometime I shall be able to see my family.'

'I don't think you should count on that,' said Bobby.

'But—'

'I don't think it'll be that kind of holiday, old girl,' said Bobby.

'No? Ah, I see. Yes, I understand, but how sad that— wait, I don't wish to be called old girl. It is a very silly English saying.'

'We're a bit like that over here,' said Bobby. 'Got to go now. Be good, don't go out with the Free French, and don't go out in the dark, either.'

'Idiot, when I next see you I am going to bite your head off.'

'Just for being an idiot?'

'Yes. Bleeding hard luck, mate. There, how do you like the silly English I have learned?'

'Love it,' said Bobby. 'So long, gorgeous, I'll catch up with you sometime.'

'Catch up with me, Bobby?'

'Yes, and your French oo-la-la,' said Bobby.

Sammy had quickly deposited the required cheque with Lady Cunningham's agent, who had said Sammy could move in his machines as soon as contracts were exchanged.

'Say a bit earlier, say tomorrow?' suggested Sammy.

'Say when your cheque proves good,' countered Mr Palmer.

'Don't offend me,' said Sammy.

'I have to guard my client's interests, Mr Adams.'

'Accordin' to my brother, Major Adams,' said Sammy, 'your client could guard her own interests and the interests of the Bank of England with only a broom handle and a coal shovel.'

'A spirited lady,' said Mr Palmer.

'Well, I'll at least get ready to move in,' said Sammy.

'No objections to that, Mr Adams.'

'Glad of that,' said Sammy, 'there's a war on, a hell of a war.'

He called on his old friend, Mr Eli Greenberg, the next day. Mr Greenberg was a sad man. His beloved old yard in Blackfriars, his living and as good as his second home in his adopted country, had been blasted by a bomb, and that had forced him to find another yard, off Camberwell Road and close to Camberwell Green. Sammy had pointed him to it.

Mr Greenberg was not only sad about the air raids and the havoc and casualties, he was sad about all the news filtering out of Germany concerning the Jews. The Nazis were terrifying the children of Israel, beating them, starving them and deporting them to regions unknown. He silently thanked his dead father for bringing the family to London many years ago.

Sammy's greeting was typical.

'How's your fine self, Eli old cock? Bearing up now, like Rachel, I might suggest?'

'Ah, Sammy, Sammy, vhen vas I not bearing up, ain't I?' sighed Mr Greenberg. 'But never did I know vorse days. Hitler, vhat a blackguard. May the Lord strike him down, and I say that, Sammy, as a man given to preaching peace and goodvill to all. But vhat goodvill could come to the blackguard who took Em'ly from us? So sad, Sammy, so sad. And then business, my boy, who can do satisfying business in such a var as this?'

'Not without headaches, Eli,' said Sammy. 'Listen, you mentioned last week that you were acquirin' transport, and I'm lookin' for selfsame. Removal firms are all full up with contracts on account of so many people movin' to where they can eat breakfast without havin' to clear their kitchens of bricks and plaster every morning. What's your transport, and where is it?'

'Here, Sammy, here.' Mr Greenberg led Sammy out to his new yard, and waved his hands in the direction of a vehicle. 'You're velcome to hire it now and immediate.'

'Ruddy bluebottles,' said Sammy, 'if I'm not mistaken, you're offering me use of a down-and-out omnibus.'

An old London General Omnibus Company open-topped omnibus was standing at the back of the yard, looking like something that ought to have died a graceful death before the wild Twenties were over.

'Still a fine vheeler, Sammy,' said Mr Greenberg. 'Vould I say othervise to a friend? Vould I offer rubbish, Sammy?'

'Yes, but is it a monument, Eli, or does it still move?'

'Sammy, I vill drive it myself for you. Say the

135

vord, tell me the job, and it vill be done.'

'Got a kettle and a gas ring in your office, Eli?'

'Ah, vhen didn't I have such things, Sammy? Didn't my mother and father find out vun should alvays have a kettle and a gas ring? And a teapot? Not a samovar, no, a teapot.'

'Right, let's have a cup of tea, then,' said Sammy, 'and I'll tell you what the job's all about.'

'Ah, a job,' said Mr Greenberg happily, 'vhat a sveet sound in these terrible times, ain't it, Sammy?'

'Look here,' said Sir Henry, enjoying a pre-dinner drink with Boots in the mess that evening, 'I need to talk to you.'

'About how to knock down German night bombers?' said Boots.

'They worry me with their persistence,' said Sir Henry, 'and I daresay they worry the Prime Minister too. But no, I've a transfer in mind for you.'

'A transfer?' said Boots.

'It's like this,' said Sir Henry, and spoke of a conversation he had had with an officer from Whitehall during the day. It related to the require-ments of the rapidly growing Commando groups, and the need for recruiting suitable men and officers. 'You know about these new shock troops, the Commandos, don't you?'

'Yes, I know,' said Boots.

'Churchill himself sees them as a way of harass-ing the Germans, damaging their complacency and striking at their sense of invincibility. Boots, I'm considering allowing a certain number of officers and men from one of our crack infantry divisions to be given the chance to volunteer, and I can arrange for you to transfer to a group as an admin. officer. You're not eligible for action, since the Commandos won't take any man or officer over forty into their fighting ranks.'

'Glad to hear it,' said Boots.

'But they need some first-class admin. officers to help with their expansion,' said Sir Henry. 'Such officers would be part of the cadre necessary at every training theatre, which would mean a permanent home base for you. I'd hate to lose you, but the Commandos would gain.'

Boots looked Sir Henry in the eye. Sir Henry cleared his throat.

'Sir, aren't you expecting the Corps to be drafted overseas as soon as our armoured divisions are up to strength?'

'True, but you needn't take that into consideration,' said Sir Henry.

'Have you been speaking to Polly?' asked Boots.

'Polly?' Sir Henry cleared his throat again. 'No, not about this. Of course, should you accept the transfer, there's no reason why she couldn't go with you.'

Boots smiled. It was quite clear now. He and Polly were being offered a permanent home posting and probably a very comfortable marital billet.

'Frankly,' he said, 'I don't know if I'm entitled to duck out of my responsibilities to you and the Corps. I ought to say no, I should say no.'

'Don't you think you should first talk to Polly?' asked Sir Henry reasonably.

'That was what I meant,' said Boots, 'I can't say no without talking to her.'

'You'll consider the transfer, then?'

'Polly and I will consider it together,' said Boots.

'Good man,' said Sir Henry. 'But I can assure you this is off my own bat. I repeat, Polly's had no hand in it.'

'I'd miss working with you,' said Boots soberly, and Sir Henry wondered then if he was doing the right thing. There were very few occasions when, out on the necessary inspection of units, he didn't have Boots among his accompanying staff officers. And at all other times, Boots was within call. Sir Henry's regard for the man Polly was so attached to was long-standing and deep-seated. Was all that inducing him to put his daughter's interests before the interests of the Corps? On the other hand, the Commando set-up would acquire an absolutely first-class admin. officer.

And Polly, after all, had waited a damned long time for a life with Boots.

Too long.

Damn all else for the time being, thought Sir Henry.

Chapter Twelve

Certain people had certain things to do the following day.

Sammy and Mr Greenberg, with the muscular help of Bert Roper and Tommy, had to transport the sewing-machines and other equipment from the Shoreditch factories to Belsize Park. And Bert was on the phone early to Sammy's home, to let him know a bomb had blown off the roof of one factory. There was no damage to the machines that couldn't be repaired, but the factory itself was out of action. Sammy said that was no more than they'd been expecting, and that he'd be there with Mr Greenberg as soon as possible. Production at both factories would have to stop for a couple of days, in any case.

Boots had to drive to 17th Infantry Division head-quarters to talk to Polly. He phoned her to let her know he'd be there by noon.

Rosie had to go and see Mr Chapman about her car, and to find out if its critical condition was in a reasonable recovery stage.

And Sergeant Eloise Adams was required to show Major Lucas that she was ready to be awarded her Army driving certificate.

* * *

As promised, Mr Greenberg himself drove the old omnibus to Shoreditch, but by a roundabout route because of new bomb damage in the City. The vehicle trundled ponderously, moving in heavyweight defiance of its age, its lower deck seats no longer existent, having been removed before Mr Greenberg bought the vehicle for a few quid.

'Eli, have you got a licence for this old heap?' asked Sammy, seated on a packing-case.

'Sammy, are you saying something vhile I am hard of hearing?' asked a pained Mr Greenberg.

'Got you, Eli, sorry I spoke,' said Sammy.

Shoreditch had been hit again last night. Buildings gaped, and the blast of high explosives had sucked out the taped windows of dwellings. People were sweeping broken glass off the pavements and workforces were replacing panes and making repairs. The Government knew that the use of these workforces was essential. It restored spirits, lifted morale and let the people know Parliament cared about them. In clearing up their pavements, they worked with a kind of grim but vociferous aggressiveness, letting each other know in the raw language of the East End exactly what they thought of the bleedin' Jerries and their equally bleedin' flying machines.

The ancient omnibus crunched its way over broken glass, and the suffering people stared at it, gaped at it, bawled at it and shouted with laughter.

'What yer got there, mate, a tupp'ny ride to 'Ackney Downs?'

'Where's its 'orse?'

'What is it, yer old lady's bathtub on wheels?'

'I dunno from 'ere if it's got wheels.'

The local grapevine buzzed then, and people started to run.

''Ere, move yerself, Nellie, there's hon'rable visitors.'

'Eh? What? Who?'

'The King and Queen, they're in Spitalfields, treadin' rubble and saying 'ello to ev'ryone, so I just 'eard.'

'Well, gawd-bleedin'-blimey, ain't that a blinder? Come on, then, Alf, but keep yer 'ands in yer pockets. I ain't 'aving you slip 'Er Majesty's crown under yer waistcoat.'

'Am I hearing vhat they're saying, Sammy?' asked Mr Greenberg, skirting obstacles.

'Drive on, Eli, business before gawpin',' said Sammy.

'Sammy, ain't ve to get vun look at Their Majesties?'

'Not now, Eli,' said Sammy, 'but on our way back we'll drop in on Buckingham Palace.'

'Sammy, ain't it sad, my boy? Vhat is more dear to me than old London, ain't it? The damage, Sammy, the damage, it gets vorse every day.'

'Don't you worry, Eli,' said Sammy, 'Fatty Goering might be big, but London's a lot bigger.'

When they reached the first factory, Tommy was there waiting for them, along with Bert and Gertie Roper. Bert and Gertie were stalwarts of a great-hearted kind.

The factory roof was a sagging conglomeration of broken tiles and cracked timbers. The interior was coated with dust and broken plaster. Tommy,

Bert and Gertie gaped at the old omnibus.

'What the hell is it?' asked Tommy.

'Our removal van,' said Sammy, 'best I could get at short notice. What's the other fact'ry like?'

'Standin' up and workin',' said Tommy.

'But this one's done for, Mister Sammy,' said Gertie.

'We've had the roof shored up,' said Tommy, 'but clearin' the place of everything we need is as much as we can risk.'

'How are the girls?' asked Sammy.

'Just about bearin' up at the other fact'ry,' said Bert, 'but them that works at this one ain't feelin' too good, not by a long shot.'

'Well, we're goin' to lift everything out of both fact'ries, and cart the lot to Belsize Park, even if it takes us all day and tomorrow as well,' said Sammy. 'Tell the girls they'll all get paid while the move's takin' place. Gertie, you go home and put your feet up.'

'I ain't goin' to do that, Mister Sammy,' said Gertie, 'I can lift sewing-machines along with you and Bert, and what's more, I'm goin' to round up some of the girls. They'll lend an 'and, them that's not 'aving to sweep up broken glass.'

'We need every hand, Sammy,' said Tommy, 'it's goin' to be a hell of a job, clearing out both factories of machines, stocks and other stuff, and loadin' the lot on that contraption.'

'Vhich contraption vill take heavy loads, Tommy,' said Mr Greenberg, clad as ever in his old round black hat and dark grey overcoat of capacious pockets. 'And I myself vill gladly lend a hand.'

'Good on yer, Eli,' said Tommy. 'Right, then, let's get busy.'

'I'll get the girls,' said Gertie.

Off she went, and the four men began the work. Thirty minutes later, as many as twenty machinists had joined them. Sammy and Tommy were touched, for these women of the East End, shaken as they were by the nightly air raids, worked with a will. But then, none of their machinists had ever failed them.

Nor had Mr Greenberg or Bert.

Boots arrived at 17th Infantry Division headquarters at eleven. Polly, knowing he was coming, was waiting for him. Out she came, and Boots, alighting from his car, saw the spring in her step, the easy movements of her body, the rhythmic swing of her skirt and her air of vitality. What other woman of forty-four could look so young?

Up she came, and she saluted him.

'Good morning, sir.'

'Good morning, Captain,' said Boots, returning the salute.

'May I say how dashing you look, sir?'

'You can say so,' said Boots, 'but I won't believe it.'

'Please yourself, you old darling,' murmured Polly, 'but I know how you look to me. How do I look to you?'

Boots smiled.

'About twenty,' he said.

'Ye gods,' breathed Polly, 'no wonder I'm infatuated. About twenty, he said. What a sport. And seeing you twice within a few days is famous, old dear. Are we going to confront the Rockbourne dragon again? You said nothing over the phone, except that you were coming to take me out.'

'I want to talk to you, Polly,' said Boots, 'and have lunch with you at Wimborne Minster.'

'Talk to me? What about?' Polly searched him. 'God, you're not going to change your mind about marrying me, are you?'

'Not unless you forget to turn up,' said Boots, and opened the passenger door. 'Get in, Polly, while I go and say hello to Rosie.'

'Yes, I think you should,' said Polly. She slid in. 'I'll wait,' she said, and Boots entered the mansion. Down the handsome staircase at that moment came Rosie, cap off and fair hair shining. Seeing Boots in the tiled hall, she quickened her descent, blue eyes alight. She flew through the hall and hugged him.

'Good morning, Lieutenant Adams,' said Boots.

'Blow that for a lark,' said Rosie, 'give us a kiss.'

He planted a warm one on her cheek. The mansion hummed with activity, and he drew her out into the open.

'How are you, Rosie?' His smile was affectionate, his love for his adopted daughter constant. 'I was just coming up to see you.'

'And I was just coming down to see you,' said Rosie. 'It's a bit thick, you know, not getting invited out myself.'

'I'll come over again one day next week and put that right,' said Boots.

'I hope that's a promise,' said Rosie.

'Cross my heart,' said Boots. He studied her. She looked a little serious. 'Rosie, you don't mind about Polly and me, do you?'

'You shouldn't have to ask that,' said Rosie, 'you should know I stand with you in whatever you do. But—' She smiled. 'But I'm not going to call her mother. Just ducky. Or old sport. Emily was my mother. You know that, don't you?'

'Yes, I know it, Rosie, and I like you for saying so.'

'Bless you, Daddy old thing, I wish you a lovely future. Now go and join Polly. She's your future.'

'See you, Rosie,' said Boots.

'You'd better,' said Rosie, 'you made a promise.'

Boots drove towards the A31, but pulled off the narrow country road into the same lay-by as before. He switched off the engine.

'Heavens,' murmured Polly, 'what am I to expect this time?'

'A discussion,' said Boots.

'Darling, you're not going to be dreary, are you? You never have been. I beg you won't disappoint me now.'

'The fact is, Polly, I've a chance of a transfer to a Commando training theatre,' he said.

'You've what?' said Polly.

Boots went into detail without mentioning her father, or the fact that the transfer had been offered to him by Sir Henry. The chance of a new job was there for the taking, he said. He pointed out it would be a home-based permanency, and that a suitable billet would be available for them. Polly stared at him, eyes wide, mouth a little open.

'But will my father let you go?' she asked.

'I've spoken to him. He'll agree to the transfer as long as he's sure I can be useful. These new Commando groups are the coming hammer of the Army. My work will mean no overseas postings. What d'you say, Polly?'

'I'm going to ask you if you'll be able to stand doing what will turn into a routine job at the same desk in the same place every day,' said Polly. 'I'm going to ask if you'll miss the mobility and the activity of being with my father's Corps, wherever it's sent.'

'That goes without saying,' said Boots. 'Shall we give ourselves time to think it over, then?'

'Yes, I think we should,' said Polly. Much as the idea of a life with Boots on a permanent home base appealed to her, she knew him all too well. Doing a routine admin. job, even with a Commando group, while her father's Corps was on active service in the Middle East or elsewhere, would not be what he would choose if he were a free agent. He was asking her to help him make his choice. 'Right now, old love, I don't feel I can decide for both of us,' she said, 'so let's give ourselves more time. Let's think it over.'

'Fair enough,' said Boots, 'but I'd like you to know you can have the casting vote, Polly. Whatever you prefer, I'll go along with.'

Polly faced him, her eyes a dark cloudy grey. Boots thought for a moment that this extrovert woman, who hid so much of herself under a brittle front, was actually going to shed a tear. But Polly was never going to let herself down in that kind of way, especially not in his presence. The clouds slipped away, and she laughed.

'Dear old thing, I love the idea of being permanently fixed up with you wherever,' she said, 'but will I have to do the cooking?'

'Wherever it is, I'll find a batman useful with saucepans, pudding basins, frying-pans,' said Boots.

'I'll see to the boiled eggs,' said Polly.

'Then I'll find a few spare chickens as well,' said Boots. 'And a chicken run.'

'What does one feed chickens on?' asked Polly.

'Among other things, eggshells, I believe,' said Boots.

'Shells from their own eggs?'

'So I believe. It provides them with needed calcium.'

'Ye gods,' said Polly, 'eating their own eggshells has to be a form of cannibalism.'

'I don't think chickens realize that,' said Boots.

'A case of ignorance is bliss?' said Polly.

'I suppose so,' said Boots.

'Well, dear old sport, we'll agree to give ourselves time to decide,' said Polly, 'but, nevertheless, when we get to Wimborne I'd like you to buy me something.'

'Such as?'

'Something to do with not wanting to permanently rely on a batman-cook,' said Polly.

'What d'you want me to buy you, then?' asked Boots.

'A cookery book,' said Polly.

Boots laughed.

'Damned if you aren't a joy, Polly,' he said.

She kissed him then, with feeling.

Rosie secured a lift to Chapman's Garage after lunch. Matthew Chapman was there, with his two veteran mechanics.

'Hello, Lieutenant, how are you?'

'I'm fine,' said Rosie, 'how's my car?'

'Better than it was,' said Matt. 'We've cleaned the chassis and body, tightened the springs, put the brakes in order and fitted a new fan belt. The ratchet that controls the opening and closing of your windscreen now works, and I've put new masks over your headlamps.' Wartime regulations required headlamps to give only slits of light.

'Mr Chapman, my Hillman's no longer dangerously ill?' said Rosie. 'I can drive it away?'

'I don't think you'll be able to do that,' said Matt. 'Well, don't you see, I've never known any car to be driven anywhere without its engine.'

Rosie smiled.

'Then I shan't try,' she said. 'Is the engine still having a bath, Mr Chapman?'

'Yes, but ready now to be lifted and serviced,' said Matt. 'I was going to show it to you, but it can't be seen. The cleansing fluid has turned into a muddy pond, and I wouldn't be surprised if a pair of ducks weren't trying to work out if it was their kind of pond.'

'I don't think I'll get in their way,' said Rosie, 'I'm happy to leave it to you to lift the engine out of its pond and service it. Somehow, I've never come round to wanting to know about cars, engines, and the way everything works. I think I'm a mechanical duffer.'

'Duffers of that kind keep garages in business, Lieutenant,' said Matt, his ready smile showing. 'So, naturally, mechanical duffers are my favourite people.'

'My word,' said Rosie, 'you're a tonic to one like me. On the other hand, I'm very good at crossword puzzles.'

'What's an old joke in five letters?' asked Matt.

'Corny,' said Rosie.

He laughed.

'About the estimate,' he said.

'Yes?' said Rosie.

'Say thirty-five quid,' said Matt.

'You're joking,' said Rosie.

'I think it's fair,' said Matt.

'I meant you're cheating yourself,' said Rosie.

'I'm happy with thirty-five,' said Matt.

'Mr Chapman, are you sure?'

'I won't lose,' said Matt. 'No, it's fair and square, Lieutenant. Let's say you can pick the car up anytime Saturday afternoon. I'll have it finished by then, or eat my boots, blow my shirt off if I won't.'

Rosie laughed. There's a regular princess, thought Matt.

An open farm truck, carrying a hundredweight of swedes in sacks and a large crate of potatoes, turned in and came to a stop on the forecourt. The driver, a woman, stepped down. Beefy, she was dressed in shirt, pullover, breeches, boots and an old felt hat.

'Got my old man's cranker, Matt?' she asked breezily.

'Ben, let's have Mr Riddle's starting handle,' called Matt.

'Comin',' called Ben.

'Is it straightened out?' asked Mrs Riddle.

'Straight enough,' said Matt, 'but it beats me all ends up, someone managing to bend a cranker.'

'I told you, Wesley did it,' said Mrs Riddle. 'You know what he's like. He'd only have to pat a Spitfire for its wings to drop off. Got no finesse, poor old sod, just a ton of muscle.' She glanced at Rosie. 'Now then, Matt, who's the lady?'

'Lieutenant Adams from Divisional headquarters,' said Matt. 'A customer.'

'How'd'y'do?' said Mrs Riddle heartily.

'Meet Mrs Doris Riddle of Puddle Farm,' said Matt to Rosie.

'Hello,' said Rosie. She smiled. 'Is there a Puddle Farm?'

'There's Puddles all over Dorset,' said Mrs Riddle, 'and one or two Piddles. But don't look at me, even if they do rhyme with my name. I'm from Hampshire. My, you're smart-looking. Can't say the same about my old man, Wesley Riddle. The last time he looked smart was on our wedding day, twenty-one years ago. Hello, that my cranker, Ben?'

'Here's it,' said Ben, arriving with a starting handle. Mrs Riddle took it and looked it over.

'Well, that's an improvement,' she said. 'How much, Matt?'

'On the house,' said Matt. 'I'd have got you a second-hand one from somewhere if I hadn't

150

known Wesley was fond of that little old lady.'

'He turned it into a bent old lady,' said Mrs Riddle. 'Thanks, Matt, very friendly. Tell you what, I'll put a couple of bob into the village Spitfire fund. Well, I'd better get these swedes and King Edwards delivered to the sergeant-cook at Manor Park.' Manor Park housed the headquarters of the 17th Division.

'Could you drop Lieutenant Adams off there?' asked Matt.

'Pleasure,' said Mrs Riddle. 'Hop up, Lieutenant.'

'Thanks,' said Rosie. 'I'll find time to pick the Hillman up first thing after lunch on Saturday, Mr Chapman.'

'See you then,' said Matt, and Rosie left, riding in the sturdy truck.

Its engine churned strongly, and Rosie smiled at the aggressive way Mrs Riddle handled the gear changes. She was probably a typical example of how no-nonsense women were dealing with what the war required of them.

'Bloody lovely feller, Matt Chapman,' said the farmer's wife. 'Family business, the garage. His dad runs another in Dorchester. Damn' shame about Matt's leg, though. I know he'd rather be in the Army or Navy, and leave Ben to look after the garage.'

'He seems cheerful enough,' said Rosie.

'Never known him with his head down,' said Mrs Riddle, powering along. 'He could have been a lawyer. Came out of his grammar school in Dorchester as top boy, so my old man said, with ideas of studying the law. But his dad persuaded him to join the business, thinking the physical side of it would strengthen his leg. It's done that all right, I'd say. He could use it to kick a mule from here to Dartmoor. His garage'll pick up after the war, when people start running their cars again. After all, he's on the main road from Poole to Dorchester. He'll make a packet from his old petrol pump alone, and good luck to him. Bloody genius with engines. Is he fixing up your own car?'

'Yes, my second-hand Hillman,' said Rosie.

'He'll do a good job on it,' said Mrs Riddle. 'Ought to be married, of course, ought to have a wife. We all thought it would be Margaret Chaise of Bere. He looked to be pretty fond of her, and she of him, but two years ago she upped and married George Bulmer, who's got a farm this side of Wimborne. Still, Matt took it like a man and went to the wedding.'

'Was it the man the lady turned down, or his lame leg?' asked Rosie.

'More like his garage,' said Mrs Riddle. 'Margaret Chaise couldn't abide grease and oily overalls, silly woman.' She chatted on, turning to the war, and what the German bombers had done to Southampton and Plymouth, the buggers. 'If you ever get to Germany, Lieutenant, forget you're a lady and make a bonfire of Hitler and his mob while they're still alive. Here we are.' She turned in at the gates of Manor Park, slowed and said hello to the sentry. He grinned and waved her through. Then he caught sight of Rosie. He blinked, came to attention and saluted. Mrs Riddle, smiling, drove on. 'I like that,' she said.

'You like what?' said Rosie.

'Men having to play second fiddle to women like you.'

'Is that what you think, that when they salute an officer, they're playing second fiddle?' said Rosie.

'Do 'em good, that's my opinion.'

'Mrs Riddle, when I salute a senior officer, I don't consider I'm playing second fiddle,' said Rosie.

'That's different,' said Mrs Riddle, and pulled up outside the main doors of the mansion. Rosie alighted, thanked her for the lift, and the lady said a breezy goodbye to her, then drove round to the huts built in the gardens. The swedes and potatoes were part of the rations for other ranks.

Rosie went back to her office, to resume her work and the supervision of the ATS personnel.

Oddly, she thought about Matthew Chapman using his lame leg to kick a mule all the way to Dartmoor. The mental picture brought a smile to her face.

Chapter Thirteen

'Eh? What?' said Home Guard Henry Wade.

'Good on yer, Henry,' said Sammy, 'it's okay to move some of our stuff in?'

'Well, Mr Adams, I ain't rightly sure Mr Palmer's advised me accordin'.'

'But you know our offer's been accepted, of course.'

'Well, yerse, I know that,' said Henry, while Hercules sat with a friendly eye on Sammy and a suspicious eye on Tommy, Bert and Mr Greenberg, all of whom were wisely staying in the background.

'We've been bombed down in Shoreditch,' said Sammy.

'Sorry for yer, that I am,' said Henry, 'it was bleedin' bad again last night.'

'So we need to move stuff in,' said Sammy, and slipped Henry a pound note.

'Yes, course yer do, Mr Adams.'

'Mr Palmer's had our cheque,' said Sammy.

'Good as yourn now, then, this place,' said Henry.

'And you're part of the fittings,' said Sammy.

'You're givin' me the job?' said Henry.

'Couldn't do without you,' said Sammy. 'I'll take

you on here and now. Well, just in case you get notice.'

'Which I might if Mr Palmer don't like the idea of you movin' in just yet,' said Henry.

'Upon me soul, I didn't think of that,' said Sammy. 'Well, consider yourself safe with Adams Enterprises, Henry, and not a word to Mother, eh? We'll get this lot unloaded, then we've got to go back for more.'

'I'll 'elp yer, Mr Adams.'

'Ta,' said Sammy. 'But could you first make sure Hercules won't bite any legs off?'

As for Sergeant Eloise Adams, she was out during the morning with Major Lucas, he himself testing her competence as a driver. She considered the exercise frivolous. She was wholly competent, her gear changes excellent now. However, silly rules had to apply, one had to obey directives and commands from everyone of senior rank, commissioned or non-commissioned. It was no good saying this or that wasn't necessary. It wasn't even necessary for Major Lucas himself to examine her, but he'd insisted.

Well, now she was out at the wheel of the car, Major Lucas sitting beside her. The road glimmered moistly under the pale afternoon sun. The heathlands were purple, and light mist hung around the Pennines, over which Roman legions had marched northwards centuries ago.

Eloise handled the car with assurance, even showing off a little. She knew Major Lucas favoured a challenging approach, that he'd mark her down if she let the snaking road reduce her self-confidence.

'Up in the air today, are we, Sergeant Adams?' he said eventually.

'Up in the air, sir?' she said, changing gear expertly as she reached a slight ascent. 'I don't know what you mean.'

'Don't you?' Major Lucas was watching her, studying her attractive profile and the little movements of her mobile lips. 'It means top of your form,' he said.

'Thank you, sir, how encouraging,' said Eloise, confident not only of her driving but of her looks. Her mirror could be delightfully satisfying. Also, her father, whom she adored, had told her more than once that she was the family's French lily. One day she would meet a man of magnificent distinction, a handsome English baronet, perhaps, who would fall madly in love with her and commit suicide if she didn't marry him. Well, she would marry him, of course. She would not want to be responsible for his death. She was not a girl any more, she was twenty-three and a woman who would know it was more intelligent to marry a baronet than to let him take poison. She had had many admirers, but could see them now as fairly ordinary men. They had all disappeared, mostly into the Services.

Reaching the top of the ascent, she began the steep descent, the glimmering road running through a valley colourful with flowering winter heather. The pale sun danced on the bonnet of the car and speckled the windscreen with little patches of light.

'Very good, Sergeant Adams,' said Major Lucas, smiling.

'Yes, sir, I am naturally very good at everything I do,' said Eloise. The car was travelling at a controlled speed in third gear, and as she reached the bottom of the descent and approached a bend, she applied a little necessary pressure to the foot-brake. To her horror, the back wheels went away from her, and the car slewed in a slow but remorseless skid on the wet road. The offside rear wheel bumped into a stone marker and its tyre at once sighed and began to subside.

'Sergeant Adams?' said Major Lucas.

'Oh, name of a thousand pigs!' gasped Eloise in French.

'I don't think that will help,' said Major Lucas, and got out of the car to inspect the offending wheel. He noted immediately that the tyre was suffering. Eloise, mortified, joined him. 'A puncture,' he said.

'Oh, it's not fair,' she protested, 'why should that silly stone be there.'

'It's an old granite mile marker,' said the Major, and looked up and down the road. There was not a soul in sight, nor any sign of a vehicle. He took off his cap, coat and jacket, and placed them on the back seat of the car. The cool, damp air embraced his shirt, tie and braces. Eloise stared at him.

'What are you going to do?' she asked.

'Change the wheel,' he said, and opened the boot. Eloise gave a little feminine yelp. She had snatched a few moments to collect her weekly laundry while waiting for the Major to appear. She intended to take it to her quarters and let it air. If one didn't air it properly, the smell of laundry soaps lingered. The Major appeared before she could even start for her quarters. She hurried back to the car, reaching it well in advance, and she placed the unrolled laundry in the boot. There it was now, slip, bra and other underwear, and he was looking at it. Oh, the fiends, he was even smiling. 'Um – Sergeant Adams, are these yours?' he asked.

Eloise rushed, snatched at the items and backed away. More horrors. Her laundered slip fell. He caught the garment in mid-air and gravely handed it to her. She looked at him over her armful of laundry.

'Major Lucas—'

'Not your day, Sergeant Adams?' He smiled. 'However, can't be helped. Life pokes us all in the eye from time to time. If it'll make you feel better, give that tyre a kick.'

Something in that appealed to her, and she recovered so well that she smiled.

'Embarrassment is very unwelcome to a woman,' she said.

Major Lucas, uncovering the well containing the spare wheel and tools, said, 'Never mind, put your embarrassment away in the car somewhere, and I'll jack the bounder.'

She folded her laundry and put it on the back seat. Then she watched him go to work. He had to go down on his knees on the damp surface of the road, to position the jack. Before he used it, however, he loosened the nuts holding the offside rear wheel in place. He worked the jack, and the wheel came clear of the ground. He soon had it off, but his hands were filthy by then. On went the spare wheel. He lowered the car, and the tyre of the spare wheel made resilient contact with the road. He finished by tightening the nuts.

'Sir, that is very good work,' said Eloise.

'I'll get the workshop staff to teach you how to change a wheel,' he said.

'Very well, sir, if you must, of course,' she said, thinking an English baronet would never ask her to do such a thing.

Major Lucas cleaned his hands on the rag that was among the tools, put everything away and closed the boot. She thought that without his coat and jacket, he must be cold, but he didn't seem so. He had a kind of exuberant, active body. He moved to retrieve his jacket from the rear seat of the car.

'I think we're ready,' he said, 'but damned if I know whether it'll be a risk or not letting you drive me any farther.'

Eloise, standing with her back to the door of the driving seat, said, 'But, sir, the fiends of fate wouldn't strike twice on the same day, would they?'

He laughed, richly. She smiled up at him. Most men would have construed it as inviting. It was certainly beguiling, and Major Lucas went so far as to give in to impulse. He kissed her, on her lips. Eloise, shocked, lost her breath. She could not believe it. She knew, he knew, they both knew, and all too well, that no officer should commit such an indiscretion. Oh, how dare he? He was not a highly distinctive English baronet, he was only one more officer and not even handsome. He was a rugged bear of a man, kissing her without permission and without the least encouragement. Tiny bright stars danced in her head, and her pulse rate galloped. He was close, very close, his body warm against hers. Oh, the brute, when would the kiss stop?

She was free then. She was also flushed and furious.

'How dare you! You kissed me! You may be an officer, Major Lucas, but you're no gentleman!'

'Well, I can't argue with that, but—'

'You are going to say I wanted you to kiss me? Did I ask you to? No, I did not!'

'Then I apologize,' he said. 'Serious mistake. Many apologies, and all sincere, believe me.'

'As a commanding officer,' she said, 'how could you do such a thing?'

'A fall from grace, damned if it wasn't,' he said. 'Hope you'll accept my apologies, Sergeant Adams.'

Ah, thought Eloise, I have the advantage now.

'Very well, sir,' she said. 'In any case, I wish to forget it. I'm ready now to go back to camp.'

'Best thing,' he said.

On the return journey, Eloise said, 'I would like to be told, sir, that the skid was not my fault.'

'Don't I remember telling you such things can't be helped?'

'It won't count against me?' she said.

'I'll be informing your sergeant-instructor you're ready to earn your certificate,' said Major Lucas. 'However, under the circumstances, I'll not land you with the job of being my driver.'

'Sir?'

'I think we both understand, Sergeant Adams.'

Utterly dismayed, Eloise said, 'Oh, that's not fair. You promised right at the beginning. Sir, is that what an officer of your rank should do, break a promise?'

'I said that under the circumstances—'

'I am to sit in an office every day?' said Eloise. 'That isn't fair at all.'

'Damn me,' said Major Lucas, 'don't you understand, after all, what I'm getting at?'

'Yes, but I'm sure it won't happen again,' said Eloise. 'I'm sure you would only make that kind of mistake once. Sir, you really could not prefer Bombardier Wright as your official driver. He's hopeless, and also boring.'

'That's the prime point, is it, that he's boring?' said Major Lucas.

'Sir, I think, don't you, that people who aren't boring, like you and I, should save each other from those who are.'

'God Almighty,' said Major Lucas and laughed.

'Excuse me, please,' said Eloise, driving in exemplary fashion towards the camp, 'but that was not a joke.'

'I know it wasn't,' he said, 'which is what made it so damned funny.'

Eloise went a little haughty.

'May I ask, sir, if I'm to be your driver or not?'

'I'll advise Captain Miller yes, you are.'

'Thank you, sir,' said Eloise, delighted. Major Lucas was out with his officers and his men most days. He did not like a desk any more than she did, not when a war against Hitler meant that practical endeavour counted for far more than orderly room work. She would be out with him, not typing away with other ATS personnel. Major Lucas was what one would call an exciting and hungry man, hungry for action, for doing things, and for making his officers and men jump to his commands. Eloise liked being with such men, vibrant and alive men, like her father and uncles, whose love of activity was infectious. Ah, how sad for people who only had dull and boring relatives. She really would forget that Major Lucas had committed such an astonishing indiscretion. He had made her very happy in appointing her his driver. He had had to, of course, after taking advantage of her. All the same, she was delighted. Further, he had promised a little while ago that when she was commissioned he would see she returned to his battery. 'Yes, sir, thank you very much,' she said, as she drove into the camp.

'I'd better assure you you're quite right, Sergeant Adams,' he said. 'What happened this afternoon won't happen again.'

'Did it happen, sir?' said Eloise. 'I've forgotten.'

'Have you, by God?' he growled under his breath. 'Well, that's one in the eye for me.'

'Excuse me, sir, but are you saying something?'

'Nothing that would interest you, Sergeant Adams.'

A memo from Brigade was waiting for him on his return to camp.

*   *   *

'Mr Adams?' said the agent, Mr Palmer, on the phone next morning.

'Hello, yes?' said Sammy.

'Palmer here. Mr Adams, I understand you've moved all your equipment into the Belsize Park factory.'

'Yes, and I'm greatly obliged, Mr Palmer, believe me I am. Our Shoreditch factory's been bombed, so I couldn't be more appreciative of your concession in letting us move everything in.'

'Mr Adams, I don't recall—'

'No, I've got to mention my appreciation,' said Sammy, his gratitude travelling unstoppably into Mr Palmer's ear. 'The work took us all day yesterday. Of course, we won't take possession until the contracts are exchanged, not unless there's another concession.'

'Possession, Mr Adams, comes with completion.'

'Don't I know it,' said Sammy, 'I've had some of that. By the way, my workforce is on war work, so you'll see we need to get production goin' pretty quick or immediate.'

'Yes, I understand that, but—'

'Can't thank you enough for your co-operation so far. It's a pleasure to know such an obligin' estate agent, and I don't say that lightly. By the way, when all these air raids stop, I'm thinkin' of castin' an eye over bombed inner London property that might be up for sale and post-war development.'

'You're serious, Mr Adams?'

'Businesswise, I don't make jokes, Mr Palmer,' said Sammy. 'I wonder, might you be able to act for me?'

'Certainly, Mr Adams, certainly.'

'I'll pop in and see you once we start workin' at Belsize Park,' said Sammy.

'Mr Adams, your cheque's good, so I think I can concede unofficial possession on behalf of my client.'

'Say unofficial immediate?' suggested Sammy.

'Um – say Monday, Mr Adams.'

'Good as immediate considering today's Friday,' said Sammy, 'and I call that highly obligin'. Highly.'

'I'll look forward to seeing you, Mr Adams.'

'Same here,' said Sammy. Well, he thought, you're on top again, Sammy Adams. I'll take some flowers home to Susie, and give her a bit of a cuddle tonight. Wait a bit, in the air raid shelter? Blow that for what it can do to my affectionate aspirations.

Chapter Fourteen

Two days later, Chinese Lady, listening with Rachel to the mid-morning news, could hardly believe how happy the wireless sounded. In Egypt a small British force of thirty thousand men under General Wavell had driven Mussolini's Italian Army of a hundred and fifty thousand men back over the border into Italian Libya, trapping hordes of surprised Italians.

'Mrs Finch, isn't that wonderful?' said Rachel. 'My life, isn't it a lovely piece of cheerful news?'

'I just hope it lasts,' said Chinese Lady. 'If it does, I'll be as surprised as those Italian soldiers. Mind, I can't think why they're fightin' us. I know they're foreigners, but I always thought them more friendly than the Germans, and when Lizzy and her brothers were young they were very partial to Italian hokey-pokey.'

If hordes of Mussolini's Italians were indeed surprised, they were neither angry nor sulky. Laying down their arms, they marched cheerfully into captivity. Happily, they accepted cigarettes from the Australian, New Zealand and British soldiers. Hitler was a gargoyle to them, Mussolini a comical kind of godfather, Britain a country in which immigrant Italian ice cream vendors made a welcome living. The badinage between captives and captors was reported as being light-hearted.

'We don't-a want to fight you, eh, English?'

'Well, good on yer, Antonio. What's yer sister like?'

'Sister? Ah, pretty nice, you bet.'

'Okey-dokey, let's have her name and address. I might just be passin' through sometime, yer know.'

General Sir Henry Simms received a friendly word to the effect that CIGS had no immediate plan for moving 7 Corps overseas. Sir Henry said he wasn't ready for any such order, anyway, that he was damned if he'd agree to putting the Corps into the field while it was still short of tanks. He hoped that after what German armour had done to the British in France, no corps or division would be required to go into battle again unless it was fully armoured. He was assured that tanks were rolling off production lines. Well, do me a favour, said Sir Henry, arrange for a hundred to roll in my direction. Can't be done quite yet, Sir Henry.

Sir Henry refrained from argument, but nothing was going to shift him from his fixed determination to get his Corps's armoured divisions up to what he considered would be full strength. The Mediterranean Basin was the coming theatre of war. Egypt, North Africa, Vichy-controlled Syria, Crete, Malta, Greece and elsewhere were all targets of possible conflict, where Britain and its Imperial allies would undoubtedly come up against Germany again, particularly if the Italian Army of Libya surrendered to General Wavell.

Major Lucas would have agreed with him. Too

urgent for action to kick his heels waiting for the regiment to be supplied with the necessary amount of new heavy artillery, he had his eye on service with the Commandos. The memo he'd received from Brigade had informed him his request for a transfer was being favourably considered. The Brigadier had no objections to losing him. He and Major Lucas did not see eye-to-eye.

'You seem remarkably happy with life, Polly,' said Rosie, as they left the Officers' Mess after lunch.

'Do I, Rosie old sport?' said Polly.

'Don't you know there's a war on?' smiled Rosie.

'I know the German *Luftwaffe* bombers are making sure none of us can forget it,' said Polly. 'What a ghastly shower of utter rotters, and may they all come down to earth with a volcanic bump.'

'What's a volcanic bump?' asked Rosie.

'Shattering,' said Polly. 'Bits of smoking sauer-kraut all over the place.'

'Sounds messy, but I think I'm in favour,' said Rosie. 'Alas that this kind of war turns us into vengeful vixens, but I still can't make out why the chaplain says it would be rewarding if we all learned to love each other. Who could love a Hitler Nazi?'

'Other Nazis?' suggested Polly. 'I've heard that some of them do.'

'I always find that very odd,' said Rosie.

'What's the latest news from home?' asked Polly.

'At home, everyone's keeping their heads down at night,' said Rosie. 'Outside of that, Emma's settled into her job at the War Office, Tim's trying to survive Commando training, Bobby's gone to

Nottingham OCTU, his French lady friend is with a FANY unit, and Eloise, I believe, is doing her best to help her commanding officer run his battery.'

'Well,' smiled Polly, 'I suppose the family—' She checked. 'Look out, old thing, here comes devoted Dicky to lay his eager peepers on your fair bosom. I think yours is tops with him.'

Lieutenant Richard Clark, the recreational officer, came hurrying up. Although in his mid-twenties, he was still boyishly enthusiastic about this, that and the other. The other included Rosie. He was eager for her favours. He was eager for everything that danced on his horizons. He organized eagerly, he offered recreational pursuits eagerly, and was, in fact, first cousin to the Eager Beaver. Enthusiastically, his eyes alighted on Rosie and her trimly-uniformed bosom.

'Hello there, just the girl I was looking for,' he said to her.

'I note you've found her,' smiled Polly.

'I was looking for both of you, actually,' he said.

'I'm spoken for, you bigamist,' said Polly.

'Er what?' he said.

'Talk on,' said Rosie.

'I say, you peach, like to spend Easter with me?' he said.

'Love to,' smiled Rosie, 'but not this Easter.'

'Bad show,' he said. 'Look, here's tickets for a hop at The Grange this evening.' The Grange was the residence of the local squire. 'Charity do for war orphans. Dances, jigs, raffles, lucky dips and other social heave-ho.'

'Could you explain heave-ho?' asked Rosie.

'I say, let's do it together,' said Eager Beaver's close relative. 'Then it'll explain itself, give you my word. Good show, eh?'

'Heave-ho's out,' said Rosie.

'Still, you can always change your mind,' he said. 'Oh, Brigadier Fraser's asking for maximum attendance, so here's your tickets. Five bob each.'

'It's blackmail,' said Polly.

'Yes, bad show,' said Eager Beaver the Second, 'but they're calling it charity. Can't stay, got to give out these other tickets to all and sundry, don't you know. What a shindig, should be good fun and all that.' His hopeful eyes caressed Rosie's appealing figure.

'I see what you're on about,' said Polly.

'You see, I see, he sees, we all see,' smiled Rosie.

'That's the stuff,' said the recreational officer. 'Cheerioh for now.'

'Love to Tipperary,' said Rosie.

'Er what? Oh, see what you mean.' Away he went, ardent to make a name for himself.

Rosie looked at her watch.

'Corporal Jones is giving me a lift to Chapman's Garage in ten minutes,' she said. 'I'm collecting my Hillman. Permission, Captain Simms?'

'That's no problem, ducky. Shoot off. I'll find a good excuse for you if the adjutant gets fretful.'

'Shan't be long,' said Rosie.

'Well, when this blooming war is over,' said Polly, 'we can all take a little more time over this and that.'

'Pardon?' said Rosie to Ben a little later.

'That's right, Matt's out and all,' said Ben, 'down

169

to Dorchester to see his dad. Won't be back just yet, miss. But your car's ready. Singing like a bird. You can take it.'

'Oh, right. Thanks, Ben, but I'm sorry to have missed Mr Chapman.' Rosie had liked his affectionate regard for her car, and the professional pleasure he had taken in doctoring it himself. 'I'll write out a cheque and leave it, shall I?'

'I never knowed a customer willing to settle that quick,' said Ben. 'Downright good of you, miss, and will please Matt.'

Will you make sure you thank him for me?' smiled Rosie.

'Well, wasn't it a pleasure for him, putting that there Hillman to rights?' said Ben. 'Labour of love, I reckon, Miss – um – Lieutenant.'

'Tell him I'm delighted the patient is fully recovered,' said Rosie.

'Miss you not comin' in any more,' said Ben.

'Will you?' said Rosie.

'Matt will and all,' said Ben.

'Give him my regards,' said Rosie.

She settled, she left the cheque with Ben, and took possession of her car. The engine fired sweetly first go, and she drove away. On her brief journey back to headquarters, the Hillman did sing like a bird, indeed it did. Oh, yes.

A labour of love?

Was that why it was singing?

The handsome, high-ceilinged hall of The Grange was crowded, and the squire and his wife,

Sir Clifford and Lady Fellowes, were themselves present. So was staff officer Brigadier Fraser and other officers, including ATS. Their khaki uniforms, well-tailored though they were, formed a subdued backcloth to the wartime glad rags worn by many of the civilian women. Colours looked to have been bravely chosen, probably because the ladies wanted to give the v-sign to the hovering spectre of Hitler. At a charity affair in aid of a new wartime orphanage, everyone was expected to give money in one way or another while enjoying the social atmosphere of the occasion and gracing it with a certain panache.

An orchestra of Dorset fiddles and accordions provided music from the gallery. The initial dances were conventional, and the Brigadier treated himself to a fox-trot with Polly. Eager Beaver the Second would have made his mark with Rosie had it not been for the fact that a senior officer intervened. For a waltz that followed, he was beaten by the squire himself. Gladly, Sir Clifford did the honours with this striking ATS lieutenant. Polly dodged the waltz to go up and talk to the orchestra.

That resulted subsequently in a mad dash by forty couples into a giddy and nostalgic performance of the Charleston. Polly wished only that Boots could have been there, for nothing would have given her more delight than to re-live this rage of the Twenties with him. The Twenties had been the sad, mad, rebellious and law-breaking aftermath of the Somme, Ypres and Vimy Ridge, when disillusionment with expensive victory had been responsible for the emergence of the wild and exhibitionist Bright Young Things, of whom Polly had been one.

Polly went through the Charleston this evening with a handsome farmer, who marvelled at her supple legs and her expertise, but had no idea that her fixed brittle smile meant her mind was not on the present but on the years when she was young, and haunted by her memories of the war against the Kaiser's Germany.

Rosie danced with a captivated staff officer, who had the devil of a job matching her extrovert rhythm. It hardly mattered. Lieutenant Rosie Adams performing the Charleston was a delight.

Matthew Chapman, sitting with Postwoman Mary Hubble and Police Constable John Rawlings beneath a large oil painting of a lady with a voluptuous bosom and bulging eyes, watched his sister performing in sprightly fashion, partnered by an Army sergeant. Constable Rawlings was also watching, but in slightly jealous fashion. He had a soft spot for Matt's widowed sister. Matt's gaze shifted and found a vision. His ready smile surfaced.

'Well,' he murmured.

'What's caught your eye, Matt?' asked Mary, a jolly woman of thirty-two in a bright blue dress.

'The Charleston,' said Matt.

'And what're you smilin' about?' asked Mary, who spread her favours around in a harmless way.

'The Charleston,' said Matt, glancing again at

the active, rhythmic and enchanting figure of a customer, Lieutenant Adams of the ATS.

'We could do it, y'know, Matt,' said Mary, 'you could manage easy.'

Matt thought about how he would look. Like a one-legged case of mistaken ambition. Barn dances were all right, and he could even manage a modern waltz after a fashion, but the Charleston, no. That was for legs supple and free-moving.

'I don't think so, Mary.'

'All right, Matt, Bob's your uncle,' said Mary. 'My, aren't some of these officers handsome devils?'

'Like me to find you one?' said Matt.

'What would I do with him?' Mary emitted her jolly laugh. 'Put him in my postbag, pop him into my letter-box and keep him for Sundays?'

'Discuss it in committee,' said Matt.

'What committee?' asked Constable Rawlings, wearing his best suit.

'Mary can think of one,' said Matt. Mary winked at him. She always thought Matt a bit of a gentleman, him being well-educated and speaking like one in that deep manly voice of his.

'Here, come on, Mary,' said Constable Rawlings, 'we can have a go at the Charleston, can't we?'

'I thought you'd never ask,' said Mary, and bounced into the dance with him.

Matt's glance returned to Rosie. She was laughing, sparkling and very free-moving.

'There you are, Matthew, just the man I want,' said someone. He looked up and came to his feet. The squire's wife, Lady Fellowes, brilliant in pale gold, was smiling at him. A woman of forty, splendid in her looks, she was good-natured, popular and immensely likeable. Her good deeds were legion.

'Just the man, am I?' smiled Matt. 'Have you lost Sir Clifford, then?'

'Yes, to some pretty young thing in the Charleston. Actually, it's your handsome looks I need.'

'You need Errol Flynn, then,' said Matt.

'You'll do, Matt. I want you to sell raffle tickets to the ladies.'

'Why the ladies?'

'Wake up, my dear man, that's where your handsome looks count, with the ladies. Sixpence a ticket, five for two shillings. Are you game? It's a good cause, really. My, thank goodness that noisy dance is finished, I can hardly hear you talking to me. Did you say yes?'

'Let's have the tickets,' said Matt.

'Well, bless you.' Lady Fellowes landed him with four books of cloakroom tickets. 'Lots of prizes. Wear your smile. Oh, and if you happen to find any lady who's just your style, good luck.' Lady Fellowes hoped he wouldn't end up with Mary Hubble. Jolly as she was, Mary wasn't his style, far from it.

Matt went amiably to work with the tickets. The Lucky Dip, under the supervision of the vicar and his wife, was going on at sixpence a dip. Matt took advantage of people putting their hands into their pockets or purses. Limping adroitly around, he reached a young woman in khaki.

'Raffle? Sixpence a ticket, five for two bob?'

Rosie turned, and a smile sprang into bright being.

'Well, it's you, Matthew, how nice,' she said, letting his name slip easily from her lips.

'You're saying you like my old school tie?' said Matt.

'Eton, you swankpot?' said Rosie.

'Old grammar school,' said Matt.

'I'm old grammar school,' said Rosie, who was also a graduate of Somerville, one of Oxford's colleges for women.

'How's the Hillman?' asked Matt, with people milling about but not interfering.

'Singing like a bird,' said Rosie. 'Thanks so much for all your work on it.'

'You're welcome, Lieutenant,' said Matt. 'Raffle tickets?'

'How much, did you say?' asked Rosie.

'Five for two bob,' said Matt.

'I'll take ten,' said Rosie.

'Lady Fellowes will like you,' said Matt, and ripped off ten tickets. 'By the way, thanks for the cheque. Sorry I wasn't there to see you myself.'

'Never mind, you're here now,' said Rosie, handing him four shillings. 'You'll ask me for a dance, I hope.'

'Come again?' said Matt.

'You can kick a leg in a barn dance, you said,' smiled Rosie.

'I'm not sure if I could manage it with you,' said Matt.

'Well, try,' said Rosie.

175

'It'll look like the wreck of the *Hesperus*,' said Matt.

'I'll wear a lifebelt,' said Rosie.

Matt laughed, shook his head at her and went on his way with his books of tickets. He didn't escape, however. Rosie appeared before him fifteen minutes later.

'Barn dance,' she said. Couples were taking the floor.

'I'm seriously considering going home,' said Matt.

'Not now,' said Rosie, 'we made a deal.'

'Did we?' said Matt. 'Lord help you, then, Lieutenant Adams.'

'Don't be so formal, old sport, I'm Rosie. Come on, shake a leg with me.'

She became quite pleased with him, for he went through all the steps, the movements and the rhythmic gallops without in the least failing her or himself. And there wasn't the faintest hint of oil or grease about him. Just the warm smell of a healthy man in active motion.

'I fluked it,' he said, as they left the floor.

'So did I,' said Rosie, 'we fluked it together. Exhilarating. Thank you so much.'

'Thank my leg,' smiled Matt.

'Thank you, leg,' said Rosie.

'My turn to thank you,' said Matt.

'Tell me,' said Rosie, 'do your friends call you Matt or Matthew?'

'You take your pick.'

Polly, curious, arrived.

'Hello,' she said.

'Oh, meet Mr Matthew Chapman, who made my wheezing Hillman sing sweetly,' said Rosie. 'Matthew, meet Captain Polly Simms.'

'My pleasure, I'll be bound,' said Matt, and shook Polly's hand.

'Delighted,' said Polly.

'So you should be,' said Rosie, 'Mr Chapman's a motor engineer doctor, a genius. He operated on my Hillman and saved it from dying a death.'

'My word,' said Polly, 'you're the first genius I've ever met, Mr Chapman.'

'Don't take Lieutenant Adams seriously,' said Matt, 'you still haven't met one.'

'Geniuses are always modest, Polly,' said Rosie.

'There you are again, Matthew.' Lady Fellowes joined the trio. 'You've found two ladies? One should be enough.'

'Oh, I'm just the gooseberry,' said Polly.

'I've memories of being a gooseberry myself,' smiled Lady Fellowes. 'Matt, have you got the stubs of your tickets?'

'In my pocket,' said Matt. He brought out the four little books and handed them over.

'Why, you lovely man, you've sold all your tickets,' said Lady Fellowes. 'Isn't he splendid?' she said to Polly.

'And a rattling fine motor doctor, I believe,' said Polly.

'Oh, yes,' said Lady Fellowes. 'Matt, what can you do with my husband's 1912 Benz?'

'Tow it to a museum?' suggested Matt.

'He won't thank you for that,' said Lady Fellowes, 'he'll take to his bed.'

'Lady Fellowes, call a doctor,' said Rosie.

'I hope it won't come to that,' said the squire's mellow wife.

'I don't mean for your husband,' said Rosie.

Matt laughed, and Polly thought how personable he was.

'I think Lieutenant Adams means the Benz,' he said.

'And you as its doctor,' smiled Polly.

'There you are, Matthew, you'll have to do something,' said Lady Fellowes.

'Fair enough,' said Matt, 'I'll come and take a good look at the beast. But if it roars at me, I'll send it to a zoo.'

'Blow your shirt off if you won't,' said Rosie.

Matt laughed again.

'It's a weakness of mine, blowing my shirt off, Lieutenant,' he said, and Rosie made a face at him for not using her name. 'Do you want the money for the tickets now, Lady Fellowes?'

'Bring it across, will you, Matt?'

With a country jig taking place, he thanked Rosie again for standing up with him in the barn dance, excused himself to her and Polly, and followed the squire's wife to a little table in a corner of the hall. Polly noticed his limp then.

'He's very pleasant, Rosie,' she said. 'What's wrong with his leg?'

'A broken ankle that was never repaired properly,' said Rosie. 'Rotten for a man like that.'

'Is he married?' asked Polly.

'No,' said Rosie, and thought about the woman

who had married someone else because she didn't like oily overalls. What a silly creature. 'His sister keeps house for him.'

'That's a man going to waste, then,' said Polly, and wondered not for the first time, when Rosie was going to respond positively to an admirer. There were several in her life, staff officers, but she never seemed to go beyond a friendly liking for any of them. There had to be some man some day, surely, who was going to strike the right response in Boots's captivating daughter. Polly was an echo of the Adams family in that she rarely thought of Rosie as Boots's adopted daughter. Rosie always seemed to belong so naturally to Boots. Her real father, now Colonel Armitage, was a remote figure, although Rosie did correspond with him. He was with Wavell's army at the moment.

The charity evening went on to its rousing end, but without Rosie and Matthew making contact again. Still, Polly won a half-bottle of gin in the raffle, and Rosie won a pair of pretty pink French garters in a little white cardboard box, so they returned to headquarters with Polly in high spirits and Rosie putting her own prize on offer.

'Would you like them for your wedding, Polly? Sell them to you for a lucky silver sixpence.'

'No, you keep them, ducky, and when you next see your motor engineer doctor, give him a treat,' said Polly.

'Are you asking me to be tarty?' enquired Rosie.

'No, I'm suggesting a garter show might work

wonders, old thing, it might make him jump a delighted mile and straighten out his crippled ankle,' said Polly. 'He seemed to me like a man who deserves that kind of cure.'

'What a lovely thought,' said Rosie, and laughed.

Chapter Fifteen

Goering's bombing squadrons were continuing to attack provincial cities as well as London. The people of the United Kingdom were appalled at the barbaric nature of Germany's assaults from the air, which were fomenting a ferocious desire to be revenged. The Mayor of Coventry had struck a more civilized note by saying his council had always wanted a site for a new civic centre, and now the Germans had provided one.

January turned grey and wet. It didn't discourage Sammy's workforce from riding to the Belsize Park factory on the tube trains each morning. Tommy arrived by car and within a week he had the machinists and seamstresses heading for maximum production. With Sammy's blessing, he gave them all a rise. Wartime wages had increased everywhere, and the new rise delighted Gertie and her girls, even if the ceaseless German air raids on inner London caused them unhappy and frightening nights in the public shelters. Sammy saw what might happen, a gradual exodus, an evacuation of their East End homes to join their kids in the country. Some of those who had been bombed out had already gone.

He had written to Boots to let him know the

purchase of the factory had been completed and production was under way. Subsequently, Boots phoned for more details. Sammy was able to assure him everything was going well, and that all contract work would soon be up to schedule. However, he mentioned the possibility that they might lose the majority of the girls. He didn't think they could put up with the air raids indefinitely. Boots gave it some thought.

'You still with me?' enquired Sammy.

'I'll be off the line in a couple of minutes,' said Boots, 'I'm under pressure here. But before I go, have you thought about an orphanage?'

'Give over,' said Sammy, 'I'm not an orphan any more than you are, or Susie is.'

'All London orphanages have been evacuated, Sammy. They're all empty. Find out if there's a large one north or west of Belsize Park. If so, rent it for the duration, either from its council owners or its charity owners. Move your workforce into it, with their husbands. It won't be like a hotel, but it'll have all the necessary amenities, and it'll be a far better bet than their present homes in the East End.'

'Well, I'll go to flamin' Kingdom Come,' said Sammy. 'What's happening to me that I didn't think of the idea myself? Ruddy hell, if I'm losin' my touch to that extent, I'll get washed down a drain with other useless leavings. Boots—'

'That's all, Sammy,' said Boots, 'I'm wanted. Love to Susie.' He rang off.

'That's him all over,' said Sammy to the dead phone. 'Springs an idea, spouts it into my ear with just a couple of full stops, then departs like Henry the Eighth for a quick five minutes with a wife who's still got her loaf of bread in place. But I'll say this much, he's still worth his director's fees. Now, about empty orphanages in north-west London. Where do I start? Local council, that's it. No, call Palmer. He might have an orphanage for sale on his books. If not, let him find one for me, rent or sale. He knows the area. That's it, let him do the work. You treat yourself to some black market chocolate, Sammy.'

'Why, Mr Adams,' said Miss Symonds, entering his office a minute later, 'you're chewing sweets.'

'Have a piece of milk chocolate, Miss Symonds,' said Sammy.

'Well, thank you,' said Miss Symonds, and took a piece. Then she moved to stand beside his chair. She placed some papers in front of him, and Sammy had a distinct feeling that the right half of her bosom was gently brushing his left shoulder. 'These need your signature, Mr Adams.'

Wait a minute, thought Sammy, what's her bosom doing on my collar-bone?

'I'll see to them,' he said.

'And thank you for the chocolate,' she said, straightening up.

'Under-the-counter stuff,' he said.

'Yes,' she said, departing with a nice smile, 'that's the only way one can get it.'

Get what? I think I'll have to watch the lady, thought Sammy. Ruddy rissoles, the things people do when there's a war on, like that case of the lonely wife in suburban Surrey who gave Sunday tea parties for Canadian soldiers. Some parties. Talk about shrimps and winkles. There weren't any, just a tea dance and the lady's seven veils, according to the Sunday newspapers.

Chinese Lady's wireless set was still so cheerful about the continuing advance of Wavell's army in Libya that she thought, in a vague kind of way, that it must have been drinking.

One more Saturday morning, one more gruelling speed march for 4 Commando. Out from the parade ground in full kit with rifles astride shoulders and into the demanding terrain of the countryside went the men and their officers. The ATS personnel watched them from their office window.

'Out for the count again later on,' commented Subaltern Felicity Jessop.

'They're a mad lot,' said Sergeant Barbara Titmus, whom the Commandos called Titters.

'Rough and tough,' said Lieutenant Pauline Cary.

'They never know when to lie down and stay down,' said Felicity.

Well, there's one or two who know how to make me do that, thought Sergeant Titmus. Talk about my honour as an NCO, they don't take a blind bit of notice of it. I might as well be anybody. Still, a girl's got to make some sacrifices for men who've got to do what real men have got to do.

On the Commandos went, with their officers, legs and feet working overtime. No slacking, no halting, no resting. Keep going, keep going, you're special, you're the guts of the Army, you're Hitler's headache.

Tim kept going, Sergeant Watts in front of him. The morning was dull and misty, the Clyde at their backs, the hills in front of them. Sweat began its assault on limbs and clothing. Rifles turned into dead weights. Thick Army boots turned socked feet hot. No-one talked. Save your breath, march on, you cowboys, think of the pints of beer waiting for you.

That was the custom, the understanding between the pub proprietors of Troon and the Commandos, that on the return of the latter from their Saturday morning death-or-glory marches, pints of beer would be waiting for them in the pubs they regularly patronized.

Sure enough, at the end of this morning's travail, when feet were on fire in redhot boots, and every limb felt as if it had been beaten by cricket bats, the pints were there. Tim, Sergeant Watts and Private Jock Murray found theirs lined up in their preferred pub.

'Get 'em doon, laddies,' said the proprietor, and down into dehydrated throats went the first pints. There were three pints for each man in all the relevant pubs.

Down went the second pints. Sergeant Watts burped.

'Canna hold it, Sarge?' said Private Murray.

'Happen I'll see you off,' said Sergeant Watts.

'No one need see me off,' said Tim, 'I'll fade out in private as soon as I get to my billet.'

He was slightly off balance when he left the pub, leaving Sergeant Watts and Private Murray still giving their feet a rest. A voice accosted his ears.

'Corporal Adams, you're squiffy.'

Subaltern Felicity Jessop materialized in front of him.

'I've had a few pints, as usual,' said Tim, 'but it's not the drink, ma'am, it's my feet. And my legs.'

'Well, try saluting,' said Felicity, 'and let's see if you fall over.' He saluted. It made him totter. 'There you are, I knew it, you blighter, you're squiffy in the presence of an officer. Let's see, what sort of punishment do King's Regulations lay down for that?'

'Don't ask me, ask His Majesty,' said Tim. 'Listen, if you had my feet, you'd be falling about yourself.'

'Don't answer me back, you lump of porridge,' said Felicity. 'Do something about your feet, then put your civvies on this evening and we'll go to the cinema.'

Off duty, the Commandos could dress how they liked, such was the unconventional attitude that permeated all ranks.

'Come again?' said Tim.

'It's an order,' said Felicity.

'I'm hard of hearing,' said Tim.

'I'm not going to shout,' said Felicity.

'Good idea, not to shout in the middle of Troon,' said Tim, 'but I'm still not sure if I heard you right. You're telling me we're going to the cinema this evening?'

'I'll wear my civvies too,' said Felicity.

'But the cinema's always full of personnel.'

'We're not going to the local cinema, you chump,' said Felicity, 'we'll take the bus to Irvine. I'll be at the stop at seven.'

'What happens when we're in the cinema?' asked Tim.

'We watch the film,' said Felicity. 'If you've got other ideas, you'd better take an aspirin. Seven o'clock, then, Corporal Adams, and make sure you're not still squiffy.'

Off she went, and Tim made for his billet.

Is she serious, or do I get another comic surprise when I reach the bus stop?

She was there at seven, and there were no Commando comedians about, just a middle-aged couple.

'Good evening, Miss McNab, a fine night, y'ken,' said Tim.

'Hello, Mr McKay, and how's your wee sister?' asked Felicity.

'Och, gang awa' to Aberdeen,' said Tim.

'Och, the puir wee lassie,' said Felicity.

If this was all for the benefit of the middle-aged couple, it hardly struck a chord. The bus arrived, the couple boarded, and Felicity and Tim followed, climbing the stairs to the upper deck after Tim had paid for the tickets. Not many people were aboard, and they secured a seat at the back. Felicity was wearing a beret, and a warm winter coat over a jumper and skirt, Tim a jacket, a cashmere sweater from the Isle of Arran and a pair of slacks.

'You're looking very informal,' he said.

'Watch your hip,' murmured Felicity, 'it's

187

crowding mine. By the way, I don't think much of your Scottish brogue.'

'Best I could do,' said Tim.

The bus pulled up at the next stop, and took on a crowd of civilians and soldiers. Lower and upper decks began to fill up. Tim whispered that he'd better not stay with her in case they were recognized.

'Righty-ho, push off,' murmured Felicity, and Tim moved to sit beside a young woman, who took one look at his civvies and sniffed at what she suspected they represented, a reserved occupation. Then, taking a look at his health and strength, she dismissed her first impression and spoke.

'You're one of them?'

'Do I look like that?' asked Tim.

'You look like a braw soldier laddie, one of the Commandos,' she said. 'Are you awa' to the cinema in Irvine?'

'Well, it's Saturday evening,' said Tim.

'I'm meeting a girl friend, but she'll no' mind if you'd like to take me with you to the cinema.'

That was the quickest offer Tim had ever experienced.

'I'm meeting a friend of my own there,' he said.

She had no hard feelings about that, and chatted to him all the way to Irvine, where almost everyone alighted. Tim did a brisk walk to the cinema to keep ahead of the mob and anyone who might know him, and Felicity, who could leg it a bit herself, caught him up there.

'You blighter,' she said, 'you were trying your luck with that girl.'

'As a matter of fact—'

'What a bounder,' said Felicity. 'Well, don't let's hang about waiting for everyone from Troon to arrive. Let's go in. Wait, whose treat is it?'

'Yours,' said Tim.

'Not on your life,' said Felicity, 'I'm a lifelong supporter of tradition in some things.'

'Meaning it's my privilege?' said Tim.

'Yes, aren't you a lucky old corporal?' she said.

Tim paid for the tickets, and an usherette about sixty years old showed them to their seats. Felicity slipped her coat off, hitched her skirt and sat down. In the semi-darkness, Tim took note of a white jumper that was much more defining than her uniform. Well, what a bonny lassie, he thought.

The film they'd come to see was *Pygmalion*, adapted from a play by George Bernard Shaw and featuring Leslie Howard as Professor Higgins and Wendy Hiller as Eliza Doolittle. It was utterly absorbing, its cockney element clashing with the highbrow arrogance of the intellectual factor. Tim thought about his cockney antecedents. He thought particularly of his paternal grandmother and her first husband, Daniel Adams, and wondered if they had known out-and-out cockneys like Eliza Doolittle and the men and women of the Covent Garden market. Then there were Uncle Tommy and Uncle Sammy, who could still sound as if they had never left East Street market. Strange about Boots, his dad, who could hold his own with anybody in well-spoken English, and in French too. There wasn't a trace of the cockney in his make-up. But poor old Eliza Doolittle, what a drubbing she received from Professor Higgins for her strangulated vowels, and not a word of thanks after she'd mastered her verbal deficiencies and convinced everyone at the ball that she was a duchess, with some Hungarian character even declaring her a princess. That made her spit in the Professor's eye, good as, but she returned to him in the end, which caused quite a few females in the cinema to blow their noses.

He and Felicity waited for the place to clear before they left.

'Ripping stuff,' she said when they were outside on the pavement.

'Yes, had me hooked from the start,' said Tim. 'Now we've got to catch the last bus to Troon.'

'We better had,' said Felicity, 'I'm not staying out all night with you, Corporal Adams. Your health and strength might get the better of both of us.'

A taxi pulled up, a well-dressed bloke alighted fast, paid the cabbie and then hurried to meet a waiting woman. They linked arms and walked away. Tim, who'd passed many an initiative test, swooped to detain the taxi.

'Tip you a quid if you'll take us to Troon,' he said to the cabbie. He was never short of funds any more than Rosie or Eloise, for he too had an allowance from Boots.

'Can I see the bawbees?' asked the cabbie.

Tim, with Felicity now beside him, fished out a pound note and gave it to the cabbie.

'That's bawbees,' said the cabbie. 'Jump in.'

In went Felicity, and in went Tim, and away went the taxi on its six-mile journey to Troon.

'My word, with taxis hard to come by, you were quick on the draw there, Tim,' said Felicity.

'Don't mention it,' said Tim.

'Wizard stuff,' said Felicity. 'What an improvement on Captain Coombes and his six hands. This taxi is a ripping end to the evening. Tell me, did the film really take hold of you?'

'All the way,' said Tim. 'Eliza Doolittle reminded me that I come from a cockney family myself.'

'Don't brag about it,' said Felicity. 'I come from two bank clerks, one male, one female, and I'm not bragging about that, am I? Or about being an old Croydon High School girl in blue bloomers.'

'Still?' said Tim.

'Still what?'

'You're still in blue bloomers?'

Felicity shrieked. The cabbie turned his head, but couldn't see into the dark interior, and returned to watching the road, a grin on his chops.

Felicity came to and said, 'Listen, what does your father do?'

'He's in the Army, same as I am,' said Tim.

'Your father's in the Army?'

'He also served in the '14–18 war,' said Tim.

'In that and this one too?' said Felicity. 'Does he like punishment?'

'He's never said so. What does your father do?'

'Grows carrots, works in the bank and serves in the ARP,' said Felicity.

'He's a useful all-rounder, then,' said Tim.

They talked on. The taxi didn't take long to reach Troon, and the cabbie, on instructions from Tim, dropped Felicity first.

'No, don't you get out, Tim,' she said, 'Lieutenant Cary might be prowling about. Lovely evening. We'll do it again sometime.'

'I'd like that in writing,' said Tim.

'No need. It's a promise, even if it's against the regulations. So long, soldier.' Felicity squeezed his knee as she got out. The cabbie took Tim on to his billet. Tim paid him.

'Thanks for the ride. Goodnight.'

'Bide a bit, laddie, are you in the Army?'

'I'm training here in Troon.'

'Wi' the Commandos?'

'Not as easy as it is with the Boy Scouts,' said Tim.

'I'll no' argue wi' that,' said the cabbie. 'Guid luck, mon.'

'So long,' said Tim.

Chapter Sixteen

At breakfast one morning with her husband and
Rachel, Chinese Lady thought it would be nice if
she could serve something a little more appealing
than the usual wartime meal of porridge and toast,
while allowing for the fact that eggs and bacon
wouldn't be suitable for Rachel. Rachel was a dear
woman, so companionable and helpful. Jewish
friends had called to see her, to offer lodgement
and assistance, but at no time had Rachel hinted
she should go and live with her own kind. Rachel,
in fact, was more than happy with the existing
arrangement. She was very attached to Sammy's
resilient Victorian mother, and was only concerned
not to outstay her welcome. Chinese Lady assured
her it was a blessing to have her for as long as it took
her to get a new home together for herself and Mr
Goodman.

The wireless was buzzing happily again. Wavell's
army was deep into Libya, the Italians in headlong
retreat. Mussolini was panicking a bit, and Hitler,
in conference with General Rommel, was
suggesting it might be necessary to go to the aid of
his Italian ally. That, of course, wasn't mentioned
on Chinese Lady's wireless. It was full of praise for
the British Army of the Nile.

'I just don't know what's got into it lately,' she said, 'it's been cheerful for days.'

'We can do with any amount of that, can't we?' smiled Rachel.

'Good news is always an incentive, Rachel,' said Mr Finch. 'I'll wager the current news is increasing production in our munitions factories by fifty per cent.'

'Tommy and Sammy will be happy if production soars in their new factory,' said Rachel.

'Rachel, how's Benjamin?' asked Mr Finch.

'He's having his plasters removed today,' said Rachel.

'Well, I'm pleased for him,' said Chinese Lady. 'All that plaster must be a heavy burden. Let's hope he'll soon be up and about.'

'Let's hope so,' said Rachel.

Later that morning, Eloise was driving Major Lucas back from another visit to Brigade. Happy in her job, she was humming a song. Major Lucas, on the back seat, stopped musing and spoke.

'Sergeant Adams?'

'Sir?'

'There'll be a new Battery Commander arriving tomorrow.'

'Which battery, sir?'

'Mine. He'll be taking over from me. I'm transferring and will be leaving the regiment as soon as my successor has a tight hold of the reins.' Major Lucas's requested transfer to a specialized branch of the Army, in which his urge for action, originality and a certain form of independence could be

194

indulged, had been finalized. Having acquired full details of his career, a specific Commando group was now eager to acquire the man. 'I'll see that you meet Major Morris, and I'll recommend you as his driver.'

Eloise, shocked, braked and brought the car to a stop on the winding ribbon of wet black road.

'I protest,' she said, turning to face him.

'It won't do any good,' he said.

'Sir, I'm *your* driver,' said Eloise, 'and don't wish to be thrown at Major Morris. No. I shall refuse.'

'You can't refuse, Sergeant Adams.'

'I insist on my right to come with you,' said Eloise, eyes hot.

'You don't have that right,' said Major Lucas.

'Sir, I do,' said Eloise.

'Damn it, woman, there are no rights in the Army that allow any of us to do as we please unless our seniors approve.'

'Sir, please don't address me as "woman",' complained Eloise. 'Also, as you're still the commanding officer, you can approve my request to be transferred with you. Yes, you must approve.'

'Must?'

'Yes. I came here only because you said you wanted me.'

Major Lucas knew it was true. At Ramsgate he'd recognized a young woman of competence and self-assurance. But he had failed to recognize what a Tartar she was. Regulations and rank meant nothing to her when she was in a temper. Then there were the occasions when she could be damnably beguiling.

195

He growled a bit.

'Damn my ears,' he said, 'if you don't try my patience and tempt me to chuck you back to where you came from, Sergeant Adams.'

'Sir, what about what is right? How would you like to be told you were going to be discarded?' Eloise was close to being charged with insolence in her temper. Boots would have seen its fiery nature as identical to that which he had encountered in her late mother, Cecile Lacoste. But he would have wondered at the root cause of it. Eloise did not know herself. She only knew that Major Lucas's willingness to pass her on to a new commanding officer made her furious. 'Am I a pair of old socks? No, I am not, and I won't be thrown away.'

'By God, if I ever meet another handful like you, Sergeant Adams, I'll blow a fuse,' said Major Lucas, thunder on his brow.

'If you shout at me, sir, I'll shout back,' said Eloise.

'I believe you,' he growled.

'I must remind you, sir, how forgiving I was on the day you assaulted me,' said Eloise.

'Jesus Christ, you're throwing that at me, you minx?'

'I'm asking you very nicely, sir, to arrange for me to be transferred with you. Then I can drive you to our new battery, wherever it is.'

'You've a deadly way of asking very nicely, Sergeant Adams, and it's not a new battery or anything to do with artillery.'

'All the same, sir, I insist on going with you,' said Eloise. 'Can it be arranged?'

Major Lucas, aggressive, vigorous and demanding, a man who could make his officers shake in their boots, stared helplessly at this tantalizing young woman who had never allowed military protocol to prevent her speaking her mind.

'Yes, it can be arranged,' he said.

Eloise's fire died down and she smiled.

'Thank you, sir, you are mostly very kind and understanding,' she said.

That helping of syrup, served with typical beguilement, made him scowl.

'I'm nothing of the sort,' he said, 'and one day, Sergeant Adams, I'll genuinely lose my temper with you.'

'Oh, that is something one expects in some men, sir,' said Eloise. 'Men who aren't boring. We are lucky, you and I, in not being boring or ordinary. Have I said so before? Well, it's quite true.'

That undid him. He roared with laughter.

When that was over, he said, 'We'll see if you like where you'll end up, Sergeant Adams. It'll be among savages.'

'Savages, sir?'

'Wild, hairy and carnivorous. They'll eat you.'

'I shall rely on you, sir, to see that they don't,' said Eloise, and put the car in motion again.

Major Lucas sat resigned. Eloise was smiling. As far as her personal contribution was concerned, the war against Hitler was to be fought in support of Major Lucas. She could imagine, with pleasure, how easily he could strangle the Nazi monster if he ever came face to face with him. While he was no gentleman, and not at all like her image of her ideal man, he knew what war was all about and how to fight it. He went around with an aura of bruising and exciting aggression, the kind that was needed to smash the power of Hitler's Germany. She felt very happy with events, even if there still lingered a touch of bitterness that he could think of discarding her.

Major Lucas perforce had to get in touch by phone with a Colonel Foster, second-in-command of the unit in question. Bring whoever you like, said Colonel Foster, but if it's an ATS sergeant, I can't guarantee she won't lose her skirt. We've already got one here who's taken to wearing a suit of armour.

Major Lucas had a grin on his face when he put the phone down.

In hospital, Benjamin Goodman had his legs out of plaster, and was undergoing a course of physio-therapy. Rachel visited him every day, pushing him around the hospital in a wheelchair after each session. Her support and help eased pressure on the busy staff, for the hospital was having to cope with a regular influx of air raid casualties.

'Next step will be walking on crutches, lovey,' she said one day.

'My life, that can't come too soon,' said Benjamin, his portly frame slightly reduced by his hospitalization. But his mood was buoyant. 'It'll be good to have my legs back.'

'Your legs are old friends of yours,' said Rachel, 'they'll catch up with you, and your crutches will always help.'

'I should want that?' said Benjamin. 'Not at any price. I haven't had the pleasure of trying them out yet, but already I'm looking forward to the day when I can say goodbye to them.'

'Make sure you give them a fond farewell,' said Rachel, her velvety good looks enjoying a recovery. Thirty-eight, a woman of lush health, her figure splendid, she was a delight to the eyes of every male member of the staff. 'Are the girls still writing to you?'

'Every other day,' said Benjamin.

'Rebecca and Leah are proud of their dad,' said Rachel, 'and so am I.'

'Believe me, I'm no hero,' said Benjamin, 'I wanted to be anywhere but where I was that night. But there it is, we can't run, Rachel, we've got to stay and fight, we can't let those Nazi swines hammer us into the ground.'

'They won't, Benjy, not while enough of us stay to fight, and not while Mr Churchill stays with us. He won't run, never. Nor will he accept losing.'

'We need an ally,' said Benjamin, not an irritable patient even in a wheelchair. He was simply glad to be alive. 'We need Russia, except that Stalin's about as trustworthy as that old diddler, Hanky-Panky Solomon, who finally did a runner from Kempton Park before the last race of the day was over, and welshed on the punters. Rachel, you're still getting looked after kindly by Mrs Finch?'

'She's a dear woman,' said Rachel.

'There are other friends, our own friends,' said Benjamin.

'I know, Benjy,' said Rachel, 'but they weren't

there that morning, they had their own worries, their own damages.'

'Well, we owe Mrs Finch, my life we do,' said Benjamin. 'I ought to put her onto a cert after the war. Say the first post-war Derby winner at long odds. Listen here, we'll need a new home when I get out.'

'Benjy, you've said that almost every day, and I do have my eye on one now. Off Brixton Hill.'

'Rent or purchase?' asked Benjamin.

'Purchase,' said Rachel, wisely refraining from mentioning that Sammy had found it for her. Benjamin was touchy about her long-standing relationship with Sammy. A little mental sigh filtered into her mind. She had nothing on her conscience, for she had never been unfaithful to her husband, but the fact was she had always loved Sammy, just as Polly Simms had always loved Boots. Polly was going to have him at last, in March. Polly, so upper class and yet so attached to the gregarious Adams family. Rachel was incurably attached to them herself, and more so now. During her stay with Sammy's mother, everyone had called more than once to see her, to offer whatever help she needed; Tommy and Vi, Lizzy and Ned, Sammy and Susie, and even old Aunt Victoria and Uncle Tom. It was not help alone that was offered, it was affection and warm undeviating friendship. And Chinese Lady and Mr Finch had been treating her like a daughter. In addition, she had received a long and splendid letter from Boots.

She heard Benjamin saying something.

'Where are you, Rachel, up on the moon?'

'No, here with you, lovey.'

'I should have to ask you twice if you like this house off Brixton Hill?'

'Yes, I do like it, and it's empty.'

'Then leave a deposit with the agent to make sure we get first option,' said Benjamin. 'I can trust you when it comes to sizing up property. I'll do a hop, skip and a jump to Brixton Hill with the help of your arm and a taxi as soon as Matron says I can. You can't expect Mrs Finch to look after you indefinitely.'

What that meant, of course, was the sooner she was out of Sammy's immediate orbit, the better Benjamin would like it. Benjamin couldn't be blamed for his suspicions.

'We'll do that, lovey, we'll buy and move in just as soon as we can.'

Benjamin smiled.

'More husbands should have good wives like you, Rachel,' he said. 'I'll get my legs back, you'll see.'

Rosie, at the wheel of her Hillman, turned into Chapman's Garage, and pulled up behind a car that was adjacent the old petrol pump. A very pretty woman in a smart leather coat and a fur hat was talking to Matthew. He said something and she laughed in delight. His broad smile was an echo of her amusement.

Rosie experienced a pang of discomfiture, a feeling that she had arrived at the wrong moment, that she was the odd one out. The woman, still laughing, handed Matthew some money. He fished into the pocket of his overalls and gave her change.

She said something to him and slipped into her car. He watched her drive away, then watched Rosie in turn as she brought the Hillman in line with the pump. She switched off the engine and got out.

'Hello,' he said.

'Hello, Matthew,' she said. His hair still needed a trim, his overalls were stained with grease, his face weathered by winter, his smile warm and welcoming. He glanced at the Hillman.

'Trouble, Lieutenant?' he said.

'With my banger?' said Rosie. 'Not on your life, it's still singing. I've come for some petrol.'

'But don't you get Army petrol from your workshop?' asked Matt.

'Oh, I have an allowance because I use the car for duty journeys,' said Rosie, 'but it's only a measly gallon once a week. I'm hoping for a few days leave soon, so could you put four gallons in, please?'

'Pleasure, Lieutenant.'

'Lieutenant?' said Rosie. 'Stop being stuffy.'

Matt, unhooking the petrol feed, looked at her. Beneath her peaked cap her eyes were stunning in their deep blue. It's a shaker, he thought, for a young woman with eyes like that to be out of my reach. I couldn't even find enough to dress her decently.

'Well,' he said briskly, 'I'm compelled to be stuffy about petrol. I have to ask about coupons. Personally, I'd like to fill your tank and let the Ministry blow its head off concerning the coupons, but then they might blow my pump up.'

'Why would you like to do that?' asked Rosie. 'Why?'

'Yes, why?'

'Fill your tank and let the Ministry go hang, you mean?' said Matt.

'Yes,' said Rosie.

'The answer's not complicated,' said Matt, 'it's simple. I like you, and it's a rare pleasure to know you.'

'Well, I like to be liked by a man as nice as you,' smiled Rosie. 'And be happy, because I have coupons, quite a few. A present from an uncle of mine.' Uncle Sammy, hearing that she'd bought a car but was restricted for petrol, had sent her a little wad of coupons, telling her in his letter that he happened to find a bundle of them in his pocket after enjoying a friendly lunch with a versatile business acquaintance. 'Here we are, old sport.' Rosie sounded like Polly sometimes. She produced the necessary amount of coupons. 'There, four gallons. Now you can look the Ministry in the eye.' Even if Uncle Sammy can't, she thought.

'Compliments to your uncle,' said Matt, and Rosie watched as he gave the old pump a bang, a crank and a needle adjustment, and began to feed in the petrol. He did everything very easily, with a kind of effortless masculine dexterity. He was a supple man, and very much like Boots with his easygoing air and the smile that always seemed close to the surface.

She had to ask.

'Who was the lovely lady, Matt?'

'The squire's daughter,' said Matt. 'She's married to a farmer. Everyone's married to a farmer or a farmhand in Dorset.'

'What did you say to her that made her laugh so much?'

'Well,' said Matt, 'there was this old man who was worried about his health. So he said to his doctor, "How do I stand?" "God knows," said his doctor.'

Rosie smiled.

'That's not actually a riotous joke,' she said.

'No, but Mrs Sylvia Manners laughs at almost anything,' said Matt. 'She was born laughing. There we are, four gallons.' He put the feed pipe back on the pump, and replaced the Hillman's petrol cap.

'Thank you,' said Rosie. Bangs vibrated through the workshop. 'How's business?'

'Up and down, here and there, what's the worry, weather's fair,' he said.

'Is that an old Dorset saying?' asked Rosie.

'No, an old Ben saying. Along with something like, cows chew grass, clouds bring rain, price of milk's gone up again.'

'Ben's a giggle, then,' said Rosie.

'Lively old codger,' said Matt. 'The petrol, let's see, two and tuppence a gallon now. Used to be one and fivepence before the war. That price is long gone and won't come back again, like a good many other things.'

'I believe you,' said Rosie, 'I believe nothing's going to be quite the same after this particular war.'

'Like women?' said Matt. He had work to do, but that took a good second place to time spent with this fascinating ATS officer.

'In what way?' asked Rosie, herself willing to linger. 'We're not going to change shape, are we?'

'I hope not.' Matt laughed. 'I'm dead against

that. No, I'm thinking that with so many women doing men's work, not all of them will want to go back to their kitchens. It's noticeable already, the change in women, particularly Servicewomen.'

'Bless the man,' smiled Rosie, 'he's painting a picture of me driving a train or working down a coal mine. Thank you, Matt, but no. I grew up enjoying the best of family life, and can't see myself ever giving that second place to a career as a train driver.'

'I don't see you as that, certainly,' said Matt, 'but I could see you running a bank.'

'You've got funny eyesight, then,' said Rosie. 'But are you against change?'

'I know I'm old-fashioned enough to be against radical changes that send women down coal mines,' said Matt.

'Snap,' said Rosie, and laughed.

'You're old-fashioned too?' said Matt.

'Excessively,' said Rosie. 'I come of a family of happy bread-winners of the male gender, and happy kitchen slaves of the female gender.' Of all the wives, Lizzy, Vi, Susie, Emily and yes, Grandma too, only Emily had preferred to go out to work. Dear departed Emily, her adoptive mother, known for being a godsend to the family in the old days. 'Happiness that's on one's doorstep can't easily take second place to being a postwoman or a plumber.'

'Or a scientist?' said Matt.

'I'll allow for some exceptions,' said Rosie.

'One should, I suppose,' said Matt. 'If a woman is a scientific marvel, she can't exercise her genius at a kitchen sink.'

'Well, we both agree that geniuses are different,' said Rosie. 'The rest of us are ordinary.'

Matt's laugh had a deep rich roll to it, which made Rosie think of Dorset rich with summer.

'Well, if you're ordinary, I give up,' he said.

'I meant in comparison with geniuses,' said Rosie.

'I still give up,' said Matt. 'You might as well say Queen Cleopatra was ordinary because she didn't invent the steam engine.'

'If you're classing me with Queen Cleopatra, I like it,' said Rosie. 'But it's far from true, of course.'

'You've met her?' said Matt.

'Well, no,' said Rosie, 'I think she's dead, isn't she?'

'I think you're right,' said Matt. 'Now I'll have to come down to being commercially-minded, and tell you you owe me eight and eightpence for the petrol.'

'Yes, of course,' said Rosie, and brought her shoulder bag out of the car. She produced a ten-shilling note from her purse, and Matt gave her change of one and fourpence.

'Fair?' he said with a smile.

'I'm happy,' said Rosie. 'I'll call in for a fill-up if I get some leave.' It occurred to her then that if the Corps ever went overseas, it would probably mean the end of her relationship with Matthew Chapman, that she'd never see this delightfully warm and refreshing man of Dorset again. Another little pang arrived. 'You don't work on Sundays, do you?'

'Only in the garden,' said Matt.

'Don't you go out?'

'Oh, some Sundays I trot out with my sister Maisie,' said Matt.

'Dorset's lovely in the summer, and not bad in the winter, either,' said Rosie. If she was dropping a hint that he might like to invite her out on one of her off-duty Sundays, he didn't pick it up.

'Thomas Hardy always thought of Dorset as his beloved county,' he said.

'Yes,' said Rosie, and smiled wryly. 'Well, I'd better go, I'm sure you've got work to do.'

'A tractor job.'

'Goodbye, then,' said Rosie, 'I'll see you when I next call in.'

'You're always welcome,' said Matt. He opened the door of her car and she slid in. Her legs in fine khaki stockings were a momentary pleasure to his eye before she tucked them in and tidied her skirt. 'By the way, if you'd like a couple of plump rabbits to take home whenever you get leave, let me know, and I'll have them ready on the day you go.'

'Matt, my family would love a couple. Thanks so much.'

'You're welcome,' he said, 'and I'll snare them myself.'

'You're really a very nice man,' said Rosie.

'I'll make a note of that,' he said, and Rosie started her car and drove out onto the road.

For the first time in many years, she felt oddly unsure of herself. She felt unsure about her developing relationship with Matthew, a man so different from the sophisticated Army officers she mixed with every day, men witty, amusing and experienced in the art of seduction. She always dealt coolly with their overtures, for she saw no point at all in giving in to cavaliers. The finale of an overture was usually expressed as 'Let's make love,' which didn't mean that at all, it meant 'let's have sex.' Rosie felt that love had more to do with deep-rooted affection and loyalty than sex. She had grown up in an atmosphere of unbreakable family loyalties. Her aunts and uncles, and Boots and Emily, had all enjoyed the kind of togetherness that survived every disagreement.

Such played a large part in Rosie's outlook on life. So did the tolerance, good nature and dry humour of her adoptive father. She would have admitted favouring a suitor who had something of Boots about him.

Perceptive Polly, who had met Matthew Chapman only once, would have said that after a fashion he was not unlike Boots.

Chapter Seventeen

'Get up, you ponce.' Sergeant 'Basher' Olney booted Corporal Tim Adams in the ribs. Tim, grounded following a hell of a blow, looked up at the man who was making the morning a misery for him. Sergeant Olney wasn't the only one, either. A cadre of violently tough NCO's at this pleasant old Scottish seaport had a single objective, to either put the training Commandos in a wheelchair for life or turn them into man-eating gorillas able to demolish German opposition without losing any sleep. 'Did you hear me?' said Sergeant Olney. 'Get up, you horrible fairy.'

Unarmed combat, except that the instructors occasionally produced wicked-looking knives, happened all too often. Tim came up on his elbows amid a ring of men all looking down at him. He saw a circle of faces and eyes, some expressive of curiosity, some of 'I'm-glad-it's-not-me-mate', and some of grinning amusement. Of sympathy there was none. That kind of thing wasn't a characteristic of the rough and tough Commandos. Tim thought that running a fast mile with a laden pack or the gauntlet of genuine bullets was easier to put up with than getting knocked about, then kicked, cursed and mocked. Sergeant Olney, wearing the uniform of a German infantryman, booted him in the ribs again. Tim decided to take him on seriously, and smash his face in for a change.

Up he came. Sergeant Olney moved like lightning, shoved the flat of his hand against Tim's mouth and hooked a foot around his leg. Down he went again, thudding onto his back.

'Sod that,' he said breathlessly.

From a first-floor window, Subaltern Felicity Jessop observed man's inhumanity to man with interest and without squeamishness. Squeamish personnel were out of place in Commando training theatres.

A large officer arrived, an oak in human form dressed up in fatigues.

'Who the hell's this layabout?' he barked, looking down at Tim.

'Just another tart dolled up as a bloke,' said Sergeant Olney.

'Jesus Christ, with two stripes?' said the officer, Captain Osgood. 'On your feet, you knock-kneed tomtit,' he bawled at Tim. Tim's vein of steel surfaced, putting a tint of blue into his grey eyes. He got up. The circle of men widened to make room for more mayhem. Captain Osgood barked an order at Sergeant Olney. 'Saw his bloody head off.'

'Best thing for a fairy,' said Sergeant Olney, drawing a sheathed knife, 'he's a dead loss to this outfit.' But Tim was first into the fray this time. His blood was up. That was an important point of the exercise, of course, to make these volunteers see red and then discover if hot blood made them effective or useless. In Tim's case, hot blood hardened his steel, and the steel controlled his temper. Lost temper never paid dividends. Up came his right foot fast and high while the sergeant's mouth was still open. The toe of the boot hit Olney fair and square in his stomach. A gasping grunt escaped him and he doubled up. Tim smashed both fists down on the back of his neck.

Felicity, ex-hockey captain, exultantly mouthed, 'Bloody good show, Tim.'

'Stay on your feet, you doughnut!' yelled Captain Osgood, but Sergeant Olney was already a sprawling heap. Tim stamped a foot on the hand that held the knife. The hand let go, and Tim kicked the knife away. Sergeant Olney turned on his back, his face a fine shade of purple. He gazed up at Tim.

'Did me, you bleeder,' he wheezed.

'Don't mention it,' said Tim.

'All right, all right,' growled Sergeant Olney, 'who's next?'

Tim wasn't deceived. He'd had some of that before, and from other instructors. Sergeant Olney might have looked as if he was climbing painfully and harmlessly to his feet, but Tim was taking no chances. He downed him again before he was halfway up, and knelt on him.

'Oh, you beauty,' breathed Felicity, and the window steamed up.

Captain Osgood shouted at the watching men.

'Well, say something, you horsebags.'

'Hoo-bloody-hooray,' said one man.

211

'What? What?'

'Hoo-bloody-hooray.'

'Stuff that hooray piddle,' said Captain Osgood. 'I want to hear some old-fashioned English, and I want to see the boot going in. If all of you don't hate that German uniform by now, I'll chop the lot of you.'

At which point, Sergeant Olney made another fast move in an attempt to throw Tim aside. Tim simply went with the movement, rolled right over, turning the sergeant with him, and again put the man on his back. He picked up the knife and pricked Sergeant Olney's throat with the point.

'Bugger me,' said Sergeant Olney, 'I'll be owing you, Corporal Adams.'

'No hard feelings,' said Tim.

'No hard feelings? What a tadpole,' said Captain Osgood. 'Send him back to Mummy, Sergeant.' But he had a bit of a grin on his face as he left to keep an appointment with a couple of junior officers who needed a few rounds with a roll of barbed wire to make them understand training here was a matter of life or death.

Tim thought of his dad, who had told him never to volunteer for anything. When Tim advised him by letter that he had volunteered for the Commandos, Boots wrote back and said well, that's one way of staying alive. Tim knew he meant simply by being tougher than the opposition. The opposition were the Germans who had knocked hell out of the BEF, and Tim, along with other Dunkirk men, was itching to get back at them.

*　　*　　*

'Corporal Adams?' It was the midday break and Tim, on his way to the canteen, stopped and turned. Subaltern Jessop, outside the admin. building, called again. 'Mail for you, Corporal Adams.'

'Coming, ma'am,' said Tim, and crossed over.

'In the orderly room,' said Felicity, looking like the best part of Tim's private dreams.

'You're very obliging,' said Tim, following her in. The orderly room was empty.

'Shut the door for a tick,' said Felicity, and Tim closed it. 'Corporal Adams, would you like a kiss?'

'Who from?' asked Tim.

'Me, you chump, who else?' said Felicity, and kissed him warmly on his mouth.

'I liked that,' said Tim, 'but wasn't it against the rules?'

'Blow the rules,' said Felicity, 'you downed Troon's number one executioner, you beauty.'

'Fluked it,' said Tim.

'No, you didn't, you laid him low like a runaway train. Rattling good show.'

'There's no mail?' said Tim.

'No, just a kiss,' said Felicity. 'That's all, Corporal.'

'What's that, then?' asked Tim, glancing.

Felicity fell for it. She turned her head. Tim swooped. Her head turned back and he kissed her smack on her lush lips. Not only that, he also treated himself to a caress or two.

After which, with the kind of umbrage befitting a wholesome ex-school captain, she said, 'Do you realize you've just committed the most frightful crime, you sex-mad shocker?'

213

'Me Tarzan, you Jane,' said Tim. 'Well, it's a fight for survival in this jungle. Glad to have met you, Subaltern Jessop, you remind me a bit of a close family friend.' He meant Polly. 'Have to push off now.'

'I'll get you court-martialled, you—'

'Mind your language,' said Tim. 'Well, that's all.' He left.

Felicity laughed.

What a goer. But she still owed him a smack in the eye for taking liberties.

A Sunday arrived. Tommy and Vi, together with Sammy and Susie, were down in Devon, visiting their children. In Dorset, Rosie had a letter to write in answer to the last one she'd received from her natural father, Colonel Charles Armitage. His address was a BFPO number, and she knew he was in the Middle East with General Wavell's army, although his letter had been carefully worded in its avoidance of his present location and any specific military matters. He asked, as he always did, for information on the latest events and happenings in her life. He mentioned that the loss of her adoptive mother had been followed by the death of his wife after a prolonged illness. It was hackneyed to call it a happy release, he said, but in this case, it was true. Rosie felt that the exercise of writing her reply would take her mind off something that was making her restless. For the first time in her adult life she had a man on her mind, a man with a lame leg, a refreshing personality and the unspoiled appeal of Dorset itself. She frankly conceded she'd have liked him to take a more personal interest in her, not treat her as just another customer. Perhaps his most personal interest was in a certain Mary Hubble, a postwoman. Rosie fidgeted and had trouble concentrating on her letter.

In Troon, the Commandos actually had a rest day. A note in an envelope was popped into Maggie Andrews' letter-box early in the morning. It was addressed to Corporal Adams. Over breakfast, he read its contents.

'Attention, Corporal Adams. Note that I have the use of a car and require an escort-driver. Meet me a quarter of a mile up from the bus stop at ten. Wear your civvies. This is an order. Subaltern Jessop.'

She can't order me, thought Tim.

'You're smiling,' said Maggie.

'Yes, I've just received an order.'

'Gang awa' wi' you, McAdams, orders don't make you laddies smile,' said Maggie.

'This is a different kind of order,' said Tim.

'There's a lassie behind it, then,' said Maggie.

'You're a clever girl, Maggie.'

'Aye, and you're an impudence,' said Maggie.

At ten, the car was there. Tim arrived beside it, and recognized it as a heap of old iron that might have been declared obsolete WD property years ago, but was meat and drink to some of the 4 Commando officers. Nothing that still moved was obsolete to them except men who wet their pants when told to swim a mile in full kit.

Subaltern Jessop was in the passenger seat. She wound the window down.

'Get in, Corporal Adams,' she said.

'It's a birdcage,' said Tim.

'Don't hang about, get in,' said Felicity.

Tim dropped a bag into the back of the car and put himself in the driving seat.

'Morning, ma'am,' he said, 'nice day.' The winter sun was sharp, the sky clear, and Scotland lay peacefully quiet. The Germans hadn't touched Scotland yet, they were still busy pulverizing Winston Churchill's backyard. The hatred of the Nazis for Churchill was paranoiac. But then, they were paranoiac in all their hatreds, and, in the eyes of Tim and Felicity, a bloody disgrace to the German people they purported to speak for.

'Well, get going,' said Felicity.

'Where to?' asked Tim, starting the engine.

'Where?' said Felicity, civilian coat again worn over jumper and skirt, and a brown beret on her head. 'How about over the sea to Skye?'

'Does this thing fly, then?' asked Tim.

'Hope not, or we'll crash-land,' said Felicity. 'Try getting away from all the mayhem. Anywhere. But keep Kilmarnock in your sights. We can have lunch at a hotel there. Everything else will be shut.'

'Off we go, then,' said Tim, and set the car in motion. It burped a couple of times, but kept going. A Commando came out of a house, and Felicity ducked out of sight.

'People will talk,' she said when she'd righted herself.

'I'm not surprised,' said Tim, 'you're the flower

of the flock out slumming with a corporal.'

'I'm what?'

'Well, I know there are only three ATS personnel,' said Tim, heading for the road to Kilmarnock, with the sun flashing light at the windscreen, 'but you're easily number one. Lieutenant Cary is actually a policewoman in disguise and Sergeant Titmus is a naughty nymph. But you're sporty and all that, pretty fair figure and all that—'

'Pretty fair? What d' you mean, pretty fair?'

'A bit of all right, say?' suggested Tim.

'What a swine,' said Felicity, 'you're out of order. Incidentally, no funny stuff today.'

'Funny stuff?' said Tim.

'Or I'll sock you,' said Felicity. Ahead, the road was clear, the view lush with wet greenery shimmering in the sunlight. 'By the way, did I see you put something on the back seat?'

'Yes,' said Tim.

'What was it?'

'A bag containing a camera,' said Tim. 'I borrowed it from Maggie Andrews.'

'For taking snapshots of lochs and glens?' said Felicity.

'They'll make fine backgrounds,' said Tim. 'I'm actually hoping to photograph you as the main subject.'

'Me? Why and what for?'

'Most of the blokes have got pin-ups of Betty Grable and Rita Hayworth on their walls,' said Tim. 'I'd like some of you on mine.'

'Say that again, Corporal Adams.'

'I don't suppose you've brought a swimsuit with

217

you,' said Tim, 'but if you're wearing a jumper or sweater, that'll do nicely.'

'I don't believe I'm hearing this,' said Felicity. 'It can't be that you're talking about making a pin-up of an ATS officer, can it? You'd have to tie me down first, and d'you know what you could get for that? Ten years in Dartmoor, you pervert. I already owe you a black eye for taking liberties with me a few days ago.'

'Sorry about that,' said Tim, 'rush of blood.'

He drove on, feeling light-hearted about the outing. In a little while, he forked left and by-passed Kilmarnock, then headed for the village of Stewarton. He stopped when they were out of the village, and from there the view of the lowlands of Scotland was of a terrain cut into dark shadows and bright greens by the sharpness of the sun.

'I say, what a ripping vista,' said Felicity.

'And no traffic,' said Tim. Traffic was always lighter in Scotland than in England. Outside its cities, it seemed to swallow cars and lorries and present an unchanging, uninterrupted panorama of hills, forests, lochs and glens. 'Like some hot coffee, Subaltern?'

'Do cows give it out here, then?' asked Felicity, spotting the dark humps of cattle.

'Not as far as I know,' said Tim. He reached over to bring the shopping bag from off the back seat. In it was a camera, a flask and two mugs. He took out the flask, then the mugs. 'If you'd like to hold the mugs, I'll pour,' he said.

'There's coffee in that flask?' said Felicity.

'From Maggie Andrews. Like some?'

'Rather.' Felicity held the mugs and Tim filled them. The coffee, made from Camp, came steaming from the flask. 'Jolly good show, Corporal Adams, if there's a wee bitty helping of sugar as well.'

'Worth a pin-up pose or two?' said Tim.

'Legs and stocking-tops, you dog?' said Felicity.

'Sweater?' said Tim, undoing a twist of paper and spilling sugar into her mug.

'Legs and sweater?' said Felicity, sipping.

'Just the job,' said Tim.

'It would have to be legs and jumper,' said Felicity.

'I'm happy.'

'Except it's not on, you rotter,' said Felicity. 'I'm not going to be pinned up in your billet for all your rubbernecked hooligan mates to gawp at. I was nearly expelled from school once for cheeking our French teacher – silly old bird – and I'm ducking the risk of being expelled from the ATS.'

'Well, look here, lovey—'

'Lovey?' said Felicity.

'It's a family thing,' said Tim. 'We originated in Walworth, where everyone's a lovey. D'you mind that I see you more as a lovey than an officer?'

'Stop trying to make me giggle,' said Felicity, 'I'll spill my coffee.'

'I was going to say I'll keep the snapshots to myself,' said Tim.

'Wait a moment,' said Felicity, 'that only applies when the snapshots are those of the owner's lady friend.'

'I know that,' said Tim.

'I'm not your lady friend.'

'I'm working on it,' said Tim.

The Sunday quiet was broken by an Army truck. It roared by.

'Shouldn't be allowed,' said Felicity.

'It's the war,' said Tim.

'Now look here, Corporal Adams,' said Felicity, 'have you got some idea that if you photograph me I can be tucked into your wallet as your heart-throb?'

'I'm working on it,' repeated Tim. 'I'm not a stuffy bloke, I'll be happy to tuck you into my wallet, even if you are an officer. You make up for that by being game for a laugh and having the right amount of whatsit.'

'Whatsit?' said Felicity.

'Bouncy sex appeal,' said Tim.

'Bouncy sex appeal? What's that exactly?'

'I don't know, exactly, but I think you've got it,' said Tim.

Felicity couldn't help herself. She laughed.

'I think I'm fighting a losing battle here,' she said. 'I might have known I was letting myself in for hysterics in consenting to come out with you.'

'You've got that the wrong way round,' said Tim. 'I received an order from you.'

'There's no need to confuse things,' said Felicity, and finished her coffee. 'It's lovely outside. Let's go for a walk.'

'I'm game,' said Tim, and finished his own coffee. They were out of the car a minute later, looking around to select the most inviting route for a ramble. 'I think that's a bridle path over there.'

'That'll do,' said Felicity, 'I'm in the mood for a brisk walk.'

'I get an overdose of that,' said Tim.

'Poor old soldier,' she said with a smile. 'Never mind, come on, let's get going.' Tim took the keys out of the ignition to lock the car. 'All right, you can bring the camera,' she said, 'I might have a weak moment.'

'The light's good,' said Tim, and fished the shopping bag out of the car.

Chapter Eighteen

They were by the loch at Burnfoot sometime later, where green hollows, lush woodlands and shimmering water seemed beautifully remote from the images of war. A felled tree, stricken with old age, and covered with moss and lichen, lay half-buried in leaves and dying ferns. Felicity sat on the smooth surface of its standing trunk, her bottom resting on the shopping bag.

'Ripping,' she said, letting her gaze wander over views bright beneath the winter sun.

'I like Scotland,' said Tim, 'it's uncrowded.'

'I feel I'm a hundred miles from anywhere,' said Felicity. 'But I'm not sure I feel safe.'

'You're safe,' said Tim, and Felicity gave him a long look. There he was, in his civvies, his head bare, his back to the sunlight, his face in shadow. He was a very masculine young man and an extremely capable NCO, she knew that. She'd seen him during much of his training, and she knew his record, his commendation for distinguishing himself as a gunner during that bitter and desperate fighting retreat to Dunkirk. They showed, those weeks of battle that had turned him into a tough and adventurous soldier with an air of bravura. He was a natural Commando.

'Just for you, then?' she smiled.

'Come again?' said Tim.

'Legs and jumper photographs?'

'Just head and shoulders will do,' said Tim.

'No, let's go mad,' she said. The sunlight was on her, turning her into a bright and colourful young woman. She unbuttoned her coat, swept it wide open and straightened her back. That did something to her yellow jumper. It tightened around her well-fitting bra. The hem of her skirt, an inch or so below her knees, allowed the sun to strike at her stockings. 'How's that?' she asked.

'I can't complain,' said Tim, liking the picture and her smile. She really was a sport.

'Well, come on, tiger,' said Felicity, 'I can't hold my breath for ever.'

Tim focused the camera. Her clinging jumper looked a brilliant gold. He snapped her.

'Lovely,' he said.

'Have fun, then,' she said. The sun was in her eyes, reflecting sparkling light. She was in the mood now, responsive to the atmosphere of fun. 'Take another one.'

Tim snapped her again, twice, from different angles. Felicity held her indrawn breath each time so that her fine figure sustained its convex curvature. Well, if he wanted sex appeal, she felt sporty enough to oblige.

'Rattling good show, Subaltern Jessop,' said Tim.

'I'm no Betty Grable,' said Felicity.

'Good as Rita Hayworth, though, who's an all-rounder,' said Tim.

'I'm an idiot to ask, but what's an all-rounder?' asked Felicity.

'A lady with no straight lines,' said Tim.

Felicity laughed and looked up at him, her smile sunlit. Tim did what came naturally. He kissed her. The crisp winter day had touched her mouth. It tingled as he laid his lips on hers.

'Is there no stopping you?' she asked after an encore that was also tingling.

'Only a sock in the eye,' said Tim.

She laughed, her face glowing, her lips moistly shining.

'How many exposures on your film?' she asked.

'Eight.'

'There's five more to go?' she said. 'Well, come on, tiger, you want legs as well as jumper, don't you?'

'It wasn't a serious request,' said Tim.

'Never mind, here we go,' said Felicity. She drew her skirt and slip high, several inches above her knees, and her stockings gleamed. 'There,' she said. 'No, wait,' she said, covering her knees, 'I don't want these snapshots pinned up on your bedroom wall.'

'I thought we agreed they were to be tucked into my wallet,' said Tim.

'Promise?'

'Promise,' said Tim.

'Take your word,' said Felicity and drew her skirt and slip high again.

Tim looked.

She was a picture of a jolly hockey-sticks type being playful. There seemed to be no suggestion of provocative sexuality about her, she seemed simply a young woman in a fun mood. All the same, it was provocative, thought Tim. And irresistible. Her legs were superb.

'That's just for me?' he said.

'Listen, I don't make a habit of this,' she said.

'Believe me, I believe you,' said Tim.

They might have heard the slight whisper of noise if they hadn't been so wrapped up in the enjoyment they were deriving from their dialogue. As it was, the interruption came with a sharp unexpected shock to them.

'What's going on, eh?'

'What's coming off, you mean.'

Felicity and Tim turned their heads and saw two men, both wearing khaki balaclavas that covered heads and faces but not bright gleaming eyes, eyes that took in the picture of Felicity's sun-dappled legs. For a moment, she was stiff with the shock of unpleasant surprise, then she snatched at her skirt and swiftly adjusted it.

'Shame you did that, you looked better with it up,' said one man. They were both bulky and muscular, wearing padded black leather waistcoats over grey jerseys and dark grey trousers.

'You push off, sunshine, we'll see to the lady,' said the other, addressing Tim.

'Who the hell are you?' asked Tim. If they were from the Troon Commando group, he couldn't place them.

'I'm Brown, he's Green.'

'No, I'm Brown, he's Green.'

They laughed, coarsely.

'Go home,' said Tim.

'See him off, Mr Green.'

'You take charge of the lady, Mr Brown.'

The menace was all too apparent, a violent and ugly thing about to uncoil itself. Both men had their eyes on Felicity, greedy eyes, the eyes of the damned. Felicity came to her feet, her unbuttoned coat dropping. Tim stood quite still as she placed herself elbow to elbow with him and drew her coat to. Both men rushed, avid for Felicity and contemptuous of Tim.

Bulk and muscle bruised the air. Felicity went rigid. Tim was lightly poised on the balls of his feet, eyes steely. One man launched himself at him, swinging a ferocious right arm and a knotted fist, his assault vicious. He struck empty air, and his impetus took him on. Then a kick, delivered high in the small of his back, sent him hurtling. Tim followed up with another lightning-like kick that hit the falling man in the back of his right knee. He followed that up too, and was merciless.

The other man had eyes only for his own target. He was at Felicity, reaching for her with hands greedier than his covetous optics. She sank her teeth into his left hand. He yelled, cursed and used his other hand to grab the front of her coat. He yanked, he pulled, and Felicity was whirled about and thrown down. She landed on her back, and he jumped her, his knees astride her hips, his hands pinning her shoulders.

'Got the lady, Mr Green,' he wheezed, and

turned his head. Unfortunately for him, he received an immediate kick in the mouth, a kick that severed four of his front teeth from his gums. The tearing wrench of that disastrous injury, which caused him to vomit teeth and blood into his balaclava, was only a precursive strike, for it was followed by a blow that almost took his head from his shoulders. He shuddered and fell limply aside.

Tim shifted the crumpled bulk and Felicity, free, came to her feet. She looked down at her unconscious assailant, and then at the other verminous creature, who lay spreadeagled on his back. Then she looked at Tim, who was breathing lightly.

'Bloody good show, Tim,' she said.

'Point is, who are they?'

'I'll tell you what they are, a couple of filthy swines,' said Felicity.

'Not Commandos, I hope,' said Tim.

'Find out,' said Felicity.

Tim first yanked off the balaclavas to reveal cropped heads and gaunt, unshaven jowls. Then he stripped the unconscious pair of their trousers, putting each man back into the land of Nod at the first signs of recovery. He searched their trousers and their other garments, but found nothing of any kind that offered clues to their identity. He tied them up back to back, lashing their arms and wrists together behind their backs with one man's braces, and using the other's to harness their legs. Finally, he tightly imprisoned their cropped bullet heads by stretching one balaclava down over both.

'Will that suffocate them?' asked Felicity.

'Not a woollen balaclava with a gap in it,' said

Tim, 'but it'll make things a lot more difficult and uncomfortable for them. Come on, let's find a public phone box in Kilmarnock, and call the police.'

Felicity smiled.

'You're in charge, oh mighty bone-crusher,' she said, and they began a swift walk back to the car.

'You all right?' said Tim.

'Yes, Tim, I'm fine,' said Felicity.

'Good,' said Tim, and she put out a hand. He took it and they walked on through the greens of Scotland.

In Kilmarnock, Tim phoned the police. To avoid the kind of fuss that would require Felicity and himself to present themselves in court, he gave false names and addresss. He informed the police of the incident in detail and upon describing the two men very accurately, he was told to hang on for a moment. The desk sergeant came back to him and said the two men were almost certainly English convicts who had escaped three days ago from Lanark Prison, where they'd been serving sentences for robbery and rape, the crime having been committed in Aberdeen two years ago. Tim said one called himself Green, the other Brown.

'Ah, weel, Mr Fielding, two more barefaced villains there never were, y'ken. One's Thomas Greenaway, the other's Henry Browning. They've a number of convictions for violent crime. You say you knocked them out and left them tied up?'

'Well, it was either them or us,' said Tim. He described the exact location, and suggested the police should get there fairly quickly to save the men freezing to death.

'Aye, we'll awa' to the place,' said the desk sergeant. 'If the rascals are who we think, we'll have cause to thank you. I canna believe, mind, that you and your young lassie dealt wi' them yourselves, but thank the guid Lord you did. Weel now, if you'll tell me where you're phoning from, a police car will pick you both up, and then we'll be sure, wi' your guidance, of going straight to the spot. Mr Fielding? Mr Fielding, are you there?'

Tim, alias Mr Fielding, wasn't. He'd hung up, and was giving Felicity details of the conversation. Felicity said thank God she hadn't known at the time they were up against convicted thugs and proven rapists. Her nerves, bad enough at the time, would have been shot to pieces.

'Well, we've done all that's necessary,' said Tim, 'and the police will chuck a posse around the area just in case those buggers have managed to break loose. Because I rang off, they might think I'm a bit of a hoaxer, but they can't risk not investigating. Let's get moving, let's see if that hotel will serve us lunch, even if it is frugal.'

The hotel did, and it wasn't frugal, either, it was very satisfying, particularly as, at Tim's suggestion, they each had a brandy before they sat down.

'Corporal Adams, I'm beginning to like you,' said Felicity.

'You're already my favourite subaltern,' said Tim.

'Where's the camera?' asked Felicity.

'In the car,' said Tim.

'Jolly good,' said Felicity.

The light was still crisp and bright when they drove out of Kilmarnock later. They toured around and stopped near a village called Craigie. Solitude was all around them. They got out to stand and observe the vista.

'Can't grumble at this,' said Tim.

'Who's grumbling?' asked Felicity.

'I'm not,' said Tim.

'I owe you for today,' said Felicity.

'No, you don't, there's no way you owe me anything,' said Tim.

'Well, as the light's still good, I'll at least let you take more snaps, if you want,' she said.

'No, I'm happy with those I've got,' said Tim, 'and any extra poses might make Rob Roy and his hairy Highlanders pop up out of the heather this time.'

Felicity laughed.

'How are you on fighting claymores?' she asked.

'Hopeless,' said Tim, 'they're not in the Commando manual. Listen, as an officer, would it embarrass you if I fell in love with you?'

'Pardon?' said Felicity.

'It could happen,' said Tim.

'You're working on it, you mean?'

'It's working on me,' said Tim, 'and I've got a feeling it might take me over.'

'It's not the time,' she said, 'wait till the war's over.'

'Fair enough,' said Tim, and they got back into the car to drive around in leisurely fashion before returning to Troon. Felicity said she'd get shot at dawn if it were known she'd been out all day with a corporal. Tim said only Lieutenant Cary would stand her up against a wall, that nobody else would worry. Fat lot of good that would do me, said Felicity, I'd still be dead. Tim said he didn't think she would be, he didn't think Lieutenant Cary could hit any kind of target, not even an elephant at close range, let alone a jumper. She might fluke it, said Felicity. Hope not, said Tim, it could spoil a jumper he was getting fond of.

The conversation was like that, friendly and chummy, but just a little guarded on Felicity's part.

Tim went to bed that night feeling he'd had more of an eventful Sunday than he had bargained for. Then he wondered when his first Commando raid would take place. The group was trained up to its eyebrows.

Chapter Nineteen

General Wavell's forces, deep into Libya, had captured Bardia, Helafaya Pass and Tobruk.

While waiting for what might be asked of them in the immediate future, most men and women in the Home Services were hoping for some leave.

Boots, Polly and Rosie were among many given four days. Bobby and Helene were offered a weekend.

On the afternoon of the day before her brief leave began, Rosie called in at the garage. She pulled up on the forecourt, and got out. There was no one visible, but a hammering noise was disturbing the walls of the workshop. Rosie walked to the wide opening and lifted her voice.

'Anyone at home?'

Matt slid himself out from under a chassis. His second mechanic, Josh Turner, kept on hammering. Matt came to his feet. His overalls were oily, his hair awry, and he looked like a man dedicated to his trade. He limped out to Rosie.

'Hello again,' he said, his smile as welcoming as ever.

'Hello, Matthew.'

'Every time you appear,' he said, 'I look like something out of a rubbish dump of oily waste, and you look like a recruiting poster for the ATS.'

'You look like a hard-working garage owner, old thing, which is much more to be admired than a recruiting poster,' said Rosie.

'I seriously doubt that,' said Matt. 'Have you called to let me know when you want the rabbits?'

'Yes, I'm going on leave tomorrow,' said Rosie.

'Then I'll snare them first thing in the morning,' said Matt, 'best time for catching them nibbling. It's a hard life for rabbits in wartime, but something's got to go into the pot besides carrots to help out with meat rationing.'

'Well, perhaps bunnies don't know about rabbit stew, perhaps they live in happy ignorance,' said Rosie. 'I'll pick them up on my way home tomorrow, shall I?'

'Do that,' said Matt, and Rosie thought it was time he helped their relationship to get off the ground and enter a high-flying phase.

Ben came out of the office. He was carrying two mugs of tea.

'Pot's done made, Matt,' he called. 'Afternoon, miss.'

'Afternoon, Ben,' said Rosie, and Ben smiled and disappeared into the workshop.

Matt, after a moment's hesitation, said, 'Like a cup of tea if you've got time?'

'Thank you, Matthew, yes, I would,' said Rosie, and walked with him to the office. It contained a little desk, an old typewriter, a phone, two chairs, a small filing cabinet, invoices stuck on a hook, a wall calendar and some odds and ends. In a corner was a gas ring, on which stood a tin kettle. On the desk was a teapot, a cup and a bottle of milk.

'Aladdin's cave,' said Matt.

'And where does the geni spring from, the teapot?' asked Rosie.

'I'm always hoping,' said Matt. 'Sit down. Now, let's see, there's another cup somewhere.' He found it in the top drawer of the filing cabinet. He inspected it, and decided Rosie should have the other cup. He poured tea for both of them, Rosie watching him and thinking how natural he was. He didn't fuss, he didn't excuse the pokiness of his office, or attempt any tidying-up because she was there, and she liked that. The last thing she wanted was to have him apologize for what, after all, was adequate for his business. She sipped the tea. It was hot and fresh and good. 'Where's your home?' he asked.

'South-East London,' she said.

'You're going home to the bombs?'

'Oh, it's the City and Central London that mostly suffer.'

'Yours is a large family house?' said Matt.

'Fairly large.'

'There's an air raid shelter?'

'Yes, in the garden,' said Rosie.

'Is something worrying you?' asked Matt.

'Worrying me?' said Rosie.

'I daresay you come up against your own kind of problems in the Army,' said Matt.

'I suppose I'm not sure how I'm going to face up to going overseas sometime in the near future,' said Rosie, and noted at once that he didn't seem at all happy about what it meant.

234

'Overseas?' he said.

'Yes, the division would go with the rest of the Corps,' she said.

'I see,' said Matt, and rubbed his mouth. A twinge of acute disappointment made itself felt. Life could deliver some very unwelcome kicks. He knew exactly how he felt about Lieutenant Rosie Adams, and what her permanent absence would do to him. He made an effort. He gave her a smile. 'I'll miss having you and the Hillman call in, blow my head off if I won't. Well, things happen, armies move around, tractors break down, Dorset lambs get taken to market and garages fall apart.'

'Fall apart?' said Rosie.

'If you ever come back to Dorset, you'll probably find this old place closed down,' said Matt. 'It's losing money. There's very little traffic on this road apart from farm and Army vehicles. My father's managing to keep his head above water in Dorchester, but we'll sink here unless I can get some capital to tide us over. I had a word with the old man a short while ago, but he needs some capital himself for new equipment. I need a lot more if I'm to keep going. There's wages for Ben and Josh, to start with. I'm scraping the barrel at the moment.'

Rosie came to quick life.

'Matt, you must keep going,' she said, 'it's your living, and you're so good at it. You're able to put any kind of damaged vehicle back on the road.'

'Unfortunately,' said Matt, 'there's this absence of passing trade, and I'm mostly dependent on the work I get from farmers.'

'But if you shut down, what would you do?'

'I think I could always get farm work,' said Matt, 'or a job in a vehicle factory.'

'A factory? A factory?' Rosie was appalled. 'Matt, you can't.'

'We'll see,' he said. 'But I'm more worried about Ben and Josh than myself. They've always been in this trade, and they've still got several years left to them as mechanics, but I'm not sure they'd get more than mucking-out jobs on a farm.'

'Matt, how much capital do you need?' asked Rosie.

'As much as twelve hundred pounds if the war lasts for another two years,' he said. 'I'm pretty sure things will improve when it's over, and I'd like to keep going until then.'

Rosie had a glad thought.

'I might be able to help,' she said.

'What?' said Matt.

Rosie remembered Mrs Riddle, farmer's wife, who had said the garage was a prime site and would thrive when the war was over.

'I might be able to help.'

'Are you talking about offering me a loan of twelve hundred pounds yourself?' asked Matt, who needed three hundred a year for the wages of Ben and Josh, two hundred for himself, and an outlay of two hundred or more for new or reconditioned equipment.

'Oh, I don't have anything like that amount of money myself,' said Rosie. 'But I have an uncle who runs a business and always has capital available.'

'But don't you see, Rosie,' said Matt, 'there'd—'

'Thanks for that,' said Rosie.

'Come again?'

'Thanks for Rosie. It means we're friends, doesn't it?'

'My pleasure,' said Matt, and smiled. 'But regarding this possible loan, there'd be only minimum repayments, probably only enough to take care of the interest until things buck up, and no businessman would make a loan where repayment of the capital looked like pie in the sky.'

'You're not pie in the sky, old sport,' said Rosie, her Uncle Sammy on her mind, 'you've got a garage that'll be a winner after the war. We'd have to arrange for delayed repayment of the capital.'

'Is your uncle more of a philanthropist than a strict businessman?' asked Matt.

'Oh, a smart businessman, I'd say,' said Rosie, 'but a good old scout as well. Will you agree to my talking to him, and will you promise not to close the garage down just yet?'

'I'd no thought of closing it down immediately,' said Matt. 'I want to keep Ben and Josh at work until the spring at least. I'd hate to lay them off in winter. But how the devil you could get your uncle to defer repayment of the loan indefinitely, I don't know—'

'Believe me, I might know,' said Rosie, and smiled.

'That's more like you,' said Matt.

'What is?'

'Your smile, it's a winner,' said Matt, and Rosie thought how absurd it was that a simple compliment from this man of Dorset could give her so much more pleasure than the far more fulsome compliments she'd had from worldly Army officers. For that matter, when had compliments been really necessary to her? Now? 'But look,' said Matt, 'I wouldn't want you to spend too much of your leave talking to your uncle on my behalf.'

'If I know my Uncle Sammy, I'd only have to talk to him once to get a yes or no,' said Rosie.

'Well, if the money ends up on the table,' said Matt, 'I'll need to do a fair amount of thinking about what it'll mean for me in the way of liabilities. I'd not want to put myself in the position of turning the loan into a bad debt. That would let you down, and your uncle, and myself.'

'No, really, old thing, you simply can't close the garage,' said Rosie, 'you must keep going until the war's over. Put your prices up, increase your charges for service and maintenance.'

'Easier said than done in rural Dorset, Rosie, but we'll see.'

'I really must go now, I've so many things to do,' said Rosie. 'I'll see you in the morning.'

'I'll have the rabbits ready,' said Matt. He saw her to her car. 'My thanks for everything.'

About to get into her car, Rosie checked to watch a horse and dogcart turn in from the road. Up on the seat, riding high, was the round-faced woman, warmly wrapped up in a long coat and wearing a brown velour hat. She hailed Matt.

'Just passing, love, on my way to Tolpuddle and all. Anything you want there?' She had a warm and rich country voice.

238

'Nothing I can think of, Maisie,' smiled Matt. 'My sister Maisie,' he said to Rosie.

'Hello,' said Rosie.

'Maisie, meet Lieutenant Rosie Adams,' said Matt, and Mrs Maisie Shaw, widow, smiled beamingly down at Rosie.

'It's good to meet the Army lady with the Hillman,' she said.

'You've heard of me?' said Rosie.

'From Matthew,' said Maisie. 'My, and that's the Hillman?'

'It was a little like an old heap before Matthew went to work on it,' said Rosie.

'Well, he knows machines and engines,' said Maisie, whose smile seemed permanent, and whose bright eyes were taking in Rosie's striking looks. 'I keep telling him they're his children, but that you can't sit an engine on your lap and tell it bedtime stories. Pleasure to meet you and all, pleasure too if we happen to meet again, that I'm sure. Up and about, Humpy. Walk on.' She shook the reins, the horse wheeled about, took the handsome dogcart onto the road and began a spanking trot. Away went the dogcart, and Rosie thought it a delight to behold.

'It's your sister's, Matt?' she said.

'Mine,' he said, 'but Maisie makes sure the nag is properly fed and watered. We keep it in a six-acre fallow field adjacent the cottage, and park the cart in the old stable there. There's a couple of other horses using the field, owned by people in Bere. The cart gives me a complete break from cars and tractors. It's my own indulgence, it's what Maisie and I use for trotting out on Sundays.'

Maisie? His sister? How absurd. A delicious vehicle like that was for a man and his favourite lady, not his sister.

'Now I understand why you said trot. But I think you're holding something back, I think you must have a lady friend in your life somewhere, someone who shares Sunday outings with you in your dogcart.'

'There was once,' said Matt, his smile wry, 'but she married a well-off farmer who owned a Sunbeam-Talbot. Well, we all win at some things, and lose at others. Up in the air, down in the hollow, headaches today are gone by tomorrow.'

'Is Dorset doggerel always philosophical?' asked Rosie.

'No, just on a par with weekly comics,' said Matt. 'You'll come in tomorrow to pick up the rabbits, then?'

'Yes, Matt, I'd love to,' she said.

'Right,' he said, and opened the car door for her. She slid in. She smiled up at him and he closed the door.

She was there again the following day, fully packed, and as soon as her car came to a stop beside the petrol pump, she saw Matthew in company with a Land Army girl who was standing beside an open farm lorry. He was smiling, the Land Army girl shrieking with laughter. Rosie slid out, and at once caught the pungent odour of farm manure. The lorry was full of it. The Land Army girl, still laughing, climbed up into the cab and drove away, giving Matt a wave. Seeing Rosie, he went into his office and came out carrying a large cardboard box. He limped up to Rosie.

'Rabbits,' he smiled. 'Four and every one plump. I'll put them in your boot.' He did so, Rosie watching him, he avoiding looking at her. But he had to when the box had been stowed and the boot closed. 'You're ready for home now?' he said.

'Yes, old thing. Listen, do you send all your lady customers into hysterics?'

'I was just sharing a farmers' joke with Lily,' said Matt.

'Share it with me,' said Rosie.

'It's near the knuckle,' said Matt.

'Well, if Lily can enjoy it, so can I,' said Rosie, 'and I can take it home with me.'

'Well,' said Matt, 'Farmer Giles needed to buy a horse, but he arrived late at the sales and there was only a zebra mare left. Hopefully, he bought it and on the way back to his farm he told it to talk to all the other animals about their work and then decide what she could do best herself. So the zebra first had a word with the chickens, who told her they cleared the farmyard of worms and laid eggs. Next, the pig told her he ate up all the leavings and had happy times with the sow. The bull was next and when the zebra asked him what work he did that was useful, the bull lost his temper. "If you'll take those silly striped pyjamas off, I'll show you," he roared.'

Rosie shrieked.

'Oh, you funny man. Yes, I will take that home with me, as well as the rabbits.'

'You're welcome,' said Matt.

'Oh, fill the tank for me, will you, please?' she asked.

He did that, and then she thought him quiet in his mood, she thought the atmosphere between them a little strained. One of them ought to say something.

Matt did.

'There we are,' he said, 'full tank. Just over two gallons was all you needed. Call it five bob, and coupons for two gallons.'

Rosie paid him and gave him one two-gallon coupon.

'Thanks, Matt, and thanks very much for the rabbits. My family will have a field day. I won't forget about the loan, and I'll see you when I get back.'

'Enjoy your leave,' said Matt.

'I will,' she said.

When she drove out, he limped onto the road to watch the car until it was out of sight. Ben called.

'Got some queer-lookin' tappets here, Matt.'

'Coming,' said Matt.

He sighed a little.

What could he offer a young woman of her kind when he also had to support his sister? As things were, he could take no more than four pounds a week from his business.

However, something promising was afoot. Constable John Rawlings was beginning to court Maisie.

Chinese Lady opened the door that afternoon. She

242

was not given to offering lavish smiles, but she did so now.

'Rosie love, you're here,' she said. 'I was expectin' you, of course, but it's still all of a nice pleasure to see you.' She kissed Rosie on her cheek. Rosie kissed her back and hugged her.

'Nana, it's lovely to be home. My word, look at you, younger than ever, bless you.'

Chinese Lady, in a blouse and skirt, was still straight of back and upright of carriage, her dark brown hair barely touched with grey, her almond eyes bright with welcome. Of them all, of all the younger generation, Rosie the adopted one commanded her deepest affections, perhaps because Rosie had always given so much affection herself.

'Oh, I don't have time to think about my years, Rosie,' she said. 'I suppose you know your dad's comin' home too.'

'Yes, I know, Nana, he'll be here tomorrow, he and Polly are driving home together. Nana, has the bombing been terrible?'

'Well, not as heavy as it was, but it's still a cruel war, Rosie.'

'But it has to be fought, there's a monster stalking the lands of Europe,' said Rosie. She picked her valise up from the doorstep, on which there was also a cardboard box, and placed it in the hall. Then she brought the box in. 'Fresh rabbits, Nana, four of them,' she said. 'They're a present from a Dorset friend of mine.' She carried the box through to the kitchen, Chinese Lady following. She placed the box on the table and lifted the lid.

The four plump rabbits, already skinned, lay packed in greaseproof paper.

'Well, bless my soul,' said Chinese Lady, 'you couldn't have brought home anything more welcome, Rosie. Is your Dorset friend a farmer?'

'No, a garage proprietor,' said Rosie.

'Well, he must be a very nice friend,' said Chinese Lady. 'I never saw such fine big rabbits. I'll bake one for supper this evening, and give Vi, Susie and Lizzy the others, if that's all right with you, Rosie.'

'Of course, Nana, they're for sharing out,' said Rosie.

'Would you put them in the larder, Rosie, while I put the kettle on for a pot of tea? You'd like some tea?'

'Bless you, Nana, you know I would,' said Rosie, and put the rabbits away while Chinese Lady filled the kettle.

'Rachel Goodman's still staying with us, Rosie, but she's at the hospital this afternoon, helping Mr Goodman to get on his feet again. She'll be with us for supper. It's nice having her here, she's such good company.'

'She's an old family friend,' said Rosie, 'and I'm glad, Nana, that it was you who took her in after her terrible time.'

'Well, I've known Rachel since she was fifteen, Rosie.'

'When she was Uncle Sammy's one and only girl friend,' smiled Rosie. 'Look, while you're making the tea, I'll phone Uncle Sammy. I want to talk to him.'

She rang him at his office.

Sammy came through.

'Hello? Hello? It's just been announced to me that Rosie Adams is on the line. Am I having the pleasure of addressin' her ladyship?'

'Yes, it's me, Uncle Sammy, I'm home on leave for four days.'

'Well, your grandma and grandad will like that,' said Sammy. 'I heard your dad's got some leave too, and Polly.'

'Yes, they'll be home tomorrow,' said Rosie. 'Uncle Sammy, can I come and see you this evening?'

'Could I say no, Rosie? Would I? Susie and yours truly will be tickled, but come early or we might have to entertain you in the air raid shelter. Jerry's usually over by not later than eight, and sometimes the buggers – pardon my French—'

'We all use that kind of French about the German bombers, Uncle Sammy.'

'Not in front of your grandma, I hope,' said Sammy.

'No, never,' said Rosie.

'Well, let's keep our fingers crossed that the you-know-whats arrive a bit late this evening,' said Sammy.

'I'll be there as soon as we've finished supper,' said Rosie.

'Rosie, don't come if the air raid's started,' said Sammy.

'I'll stay here with my head down and phone you again,' said Rosie.

'You do that, Rosie.'

Miss Symonds came in as Sammy put the phone down.

'Your tea, Mr Adams,' she said, placing on his desk a tray containing the cup of tea and a plate of biscuits. She had taken to bringing his tea in herself.

'Much obliged,' said Sammy. 'Hold on – biscuits?' Biscuits were now out because of the war.

'They're oatmeal biscuits, Mr Adams, I made them myself,' said Miss Symonds, looking quite fetching in a smart skirt and lace-trimmed blouse. Sammy kept his eyes off her blouse in case it tempted her to let one half of her bosom come to rest on his shoulder again. Well, it could happen. She was standing beside his chair.

'Well, good for you, Miss Symonds, I'm frankly partial to a biscuit with my afternoon cup of tea.'

'You're very welcome, Mr Adams.' Miss Symonds leaned, took the plate of biscuits off the tray and placed it in front of him. Her blouse whispered in its moving contact with the point of his left shoulder. A delicate scent reached Sammy's handsome nose. Blind me, he thought, what's going on? The blouse retreated. 'I do hope you enjoy them, Mr Adams.'

'I'm sure I will,' said Sammy.

Miss Symonds glided out.

Ruddy bananas, I think her bosom fancies my shoulder to sigh on, thought Sammy. When do I call for help?

The baked rabbit that evening was delicious, on a par with roast chicken. Mr Finch and Rachel were

246

both delighted to see Rosie, and to enjoy her presence and the meal. Rachel thought her the bright star of the Adams galaxy, a fascinating and lovely young woman whose effervescent personality always seemed to reach out and embrace family and friends alike.

When, wondered Rachel, would some distinctive man enter Rosie's life? He would have to be very distinctive to match the extraordinary appeal of Boots's adopted daughter.

Chapter Twenty

The car, an Army vehicle overdue for retirement, had come to a stop outside the admin. block earlier that day, and Major Lucas eased himself out. So did Major Campion, the new OC. He nodded genially to Major Lucas, then disappeared. Major Lucas spoke to Eloise.

'Shan't need you again this afternoon, Sergeant Adams.'

'Very good, sir,' said Eloise. 'May I remind you, you promised me three days leave beginning tomorrow?'

'You reminded me of that yesterday,' said Major Lucas. Formidably physical in his rugged build, he leaned to look her in the eye through the open side window.

'Yes, I know, sir,' said Eloise, not quailing in the least.

'And what did I say?'

'You made frightening noises in your throat, sir.'

'I did what?' said Major Lucas.

'That's as much as I dare say, sir, except that I thought it was fair to remind you again,' said Eloise.

'Very well, Sergeant Adams, you can have your three days leave from tomorrow. I'll speak to Captain Miller.'

'Thank you, sir, how kind,' said Eloise.

His lips twitched. What a young madam she was with her precise speech, her air of being above the *hoi polloi*, and the little war she was always conducting with him.

'You can catch the first train to Leicester in the morning,' he said, 'and change there for the London express. Remember we'll be travelling to the new unit the day after you return.'

'Yes, sir,' said Eloise. 'May I ask what kind of unit it is?'

'I told you, a unit of man-eaters. That's all, Sergeant Adams.' Major Lucas took himself off.

Really, what a very awkward and provoking man he was, thought Eloise. However, he had kept his promise, and arranged for her to be transferred with him.

Rosie, driving her car through the darkness of a February evening, arrived at the house on Denmark Hill just after seven. The whole neighbourhood was masked by blackouts, every house a looming bulk showing not the slightest chink of light for the benefit of Goering's bombers. A bus, trundling up the hill from Camberwell, was a dim moving carrier of people anxious to get home. London's heart was riven, wounded and suffering, its outer arteries damaged in places but still pulsing strongly, even if the system was sometimes erratic with nerves. The bus passengers talked to each other, cheerfully and encouragingly, hiding their anxieties. Out of the hideous battles of the Great War had come an incredible and enduring comradeship. Out of the German air blitz on London and other cities had come a drawing-together of the British people. Every neighbour in every city under assault had become a friend, a help and a sustainer of morale. London itself, the battered capital of the Empire, was now the home of a great family of resilient people.

Rosie parked her car in the drive. She alighted, peered, made her way to the front door and rang the bell. So far, no sirens had sounded.

The door opened. The hall beyond was dark.

'There you are, Rosie,' said Sammy. 'At least, I think it's you. The blackout can leave a bloke guessing.'

'You've guessed right this time,' said Rosie, and stepped in. Sammy closed the door, shutting out the nervous atmosphere of the unprotected hill. 'How are you, Uncle Sammy?'

'All the better for seeing you,' said Sammy, and gave her a warm hug and a kiss. 'Come through, Rosie. We live in the kitchen in the evenings. It's nearest to the air raid shelter.'

'You lot are all far worse off than I am,' said Rosie, a brown paper carrier bag with her. 'Dorset is almost tranquil – hello, Aunt Susie.'

Light flooded out from the kitchen as its door opened wide to reveal Susie.

'Rosie love – come in – it's warm in here.'

Rosie kissed her aunt, and Sammy closed the door, shutting them into a haven of homely comfort that was so typical of people brought up to hug their kitchen firesides, except on Sundays, when the parlour was used.

'Aunt Susie, lovely to see you and Uncle Sammy,' said Rosie.

'Look at you,' smiled Susie, whose fair hair and blue eyes matched Rosie's. 'Sammy, did you ever see a smarter or better-looking lady officer?'

'Well, to be frank, Susie,' said Sammy, 'I don't make a practice of going round examining women in uniform as I like them best in nice Sunday frocks. Mind, I grant you Rosie is special. I'd like her in anything, even a grass skirt.'

'Draughty on a February night, Uncle Sammy,' said Rosie.

'Sit down, Rosie,' said Susie.

'Where's Paula?' asked Rosie, as she seated herself at the table with Susie and Sammy.

'In bed,' said Susie. 'I put her down early now, to make sure she gets some sleep before we have to wake her up and take her to the shelter. There's a pot of coffee on the stove. It's made from Camp, but would you like a cup?'

'Thanks, yes,' said Rosie.

Sammy got up, took the pot from the range hob and placed it on a table mat. Susie did the honours, pouring a cup for each of them.

'Will you be going overseas, Rosie?' she asked.

'Sometime, I think,' said Rosie.

'That will mean your dad and Polly too,' said Susie.

'Yes,' said Rosie. 'It's this rotten old war.'

'Not my idea of fam'ly togetherness, all three of you going,' said Sammy.

'Nor mine, Uncle Sammy,' said Rosie. 'Look, I want to ask you a favour without taking too much time about it in case the bombers come.'

'Fire away,' said Sammy, and very concisely Rosie told him about Mr Matthew Chapman and the garage in Dorset. She touched on Matthew's expertise as a motor engineer, the goodwill he had built up, his post-war prospects and his need of capital. Susie listened, and Sammy was all ears. 'And what's the favour, Rosie?' he asked.

'Uncle Sammy, could Adams Enterprises make the loan?' asked Rosie.

'Pardon?' said Sammy.

'Mr Chapman's such a nice man,' said Rosie, 'with two elderly mechanics who need their jobs with him. His garage is on the main road from Poole to Dorchester, and will make huge profits after the war when traffic starts to multiply. Uncle Sammy, it's only twelve hundred pounds he needs.'

'Rosie, these days I could buy a small garage itself, especially one in the wilds of Dartmoor—'

'Dorset, Uncle Sammy, and not in the wilds,' said Rosie.

'Well, wherever, Rosie, I could still buy it lock, stock and barrel for twelve hundred quid,' said Sammy.

'But you couldn't buy Mr Chapman and his expertise,' said Rosie.

'Who is this bloke?' asked Sammy.

'A friend,' said Rosie. 'Oh, come on, Uncle Sammy, the firm can lend the money, can't it?'

'Let me get this straight,' said Sammy. 'You're asking the firm to make a loan of twelve hundred pounds without any idea of when it'll be paid back?'

'Oh, you'd receive the interest until repayment,' said Rosie.

'Glad to hear it,' said Sammy, 'but the firm might have to whistle for repayment. Did he offer any security?'

'Yes, of course he did, his honesty and integrity,' said Rosie.

'Unfortunately, I don't happen to be personally acquainted with his honesty and integrity,' said Sammy, while Susie eyed Rosie with a faint smile.

'Uncle Sammy, d'you want me to lose face?' asked Rosie.

'Susie, what do we know about losing face?' asked Sammy.

'It means blushing humiliation,' said Susie.

'Am I acquainted with occasions when I've seen Rosie blush?' asked Sammy.

'Well, Rosie's never been shy enough to blush, and anyway, blushing went out when Queen Victoria passed on,' said Susie. 'But humiliation, well, awful humiliation could still make anyone turn all pink and hot.'

'There, you see, Uncle Sammy, I simply can't lose face,' said Rosie. 'I don't want the money to come out of your personal pocket or Dad's, just out of the firm's bank account. I know it'll be repaid eventually.'

'Do you know that, Rosie?' asked Susie.

'I'm sure of it,' said Rosie.

'This feller Matthew Clapham,' said Sammy, 'what—'

'Chapman, Uncle Sammy, if you don't mind,' said Rosie.

'Yes, what sort of a friend is he?' asked Sammy.

'Uncle Sammy, a friend's a friend,' said Rosie guardedly.

'We can't argue with that, Sammy,' said Susie.

'I picked up four fresh rabbits from him this morning,' said Rosie. 'Presents for our families. I've brought yours, Aunt Susie.' She handed the carrier bag to Susie. It was weighty. Susie opened it up and inspected the contents.

'Rosie, lovely, it's twice the size of any rabbit we can get from our butcher,' she said. 'Look, Sammy.' Sammy peered into the bag.

'Have I got a feeling it's going to cost me twelve hundred quid?' he mused. Rosie smiled at him, her eyes as deeply blue as Susie's. Sammy felt that for most of his life he'd been trapped by deep blue. Rosie felt that for nearly all her life she'd known love and security and trust. Uncle Sammy was going to trust her now, wasn't he? He was still as family-minded as his brothers, still a man with a look of electric mental energy. But he was also still sharp with business acumen. 'Frankly, Susie,' he said, 'it's not a loan the firm could make without the approval of the board, nor without security. So I'll lend you the money myself, and rely on you to get the best deal you can out of Mr Chapman, bearing in mind you're responsible for paying me back.'

'Uncle Sammy?' said Rosie.

'If you don't pay me back I'll lose face with your Aunt Susie,' said Sammy.

'And turn a hot pink all over,' said Susie.

'Uncle Sammy, if it's to be a personal loan, perhaps I should ask Boots, my dad,' said Rosie.

'Your dad's got all kinds of future expenses to take care of,' said Sammy, 'and while he gets director's fees, I get that and a managing director's salary as well. I'll draw a cheque in your favour now.'

'Oh, Lord,' said Rosie, 'now I'm not sure I haven't been guilty of an unpardonable imposition.'

'Is that educated language which I'm unfamiliar with?' asked Sammy. 'Hold on.' He left the kitchen, and came back with his pen and cheque book. He sat down again, and opened the book.

'Uncle Sammy, are you really going to do this?' asked Rosie.

'Rosie, you and the fam'ly go back a long way,' said Sammy, 'and that takes in the time when you might have gone off to live a rich life with your natural father. But you didn't, Rosie, you stayed with the family and showed us you were an Adams.' He reached across the table and pressed her hand. 'That was highly welcome to me and your Aunt Susie, and to Boots especially. It's no hardship to write this cheque, Rosie, and if I know you, it's a cert you won't be throwing the money into a bucket with a hole in it.' He wrote the cheque, ripped it from the book and gave it to her.

'Uncle Sammy, I don't know if I should—'

'Take it, Rosie,' said Susie, 'I'm sure you've got trust in Mr Chapman. Um – how old is he?'

'Oh, about thirty,' said Rosie.

'Does he have a family?' asked Susie.

'No, he's a bachelor,' said Rosie. 'His widowed sister keeps house for him.'

Susie smiled.

Sammy said, 'Well, as an unmarried bachelor, he'll be able to give all his time to saving his garage from sinking.'

'Oh, he'll do that,' said Rosie. 'Uncle Sammy, you're a darling. Aunt Susie, you don't think I've been out of order in asking, do you?'

'Not in this family,' said Susie. 'We – oh, here it goes, blow it.' The air raid warning was suddenly blasting away in staccato fashion. 'Sammy, bring Paula down, quick.' Sammy leapt up and ran. 'Rosie, you be quick too. Get away before the bombers arrive, it'll be any minute. They'll be over the coast already. We'll be seeing more of you while you're on leave.'

'I'll dash, I've got my car outside,' said Rosie. 'Take care, Aunt Susie. Thank Uncle Sammy for me—'bye.' She hurried out of the kitchen and out of the house, the sirens still going. In her car, she switched on the ignition, fired the engine and reversed out of the drive into the road, the night still an inky darkness. She switched on her masked headlamps, and the feeble slits of light pointed a faint way for her. She straightened up, angled across to the lefthand side of the road, and motored up the hill in churning third gear.

Above, the night sky began to fill with sound, with the droning of Heinkel and Dornier bombers heading for Central London.

Rosie heard an enormous noise then, ahead of her. She searched the sky, her heart suddenly beginning to hammer, hands gripping the wheel. She glimpsed lights, tiny lights, moving towards her from the sky low above Herne Hill. The noise became a huge inferno of sound. She saw it then, a crippled Heinkel made visible by darting flashes of fire that were sucked by the slipstream from its blazing tail. The plane was coming straight at her, its engines roaring as its pilot made desperate efforts to keep the bomber afloat. Rosie was appalled. If it hit the hill and its cargo of bombs all exploded, the devastation would be horrifying, and take in the houses of Uncle Sammy and Uncle Tommy. Her car would vanish, blown to bits. She jammed her foot hard down on the accelerator as the stricken bomber, rocking and floundering, passed directly overhead, its tail burning, the tongue of flame streaming like that from a hurtling comet. She motored frenziedly up the hill, but stopped at the turn into Red Post Hill, wherein was sited the family house in which she had spent so many happy years.

Her stop was compulsive. She simply could not help herself. She scrambled out and turned and looked. She saw the Heinkel's fiery tail, the elongated tongue of flame that itself seemed to dance and waver. The drunken bomber was passing over the east side of Denmark Hill, over its houses, over the houses of adjacent roads and streets, in the direction of East Dulwich. The fading vision of the flame disappeared, and moments later Rosie heard a noise like muffled thunder. Everything that stood between her and the crash stole from her the sight of what had happened.

The Heinkel smashed itself into fiery oblivion as it plunged into the playing fields close to North

Dulwich railway station. It gouged a huge pit in the soft wet muddy ground, and deep in the pit its bombs exploded. Amid a blinding inferno of fiery light, the explosion took a totally upward path, hurling the disintegrating plane in bits and pieces high into the sky. A sports pavilion shuddered, and its windows shattered. Down on the roofs of surrounding houses descended thousands of tiny bits, and the running vibrations of the explosion drummed against exterior walls in successive waves.

If the sky itself had burst apart, the damage inflicted on houses was no more than a scarring of roofs and outside walls, and the only windows broken were those of the pavilion. Rosie did not know that at the moment, but subsequently she often wondered if this was an instance of a pilot who, despite being on a bombing raid against an obstinate enemy, had done what he could to avoid a terrifying crash-landing on houses and homes. Rosie, remembering the desperate roar of the engines and the rocking wings of a plane trying to maintain height, was inclined to give the destroyed pilot the benefit of the doubt.

As it was, she threw herself back into the car and motored home in a rush. There was no-one in the house. Her grandma, grandpa and Rachel were in the garden shelter. She rang the police. It took her some time to get through following a succession of engaged signals, when she was then able to inform them of all she had seen and heard.

'Thanks, miss, I think we've got calls and messages coming through by the dozen now, but much obliged for your own call. You get your head down.'

'Wait, what about the damage? It must be frightful.'

'Grace of God, miss. Hit the North Dulwich playing fields, by all accounts, and that saved the day for residents, apparently. Well, it saved the night, that is.'

'Thanks for that enormous relief,' said Rosie.

The bombers were arriving in desultory fashion, for Goering no longer had command of limitless squadrons. Nevertheless, the City of London and the docks were again under assault from above. Rosie undressed and put on some old clothes, then joined the others in the air raid shelter, keeping as quiet as she could as she wrapped herself in a blanket and lay on a mattress. She said nothing about the crashed bomber. She said nothing at all, in fact. She was sure Chinese Lady and Rachel were actually asleep. They were used to these raids, but their disturbed nights brought tiredness by evening. Their sleep in the shelter would become fitful, and Rosie made sure she did not wake them now. She was not tired herself, and her heart was still beating a little fast.

A hand touched hers. By a slight pressure of his fingers, Mr Finch let her know he knew she was there, safe with them, and Rosie melted.

'Bless you, Grandpa,' she whispered.

Chapter Twenty-One

The morning arrived, and with it news of the war and the results of another night's bombing. Again, there was a cheerful note. General Wavell's small but intrepid army had taken Derna and was actually advancing on the main Italian base at Benghazi. Wavell had split his force and was attempting a pincer movement. Winston Churchill was triumphantly smoking large cigars and toasting Wavell in whisky. Mussolini's portly frame was sagging.

At breakfast with Sammy and little Paula, Susie said, 'Well, after all that happy news, Sammy, tell me exactly what you thought of Rosie's need to help this man Matthew Chapman.'

'At this exact moment, Susie, I can only think that somehow I parted with twelve hundred smackers like a geezer with no tomorrow,' said Sammy, treating Paula to a little more precious sugar on her hot porridge, for which the girl rolled happy eyes at him. 'Yes, you can smile, Plum Pudding the Second, but it's a mystery to me how it happened. Susie, did I do any heavy drinking before Rosie arrived? Was I rolling a bit?'

'No, Sammy, you weren't,' said Susie, 'and you know I don't allow any heavy drinking on account of having seen Mr Goodboys fall drunk all the way down the stairs of Peabody Buildings when I lived there in my young days. It did him a lot of damage. I don't want you damaging yourself, Sammy. Now, what about Rosie, then?'

'Like I've just said,' remarked Sammy, 'I'm vague about how it happened.'

'No, you're not,' said Susie, 'you're a softie where all the girls are concerned. Wedding presents of generous cheques for Annabelle and Cassie—'

'Annabelle and your brother Freddy, actu'lly,' said Sammy.

'Same thing,' said Susie. 'What was Freddy's was always Cassie's, even before they married. Sammy, I'm not asking you about your generosity to Rosie, I'm asking what you thought of her wish to help Mr Chapman in such an extravagant way.'

'Friendly gesture?' suggested Sammy.

'A bit more than that, surely,' said Susie.

'Yes, got to be,' said Sammy. 'Shall I cut your toast up for you, Pudding?' he asked Paula.

'Daddy, I'm five years old, I go to school, and I'll be six soon,' said Paula.

'I don't like the way time flies,' said Sammy. 'I was six myself once.'

'Sammy, I'm talking to you,' said Susie.

'Well, it did occur to me that Rosie's going out on a limb for a Dorset bloke who's just a friend,' said Sammy.

'Yes, very odd,' said Susie.

'Odd?' said Sammy.

'I think it might just have happened at last,' said Susie, 'I think our Rosie might be in love.'

261

'With a bloke who's got a run-down garage?'

'Sammy, when I first came to care for you, you had a grotty old stall in East Street market.'

'But prospects, Susie, prospects. And no debts.'

'It wouldn't have made any difference if you'd had a hundred debts,' said Susie. 'Not every woman falls in love with a man's prospects and his bank balance. Sometimes it's just the man himself.'

'Crikey, Mummy,' said Paula, 'did Daddy have a bank balance before he got old?'

'Who said that?' asked Sammy.

'Me,' said Paula, beaming. 'Well, I'm nearly six.'

'Listen, Plum Duff, I'm not in a bathchair yet,' said Sammy.

'Fank goodness, we'd have to push you,' said Paula. 'Mummy, I've finished. Can I go up and say goodbye to Teddy before school?'

'Yes, up you go, sweetie,' said Susie, 'and I'll be ready to take you when you come down.'

Paula scrambled from her chair and went upstairs to talk to her teddy bear.

'Susie, you reckon Rosie might seriously fancy her Dorset bloke?' said Sammy.

'I think so,' said Susie. 'Rosie could take her pick of eligible men, and any one of them would be glad to have her. But she's not the kind to be impressed by wealth. She's never aimed for the stars or wanted the moon. Her star was always Boots. She told me years ago, when she was fifteen, that she wasn't going to bother to get married, she wanted to be free to look after Boots when he was old. But there's a look in her eye now, I'm sure of it.'

'Knowing Rosie and how forthcomin' she's

always been,' said Sammy, 'I'd say she'd have told us if there was anything serious between her and this Dorset bloke.'

'Sammy, perhaps Mr Matthew Chapman is holding back.'

'Think so?' said Sammy.

'Perhaps a man with a run-down garage and only hopeful prospects wouldn't dream of making a serious approach to a young woman who looks as high-class as Rosie does,' said Susie.

'Ruddy goldfish,' said Sammy, 'is she going to lend twelve hundred quid to a no-hoper who treated her to four rabbits?'

'Yes, isn't it interesting, Sammy love?' said Susie. 'But we'll get our money back. Rosie will see to that, one way or another.'

Boots and Polly were away, heading for home.

'Boots, has Rosie mentioned a Mr Chapman to you?' asked Polly.

'No, I don't think so, although I've had lunch twice with her recently,' said Boots.

'I think the gentleman has made a distinct impression on her,' said Polly.

'Who is he?' asked Boots, heading for Winchester without the aid of signposts. Signposts had been removed everywhere following the threat of a German invasion.

'He runs a garage near the village of Bere Regis,' said Polly. 'A very pleasant man, with a lame leg and a gift for putting damaged vehicles back on the road. He put life back into Rosie's Hillman when, according to Rosie, it was at death's door.'

'Was that what impressed her?' asked Boots.

'That and the man, I think, old dear,' said Polly. 'He's a little bit like you.'

'I pass on that,' said Boots, 'except to suggest it can't be in his favour.'

'Well, it is, old darling, very much so,' said Polly. 'She's been immune up to now, but she's not quite her usual self, and I really do suspect she's got Matthew Chapman on her mind. I think it's confusing her.'

'Old-fashioned fate confuses all of us,' said Boots.

'It did a lot more than that to me when it hit me over the head,' said Polly. 'It scuppered me. I wonder, will Rosie say anything to you when you get home?'

'I'll wait and see,' said Boots.

'Darling, you'll have to let her go sometime, you know,' said Polly.

'I've never wanted to chain her,' said Boots.

'Try me,' said Polly.

'You, Polly?'

'Yes,' said Polly, 'you can chain me for the rest of my life. Mrs Pankhurst wouldn't approve, but as she's riding her fiery chariot up in the sky now, I'll turn a deaf ear to her.'

Boots laughed. She lightly caressed his thigh.

The car engine stuttered a bit, and the wheels seemed to wobble.

The lightest caress from Polly could be touchingly off-putting.

*   *   *

264

'Matthew?'

'I think I know that voice,' said Matt over his office phone.

'Yes, it's all my own,' said Rosie.

'How were the rabbits?' asked Matt.

'We had ours baked last night,' said Rosie. 'Delicious. The others are being shared out. We're a circle of four families, a close circle.'

'Pleased to hear it,' said Matt. 'Related families should be close as long as they don't sit on each other's lap. That's when the dogfights break out.'

'Pardon me,' said Rosie, 'but my father's mother, everyone's arbiter, would never allow dogfights.'

'Is she the families' matriarch?' asked Matt.

'Yes,' said Rosie, 'and everybody ought to have one like her. If Hitler had had one, he wouldn't have been allowed to grow up thinking he was Germany's fiery Messiah. And certainly, one like ours would never have let him sport that silly moustache.'

She heard Matthew laugh.

'Point taken, Rosie,' he said. 'Did you get touched by the raid last night?'

'You'll never believe it,' said Rosie, 'but I was on my way home from my Uncle Sammy's, and I actually saw a Heinkel bomber pass overhead, terribly low. It was on fire, and it crashed in some playing fields and blew up. Miraculously, the houses around escaped damage and there were no casualties.'

'At this time of the year,' said Matt, 'a plane crashing down on a damp playing field would have made a large hole for itself, and that would have

265

minimized the effects of the bombs blowing up. But what were you doing out in the open with a raid on?'

'I told you, I was on my way back home from my Uncle Sammy's,' said Rosie.

'Your Uncle Sammy needs his head examined, then, for letting you go with an air raid on.'

'Should you say that about an uncle I love?' asked Rosie.

'Excuse my feelings,' said Matt.

'Oh, I'm touched, old sport,' said Rosie lightly, and waited for a response to that.

'Don't do it again,' said Matt.

'Oh, dear,' said Rosie wryly.

'Pardon?' said Matt.

'Listen, Matt, I actually have the money you need.'

'You've got twelve hundred pounds?'

'Yes, it's from that uncle of mine who needs his head examined, and I'm free to let you have it,' said Rosie. Silence at the other end. 'Matthew?'

'Rosie, I can't take it, either from you or your uncle,' said Matt. 'It's not on.'

'But—'

'No, Rosie. I've given it a lot of thought, and since I can't see the wood for the trees in regard to repayment, I must say no.'

'You'll close the garage down?' said Rosie, disappointment bitter.

'No, blow my shirt off if I will,' said Matt. 'I'll keep going. The garage is all I've got. I won't say I couldn't turn my hand to other kinds of engineering, or hold down a job in a warplane factory, but motor engineering is my first love. Further, I'm my own guv'nor, I like it that way, and I'll hold on, damned if I won't. I'll manage. Don't think I don't appreciate your offer. I do, and you can believe that. But I can't accept a loan that I might not be able to repay. D'you see that, Rosie?'

'Yes, Matt. You're a very honest man.'

'You're a friend in a thousand,' said Matt, 'and the finest young lady I'll ever get to meet.'

'Could you write that down sometime?' asked Rosie.

'It stands, whether it's written down or not,' said Matt. 'You're worth all the luck that's going, and I hope most of it comes your way. Enjoy your leave, but for God's sake don't go out again when there's a raid on.'

'I won't,' said Rosie, who felt, not for the first time recently, that her facility for finding the right words for all occasions had deserted her. Why? Matt wasn't intimidating or awesome. He was a man of Dorset, a man of the countryside who knew about farm tractors and combine harvesters, how to put them right when something happened to the works and how to make people feel happy. He might have been a barrister if he had studied the law, but she still wouldn't have found that intimidating. 'Well, I must ring off now, I suppose, and let you get back to your work – oh, I do wish you well, I do hope you can keep the garage going.'

'I promise you,' said Matt.

'Is that really a promise?'

'Hook or crook, Rosie.'

'That really pleases me,' said Rosie.

'Noted,' said Matt. 'Goodbye now.'

'Goodbye, Matt. I'll call in for some petrol when I get back.'

'I'll keep the old pump going,' said Matt, and Rosie hung up.

She was sure of one thing now, that that kind of conversation simply wasn't good enough.

The London express, which Eloise boarded at Leicester, was packed. Trains everywhere were packed these days, especially with men and women of the services. There was no seat to be had, and the corridors were crammed with standing passengers. Eloise received boisterous invitations from various groups of Servicemen to join them as she walked along the platform, but ignored them all. She reached the first-class coach and spotted a compartment occupied by only one person. She boarded. If a ticket inspector came along, well, she would pay the difference.

In the corridor, she pushed back the door of the compartment. Its lone occupant looked up. A handsome, slender man in his thirties, he was so well-dressed she knew at once that he must be a gentleman of culture and means. His hat and coat were on the rack, his charcoal-grey suit elegantly tailored, his shoes spotless. His inspection of Eloise was not in the least impolite or discouraging. There was, in fact, the hint of a smile.

'Good morning,' he said, his pleasant voice slightly languid.

'Oh, good morning,' said Eloise.

'Allow me,' he said. He stood up, took her valise

from her and placed it on the opposite rack. He also pushed the door to.

'Thank you,' said Eloise, and took a corner seat, beside the window. The gentleman reseated himself opposite her. Moments later, the train was moving, steam hissing, wheels grinding and couplings straining.

'You're a sergeant, I see,' said the gentleman, his slight drawl fascinating.

'Yes, but I'm being recommended for a commission very soon,' said Eloise. 'My father and sister are both commissioned, and I'm naturally eligible.'

'Yes, you have the air,' smiled the gentleman.

The door was pushed back and Eloise looked up at the all-too-soon intrusion of a ticket inspector. He eyed her with patent disapproval.

'What're you doing in this compartment, miss?' he asked.

Eloise, vexed about being found out in front of the charming gentleman, put her feelings aside and said with a smile, 'Oh, I'll pay the difference, I'm happy to.'

'I'm referring, miss, to the fact that this compartment is reserved exclusive to this gentleman, Sir Richard Nott-Bailey, as is posted on the door.'

Sir Richard? An English baronet? Could it be? Eloise experienced a sense of exciting fate and a delicious flutter.

'Oh, I'm so sorry, I failed to notice,' she said.

'I must ask you, miss, to kindly leave,' said the ticket inspector.

'Permit me to accept this young lady as my guest,'

said Sir Richard. 'However, the difference will be paid. How much?'

'Six shillings and sixpence, sir.'

'Allow me,' drawled Sir Richard.

'No, no,' said Eloise. She knew instinctively that the right thing to do was to pay the amount herself. 'Thank you, how kind, but no.' She extracted a pound note from the wallet section of her purse and gave it to the ticket inspector, who wrote out an excess fare form and handed it to her, with the change. 'Thank you,' she said, smiling at him. It was one of her nicest smiles, ostensibly to charm the railway official, but actually for Sir Richard to take note of and to remark how gracious she was. Which she was, of course. She was a long way now from her time in Uncle Jacques's wine bar in Albert, having learned much from her English father and his adopted daughter Rosie. Her father was extremely civilized, Rosie a young woman of grace which, Eloise was sure, came from the fact that her natural father was an aristocrat.

'Sorry to have bothered you, Sir Richard,' said the ticket inspector.

'No bother,' said Sir Richard, and the official left, pushing the door to. The train had picked up speed and was running fast through countryside damply and limply green, the vivid colours of autumn having long collapsed and died under the onslaught of melancholy winter. 'Well, now we may settle ourselves, young lady.'

'Thank you for being so kind,' said Eloise.

'Not at all, I'm happy to have your company.' It was on the cards, of course, that ATS sergeants did not often cross Sir Richard's path, especially one like Eloise. Despite the utilitarian nature of her uniform, Eloise looked altogether a most attractive young woman, her peaked cap, worn as usual against the regulations at a slight angle, adding its touch of piquancy to her features. 'Would you care to talk?' he asked. 'That is, providing my own part won't be boring.'

'Oh, I much prefer conversation to dull silence,' said Eloise.

Sir Richard smiled.

'Silence is sometimes not as dull as some conver-sation,' he said. 'Shall you make the choice and risk the consequences?'

'I'm sure there'll be no boring consequences,' said Eloise.

'Then, to begin with, as you know my name, may I know yours?'

'I'm Eloise Adams. I'm – oh, perhaps I should tell you my father is Major Robert Adams, serving on the staff of General Sir Henry Simms. Would you know Sir Henry?'

'I'm afraid I haven't had the luck to meet him,' said Sir Richard.

'He's a great friend of our family,' said Eloise. 'I'm on my way home for three days leave.'

'Then I wish you a happy leave, Sergeant Adams, soon to be commissioned,' smiled Sir Richard. 'I'm woefully ignorant about ATS officer ranks. What are they?'

'Oh, subaltern, lieutenant, captain, major and so on up to commandant,' said Eloise.

'No generals?'

'No, but you may believe me, Sir Richard, when I tell you I've known some ATS officers who would make awesome generals.'

'You alarm me, young lady.'

'They alarm everyone,' said Eloise. 'Dragons do, don't they? Fortunately, I'm not like that myself, no. My disposition comes from my father. He and I are the most agreeable people you could wish to meet. He's a very exceptional man, and my battery commander acknowledges I take after him.' Eloise's air of smiling self-belief was sweetly tempered by a modest flutter of her eyelashes. 'That's why I'm his personal assistant. He would instantly dismiss anyone ordinary.'

'Fascinating,' murmured Sir Richard.

'Really?' Eloise was delighted. 'Do you think so?'

'Indeed I do. Tell me more, young lady.'

The train thundered south, faint sunlight beginning to brighten the morning. Happily, Eloise made herself very comfortable. She crossed her legs. Her khaki skirt, hitched, sighed to the movement. Her regulation stockings, which she thought more of an insult than an adornment, were nevertheless not unattractive on her slender legs. Sir Richard smiled. Women on the whole were exhibitionist, even ingenuous young women like this one.

'Well,' said Eloise, 'Major Lucas—'

'Major Lucas?'

'Our battery commander,' said Eloise. 'He's a very demanding man, with no time for incompetence. Too much of that, he says, will lose us the war, oh, yes.'

272

'A correct conclusion,' said Sir Richard.

'Yes, I agree,' said Eloise. 'Major Lucas was furious about our defeat in France, and raged about like an angry bull on his return from Dunkirk. I met him at Ramsgate, you know, where I helped him with one or two matters, and he was so impressed with my competence that he insisted on having me posted to his battery.'

'A discerning gentleman, undoubtedly, even if demanding.'

'Fortunately, I'm very good-natured and am able to put up with his tempers, although he makes other ATS personnel quake.'

'Quake?' murmured Sir Richard.

'Yes, you may believe me, Sir Richard, but of course the thing always to do with Major Lucas is to stand up to him. I would never let my father down, or my late French mother, by quaking.'

'You had a French mother?' said Sir Richard.

'Yes. She died some years ago. My father was very sad about that.' Eloise wasn't going to mention she came of unmarried parents, especially not to this cultured English baronet. Imagine – she had actually met one. Did he have a wife? 'Do *you* have children, Sir Richard?'

'At the moment, I'm still a bachelor.'

How amazing. A bachelor baronet. Eloise gave him the benefit of the doubt in respect of a baronetcy.

'I'm single myself, Sir Richard. Of course, I've had offers of marriage.' That was true. 'But I know my father wouldn't like me to marry someone ordinary.'

'That would be the natural wish of a father with an exceptional daughter.'

'Oh, I must tell you that as a widower he's engaged to the daughter of Sir Henry Simms,' said Eloise, thinking it an impressive piece of information.

'Ah, yes, I think you mentioned the gentleman before,' said Sir Richard.

'Yes, and I mentioned my father was on his staff.'

'Your family moves in exalted circles, it seems,' said Sir Richard, his languid air pleasantly imbued with good humour.

'Oh, I don't care to go about giving people that impression,' said Eloise. 'It would be much too pretentious and ill-bred. Also, I never think of my friends and acquaintances like that, no, no.'

'Fascinating,' said Sir Richard again.

Eloise uncrossed her legs and tucked one ankle behind the other, thereby taking up the seated posture of a very well-bred young lady, her smile all of beguiling. Major Lucas would have been sorely tempted to smack her bottom.

'I have a lovely sister and a very good-looking brother,' she said.

'Then permit me to say your father has two exceptional daughters,' said Sir Richard.

'How kind,' said Eloise. 'Of course, my sister is much older than I am.' Rosie was two years the elder. 'That's why she already has a commission. My brother is also in the Army, you know.'

'Yours is a military family, young lady?'

'Only because of the war,' said Eloise. 'What

274

dreadful people the Nazis are, don't you agree, Sir Richard?'

'There's little to be said in their favour.'

'I really feel quite sorry for the German people, forced to obey a leader like Hitler,' said Eloise, sure that cultured people liked to broaden a conversation. 'My grandmama often says such a man was a dreadful mistake on the part of his parents.'

'I believe drowning at birth is the recommended way of disposing of such mistakes,' said Sir Richard, 'but of course, at birth a mistake isn't recognized as such.'

'Oh, that's very true,' said Eloise.

The conversation went on and on, and so did the train. Eloise was forthcoming, loquacious and engaging, Sir Richard responsive in his nods, smile and comments, and altogether most agreeable.

Nearing London, he asked, 'When do you return to your unit and your formidable battery commander?'

'On Monday,' said Eloise. Today was Friday.

'I'm returning home myself that day,' said Sir Richard. 'Would you care to share the journey back with me as far as your stop at Leicester? I'll be catching the eleven-thirty. May I have the pleasure of reserving a compartment for both of us, Miss Eloise Adams?'

'Oh, please do,' said Eloise, 'I should like that very much.'

'Unfortunately, because of the war, there's no dining-car, and we shan't be able to enjoy having a civilized lunch served to us. However, I'll bring a bottle of wine and some excellent sandwiches. My London club will provide them. That might be fairly enjoyable, fairly civilized.'

'Thank you, Sir Richard, I'm sure it will.'

They parted when the train reached the London terminal, Eloise having promised to meet him there at eleven-fifteen on Monday morning.

She made her way home in a very happy frame of mind.

Chapter Twenty-Two

Lieutenant Cary, earnest in her commitment to duty, took an opportunity to have a word in private with Subaltern Jessop.

'Hello, what's up?' asked Felicity, noting that earnestness was wearing a frown.

'This is an official conversation,' said Lieutenant Cary. 'You're being posted to ATS Area Command.'

'No, I'm not, I haven't made a request for it,' said Felicity.

'I made the request on your behalf,' said Lieutenant Cary.

'Then unmake it,' said Felicity.

'Don't be impertinent,' said Lieutenant Cary.

'Look here, stop taking yourself so seriously,' said Felicity. 'We're not at Aldershot.'

'That's irrelevant,' said Lieutenant Cary, 'and I have to tell you that even here there are some regulations I won't allow to be broken. You spent last Sunday, all day, in the company of a male NCO.'

'Who told you that?' asked Felicity.

'I saw you,' said Lieutenant Cary, 'I saw him join you in the car in the morning, and I know you didn't get back until late afternoon. That was a flagrant breach of regulations. I took time to think it over, and am now telling you, you're being posted.'

'Jolly good show, I don't think,' said Felicity, and went immediately to see Colonel Foster, a figure of no-nonsense authority. He was in some dilapidated room he referred to as his mousehole.

'Come in, whoever it is,' he called in answer to her knock on his door.

Felicity entered. He looked up from an examination of an array of daggers and knives on the bare table he used as a desk. His cap off, he was in fatigues, his jaw marked by a five o'clock shadow. He had a long face and great black eyebrows.

'Oh, it's you, Felicity. What's on your mind?'

'Sorry to bother you and all that, Colonel, but Lieutenant Cary is after giving me the boot,' said Felicity.

'Is she? What for?' He picked up a dagger, and tested its sharp point with the tip of a finger. A tiny bead of blood sprang. Felicity explained briefly but truthfully. 'Can't you plan a social excursion better?' asked the Colonel.

'I will next time,' said Felicity.

'I'll chop your head off myself if you don't. Feeble planning is no better than mucking about. All right, dismiss, you scatterbrain. You can't leave 4 Commando. You're a tonic. I'll speak to Lieutenant Cary.'

'She might stand her ground, sir.'

'I wouldn't advise her to. By the way, who was the NCO?'

'Permission to keep that to myself, Colonel,' said Felicity.

278

'Well, it's your funeral if you lose your shirt buttons to an NCO,' said the Colonel. He picked up the phone, and as Felicity left she heard him say, 'Give me Lieutenant Cary, admin.'

He fixed it, but it was a narrow escape for her, and Lieutenant Cary, of course, didn't like being the loser. She wouldn't have been in a conventional unit, and in the same kind of outfit Felicity might well have found herself reduced to the ranks.

Bobby Somers, given a weekend's leave from OCTU, was on his way to meet Helene, on leave from her FANY unit. He had phoned her, and he had also phoned home.

Chinese Lady experienced what she called a bit of a flustering if enjoyable morning. First, not long after breakfast with Rosie, Rachel and Mr Finch, there was a visit from Lizzy and Vi, who wanted to see Rosie. Rosie happened to be in Mr Finch's study, talking to a friend in Dorset on the phone. When she'd finished her call, she enjoyed a lively reunion with Lizzy and Vi. Then everyone, except for Mr Finch, at work by then, spent half an hour all talking at once, although Chinese Lady, with so much to do, said she just couldn't spare any time for talking at all. But she managed it, and afterwards Lizzy, Vi, Rosie and Rachel went to Brixton together to do some shopping.

Just before noon, Boots arrived with Polly, Polly bearing a huge bouquet of flowers for Chinese Lady, her future mother-in-law. She presented it to her with an affectionate smile.

'For you, Maisie, with my love and my best wishes,' she said without affectation, which was very flustering indeed for Chinese Lady, although Polly used her name so naturally and easily that it didn't seem disrespectful. Boots had warned her Polly wasn't going to call her mother. Coming out of her fluster, she thanked Polly for the lovely flowers and asked her if she would stay and have lunch with them, and Polly said she'd love to, and that Boots would take her home after the meal.

Then Boots produced four large plump Dorset chickens, fully plucked, one for each family. Chinese Lady said she was overcome because Rosie had brought rabbits for everyone yesterday . . .

Lizzy, Vi, Rosie and Rachel returned from shopping then, and there were more minutes when everyone seemed to be talking at once. Lizzy, a little guarded at first with Boots and Polly, put her reservations aside quite soon, however, and became her usual outgoing self. The fact was, she had always liked Polly, just as she had always been on close terms with Boots. She and Vi were both delighted to receive a fat Dorset chicken each before they left. Lizzy especially needed to be back home in time to welcome Bobby and Helene.

As for Rachel's interest in the future of Boots and Polly, she thought Boots singularly himself, considering what he was going to take on in the person of a woman as brittle, temperamental and sophisticated as Polly. But then, it was obvious Polly was already much less brittle and much calmer. Dear God, thought Rachel, is she actually going to promise to love, honour and obey Boots, is she going to play his little woman? I doubt it, and would Boots like her as such? No, not Boots, he likes a woman to be her own true self, and not to let feminine tantrums upset him. She'd known him to smile at some of Emily's sharp outbursts. He always found people's tempers amusing rather than provoking.

Just after Lizzy and Vi had departed, Eloise arrived, having advised Chinese Lady by phone yesterday evening that she'd be home for three days. Her arrival didn't quieten things down. Far from it. She was in an excited and happy mood, ready to entertain everyone over lunch. Chinese Lady had baked a very large pie of mashed potatoes, cheese and onions, well peppered, using a wartime recipe and the family's cheese ration for a week.

Everyone sat down to it, and at once Eloise said how amazing her train ride to London had been.

'The wheels fell off?' said Rosie.

'No, no, how could they fall off a train?' said Eloise.

'Next question, Rosie,' said Polly.

'I give way to you, Polly,' said Rosie.

'No, I'm going to tell you why it was amazing,' said Eloise, and went into the details of how she met a gentleman called Sir Richard Nott-Bailey and how they shared a first-class compartment all the way from Leicester to London. Chinese Lady expressed astonishment.

'Yes, Grandmama, who can believe it?' said Eloise, eyes alight.

'Can you believe it, Daddy old love?' asked Rosie.

'Can you, Rachel?' asked Boots.

'My life, can I, should I?' asked Rachel. 'Can you, Polly?'

'Rachel, old sport,' said Polly, 'I'm willing to believe anything can happen in a first-class compartment on a train journey from Leicester to London.'

'You're all laughing at me, but it's true,' said Eloise.

'No, we're all happy for you,' smiled Boots, who knew, as did Rosie, that Eloise indulged in ingenuously extravagant ideas about suitable men.

'Thank you, Papa,' she said, 'but of course I don't know if anything will come of it.'

'Are you expecting it might?' asked Rosie, with Chinese Lady looking a bit dubious.

'Oh, I don't have definite expectations,' said Eloise, 'but I can tell you he's invited me to be with him on the journey back to Leicester.'

'On the strength of that,' said Polly, 'one could have all kinds of expectations.'

'There's a possibility, isn't there, that the gentleman might be married,' said Boots.

'No, he's a bachelor baronet,' said Eloise.

'A bachelor?' said Rosie. 'Well, things do look promising, don't they, Nana?'

'I just don't know,' said Chinese Lady uncertainly, 'I just don't know what to say.'

'I should be lost for words myself,' said Rachel. 'I am.'

'I'm all agog,' said Rosie.

'We all are,' said Boots.

'Yes, isn't it exciting that Sir Richard is so taken with me?' said Eloise.

'We all wish you luck, my French chicken,' said Boots.

'My word,' said Rachel, 'have you got a promising future with a baronet, Eloise?'

'Oh, how can I answer that, Rachel?' asked Eloise.

'Everything depends on what happens on your journey back to Leicester, doesn't it?' smiled Rosie.

'Yes, I think so, don't you?' said Eloise.

'My life,' said Rachel, 'we shall all spend the day holding our breath for you.'

'Well, I don't know about holding my breath,' said Chinese Lady, 'I'm not sure I like people meetin' on trains without being introduced proper. I suppose I'm old-fashioned.'

'So am I,' said Rosie.

'So am I,' said Rachel.

'And what are you, Boots?' asked Polly.

'Airy-fairy,' said Rosie.

Chinese Lady showed one of her rare smiles.

'There you are,' said Rosie.

'Yes, here I am, poppet,' said Boots. That was his old pet name for her. He was in the sitting-room, in a fireside armchair, and relaxing with the day's newspaper. He was interested in General Wavell's continuing offensive against the Italians in Libya, since he was sure Sir Henry's Corps was destined for the Middle East.

Rosie sat down. She gave the fire a little poke before she spoke.

'Can I talk to you?' she asked.

'Of course you can,' said Boots. 'Is there a problem, then?'

'Yes, in the shape of a Mr Chapman,' said Rosie.

'Have I heard of him?' said Boots. He had, through Polly.

Rosie painted her own picture of Matthew, his refreshing personality, his garage, his expertise, and her meetings with him following his first inspection of her misbehaving car.

'So you see?' she said.

'Um – what should I see?' asked Boots.

'Me in a fix,' said Rosie.

'What kind of a fix?'

'Well, how do I get him to recognize I'm not just another customer?'

'Don't tell me you haven't found it possible to let him know that,' said Boots.

'Well, I haven't,' said Rosie, 'I've begun to stutter.'

Boots regarded her in amazement. Rosie at twenty-five was a young woman capable of dealing with all the variations of life. She had dealt in remarkably effective fashion with her natural father, the owner of a large Surrey estate, who had thought all the riches he could offer her would be irresistible. She did not consider them irresistible, and she opted to remain with her adoptive family. Boots could hardly believe the owner of a small country garage had her in a state of confusion.

'Rosie?'

'Do you think I'm in love?' she asked.

'You're asking me?' said Boots.

'Well, I feel so unsure of myself that I don't know how to hold the right kind of conversation with Matthew. I need you to tell me I'm not going potty. Emma, you remember, said Jonathan made a potty girl of her. But it's absurd in my case, I'm long out of school, and I ought to be able to make a conversation go my way, unless I've gone soft in the head.'

'What way is your way, poppet?'

'Wake up, old thing,' said Rosie. 'I told you. I want to be recognized as special.'

Boots smiled.

'If Mr Chapman can't recognize that, Rosie, he's a blockhead.'

'He might be short-sighted, but he's no blockhead,' said Rosie. 'He's well-educated and very articulate, but his garage business is a little rocky. It made me do something impulsive, something you might think rather silly.'

'Except for bank managers, we've all had those kind of moments,' said Boots. 'What was yours?'

Rosie told him about the capital Matthew needed, how she had wheedled a cheque out of Sammy and then discovered, over the phone, that Matthew simply wouldn't accept it. Boots said that was a commonsense decision, and one that probably took into account his feelings for her. Rosie said he was keeping all his feelings dark. Boots suggested that was possibly because a struggling garage owner felt he couldn't afford to let them show, that a man of Dorset might, in fact, be more old-fashioned than a town man.

'Meaning what?' said Rosie.

'That because he can't offer you very much, he's

keeping his distance,' said Boots. 'As an officer, Rosie, you look pretty well-off yourself.'

'That's ridiculous,' said Rosie.

'You might think so, he might not,' said Boots. 'It's a classic situation.'

Rosie fumed.

'Could anyone be so old hat?' she said. 'It's 1941, not 1841. Look at Tim as an example of the modern man. He mentioned in his last letter that he's got a stunning ATS officer in his sights, even if he is only a corporal.'

'I fancy some regulations go by the board in a Commando unit,' said Boots.

'Well, something's going to go by the board down in Dorset when I get back,' said Rosie, and Boots wondered just what kind of a man Matthew Chapman was, since he was the only one in whom Rosie had ever shown real interest.

'If you go overseas with the Corps, Rosie, this Dorset gentleman is going to disappear from your life. How would you feel about that?'

'Oh, rats to letting him disappear,' said Rosie.

'I see.' Boots smiled. 'It's serious, then?'

'Well, it's not funny, I can tell you that,' said Rosie.

'If his principles are holding him back,' said Boots, 'help him to ditch them. Some principles just get in the way of a relationship. And as your Uncle Sammy would tell you, if a man's got prospects – post-war prospects in this case – who needs principles of the kind we're talking about?'

'Daddy old sport, you're a girl's best friend,' said Rosie. 'Oh, would you like to hear a farmers' joke?'

'Dorset farmers?' said Boots.

'Any old farmers,' said Rosie.

'Try me,' said Boots, so Rosie told him the one about the farmer who bought a zebra mare. Boots laughed his head off.

'There, you see, Matthew told me that,' said Rosie.

'And what am I supposed to see about it?' asked Boots.

'Well, a laugh like that made you happy, didn't it?' said Rosie.

'You could say so, Rosie.'

'Yes, that's what Matthew does to me, he makes me feel happy, even if unsure of myself,' said Rosie.

Chapter Twenty-Three

There was no respite for one of 4 Commando's platoons. The weather first thing had been bright, the Firth of Clyde calm. It changed midway through the morning. Clouds rolled in, and a cold blustery wind disturbed the waters.

A makeshift landing-craft that had been launched in calm conditions was now rocking and bucketing on the grey heaving sea, at a short distance from a strip of beach on the east side of the Isle of Arran. Beyond the strip were steep, rugged cliffs. The men, chucked into the hazards of a beach-landing exercise, were holding on for dear life, the craft at the mercy of the running swell, the outboard engine's propellor repeatedly lifting clear of the surface. Control of the craft was lost each time, and as the minutes passed the beach was no nearer.

'Who bloody chose to make a bloody practice landing in a sea like this?' hissed one man.

'Ask my Aunt Fanny,' said another.

The green of seasickness was touching some men. Tim and Sergeant Watts, two of the four NCO's aboard, felt the onset of a stiff breeze and a rising swell had made conditions dangerously unfavourable to the exercise. The Commandos would make their leap from the craft without hesitation, once they were close enough to the beach, but the chances of reaching it were receding rapidly, and several men were cursing the arrival of bilious symptoms. The heaving and plunging movements of the craft had everyone reeling and slipping.

It's got to be aborted, Tim told himself. We'll never make it.

Someone put those thoughts into words.

'Shut your mouth!' shouted Captain Coombes, the officer in charge.

The craft tipped violently, and an off-balance man, one Private Morgan, fully kitted, was catapulted over the side of the craft into the freezing, tumbling waters. The helmsman, fighting the onslaught of increasing turbulence, did what he could to keep the craft close to the man overboard. The leaden sky opened up and poured down sheets of rain. Private Morgan struggled, clawing at the heaving surface, and the helmsman gritted desperate teeth at the failure of the craft to stay close. The threshing Commando was losing touch, the sea dragging and pulling at him.

'A rope, for Christ's sake!' shouted Captain Coombes, white with fury and a sickening realization that responsibility for any adverse consequences of the exercise were going to be laid at his door. 'And stay where you are, all of you! I'll court-martial any man who goes in after Watkins!'

But Sergeant Watts had already slipped over the side, having whipped off his pack. With one hand gripping the gunnel, he received an uncoiled rope that Tim flung at him. He grabbed one end of the rope. Tim and another man took hold of the other end. Sergeant Watts let go of the gunnel and lashed the rope fast around himself before the sea laid claim to him. Then he struck out towards Morgan, who seemed to be rolling over and over in the restless waters. The rope played out, Sergeant Watts using a powerful crawl. Morgan went under, dragged down by his pack. Sergeant Watts plunged after him and hauled him up. Freezing cold attacked both men, Morgan now unconscious. Tim and others strained on the rope and pulled, the craft swinging and rolling. Four men vomited. The officer roared at the helmsman.

'Hold it steady, man!'

'Do me a favour,' grated the helmsman. The rain and the wind threw his words away.

The rope was taut, the pull desperate, men bunching around Tim and the others to give them purchase as they strained with arms and limbs. The whole platoon formed a dark conglomerate of jerking, heaving men fighting to keep their balance, fighting to bring Sergeant Watts and the unconscious Morgan in before the NCO was forced by frozen hands and arms to let go of the latter.

'Pull, you buggers!' bawled Tim. They pulled, he pulled, and Sergeant Watts was close to the craft then. Over the side a man bent double, another man took hold of his ankles, and down he went, near enough to grab at Morgan. His knife glinted and he cut the man's pack free. It sank. He took hold of Morgan with both hands, and let Sergeant Watts go free of him. Tim, hanging over the gunnel, grabbed the sergeant. The rain stopped.

It took time and intense effort to drag both men aboard. Morgan was landed on his back, and Captain Coombes hammered him as the craft turned for home. The half-drowned man lay limply jerking to the violent motions of resuscitation. Men made themselves heard.

'Get him to vomit, Captain.'

'Someone jump on him, for Christ's sake, that'll make him disgorge.'

'He's bloody gone, mate.'

'Course he bloody hasn't, not Morgan, he's a Welsh Commando.'

'Shut up!' hissed Captain Coombes, City of London Territorial. Astride Morgan, he heaved, pushed and pummelled.

Morgan dribbled water. He coughed and retched. He vomited. Captain Coombes slapped the white face, and Morgan came to. Men made themselves heard again.

'Told you, he's a Welsh Commando.'

'So what, you berk?'

'You can't drown a Welsh Commando, Smithy.'

'Why can't yer?'

'Sergeant Watts won't allow it. He's got a Welsh grandmother. He'd let you sink, of course, Smithy, you being just a gormless cockney.'

'Ha-ha, bleedin' funny, I don't think.'

When the platoon landed at Troon, both Sergeant Watts and Private Morgan were hospitalized to receive treatment for hypothermia. Captain Coombes sorted out Tim, and took him aside.

'What's your bloody game, Adams?'

'Don't I get a commendation for being quick with the rope?' countered Tim.

'Want a medal, is that it? Well, I'm not talking about medals, I'm talking about Subaltern Jessop. Hands off, you bugger. She's my piece of fruit cake, and you're not even eligible. She's out of bounds to you, got it, sodface?'

'Not up here,' said Tim. 'Up here, it's every man for himself. Also, I object to your language.'

'Object to what?'

'To your language. Sir.'

'Would you care to explain that, you jumped-up pillock?'

'Yes. Subaltern Jessop is not a piece of fruit cake. She's a very nice young lady. Sir.'

'There was very nearly a nasty incident this afternoon, Corporal Adams. There'll be one for certain in a minute, and you'll be buried tomorrow. I have it on good authority that you've been consorting with Subaltern Jessop. All ATS officers are out of bounds to you, particularly Subaltern Jessop. You hear me?'

'Well, the fact is, sir,' said Tim, 'you know as well as I do that up here it comes down to may the best man win.'

'You're a bloody also-ran from this moment on,' said Captain Coombes. 'By the way, yes, you were quick with the rope. Bloody good show, Adams, but watch where you point your overrated virility in future. Dismiss.'

Tim made for his billet. Maggie was there to inspect him on his arrival.

'What will your boots be like, McAdams?' she asked.

'Wet, Maggie, but not muddy,' he said, and Maggie peered.

'Och, aye, wet it is, laddie,' she said. 'They'll be needing a wee bitty polish again when they're dry, I'm thinking. Off wi' them.'

'I'm wet myself,' said Tim. 'It sheeted down for five minutes.'

Maggie looked at him, a young man brown and weathered by the elements, a young man training to carry war to the Germans. Maggie knew what that training was all about. The Commandos, a mixture of hardy Scots, Welsh, English and Ulstermen, had singular jobs to do, and like all the landladies of Troon, Maggie had a soft spot for them.

'I heard a rumour you lost a man out there,' she said.

'Just a rumour,' said Tim, his boots off. 'Any tea going?'

'Will you no' take a hot bath first?' said Maggie. 'Aye, you will. Up you go, McAdams, and I'll bring the tea when you're oot and resting.'

'What an angel,' said Tim. 'I'm going to adopt you as my favourite Scots aunt.'

'Awa' wi' you,' said Maggie, and up he went.

Maggie answered a knock on her front door an hour later. From out of the darkness, Subaltern Jessop addressed her.

'Good evening, Mrs Andrews. Is Corporal Adams here?'

'Och, aye,' said Maggie.

'I have to see him,' said Felicity, her ATS trench coat wet with rain. She had just come off duty for the day.

'You'll step in?' said Maggie. Felicity entered and Maggie closed the door. She turned and called. 'McAdams?'

'I hear you, Maggie,' called Tim from his room.

'It's Officer Jessop wishing to see you.'

'Officially?' called Tim.

'Of course,' said Felicity.

'Aye, officially,' called Maggie.

'Can she come up?'

'I'm on my way,' called Felicity, and climbed the stairs. Maggie smiled. Something was going on between these two. Whatever it was, she wasn't going to interfere, even if she was expected, as Tim's landlady, to discourage an ATS officer or any woman from going up to his room. Maggie was no prude, no busybody. Nor was she likely to be indiscreet and spread the news of the ATS officer's visit.

Felicity reached the landing.

'In here,' said Tim. His door was ajar, and Felicity went in. She came to an immediate stop. Tim was relaxing on his bed, sparsely clad in just his brief white pants. His body looked firm, brown and muscular. And his pants, well, what a show-off.

'You blighter,' she said.

'What for?' asked Tim.

'How dare you invite me in, you bounder, when you're not dressed? That's the giddy end.' Felicity examined his legs, thighs and torso like a PT instructor looking for faults. 'Disgusting. You ought to be charged with indecency. Aren't you cold?'

'Not yet,' said Tim, who seemed perfectly at ease. 'I'm still cooling down from a long hot bath and a pot of hot tea.' The pot, together with cup and saucer and milk jug, was on a tray on the bedside table. 'Make yourself at home, Subaltern Jessop.'

'You're supposed to get on your feet and stand to attention in the presence of an officer,' said Felicity.

'Can't we be informal?' suggested Tim. 'Take your coat off.'

'I'll stay all in one piece, if you don't mind,' said Felicity. 'Listen, I was nearly posted out of Troon on account of last Sunday, when you put yourself in the car and drove off with me for the day. Lieutenant Cary read me the ATS riot act for allowing myself to be kidnapped by an NCO.'

'Hard luck, mate,' said Tim, 'that's the Army for you. Mind you, there's another version of events.'

'Who's going to believe you, you blighter?' said Felicity.

'Good question,' said Tim. 'Anyway, what happened that you didn't get posted?'

'Fortunately,' said Felicity, 'Colonel Foster saved my bacon, bless him. Look here, Corporal Adams, if you don't put something on, I won't be responsible for what I'll do to you.'

'I've got something on,' said Tim. 'By the way, if Lieutenant Cary read you the ATS riot act, Captain Coombes read me the grittiest part of the King's Regulations. I'm in line for a soldier's burial if I consort with you again. He says you're his piece of cake, not mine.'

'Bloody cheek,' said Felicity. 'Consorting with Captain Coombes is like being in a rugby scrum. What did you say to him?'

'I said that in this outfit it was a question of may the best man win.'

'Oh, rattling good show, Tim.' Felicity laughed. 'I expect Lieutenant Cary blabbed to Captain Coombes about you, and I expect Captain Coombes sees you as a tinpot interloper. Well, corporals are ten a penny, I suppose.'

'So are ATS subalterns,' said Tim.

'Yes, aren't we?' said Felicity. 'But I'm up for my second pip in a month or so, if Lieutenant Cary doesn't kybosh it. Talk about bossy prefects, she's the mother of all.'

'It'll make no difference, your promotion,' said Tim, 'I've still got a feeling I might fall in love with you.'

'Oh, well, I'll have to learn to live with the possibility,' said Felicity.

'I've got the same problem,' said Tim.

'Well, all right,' said Felicity, 'we'll both try to live with it. But I owe you something for being improperly undressed in front of an ATS officer. How'd you like this for starters?' She put a hand high up on his thigh and squeezed. Tim took off. He was still up in the air when she squeezed again.

'Hell's bells, was it you who did that?' he asked.

'It ruddy well was. You're a bit larky for an old Girl Guide, aren't you?'

'Oh, well, fun and games and all that, you know,' said Felicity. 'I'm not in favour of having a miserable war.'

'Watch out if I have my own back,' said Tim, tempted to try five minutes of happy war with her.

'I'm out of bounds,' said Felicity. 'Well, have to go now. Had to let you know I've been ordered off consorting with you.'

'I'll try working a flanker on that order,' said Tim.

'No, try to forget me,' said Felicity.

Tim slipped off the bed. Felicity watched the quick supple movements of his body for an eye-catching moment, then fled. He heard her laughing as she went down the stairs.

What a peach, what a sport, what a provocation.

He'd had a girlfriend before the war. Fanny, a sister of Nick Harrison, cousin Annabelle's husband. But it had never been more than an easy-going relationship, and Fanny was in the Wrens now and he'd lost touch with her.

He'd found Subaltern Jessop instead.

Was it a lucky find?

Only time would tell with a young woman who didn't take anything very seriously.

Life might be a game, but war certainly wasn't. He wondered if one day she'd find that out.

A little frown disturbed him.

Chapter Twenty-Four

Bobby had kept his rendezvous with Helene in London. They met at Lyons Corner House in Coventry Street, Bobby attired as an officer cadet, Helene in her FANY uniform, with its khaki beret.

'Bobby!' In the foyer, Helene, demonstrably French, put her valise down and wrapped her arms around him. 'Ah, how nice you smell, like a healthy man, much better than horsy women.'

'Put me down,' said Bobby, 'people are looking.'

'Ah, you English with your – wait, put you down? Who is holding you up in the air, then?'

'Fair question,' said Bobby. He gave her a kiss and released himself. The foyer was full of people and uniforms. 'Let's see if we can get a coffee.'

'Coffee is first?' said Helene, tall, full-bodied and excited. 'I am second?'

'Not to me,' said Bobby.

'Then aren't you going to ask me how I am?'

'How are you, you lovely French hen?' said Bobby.

Helene laughed. What a difference, thought Bobby, from the angry and quarrelsome young woman he had first encountered on her parents' farm. Since arriving at Portsmouth with her, she'd changed into an entertaining French minx, teasing, flirtatious and capricious. It was as if hard and daily farm work had repressed her natural Latin exuberance, and miraculous escape had released it. Helene could have told him he alone was responsible.

'Ah, you adore what I mean to you?' she murmured in French.

'We'll discuss it over coffee,' said Bobby. 'Come on.' He picked up her valise and carried it with his own.

They found the restaurant that served coffee and light snacks. Bobby, who hadn't had much breakfast, ordered four rounds of toast with his coffee, and Helene, who had hardly touched her own breakfast because of the excitement of anticipating the reunion with her crazy English soldier, ordered the same. Over the light meal they talked of the war and what might be happening to the people of occupied France, especially to her parents. They talked in French because Helene frequently liked to revert to her own language. Among other diners were two sergeants of General de Gaulle's Free French Army, who kept glancing at Helene.

Bobby let her know he'd phoned his mother yesterday afternoon, and that she was expecting them by lunchtime. Helene, of course, was to stay at his home for the weekend. Helene said she was very much looking forward to seeing his parents again.

When they left, the Free French sergeants followed them out into the street, and there one of them spoke to Helene in her own language.

'You are French?'

'Yes, and who are you?'

'Soldiers of de Gaulle. Is this man in a British uniform also French?'

'Is that your business?' said Helene. 'No, it isn't. Go away.'

'Why are you wearing a uniform of the English? You should be with de Gaulle. What is your name?'

'That also isn't your business,' said Helene haughtily.

'This lady has papers issued to her by the French Embassy,' said Bobby. Helene had presented herself there before the fall of France. 'Her papers entitle her to serve France in her own way. That's all. Dismiss.'

The two sergeants looked at each other, then one spoke to Helene again.

'This man uses French, but he's English. We can tell that. You should be with the Free French.'

'And you should be in a place for impertinent imbeciles,' said Helene. '*Marchez!* Go!'

They stood their ground, so she and Bobby departed. The sergeants began to follow. Helene fumed. Bobby took no notice. 'Do something,' she said.

Bobby simply kept his eyes open. He spotted what he was looking for, a taxi coming from the direction of Piccadilly Circus. For hire. London was a badly bombed city, but taxis still served the West End, and the West End still served the escapist demands of people and the many men and women of the services who always abounded there. Bobby waved the taxi down. It pulled up.

'Where to, Colonel?' asked the cabbie.

'Charing Cross station,' said Bobby.

'Won't do yer no good, General, no trains running from there today. It's the ruddy war, yer know. Take yer there tomorrer if I spot yer.'

'How about London Bridge?' asked Bobby.

'Trains from there all right, but you'd 'ave been unlucky yesterday. Hop in, Brigadier, and yer lady FANY.'

Bobby and Helene got in. Up came the Free French sergeants. One tried to open the door. Bobby held it shut. Away the taxi went, and both Frenchmen shouted.

'De Gaulle will have you!'

'What do you think of such men, Bobby?' asked Helene, flushed.

'That some Frenchmen are as crazy as the English,' said Bobby. 'And a lot more jealous. It's the hot blood of France.'

Helene hugged his arm and said, 'Ah, you are always good for me. See, no wonder I shan't mind marrying into an English family. When will it be?'

'Didn't we decide months ago?' said Bobby, noting bomb damage here and there. But despite everything of a discouraging nature, the streets were alive with hustle and bustle, and the taxi, along with the rest of the traffic, was reduced to a crawl. 'Didn't we say when the war's over?' Bobby, a practical man, was against the uncertainties of a wartime marriage.

'But we need not wait until then to make love,' said Helene.

'Now, you mean? Before we get to London Bridge?' said Bobby.

'Now? In this taxi?' Helene rose to the bait. 'What do you think I am, a Paris tart?'

'I know what I am for suggesting it,' said Bobby.

'Yes? What are you?'

'An idiot,' said Bobby.

Helene laughed. There was no one quite like this particular idiot to Jacob Aarlberg's resilient daughter.

At London Bridge, they caught a train that would take them to Champion Hill station, only a stone's throw from Bobby's home off Denmark Hill. They found a compartment to themselves, and Helene immediately asked to be kissed. Bobby obliged. Helene melted. The train drew out. A soldier, walking the corridor, stopped at the compartment and pushed the door back. The train rattled over a cluster of points as Bobby and Helene looked up into the face of one of the Free French sergeants.

'I followed you, you see?' he said. 'In another taxi. My comrade did not have the time himself.'

'Well, now you're here,' said Bobby in his fluent French, 'sit down and tell us what's bothering you.'

'You are. You have a young French lady. You have put her into an English uniform and stolen her from General de Gaulle, the only general who can win this war for the British. At the next station I shall take the young lady off this train, and deliver her to the barracks of the Free French Women's Army in Down Street. I caution you not to interfere.'

Bobby looked at Helene.

'What do you say to that, *mademoiselle*?'

'What can I say? I am speechless.'

Bobby turned to the sergeant.

'You have no authority,' he said. 'You know it and we know it. Leave the train as soon as it stops.' The first stop was South Bermondsey, only minutes away.

'My authority is General de Gaulle of Free France,' said the sergeant. 'Get up, if you please,' he said to Helene, who spoke to Bobby.

'This one is worse than the other, a peasant,' she said.

'However, do as he asks, *mademoiselle*, get up,' said Bobby. Helene saw his expression. She knew Bobby very well now. She came to her feet. So did Bobby himself. The sergeant was never quite sure what hit him. He was left only with a vague impression that the English soldier and the young Frenchwoman acted together, as one.

When the train stopped at South Bermondsey station, a grey and suffering place, but bustling with repair workers, a door opened. Moments later, a Free French sergeant was on the platform, but not upright in the tradition of Gallic sergeants. He lay like a drunk sleeping off a long and liquid night. The door closed and the train went on. A worker, spotting the recumbent man, spoke to a mate.

'What's that bleedin' heap over there, Sid?'

'Search me, Baldy, I didn't put it there.'

'I think it's movin'.'

'Well, if it's breathin' as well, it don't need any help from me.'

Helene was laughing softly.

'Bobby, what a terrible man you are.'

'You can talk, you iron maiden. Did you use both knees?'

'Yes, but only one at a time. We are a fine team, yes?'

'Pretty good.'

'We have to be very good if we're sent to France,' said Helene a little soberly.

'I don't think they'll send us unless they're sure we will be,' said Bobby.

'I'm hoping many French people will be bravely resistant, so that we shall be happy to help them. Bobby, do you want to kiss me again?'

'I can't say I don't.'

'We're alone, aren't we?' said Helene.

'We might not be in a moment,' said Bobby as the train pulled into Queens Road station at Peckham. 'What a surprise packet you are. On the farm, you gave me the impression you were a manhater in iron corsets.'

'That is a lie!'

'No iron corsets?'

'Oh, pig of an Englishman, take that!'

She was pummelling him when the train drew out. Bobby's broad chest bore it without caving in.

It was Lizzy who opened the door to them a little later, having just returned from her outing. At forty-two, with her chestnut hair and brown eyes, she was still a richly-endowed brunette, her Edwardian hour-glass figure still entirely admirable.

'Helene? Bobby? Lovely that you're here. Come in.' She welcomed Helene with a kiss, and Helene

304

warmed, as she always did, to the affectionate hospitality of Bobby's attractive and generous-natured mother. 'Helene, don't you look nice in your uniform? Bobby said on the phone you're a FANY, which I heard about in the last war. They were ladies doing special jobs, my husband said.'

'Yes,' said Helene, 'I am now a special lady myself.'

'Don't argue with that, Mum,' said Bobby. 'Helene's as definite about her speciality as Eloise is about hers. It's a kind of French belief in themselves.'

'I'm not goin' to do any arguing,' said Lizzy. 'My goodness, don't you look grand too, Bobby? An officer cadet, won't your dad be pleased? Well, don't let's stand here. I'll serve a pot of tea and some cake in a few minutes, but first I'll take you up to your room, Helene, and Bobby can bring the bags.'

'I'm so pleased to be here,' said Helene.

'We're all pleased you and Bobby are here for the weekend,' said Lizzy, leading the way up the stairs of the pretty suburban house she and Ned had lived in all their married lives. She read mocking comments about suburban houses in the newspapers sometimes, and wondered if the writers understood that a house was a treasured home whatever and wherever.

She installed Helene in Annabelle's old room, as on other occasions, and Helene now saw it as a friendly and comfortable haven. Its decor and furnishings were feminine-inspired, and Helene, once as hard a farm worker as any man, liked to feel feminine whenever she was close to Bobby.

In his home, she was happily close.

'Madame Somers – oh, Mrs Somers, yes – you are so kind,' she said.

'Well, you're as good as one of the fam'ly now,' said Lizzy, who took it for granted that there would be a wedding sometime. Bobby came in from his own room. 'Bobby, I'll leave you two to unpack while I get some lunch. Your dad will be home later today, and so will Emma. Now, will some nice poached haddock be all right for your suppers?'

'Serve it with a creamy sauce,' said Bobby.

'Creamy?' said Lizzy. 'Excuse me, but there's a war on.'

'So there is,' said Bobby. 'Well, use some milk and cornflour, some parsley, and a bit of salt and pepper. And as I don't suppose you've got any lemons, add a couple of spoonfuls of white wine. Tablespoons.'

'I've got some dried parsley from plants your dad grew in the garden,' said Lizzy, 'but wine in a sauce? Is that French?'

'It's tasty, and it'll perk up the haddock,' said Bobby.

'I didn't know any haddock of mine needed perkin' up,' said Lizzy.

'Like me to do it, Mum?' asked Bobby.

'Bobby Somers,' said Lizzy, sounding like Chinese Lady, 'when I can't do my own cookin' and my own sauces, I'll be in a wheelchair in an infirmary somewhere. Did you say two spoonfuls of wine?'

'Well, Dad's usually got a bottle or two of white wine in the house, hasn't he?' said Bobby.

306

'All right, I'll open one,' said Lizzy.

'Good idea,' said Bobby, 'we can drink the rest with the meal.'

'Well, I don't mind being a bit French with Helene here,' said Lizzy. 'Oh, Rosie and your Uncle Boots are home, and so is Eloise. And Polly. Oh, Boots has given us a lovely big chicken for our Sunday dinner. Now, see to Helene, Bobby, make her at home, while I put the kettle on.' She smiled at Helene and went downstairs, murmuring, 'French sauce? I don't know what's wrong with poachin' haddock in milk and water. Next thing, I'll have to do French bread sauce with the chicken tomorrow, I suppose. What's French bread sauce?'

'Your mother is such a nice woman, Bobby,' said Helene.

'So is yours,' said Bobby. 'Like me to unpack for you while I'm here?'

'No, go away, it's too intimate,' said Helene.

'You don't want to undress for me?' said Bobby.

'Here, in your mother's house?' said Helene indignantly, and chased him out of the room.

There were no air raids that night. The skies over Britain were quiet for once. In Berlin, however, a certain quarrelsome element pervaded the atmosphere. Goering was still failing in his promise to bring about a state of capitulation in London, which meant he could not deliver a cowed Winston Churchill to Hitler. Hitler, his mind on Russia, anyway, was contemptuous. Goering's medal-encrusted corpulence suffered dire mortification.

For Chinese Lady and her family, the weekend

was what she called very sociable, especially as Polly and her mother, Lady Simms, joined them for the Sunday dinner of roast Dorset chicken. Later, while Polly and Lady Simms were still there, everyone came for Sunday tea. Tommy and Vi, Susie, Sammy, little Paula, Lizzy, Ned, Emma, Bobby and Helene, all arrived. Only Rachel was absent, being at the hospital and taking tea there with Benjamin.

Polly might have thought the whole thing tedious, but didn't. Her affinity with these families and their zest for living was long-established. Helene thought them all infectiously outgoing, with none of the traditional reserve of the English. Such a way they had for talking, joking and laughing.

Chinese Lady and Boots exchanged glances amid table chatter. His little smile told her his thoughts might be coinciding with hers, thoughts of the years of struggle when their kitchen was their dining-room and their living-room, invaded on Mondays by the smell of washing from the scullery, and sometimes only Sammy knew where the next pennies could be found. In one of his old socks, and loaned at exorbitant interest rates. Now look, they were actually entertaining Lady Simms to tea.

Lady Simms, as outgoing herself as these people, had never voiced any objections to Polly marrying into the Adams family. She was aware that Boots's mother had cockney origins and many little ways that could be associated with the plain-speaking, no-nonsense working-class women, but Polly saw her only as likeably honest and quaintly Victorian. Lady Simms thought the husband-and-wife relationship of the Finches quite intriguing, for Edwin Finch was so obviously a man of intellect and sophistication.

As for Boots himself, Lady Simms knew him well enough to understand why Polly had always wanted him. In his looks, mannerisms and character, he had instant appeal, and he had served, as Polly had herself, in the Great War. Not that he was perfect. What man was? Indeed, Polly had once said he was a little strait-laced, with something of his mother's Victorianism. And on another occasion she said he was a prig, a stuffed shirt and an unfeeling swine. Why do you love him, then? Because I'm a bloody idiot, said Polly.

Now, however, she would hear nothing against him. He's not a prig, a stuffed shirt and an unfeeling swine, my dear? May God forgive you, Stepmama, how can you say such a thing? Why did you once say that yourself? Because I was off my silly chump with frustration, said Polly. Well, said Lady Simms, I've never regarded him as a stuffed shirt myself.

The table chatter went on. Rosie asked for everyone's attention and told her story of the zebra mare. The company erupted. Only little Paula and Chinese Lady failed to split their sides.

'I don't know why everyone's laughing,' said Chinese Lady. 'What did the bull mean about striped pyjamas?'

'He was probably shortsighted,' said Boots, 'and I daresay it was that which created problems for the lady zebra.'

More eruptions.

'Boots, did you have to crown it?' smiled Lady Simms.

'The bull?' said Mr Finch.

'No, the story,' said Lady Simms.

Chinese Lady still looked slightly puzzled.

'How d'you feel, Helene?' asked Ned, when the party was breaking up and the evening untroubled by bombers.

'Oh, m'sieur, I am tired, yes, but very very happy,' said Helene.

'Sure?' said Ned.

'I am only sad that my parents could not be here,' said Helene.

'Understood,' said Ned. 'We'll go home now.'

Chapter Twenty-Five

Eloise could hardly believe her ears. Everything had been delightful until now, some happy conversation, an alfresco lunch of smoked salmon sandwiches and wine, with the blinds of the compartment drawn down for privacy, and then the sudden movement of Sir Richard Nott-Bailey that had him seated close beside her and offering her an intimate relationship.

'You are quite lovely, quite charming, and the apartment I use in Leicester will complement your charm. Come whenever you can obtain weekend leave, and I shall dress you in exquisite clothes in place of your drab uniform. I shall, of course, give you an allowance that will take care of any expenses you may incur in travelling and so on. Perhaps a kiss now to—'

'Stop!' gasped Eloise.

'You are surprised? Well, as I said to begin with, I've taken a great fancy to you, and a kiss now to seal the arrangement would be appropriate, I think.'

A wine-tasting mouth landed on hers, and a hand actually stole up inside her skirt and slip. Oh, the beast, is this what one must put up with from an English baronet, his groping hand and his offer to make her his mistress? How disgusting. She was not that kind, no, never. Ugh, his mouth was wet with wine.

Sensibly, she waited until he broke the kiss to draw breath. Then she hit him, she smacked his face hard with the flat of her hand. It rocked him, staggered him, and left an angry-looking weal.

'You are a pig, do you know that?' she breathed furiously. 'If you think yourself a gentleman, let me tell you my father is a hundred times more so. How dare you offer me money to sell myself to you? Go away.'

Vibrating, he came to his feet.

'Get out, you stupid bitch, get out!'

'I am to get out, I am to leave this compartment, I myself?' Eloise was finely scathing as she stood up. 'No, you are the one to go, or I will pull the cord and stop this train, and believe me I will.'

'Damn you, you hussy!'

'Damn you twice over,' said Eloise, her hand reaching.

Sir Richard Nott-Bailey flung himself out of the compartment, and went in search of another, almost hissing with spite.

Me to be a pig's mistress, me myself, the daughter of my mother and father? Eloise was shocked and disillusioned. What would Major Lucas say if he knew about this?

She felt he would say what a damned fool of a woman she'd been. Yes, he would say that, or something like it. He wasn't a gentleman, either.

Rosie was back in Dorset by early afternoon. She

drove straight on through Bere Regis, passing Matthew's cottage and turning in at the garage. As she alighted, out of the workshop limped Matthew in his overalls.

'Hello there,' he said.

'Hello,' said Rosie.

'Pleasure to see you again,' he said.

'Tell me more,' said Rosie.

'How was your leave?' he asked.

'Lovely,' said Rosie, 'and so were the rabbits. I'm sorry you weren't able to accept the loan, and I returned the cheque to my uncle.'

'Rosie, did you think me ungrateful?'

'Ungrateful?' said Rosie. 'No, of course not, I simply felt you'd decided to fight your battle in your own way, and after I'd thought about it, I found I liked it. I didn't at first.'

'It may sound hackneyed,' said Matt, 'but there *are* times when a man has to stand on his own two feet.'

'A man has to do what a man has to do,' smiled Rosie. 'That's even more hackneyed.'

'It's how the West was won,' said Matt.

'By the American pioneers?' said Rosie.

'I thought it was Gary Cooper and John Wayne,' said Matt.

'And Colonel Custer?' said Rosie. 'Oh, no, he lost, didn't he?'

'There are always some who fall by the wayside,' said Matt.

'I don't think you will,' said Rosie, 'I think you'll win.'

'I treasure your faith in me,' said Matt.

313

'I should hope you do,' said Rosie, 'it's gold-plated.'

'Then it's worth a lot more than a loan,' said Matt.

'Are you sure it is?' asked Rosie.

'As sure as my sister's chickens lay eggs,' said Matt.

'Well, I'm happy for your sister and her chickens,' said Rosie, 'and about you being sure. So next Sunday, if it's fine, I'd like to be taken for a ride in your dogcart.'

'Are you serious?' asked Matt.

'Is a ride in a dogcart serious?' asked Rosie. 'I'm hoping it'll be fun.'

'It's a way of getting out and about like our grandfathers,' said Matt.

'Well, bless our grandfathers,' said Rosie. 'Now look here, old thing, I don't mind people being old-fashioned. I'm old-fashioned myself about some things, but there's a limit, you know. Throw your old hat away.'

'Come again?' said Matt, thinking her a picture against the background of the old petrol pump. 'My old hat?'

'Yes, your Victorian one,' said Rosie, 'and stop treating me as if I'm just another customer.'

'If you're just another customer, I'm a haystack,' said Matt.

'I like haystacks, they're part of a country landscape,' said Rosie, enjoying the fact that she was at last making the conversation go her way. 'Matthew, are you with me?'

'I think I've fallen behind,' said Matt.

'No, you haven't, you're still dodging the issue,' said Rosie, 'so bring your dogcart to headquarters at ten next Sunday morning and pick me up there.'

Matt looked uncertain.

'What's going on?' he asked.

'Nothing so far, nothing at all,' said Rosie, giving him a direct look. Matt avoided the challenge, and eyed the petrol pump. 'Matthew, would you mind looking at me when I'm talking to you?' Matt, helpless, looked at her, and her eyes held his. A little sigh escaped him.

'Rosie, damn all if you don't stand a man on his head,' he said.

'Is that a compliment or a complaint?' she asked.

'It's no complaint, far from it,' said Matt.

'So will you take me out next Sunday or won't you?'

'I can't think of anything I'd enjoy more,' said Matt.

'Well, try inviting me, old thing,' said Rosie, 'it might make next Sunday mean something.'

'Such as?' said Matt guardedly.

Rosie smiled.

'How about the beginning of a happy friendship?' she said.

'What kind of a friendship have we had up to now, then?' asked Matt.

'Generally speaking, just a stuffy one,' said Rosie.

'Objection,' said Matt.

'You can't object,' said Rosie, 'it's true.'

'I'm not accepting that,' said Matt, 'it's making me sound like my bank manager. It's slander.'

'And rats to you too,' said Rosie.

Matt's deep rolling laugh arrived.

'I think I'd like to have the pleasure of calling for you in the dogcart at ten next Sunday morning, Lieutenant Rosie Adams,' he said.

'Why, Mr Chapman, how kind of you,' said Rosie.

Matt laughed again.

Rosie congratulated herself on inducing such a warm response in him.

Matt, of course, still wondered what he had to offer a young woman who looked as if her world was very different from his.

If he had met any of her close relatives, if he had met Tommy and Vi, and Sammy and Susie, and most of all Grandma Finch, he would have known what her real world was.

Very much the same as his, allowing for the fact that he was a man of the country and she was a Camberwell rose.

4 Commando was ready to fall flat on its back. It had rained all morning, adding extra discomfort to another crucifying exercise over ground that was wet, muddy, hilly and leg-wrenching. But the clouds broke up in the afternoon and the sun showed itself. It made hot bodies steam.

Lieutenant Cary and Subaltern Jessop watched the return of officers and men close to collapse. Out of the pale sunshine they came, a long trailing single file, the last man far behind the first, and all required to form up on the parade ground before they were given the relief of being dismissed for the day. It took time for the last man to complete the formation, and still there was another fifteen minutes of exhausted suffering to endure.

'I wonder if it's wise to try to kill them off,' said Felicity.

'No good being soft,' said Lieutenant Cary, 'no good temporizing with men of any Commando group. The Germans won't hand out soft options.'

'Well, I'm proud of our hairy old blighters,' said Felicity, 'and I'd like to be there when they jump Hitler's stinkers on their first raid.'

The men were finally dismissed. Some wondered if they wouldn't feel better if they just dropped where they were and passed on. Tim decided, however, that dying in lingering puddles would be too ruddy wet.

'I'm going to my billet for some hot tea,' he said.

'Only thing to do, by gum,' said Sergeant Watts.

From the window, Felicity watched the men dispersing. She picked out Tim, limping a bit, rifle in his hand. She smiled. There he was, a born survivor of this life or death training, but still a more civilized man than Captain Coombes, too earthy and unsubtle for her liking.

Lieutenant Cary returned to her cramped office, and Felicity wandered outside just as Tim and Sergeant Watts came up. Sergeant Watts trudged on. Tim stopped.

'Afternoon, ma'am,' he said.

'Afternoon, Corporal Adams. Any complaints?'

'Yes, I'd like a new pair of feet,' said Tim.

'They're not on issue,' said Felicity.

'Ruddy criminal, then,' said Tim. 'Listen, can we sneak off to the Irvine cinema again on Saturday evening?'

'Well, I'm blessed,' said Felicity, 'don't you still not know ATS officers are out of bounds to you? I'm especially out of bounds in case I get reduced to the ranks.'

'Right, understood, ma'am,' said Tim, and went on his way.

Felicity frowned. She saw Sergeant Barbara Titmus approaching, some papers in her hand. The plump-fronted ATS sergeant stopped to speak to Tim. In a moment or two she was laughing. Felicity went back into the office she shared with Titmus, who appeared after five minutes, smiling all over.

'What's amusing you?' asked Felicity from her desk.

'Tim Adams,' said Sergeant Titmus.

'Corporal Adams?'

'Yes, what an entertaining bloke,' said Sergeant Titmus.

'You'd know about entertaining blokes, of course,' said Felicity.

'Is it my fault they creep up on me?' said Sergeant Titmus.

'It's your fault that you let them,' said Felicity.

'Well, they're going to fight a special kind of war,' said Sergeant Titmus, 'and a girl's got to show sympathy.'

'Sympathy's the least of it,' said Felicity.

'Still, Corporal Adams hasn't ever crept up on me,' said Sergeant Titmus, 'but he has asked me for a date. I'm going to the pictures with him next Saturday.'

'Congratulations,' said Felicity.

318

'He's—'

'Never mind the details, I'm busy,' said Felicity.

Colonel Dudley Lister, commanding officer at Troon, and his deputy, Colonel Foster, had two visitors from London the following day, two senior officers who were among the leaders of the Commando movement, a movement that had the full and enthusiastic backing of Churchill.

When they left, which was not until the next day, the colonels were in possession of every specific detail concerning the first raid to be made by 4 Commando. It was to take place as soon as possible, and the target was not the French coast but the German-occupied Lofoten Islands of Norway.

Major Lucas began his journey to his new unit early in the morning, Eloise at the wheel of the car, their kit stowed partly in the boot and the rest on the back seat.

'Instructions, please, sir?' said Eloise.

'Sheffield, Bradford, Carlisle, to begin with,' said Major Lucas, seated beside her.

'Carlisle? Carlisle?' Eloise was astonished. 'Isn't that close to the border of Scotland?'

'Quite correct, Sergeant Adams, and a good hundred and fifty miles,' said the Major.

'And it's only to begin with?' said Eloise.

'We've another seventy-odd miles to cover through Scotland,' said Major Lucas.

'We're going to finish up in Scotland?' said Eloise.

'Correct again, Sergeant Adams.'

'Well, I consider it very unfair, sir, that I haven't been told.'

'In some way,' said Major Lucas, 'you'll have to get to understand sergeants aren't told everything.'

'Well, I think I should have been told I'm to be hundreds of miles from my home,' said Eloise, starting the car.

'Do you wish to remain with the battery, after all?' he asked.

'I don't wish to have another unfair argument with you, sir,' she said.

'Unfair to you?' said Major Lucas.

'Yes, sir. Because of your rank, you always have the advantage.'

'A man in argument with you, Sergeant Adams, needs God on his side,' said Major Lucas. 'Get going. The time's coming up to 0-eight-hundred, and it'll take us six or seven hours to reach Carlisle, and we've probably got another three hours on top of that.'

'Sir, I've no idea of the route,' said Eloise, 'and there are no signposts.'

'I know the way,' said Major Lucas, 'and we'll share the driving. Off you go.'

He gave her instructions that took them onto the A38 and north to Sheffield. Then he asked her if she had enjoyed her leave. Eloise, always willing to talk, launched into a flow of words. She hadn't intended to tell him about Sir Richard Nott-Bailey, but somehow every detail of her journey from Leicester to London came out. Major Lucas listened like a man who, amused at first, found his sense of humour beginning to come under attack from an awakening sense of exasperation.

'There, what do you think of that, sir?' said Eloise, motoring steadily, the wartime traffic not at all heavy so far. 'Imagine my meeting such a cultured and intellectual gentleman who insisted I should share the return journey with him.'

'I go out of my way not to meet that kind,' growled Major Lucas. 'Most of them are damned pacifists who'd have handed this country over to Hitler and his Nazi culture if they'd had the power to.'

'Perhaps this one might,' said Eloise, 'for he proved to be a man of disgusting deceit. On the return journey, I was amazed to find out he wasn't a gentleman at all.' Driving through a village in which a newsagent's placard announced BENGHAZI CAPTURED, she described the horror of finding herself being kissed, fondled and offered money to become the dreadful man's mistress. 'Major Lucas, oh, the humiliation.'

'How much did he offer?'

'How much?' said Eloise.

'Yes, was it a miserly amount?' asked the Major.

'Do you mean to insult me?' demanded Eloise, out of the village and driving through winter's countryside. 'Wasn't I insulted enough by that deceitful beast?'

'Serve you right,' muttered Major Lucas.

'Sir, I didn't hear that. What was it?'

'Never mind. What happened next, Sergeant Adams?'

'I threw him out,' said Eloise.

'You kicked him off the train?'

'No, no, how could I do that? I am not a weight-lifter. I ordered him to leave, I told him I would pull the cord and stop the train otherwise. He left to find another compartment, but I am still burning at having been so humiliated.'

'I feel for you, Sergeant Adams, in your innocence,' said Major Lucas.

'Sir, I'm very suspicious of that remark,' said Eloise.

'I'm damned if I know exactly what to make of you,' he said.

'Then I cannot comment,' said Eloise huffily.

'And I take that with a pinch of salt,' he said.

'Sir, don't you realize how shocked and upset I am?' she asked.

'Are you? It doesn't show.'

'Am I to have no sympathy from you, Major Lucas?'

'You don't need any. Get a move on, the road's clear.'

Eloise compressed her lips, put her foot down and the car rushed on its way north, towards Carlisle and Scotland.

In Libya, General Wavell's army had broken out of Benghazi to head south in its conquest of Italian Libya. Mussolini's army, routed, was surrendering by the thousand. Hitler was arranging for General Rommel to have every assistance in the formation of the Afrika Korps. Germany's uncontradictable Fuehrer insisted that the Third Reich must rush to the aid of Mussolini.

*　　　*　　　*

322

In Carlisle, the rain was sheeting, the afternoon infamously wet and murky. Major Lucas, having decided to complete the journey tomorrow, found a hotel in which he and Eloise could stay the night.

'A double, sir?' enquired the reception clerk, who thought the attractive ATS sergeant was just what the rugged Army officer fancied for the night. Eloise, attacked by her own thoughts, stiffened.

'No, two singles,' said Major Lucas brusquely, and that was that.

Eloise escaped having to scream, kick and fight in defence of her honour. Indeed, over dinner together in the hotel restaurant later, Major Lucas was almost the gentleman in his civility and good humour, as well as not being in the least concerned that it was against the regulations for him to dine with an ATS sergeant. Further, because she was tired, he allowed her to retire early. His courtesy lapsed then, for he made no attempt to see her up to her room. A true gentleman would have done so and not left her to find her own way through the corridors and up the stairs of a strange hotel.

She felt huffy about that, and kicked a shoe off when she arrived in her room.

Anglicized though she was, Eloise Adams still had much of the temperament of her French mother.

It was noon when they arrived at their destination the following day, with Major Lucas at the wheel, and Eloise staggered to be informed it was Troon.

'I am amazed not to have been told,' she said.

'I did mention Scotland.'

323

'You didn't mention Troon, sir. Troon is most amazing, for it's where my brother Tim is stationed.'

'Call it a happy coincidence, and stop tearing your hair,' said Major Lucas, pulling up outside a building marking the beginning of Troon's promontory. There were a number of soldiers about.

'Tearing my hair?' said Eloise. 'Really, Major Lucas, no-one could fail to notice I'm too good-tempered to do a thing like that.' Major Lucas let that go, and Eloise studied grey heaving waters. 'It's the end of the earth,' she said.

'It's a Commando training theatre, full of wolves, as I think I told you,' said Major Lucas.

'Sir, you said nothing about Commandos, only about savages and man-eaters,' complained Eloise.

'Same thing, Sergeant Adams. Now, I have to see Colonel Foster, second-in-command. You have to report to the senior ATS officer here.'

'I am still amazed to find myself here, where my brother is,' said Eloise. 'Of course, I shall tell the ATS officer I'm reporting only as your driver and not as a clerk.'

'You won't be doing much driving,' said Major Lucas, but she was out of the car then. From the office window, Subaltern Jessop watched the Major emerge.

Eloise looked around. Incredibly, her glance took in a familiar figure.

'Tim!' Because she sometimes gave in to impulses instead of following orders, she rushed. Tim, coming up from the promontory, found himself wrapped in the arms of an ATS newcomer.

'Here, steady—'

'Tim!' For all her little foibles, Eloise loved her English family and showed it.

'Jesus Christ,' said Tim, 'this is you, Eloise?'

'Yes!' Happily, Eloise kissed him. Felicity, at her window, said to herself, 'God, what a rat, he's now got a thing about ATS sergeants.'

'What the hell are you doing here?' asked Tim. Commandos were coming up, all with their eyes on Eloise.

'We've been transferred, my battery commander and myself,' said Eloise, 'but I knew nothing about finishing up here until we arrived a few minutes ago. He's a terrible man, Major Lucas. Tim, see how well you look, so brown and healthy.'

'Who's the sergeant, Corp?' asked a man.

'Aye, who is the lassie?' asked a Scot.

'A new arrival,' said Tim, 'who happens to be my—'

'New? Up wi' the lassie,' yelled the Scot.

The next few moments were utterly dreadful for Eloise. A dozen hands took hold of her, hoisted her high and carried her horizontally around, her skirt riding up in rumpled folds. She shrieked. The Commandos sang.

'She'll be coming round the mountain when she comes,
She'll be coming round the mountain when she comes,
She'll be coming round the mountain, coming round the mountain,

325

Coming round the mountain when she
   comes.
She'll be wearing silk pyjamas when she
   comes,
She'll be wearing silk pyjamas when she
   comes,
She'll be wearing silk pyjamas, wearing silk
   pyjamas,
Wearing silk pyjamas when she comes . . .'

Eloise, shrieking her head off, saw Major Lucas,
watching from a door in the building.

'Major Lucas! Help me!'

Major Lucas's brief grin was equivalent to saying
'I told you so.' Then he disappeared. Oh, name of
a dog, what a beast. It was Tim who rescued her.

'Such disgusting men are Commandos?' she
said, furious.

'Well, we're all much the same, all pretty
disgusting,' said Tim. 'Can't be helped, all part of
the fight for survival. If you're joining admin. here,
you'll get used to blood and thunder. We bury dead
men almost every day.'

'Men die in training here?' gasped Eloise. 'No,
no, I don't believe it.'

'You'll get used to it,' said Tim.

'Never! Oh, that brutal beast, Major Lucas,
bringing me here to see men die. No wonder he was
so secretive about it. I'm going to—' Eloise
checked. She knew her half-brother. 'Are you
having a joke with me?'

'It helps, a joke or two,' said Tim.

'Oh, I forgive you,' said Eloise, 'it's the happiest

thing, seeing you, Tim.'

'Great to see you, Eloise, but I think you'd better go and report,' said Tim. 'Then I'll take you to the canteen for some eats. That door there for admin. Ask for Lieutenant Cary.'

A few minutes later, Lieutenant Cary, the earnest ATS officer, was telling Eloise that she'd never heard of her, had not been advised of her coming, didn't have a job for her and didn't know what to do with her. Eloise began to expostulate in her own kind of way, beginning, of course, with the fact that she was here as the assistant of Major Lucas.

Outside, the Commandos had disappeared. They were all in the canteen, except for Tim. Felicity was giving him a verbal hiding while he was waiting for Eloise.

'What a specimen, what a bloody traitor, what an unprincipled blighter you are, Corporal Adams. First Sergeant Titmus, now this new sergeant, are you carrying on with both?'

'The new sergeant's my sister,' said Tim.

'Your what?'

'My sister Eloise,' said Tim.

'How the devil did your sister get here?' asked Felicity.

'Got herself transferred, apparently,' said Tim.

'Oh, sorry I spoke out of turn about her,' said Felicity. 'But regarding Sergeant Titmus, you won't be taking her to the cinema on Saturday evening. She'll be on duty.'

'On duty?' said Tim. 'Who fixed that?'

'I did, you bloody rotter,' said Felicity.

'I can't think why I fancy you,' said Tim, 'you're

not much of a lady considering you were once captain of your school.'

'Listen, you blockhead,' said Felicity, 'you know as well as I do that up here in Troon there are no ladies. And no gentlemen, either. Up here in Troon no-one thinks of anything except how to win the war.'

'You sure?' said Tim. 'I mean, I often think of what you look like when you're just slipping out of your nightie. Would it be something like Venus?'

Felicity choked, but quickly recovered.

'Don't you know you're not permitted to think things like that about an ATS officer?' she said.

'Makes a nice change from thinking about Hitler, though,' said Tim. 'Now be a good girl and let me know sometime when we can meet at midnight in your billet. What won't you be wearing?'

'I'm going to report you, you pervert,' said Felicity, and went back inside to choke down hysteria. Corporal Adams. What a stinker, what a specimen, what a danger to a woman. He was getting very advanced ideas about her.

Eloise, out of Lieutenant Cary's office, bumped into Major Lucas. She informed him that the ATS officer knew nothing about her, had no work for her and hadn't arranged a billet for her. Major Lucas said Colonel Foster, deputy to a Colonel Lister, would see to it that a billet was provided, and give her work to do. Eloise asked what kind of work?

'Admin. work, office work,' said Major Lucas.

'I am to be given boring work that anyone could

do?' said Eloise. 'Sir, I wish to say that sometimes my worth is not appreciated.'

'Damn it, Sergeant Adams, stop behaving as if you're a counter assistant in an Oxford Street store and I'm your department supervisor. You're in the Army, there's a war on, and of course your worth is appreciated, as much by me as anybody. Why else d'you think you're here, where a special kind of war is being planned? You're here because I think you can make a contribution. You'll do any kind of work you're asked to, and without flouncing about as if I've set your petticoats on fire. Is that clear?'

'Yes, sir,' said Eloise. 'My petticoats, sir?'

'You know what I mean,' said Major Lucas. 'Or d'you want me to be blunter and say your khaki pants?'

'No, sir, I don't,' said Eloise. 'Thank you for believing in me. I shan't let you down.'

'Right,' said Major Lucas, 'now go and get something to eat, and afterwards a billet will be found for you.'

'Very good, sir,' said Eloise, and saluted and went in search of Tim.

Over the meal in the crowded canteen, men of aggressive health and strength kept coming up to let her know she needn't ever be alone at night. She responded to all such overtures in the haughty negative. On the other hand, she was delighted to be among the kind of men who, like Major Lucas, looked as if they knew how to fight Hitler's jack booted Nazis. Tim himself looked superbly fit and teak-brown.

Her teasing brother had become a man.

Chapter Twenty-Six

4 Commando teamed up with 3 Commando for the raid on the Lofoten Islands in early March. The purpose was to destroy the many factories producing huge quantities of cod and herring oils, which were used to make glycerine for Germany's explosives and to provide vitamins A and B for Hitler's armies. The combined groups were escorted into Norwegian waters by two cruisers and five destroyers. The men behind the creation of the Commandos were firmly backed by Winston Churchill in this first really significant venture, and the presence of the Royal Navy warships signified the extent of Churchill's support.

The going was hazardous for the landing craft, launched from cross-channel ferries once the force was well into Norwegian waters. The sea was rough and the unexpected brightness of early morning exposed them to the possibility of discovery and attack from the air. The first danger, however, came from an armed German trawler, which opened fire. One of the British destroyers promptly rushed to engage it and to put it out of action. From a landing craft, Tim and other Commandos watched the brief but successful action. On ploughed the craft of 3 Commando towards their objective, the harbour of Stamsund. From there they were spotted by Norwegian fishermen, and moments later fishing boats were hoisting the national flag in welcome, and in defiance of the German overlords. Minutes later, the Commandos were effecting a landing.

On went the landing craft of 4 Commando towards their own objective, Svolvaer, the capital of the Lofoten Islands. At Svolvaer's harbour, Tim, heart beating fast but his body almost perishing from the icy coldness of the morning, leapt with other men onto the jetty. They expected to be met with German fire but Svolvaer lay stark, bleak and apparently empty. Then Norwegians materialized to stare at the swarming Commandos, among whom were Major Lucas and Colonel Foster, acting under the command of Colonel Lister, a Commando to the core. Patriotic Norwegians immediately offered to help them locate units of the Gestapo, German barracks, oil installations and factories. Similar help was offered in Stamsund, and in Brettesnes, another objective.

The Commandos went to work. Norwegians joined forces with them and enthusiastically helped to hunt down collaborators known as Quislings after the puppet leader of German-occupied Norway. Tim was among the men who exchanged fire with personnel of the *Luftwaffe*, pinned them down and quickly made prisoners of them. Units of the German Army, totally unprepared for a raid, were at a base too far away for them to reach any of the affected ports in time to fight off the British. The few German soldiers who did show themselves, surrendered without resistance.

Up went oil installations, up went a great oil dump, and up went factories, blown to smithereens. Everything useful to the German war machine was destroyed, including shipping. The Royal Navy's warships stood off, waiting, watching and prowling, guarantors of a return passage home for an invading Army force that had quick work to do.

Tim lost all sense of being cold in the speed of the action. He was sweating long before destruction was complete. If there was relief among the Commandos that German Army units were absent, a number of them expressed regret that they hadn't had the chance to do some serious work on Hitler's jackbooted robots.

'Tell me another,' said Tim.

'Any road, your shout when we get back,' said Sergeant Watts.

Before the last of the Commandos left the islands, a young lieutenant used a post office to send a telegram.

YOU SAID IN YOUR LAST SPEECH GERMAN TROOPS WOULD MEET THE BRITISH TROOPS WHEREVER THEY LANDED STOP WHERE ARE YOUR TROOPS?

The addressee was Adolf Hitler, Berlin.

The men and women who had been left behind at Troon could only wait. Felicity waited, restless and fidgeting. Lieutenant Cary waited, but without fidgeting. She attended to her work in apparent calm. Eloise waited, walking up and down the promontory, khaki overcoat buttoned to the neck against the cold, and she did not know for whom she was worrying most, Tim or Major Lucas. Admin. and maintenance men waited, chain-smoking. Maggie Andrews waited and worried, and so did many of the other landladies of Troon.

Not until the first evening news was broadcast on the radio did an announcement come to the effect that a force of British Commandos had mounted a successful raid on the Lofoten Islands. Details included the fact that there were no fatal casualties, that two hundred and sixteen Germans had been taken prisoner, and that a large number of volunteer Norwegians were aboard the returning ships.

At Troon, the ATS personnel celebrated by taking one drink too many and getting squiffy. And some of the landladies baked cakes from wartime recipes.

Listening at home, Chinese Lady said to her husband, 'I just don't know what's got into that contraption lately, it's gone all cheerful again.'

'Well, to mark the occasion, Maisie, would you like a glass of port?' smiled Mr Finch.

'Yes, I would, Edwin, what a nice thought.'

'May I have one too?' asked Rachel, happy that daily physiotherapy was doing wonders for Benjamin's legs and that he was getting about on crutches.

'We'll all celebrate,' said Mr Finch.

4 Commando group returned to Troon, most of the men with extravagant ideas of spending the

next twenty-four hours in their beds, whether or not they could get their boots off. First, however, they assembled on the parade ground to await dismissal in the usual way. Colonel Lister addressed them and from the building, admin. personnel were at the windows watching. When dismissal came, the Commandos swarmed through the streets of the ancient port to their billets under the eyes of Scots of all ages.

'Ye're hame again, laddies,' called a woman.

'Aye, hame is here,' called another. Many inhabitants considered 4 Commando belonged to Troon and nowhere else.

Young women swooped in glad welcome of returning sweethearts.

In a while, Maggie Andrews opened her door to Tim.

'So there you are, McAdams, and bringing your boots back again into my hoose.'

'Only God knows how they've got here, Maggie.'

'Well, off wi' them when you're free of your visitor,' said Maggie. 'They'll need more than a wee bitty spit and polish, I'm thinking.'

'Did you say there's a visitor?' asked Tim.

'Och aye, she's in the parlour,' said Maggie.

Tim, looking forward to a bath and to letting a good night's kip take care of the flatness of reaction, went in. Felicity, who had made her way to his billet while the Commandos were awaiting dismissal, turned from the window.

'Hello,' she said, 'how long has the group been away?'

'Several days,' said Tim.

'Seemed like a fortnight,' said Felicity. 'Still, here you are. Glad to see you're still in one piece.'

'So are you,' said Tim, 'and I've always thought nature fitted you together very nicely.'

'Well, I'm happy about that,' said Felicity. 'I thought I'd drop in and congratulate you on a rattling good show, although I can't hang about. Lieutenant Cary's bound to have her gimlet eye on me, she being a dog in the manger.'

'Well, none of the men would want you sent to the bottom of the class,' said Tim. 'I certainly wouldn't. So don't hang about, then, slide off.'

'Wait a minute,' said Felicity, 'I can stay long enough to hear all the exciting details of the raid from one who was there. I hope it's going to make your funny sister proud of you.'

'I'm foggy about the details at the moment,' said Tim. 'Listen, how are your personal feelings coming along?'

'What personal feelings?' asked Felicity.

'Well, do you feel sort of rapturous that I've come back alive?'

'Steady, tiger, you're getting ideas again,' said Felicity.

'Still, you missed me a bit, didn't you?' said Tim. Felicity fidgeted. Tim knew the type. Jolly hockey sticks female, playful and larky, but not sure that her best bet for a future wouldn't be as a paid leader of a group in Prunella Stack's League of Health and Beauty. Someone ought to save her from that. She'd already got her full quota of health and beauty. 'Did you miss me?'

'Yes, of course, you and everyone else,' she said.

'Well, old soldier, I think I'll push off now.'

'See you Sunday?' suggested Tim.

'Where?' asked Felicity, crossing to the door.

'In your sweater,' said Tim.

She laughed then and turned.

'By the way, I hear you're going to be recommended for a commission,' she said.

'Is that a fact?' asked Tim.

'Colonel Foster mentioned the possibility to you a little while ago, didn't he?' said Felicity.

'In a casual kind of way,' said Tim.

'Well, I think you'll find Colonel Lister's going to confirm it in a definite kind of way,' said Felicity.

'With a commission, I could do some serious work on you, Subaltern Jessop,' said Tim. 'That reminds me, didn't you once say that if I were commissioned I could make an appointment to come up and see you in your billet for several hours?'

'Good grief,' said Felicity, standing with her back to the closed door, 'I don't know why you've been waiting for a commission. With your kind of nerve, what's been holding you back, even as a ten-a-penny corporal? Come up and see me Sunday afternoon. I'll be wearing a Betty Grable sweater.'

'I'll be cockeyed,' said Tim.

In the kitchen, Maggie clearly heard Officer Jessop's peal of laughter. She looked at Tim's boots, and the open box containing brushes and polish. She addressed the boots.

'I dinna think he'll be wanting you just yet,' she said.

*   *   *

Eloise spotted Major Lucas on his way to his billet, which was in one of Troon's very handsome houses. She herself was billeted in the same house as Sergeant Titmus, and was already the superior presence there. She intercepted the Major, who looked as challenging as ever. That was something that always struck a chord in her. She saluted. He stopped and returned the salute.

'Sir, welcome back,' she said.

Major Lucas, a man of action who was certain every officer and every man of the British Army needed to acquire a tenacious spirit of disciplined aggression in order to match the dedication and efficiency of the German Army, eyed Eloise with a slight smile.

'Everything going in your favour here, Sergeant Adams?' he said.

'Everything has been worrying,' said Eloise.

'Who's been upsetting you this time?' he asked.

'Upsetting me, sir?'

'Well, you seem to suffer from men who kiss you when you haven't asked them to, or carry you about like an effigy of Mademoiselle from Armentières,' he said. 'That's been happening fairly frequently, has it?'

'I wasn't referring to such things, sir, but to the worry of waiting.'

'Waiting for what?'

'Waiting to know about the raid and for the group to return,' said Eloise. 'We're all very glad there were no casualties, sir. Was it as dramatic as it sounded on the radio news?'

'Well, if you can call a large amount of seasickness dramatic, the answer's yes,' said Major Lucas. 'Otherwise, everything went to plan.' He thought, realistically, that the absence of German Army units had deprived the Commandos of the chance to undergo a necessary baptism of fire, shot and shell. 'Myself, I was there only with special permission, since I hadn't been here long enough to fully adapt myself to landing craft exercises. However, I came off the craft without falling flat on my face.'

'I'm sure you did, sir,' said Eloise, 'and I'd like to be allowed to say you aren't the sort of man to falter when in action, and that it's your kind who'll do most to help us beat Hitler and hang him.'

'You'd hang Hitler, would you, Sergeant Adams?' Major Lucas asked the question encouragingly.

'Well, sir, I'd like to be there when you hang him yourself,' said Eloise. 'I'm sure you'd make a far better job of it than any other officer I know.'

'You see me as a natural-born hangman, do you?'

'Only in respect of Hitler, sir.'

His mouth twitched. There she was, at her most beguiling, and damned if he didn't feel like carrying her off to his billet and proceeding from there. His feelings for this young woman of self-declared excellence weren't of a light kind.

'I've got the picture,' he said. 'Now, if you don't mind, I'm going to find a hot bath.'

'Sir, just one more thing,' said Eloise.

'What is it?'

'I wish to say I hope we shall see the war through together.'

'Are you sure you hope that?' he asked.

'If I may say so, Major Lucas, I'm sure we'll get along very well together from now on.'

'What are you talking about now, Sergeant Adams?'

'Well, sir,' she said, 'I'm sure that whatever brought us together at Ramsgate meant us to be a great help to each other all through our fight against the wickedness of Hitler and his Nazis. I've decided I like it here, and that I admire the Commandos.'

'Glad to hear it,' he said.

'Thank you, sir,' said Eloise. 'Sometimes you are almost as agreeable as my father, and I'm pleased to tell you so.'

Major Lucas did not receive that at all agreeably.

'If you don't stop throwing your exceptional father at me, Sergeant Adams, I'll begin to wish he'd never been born,' he said.

'Oh, no, sir, you would like him if you met him,' said Eloise.

'I doubt it,' said Major Lucas, and off he went, feeling he'd never make head nor tail of Sergeant Eloise Adams, which was an unusual state of mind in a man as aggressively sure of himself as he was. Of course, one could have said that while he didn't favour meek and mild women, neither did he favour the kind who made him feel he was being turned upside-down.

If he didn't get the better of Sergeant Adams one day, he'd lose the war.

'Good morning, Mr Adams,' said Miss Symonds on Thursday morning.

339

'Not a good one,' said Sammy.

'No. Those dreadful Germans, now look what they've done.'

The Germans had widened the scope of their air raids, making only nuisance attacks on London while they ranged over the industrial centres of Britain. They had just bombed Clydeside and Merseyside. Damage had been frightful, casualties heavy.

'Liverpool and Glasgow, eh?' said Sammy. 'Well, it's hurt a lot of people, Miss Symonds, it's hurt them considerable. But what profit is there in it for Hitler in the long run? I'll tell you, Miss Symonds, it's the kind of profit that in the end is goin' to turn into a bad debt. Bound to. Stands to reason. It's like business. Run a business that hits your rivals unfairly week after week, and one day your rivals are goin' to hit you back, and they're not goin' to play by the rules, either. What a daft shortsighted lot the Germans are, cheering Hitler, throwing flowers at him, loving him as their warlord, letting him kiss their kids, and not seeing what's goin' to be thrown at their own selves one day, the silly sods. It won't be flowers. Now, if you'll excuse me, I've got to get to Belsize Park to see a bloke about an empty orphanage that happens to be up for rent for the duration of the war.'

'A very good speech, Mr Adams. Your coat?' Miss Symonds took it from the stand and helped him into it. In doing so, she managed to effect a few caressing touches. Sammy blinked.

'I've got to ask, Miss Symonds,' he said, 'have you got designs on my physical framework? I know

340

there's a war on that's makin' people act very peculiar, but I happen to be married to Mrs Susie Adams and she's not in favour of anything I can't explain.'

'Why, Mr Adams, I'm not in the habit of acting peculiarly,' said Miss Symonds.

'Well, good, we've cleared that up, then,' said Sammy. 'I'm off now, and I'll be back this afternoon.'

'Quite so, Mr Adams,' said the handsome but odd Miss Symonds.

Sammy went home and picked up Susie. He took her with him to meet Mr Palmer, the agent, at the agreed rendezvous north of Belsize Park, the entrance to a huge three-storeyed mansion that had been converted into an orphanage. It was unoccupied and up for renting until the war was over. An inspection convinced Sammy and Susie that if the many dormitories could be divided into bedrooms it could house a large number of his machinists and their husbands.

It was a proposition that he'd have to discuss at length with Gertie and the girls, who would then have to talk to their husbands about it, those whose husbands weren't away serving with the Forces.

Susie told him to take his time, and meanwhile to find out if Adams Enterprises, as tenants, would be allowed to do a conversion job on the dormitories.

'You're a wise girl, Susie.'

'Yes, I know,' said Susie.

'I often feel I made the best move of my life when I married you,' said Sammy.

341

'Well, you did, Sammy, and you can believe that,' said Susie.

The following day, during a conversation about the orphanage with Bert and Gertie, Sammy found himself up against a no-go situation. Bert and Gertie said they appreciated his thoughtfulness on behalf of the workforce. Well, Bert said it was a bleedin' nice thought at heart, and Gertie said blimey, not half, which amounted to the same thing. But, said Bert, it'll turn into bedlam, all the women, including those with young kids and those who'd have husbands there as well, living together, I ask you, guv'nor, where's the privacy coming from? There'll be spitting and scratching after only a couple of days, he said. Their homes ain't much, said Gertie, but they're still their homes as long as they keep standing up, with backyards to hang out their Monday washing. That's right, said Bert, and at this here orphanage who's going to look after the young kids while their mums are at work? There's neighbours or grandmas that look after them at the moment, said Gertie.

'So yer see, Mister Sammy,' she said, 'Bert and me feel murder's goin' to be done if all the girls live under the same roof, like.'

'Got you, Gertie,' said Sammy, 'see what you mean.'

'Well, we give it a lot of thought, guv,' said Bert, 'but don't reckon it'll work.'

'I take your point, Bert,' said Sammy, 'we'll just have to hope Shoreditch can keep standing up to the bombing.' Pity the idea's fallen off a cliff, he thought, but it does occur to me that for once Boots has come up with a dud. That made him grin to himself. It wasn't often that the mental equipment of the family's Lord-I-Am seized up.

Susie, when told that evening, said she and Sammy, and Boots as well, ought to have realized that even though the air raids were giving them nightmares, as long as there were safe public shelters, the women of the East End would always cling to their own doorsteps.

'Just like our old friends and neighbours in Walworth, Susie?' said Sammy.

'Yes, just like them, Sammy love,' said Susie, thinking of her mum and dad still clinging to their own doorstep in that little close off Browning Street. Her dad was now a full-time ARP warden at three pounds a week, having lost his job with the firm's Southwark brewery. The brewery had been bombed flat. Sammy said he was going to use the site to build a three-storey block of commodious flats for workers after the war. Sammy wasn't a man with a little mind, thought Susie. Thinking in terms of the commodious was typical of him.

'By the way, Susie,' he said, 'these contracts we've got with the Army and the Air Force.'

'Yes?' said Susie.

'It's makin' us war profiteers,' said Sammy.

'Sammy, I told you ages ago I'm against war profiteers,' said Susie.

'Yes, I know,' said Sammy, 'so don't tell Chinese Lady. She's against them too.'

Chapter Twenty-Seven

The wedding of Polly and Boots took place at noon on Saturday, March 22, at Polly's parish church in Dulwich. By request of the bride and groom, it was a quiet wedding with only the closest relatives in attendance and no bridesmaids. On Boots's side, his mother and stepfather were there, along with Tommy, Vi, Sammy, Susie, Lizzy, Ned, Emma, Rosie, Tim and Eloise. Rosie, Tim and Eloise had all managed to get special leave for the wedding weekend.

There was just one favoured guest: Rachel.

Boots was in uniform, Polly in a classical dove-grey costume, and Sir Henry Simms had taken time off to give the bride away. The ceremony was orthodox, and Rachel smiled as she heard Polly promise to love, honour and obey her husband. It was spoken almost demurely, and Rachel knew what that meant. Polly would always be her own woman, however devoted she was to Boots.

Chinese Lady couldn't help thinking of Emily. Nor could Lizzy, who hoped her late sister-in-law wasn't turning in her grave. She'd always shown a little bit of the tigress whenever Polly was present. However, Ned, the best man, thought Boots and Polly so well suited to each other that marriage had been inevitable sometime or other after Emily had gone. Susie thought Polly looked almost too good to be true for a woman of forty-four. With her wit and her vivaciousness, she was going to be a delight to Boots, Susie was sure of that. Gentle Vi felt a surge of sentimental empathy with the bride and groom. Tommy and Sammy got rid of the last of their reservations and whispered to each other as Boots kissed his new wife.

'I can't help likin' her, y'know, Sammy.'

'Well, y'know, Tommy, Polly's been a help to the fam'ly business more than once.'

'And she'll make an entertaining sister-in-law.'

'Classy, Tommy, classy. Polly's got style.'

'I don't think Em'ly would really mind, Sammy.'

'Hope not, Tommy, hope not.'

Emma, Rosie and Eloise were all delighted with everything. Emma thought Polly a fascinating woman, Eloise regarded her as excitingly aristocratic and Rosie saw her as a lifelong friend and confidante, just as much as cousin Annabelle was. Rosie kept in regular touch with Annabelle. As for Tim, he had long decided that Polly would make a very acceptable stepmother. He wasn't to know that Polly, fighting to keep age at bay, didn't want to be thought of as anyone's stepmother, whatever the facts were.

The reception was held at the Simms' mansion in Dulwich Village. Boots and Polly, due to leave for Devon, stayed long enough to talk to everyone in turn, and to help themselves to a little snack from the wedding breakfast buffet, somewhat limited because of the wartime shortage of exotic foods that at some weddings excited gourmet guests more than the ceremony itself.

Rosie managed to get Boots to herself for a few moments.

'Good luck, Daddy old love, have a very happy new married life, and don't worry about me. I've solved some of the problems I was having with Matthew Chapman.'

'What did you do, then?' smiled Boots.

'Talked to him,' said Rosie.

'He's now fully aware you're not just another customer?' said Boots.

'You can be sure of that,' smiled Rosie.

'But there are still a few problems, poppet?'

'Yes, he hasn't come round yet to putting on a new hat,' said Rosie.

'And you want him to?' said Boots.

'Daddy old love, I think I want the man himself,' said Rosie, 'and I think I'm going to win.'

'Sure?' said Boots.

'Well, he's still stuck with his old-fashioned principles,' said Rosie, 'but he's taken me for a ride in his dogcart, and informed me his sister's going to marry the village policeman.'

'That's in your favour?' said Boots.

'Yes, I'll take her place in the dogcart whenever I've an off-duty Sunday,' said Rosie. 'A dogcart in Dorset is out of this world. Also, he can't escape the fact that he loves me.'

'He's told you so?'

'He doesn't have to,' said Rosie. 'I know.'

'How'd you know?'

346

'He can't look me in the eye,' said Rosie.

'I'll find an opportunity to call in at his garage one day,' said Boots. 'I'd like to meet the man who—'

'Papa?' Eloise edged in. 'Ah, how splendid you look, doesn't he, Rosie?'

'It isn't his looks that make him our favourite person, Eloise,' smiled Rosie, 'it's much much more than that.'

'Oh, he is very exceptional,' said Eloise, 'and much to be congratulated on marrying Lady Polly Simms.'

'Ducky, she isn't Lady Polly Simms,' said Rosie.

'No? But she looks as if she is,' said Eloise.

'I'm reminded to ask you about your cultured gentleman,' said Boots. 'I don't think I've been notified of developments.'

'Papa, there aren't any,' said Eloise. 'My first impressions deceived me. I found out he was a dreadfully boring man.'

'The ultimate crime,' said Rosie, and Polly arrived along with close relatives who wished to meet Boots's daughters.

The newly-weds were almost ready to leave ten minutes later. Lady Simms snatched a few words with Polly in her stepdaughter's bedroom.

'Well, my dear, no more gnashing of teeth, no more throwing of cushions and no more frustrations?' she said.

'Stepmama, if you think I'm going to have a dull and quiet life with Boots, you're mistaken,' said Polly. 'Ye gods, who wants to be his little woman? I'll fight that every inch of the way.'

'In any fight between you and Boots,' smiled Lady Simms, 'my money's on Boots.'

'It's the excitement that counts, not who wins,' said Polly, and she and Boots left soon after that, to motor down to a hotel in Salcombe. He was familiar with Salcombe, a pretty little resort in Devon, he and his family having spent summer holidays there. He had suggested Polly might like what the renowned Palace Hotel in Torquay could offer them. No, let's opt for Salcombe, where it will be lovely and quiet and we can walk the cliffs every day for a week, said Polly. I hope that won't tire me out, said Boots. Darling, I'll look after your health and strength, and take very good care of it, said Polly. After all, she said, I'm now married to it.

'Sammy,' said Susie, when they were on their way home, 'things are happening with Boots and his family.'

'It's already happened with Boots, he and Polly are legally churched now,' said Sammy.

'Yes, and then there's Tim,' said Susie.

'There's a chip off the old block, if you like,' said Sammy.

'Did you know he's got his eye on an ATS officer up in Scotland?' said Susie.

'I haven't been notified official,' said Sammy.

'Oh, I had a chat with him,' said Susie, 'and I think we can look out for interesting developments unless Tim gets sent overseas.'

'Which he might,' said Sammy. The war in the

Middle East was hotting up. General Rommel and his Afrika Korps had entered the fray. 'Still, keep me informed, Susie, I don't like being ignorant of interesting developments.'

'As for Eloise,' said Susie, 'from what she told me, it seems she's helping her commanding officer to run the Army in Scotland.'

'Poor bloke,' said Sammy. 'If I know Eloise, he's goin' to find himself surplus to requirements.'

'Eloise says he's a very aggressive man.' Susie smiled. 'Perhaps he'll turn round and bite her.'

'She'll bite him back,' said Sammy. 'She's an Adams now, and we all bite back.'

'Lastly, can you take a blow, Sammy?' said Susie. 'I think we're going to lose Rosie.'

'Here, steady,' said Sammy. 'I can take a blow but not under me belt when I'm drivin'. What d'you mean, lose her?'

'I think from what she told me this afternoon that she's going to finish up in Dorset with her hard-up garage proprietor.'

'Our Rosie?' Sammy's electricity nearly short-circuited. In his regard for the value of family togetherness, he had more of Chinese Lady in him than he realized. On top of that, Rosie was a particular favourite of his. He'd have stood with Rosie to fight demons. 'Our Rosie in Dorset?'

'It's not Timbuctoo,' said Susie.

'Good as,' said Sammy, 'and I'm against it. I'll have to think of something.'

'Sammy, don't you dare interfere,' said Susie.

'Interfere? Me?' Sammy sounded aggrieved. 'I'm not that kind of a bloke, Susie.'

'Yes you are, where the family's concerned,' said Susie.

'Now, Susie, is thinking of something the same as interfering?'

'The way your thinking runs, yes,' said Susie.

'I'll think of something else, then,' said Sammy.

'Heaven help Rosie's hard-up Dorset man,' said Susie.

The dawn broke in Devon and touched the curtained window of a hotel bedroom with faint light. Polly awoke, stretched in a dreamy and luxuriating way, and looked at the man beside her. He was deeply asleep, his breathing even, his dark brown hair untidy from its contact with the pillow.

'Hello, lover,' she whispered.

He hadn't failed her, he had given her all that she had expected and wanted, himself first and foremost. Everything else followed from that. How wonderful to be made to feel twenty-one again, with life and passion so resurgent.

She slipped quietly from the bed, and crossed to the window. She drew back the lace curtains, and there it was, the dawn-pearly sea, just visible.

This is my dawn. Ye gods, at forty-four my dawn has only just begun? She laughed to herself at the absurdity of it. What do I do now, make every remaining year last a decade or try to grow old gracefully?

'Polly?'

She turned and in her nightdress her slender body stirred. Boots, awake, was watching her. She moved until she was gazing down at him, noting the

350

lazy look of his impaired left eye.

'Hello, old sport, do you want to say something?' she asked.

'Yes, what happened last night?' asked Boots.

'Oh, nothing very much,' said Polly, 'just some long-delayed flashes of lightning.'

'Any sparks?' asked Boots.

'Several hundred,' said Polly. She didn't want to ask the standard question of a bride, but she did. 'How was I? Up to expectations?'

'Over and above,' said Boots, his smile that of a man entirely relaxed and with no complaints to make.

'And how do you feel about me as Mrs Robert Adams?'

'Well, if you'd like to get back into bed,' said Boots, 'I'll let you know.'

Polly laughed softly.

'I've got you at last, haven't I?' she said.

'You can look at it like that, if you want to,' said Boots, 'but as I see it, the best of the bargain is mine.'

Polly didn't think she needed to tell him she loved him. God alone knew how many times she'd told him so in the past. But the other side of the coin ought to be considered, so she said, 'Love me dearly, do you, old sport?'

'Dearly,' said Boots.

'I can believe that?' she said.

'I thought you did believe it,' said Boots.

'Oh, I do, darling, but my belief sometimes needs reassurance,' said Polly.

'Be reassured,' said Boots.

Mrs Robert Adams the Second slipped back into the bed.

On his return to Troon from his weekend leave, Tim found a note from Felicity awaiting him. He knew she'd gone on leave herself today, for a week, to her home in a South London suburb. The last time they'd enjoyed a get-together had been two Sundays ago, and although she was her usual playful and non-committal self, there'd been one or two moments when he felt she was actually on the verge of chucking her restraints overboard. She held on to them, however.

Accordingly, her note was a very welcome one in its contents.

Tim darling,

I didn't say so at the time, but I had a bad few days waiting for you to come back from the Lofoten raid. Silly me for refusing to acknowledge my feelings. So now I'm saying yes, I'd like it if you'd fall in love with me. In fact, I want you to, and I'll be spending my leave hoping that when I get back you'll tell me you have.

We're only young once, aren't we?

Love, Felicity.

Tim lamented the fact that he had to wait a week before being able to deliver a personal response to the note.

In London's West End, the Windmill Theatre, renowned for its saucy girls and saucy revue, was alive, kicking, and determined never to close throughout the war. Some theatres, damaged, were empty of shows and audiences. Others were doing their best to offer their escapist elements nightly to people willing to risk an air raid.

On Saturday evening, Felicity was at the theatre that was staging Ivor Novello's most popular musical, *The Dancing Years*. She was with an old school friend, now a Wren officer, and their escorts were two Admiralty-based Navy officers who, now that the interval had arrived, were striving at the crowded main bar to obtain drinks. Felicity had been talking to her friend, Pauline Clewes, about the show and its melodious music, so typical of Ivor Novello. She was on the sixth day of her leave, and would be returning on Monday. She was thinking now of Tim, and his gift for amusing repartee.

'What's that smile for?' asked Pauline.

'Oh, for one of the blokes,' said Felicity.

'What are they like up there?' asked Pauline.

'A ferocious bunch of bruisers, cowboys and desperadoes,' said Felicity, 'and God knows what they'll do to Hitler and his gang if they ever catch up with them.'

'Is yours a bruiser, a cowboy or a desperado?' asked Pauline.

'Oh, just a lovely bloke,' said Felicity.

'I thought you were going to stay clear of that kind,' said Pauline.

'I've done my best, believe me, in my wish to be a free spirit,' said Felicity, 'but if I'm not careful some sneaky female will pinch my bloke, and I know I'm dead against that.'

Their escorts arrived with the drinks then.

Afterwards, they returned to the auditorium for

the second half of the musical. Outside, the evening was relatively quiet.

It was when the show was over and the audience was streaming from the theatre that the air raid warning sirens sounded. In the darkness, people jostled and took startled note of the sirens.

'Public shelter or a dash home for you girls?' asked Pauline's escort, who had brought them to the West End in his car.

'A dash home,' said Felicity. She and her old school friend were near neighbours in Streatham.

'Right, a dash for the car first, then. Come on, Jerry's not here yet.'

In the darkness, made solid by the blackout, other people were feeling their hurried way towards public shelters or underground railway stations. Felicity and her companions made a blind run for the car. It was parked in Savoy Street. They reached it, piled in, and the car began its helter-skelter journey to Streatham. The German bombers arrived as it came racing out of Savoy Street into the Victoria Embankment to head for Westminster Bridge.

High explosives began to drop in inner and central London. The car raced on.

'Go, man, go!' exclaimed Pauline.

'Yes, don't hang about,' said Felicity.

Both young women were willing to run the gauntlet.

A bomb struck the road some way in front of them. The explosion produced a great roar of sound and a blinding sheet of flame. The fiends of hell took hold of the car, lifted it and smashed it down.

Felicity did not arrive back in Troon on Monday. Nor had she put in an appearance by Tuesday afternoon. Tim wondered if she had asked for an extension to her leave for some family reason. Happenings of a critical kind were becoming common to families. He enquired of Captain Cary, recently promoted to that rank. The answer was in the negative. Captain Cary informed him, in fact, that Lieutenant Jessop, also recently promoted, would be officially listed AWOL if she was not back by tomorrow.

'Don't be daft,' muttered Tim.

'Pardon?'

'I didn't say anything,' said Tim and went on to his billet.

Major Lucas called on him later. The Major, now in command of one of the Commando detachments, liked Tim and admired his qualities as a do-or-die NCO. He had spoken to Colonel Foster about a third stripe for Corporal Adams. Not necessary, said Colonel Foster, he's in line for a commission.

Maggie showed the visitor into the parlour, and called up to Tim, who came down.

'Hello, Major, something in the wind?'

'I think you've a relationship going with Lieutenant Jessop,' said Major Lucas, looking sober.

'On the quiet,' said Tim. Not so quiet, thought

Major Lucas. Most of the men close to Tim were aware of his feelings towards Felicity Jessop. 'Is she back, sir?'

'No, Tim, she isn't,' said Major Lucas. 'There's been a phone call to admin. from London. She was caught in an air raid on Saturday, and she's on sick leave until further notice. That, at least, is the official line for the time being. She has a fractured hip, broken ribs and eyes full of glass fragments.'

'Jesus Christ,' said Tim, his blood draining, 'does that mean what I think it does?'

'I've brought some Scotch,' said Major Lucas, and drew a half-bottle from his greatcoat pocket. 'Any glasses?'

Tim, floundering, hardly heard the question. Major Lucas found two glasses himself. He poured a generous measure of Scotch into each. He handed Tim one, and Tim took a needed gulp.

'Jesus Christ,' he said again, and drew breath. 'Is this whisky a way of telling me Felicity's been blinded?'

'Damned unfair on a young woman like her,' said Major Lucas.

'Unfair?' said Tim. 'Is that a real word right now? Wouldn't crucifying be more like it? Major, I'm shot to pieces.'

'You're not the only one, take my word for it,' said Major Lucas.

Tim gulped more whisky and fought the numbing assault of shock. Blinded? Felicity? God, war certainly wasn't a game, it was murderous. What could a woman like Felicity get out of life when the whole world had become invisible to her?

'Major, I've just had forty-eight hours leave to attend a family wedding. Can you arrange for me to have a few more days?'

'So that you can go down to St Thomas's Hospital and see her?' said Major Lucas. 'I could, but I don't think it would be a very good idea. Not at the moment. It's too soon, Tim. She's bound to be very ill, and not up to visitors. Wait a while, wait a couple of weeks or so. Then, if there's nothing on up here, I'll see you get a few days leave. Will you settle for that?'

'Is that the best advice you can give me?' asked Tim.

'I think so,' said Major Lucas, 'I think you'd be wise to settle for a waiting period.'

Tim finished his whisky and looked blankly at the empty glass.

'I suppose so,' he said, 'but I'm going to have a lousy time waiting.'

'Understood,' said Major Lucas, regarding this fine-looking young man and his undisguised sadness with the realization that his feelings for Felicity Jessop were far deeper than mere affection. The Major, very much a rugged character and a wholly practical man, could nevertheless identify with him. He had his own deep feelings for Tim's sister Eloise who, only a few days ago, had departed for an ATS officer cadets training unit near Carlisle. He frequently looked wincingly back to a day when she had made it clear to him she had no wish for a close relationship with him. 'Let's bite the bullet, Tim,' he said, and poured more Scotch for both of them.

Tim said nothing. He was thinking of his father and of the fact that for four years after the first battle of the Somme in 1916 he had been blind. Tim knew, along with the rest of the family, that his mother Emily had not hesitated to be wife, guide and godsend to his father during those afflicted years. His reflections pointed him to what he himself wanted to do, should do and would do. Felicity's note and its meaning couldn't be put aside.

In early April, Bobby Somers received the King's commission, along with other successful cadets. He survived the liquid celebrations and the following morning his head was fairly clear. It needed to be, because an officer in mufti arrived to talk to him, a Colonel Ross. The interview was private.

Bobby had leave due, beginning tomorrow, and Colonel Ross advised him that at the end of it he was required to report to a certain address in London and ask to see a Mr Small. Colonel Ross quoted the address.

'Memorize it, Lieutenant Somers, but mention it to no-one. Shall I repeat it?'

'No need, sir,' said Bobby, 'it's already memorized.'

'Good,' said Colonel Ross, a man of precision. 'You'll need to commit any amount of stuff to memory. Now, you've just been commissioned as a second lieutenant. If you come out of specialized training with top marks, you'll be promoted to captain. Not that you'll enter France as Captain Somers. Obviously you'll carry no evidence whatever of your real identity.'

That, of course, related to the purpose behind Colonel Ross's first meeting with Bobby and Helene in the late summer of 1940, to recruit them for the organization that had come into being with the wholehearted approval of Churchill. Special Operations Executive (SOE) was designed to encourage and help the growth of a movement termed 'French Resistance'. Colonel Ross was Churchill's man, a shadowy figure who slipped in and out of his role as a roving recruiting officer for the SOE, the active head of which was a Major Buckmaster.

'Can I ask about Helene Aarlberg, sir?' enquired Bobby, as much of a physical stalwart as his Uncle Tommy, and as mentally alert as his father. He also had a determination of a rugged and obdurate kind, and his French was close to being fluent.

Colonel Ross, who regarded him as first-class material, said, 'I've seen Mademoiselle Aarlberg. She's just completed her course with FANY, and she too will be going on leave tomorrow. It will mean you can go together to see Mr Small the day after your leave ends. In civvies, by the way, at three in the afternoon. Any questions?'

'Only to ask if there's anything else we need to know,' said Bobby.

'Nothing for the moment, except neither of you must talk about this to anyone. Anyone. That's understood?'

'Yes, sir,' said Bobby.

'If at any time during your training, you wish to change your mind about what it all means, you may do so,' said Colonel Ross. 'There'll be no hard feelings, and that goes for both of you. I hope, however, you'll stay with us, in which case I wish you and Mademoiselle Aarlberg good luck and safe hunting.'

'Thanks,' said Bobby, and Colonel Ross shook hands with him and departed. Later, Bobby phoned Helene.

'Bobby, why haven't you phoned me before, what have you been doing?' asked his young French lady.

'Getting commissioned as a second lieutenant,' said Bobby. 'I meant to ring you last night, but got caught up in a passing-out shindig.'

'Excuse me?' said Helene.

'A celebration party,' said Bobby.

'I forgive you, then,' said Helene. 'Oh, and I am myself now an approved FANY officer. Bobby, am I to meet you tomorrow? Colonel Ross came to see me yesterday, and he said—'

'Yes, I know,' said Bobby. 'Meet me at Charing Cross station about twelve, and we'll go home on leave from there.'

'Yes,' said Helene, 'but did you know that at the end of our leave we have to—'

'Yes, I know that too,' said Bobby.

'Must you be speaking before I have finished?' asked Helene.

'Yes, sometimes,' said Bobby.

'Bobby, the air raids are still bad, and I feel for the people,' said Helene. 'Ah, those Nazi Boches, ever since they dropped bombs on Warsaw they have been making war on women and children.

How I should like to lock Hitler in a small cellar with a live grenade. It would give him seconds of unbearable fear and panic before it blew him to pieces.'

'And I daresay some people would gladly feed the pieces to his own dogs,' said Bobby.

They talked soberly for a few more minutes before they hung up. Ahead of them was a new challenge, an entry into an organization that was secretive and dedicated, that would train them and, if they passed all tests, send them as agents into German-occupied France.

They would go together, as a pair, for it was certain one would not go without the other.

Chapter Twenty-Eight

Early April.

Tim had his special leave and called first on Felicity's parents in their neat suburban house. He introduced himself, and they said they had heard of him through Felicity. They confirmed, sadly, that two specialists had diagnosed Felicity's blindness as a regrettable permanency. She had been moved from St Thomas's to a hospital near Farnham in Surrey, where she would receive the kind of therapy and care that would help her adjust to her disability. At Tim's request, Mr Jessop gave him the address.

The following day he travelled down to Farnham, and managed to get a taxi outside the station. It took him to a converted mansion used as a convalescent hospital by the RAMC. The day was breezy but warm, white clouds running under the blue sky, and there were daffodils lifting their heads in the hospital grounds. In reception, he was given a cheerful welcome and a nursing sister herself took him along a corridor to the rear of the building. She led the way out onto a long paved terrace, and there in the sunshine were a number of patients resting in lengthy and cushioned cane chairs.

'This way, this way, corporal,' said the brisk sister,

and Tim followed her to the end of the terrace. He saw Felicity then, reclining. She was wearing a blue hospital dressing-gown, and there was a bandage around her eyes. 'Here we are, Felicity,' said the sister, 'I've brought you a visitor.'

'The Prime Minister?' said Felicity. 'Well, I've always wanted to meet him, of course.'

'Mr Churchill's a little busy today,' said the sister, 'so he's sent a corporal. Quite a nice-looking one, with very good manners. I'm sure you'll like him.' She smiled at Tim. 'Treat her gently,' she murmured, and left them alone.

'Hello, love,' said Tim.

Felicity sat upright.

'Tim? Oh, good grief,' she said, and made a little face. Tim pulled an unoccupied cane chair close and sat down on the edge of it. He reached, took hold of Felicity's hand and squeezed it. 'Thanks,' she said, 'but sorry I came a cropper. Should have known better than to be out late at night in London.'

'Bloody hard luck, Felicity,' he said, 'and I know that's putting it mildly.'

'Suffering cats,' said Felicity, 'don't talk like a banana. Say something that'll make me laugh.'

'Could you laugh?' asked Tim.

Felicity, face turned towards him, the bandage blanking out her eyes, said, 'Not much, to tell the truth. I'm wallowing in murk, and I don't care who knows it. But tell me a funny story.'

Her brittleness reminded Tim of that which Polly had often shown.

'Well,' he said, 'the new recruit looked a bit

uncomfortable when the brigadier stopped in front of him. "Aren't you happy, man?" snapped the brigadier, and the new recruit nervously said he was. "And what were you in civvy street?" asked the brigadier. "A bleedin' sight happier," said the recruit.'

'And that's funny?' said Felicity.

'It was in the Great War, according to my father,' said Tim. 'Anyway, damn good to see you, Felicity.'

'Is it?' she said. 'How do I look, then?'

'Same as usual, pretty sexy,' said Tim, and leaned and kissed her on her lips. 'How's that for starters?'

'Not bad,' said Felicity. 'You've got a man's smell, did you know that?'

'BO?' said Tim.

'No, pretty sexy,' she said, and a little sigh escaped. 'You're a good old scout, Tim, to come all this way to see me, but let's face it, I'm now one of the ruins Oliver Cromwell knocked about. Except that he calls himself Hermann Goering now, the rotten swine.'

'Don't let's get gutted,' said Tim. 'Let's think positive. What plans do you have?'

'Plans?'

'Yes.'

'Right now,' said Felicity, 'my one plan is how to stop walking into furniture.'

'That's the stuff,' said Tim. 'But you'd like to be close to 4 Commando, wouldn't you?'

'Have a heart,' said Felicity, 'that's all over. I'm going to have to learn blind knitting for the troops. What size socks would you like?'

Tim thought her great. She had to be suffering,

she had to be desperate about her blindness, but, apart from the brittle edges, she was doing herself proud. What a lovely warrior.

'Well, I daresay we could think about a bit of domestic knitting later on,' he said.

'Domestic knitting? I'm a bit in the dark,' said Felicity, and a little brittle laugh arrived. 'What's domestic knitting?'

'Oh, that's something a lot of married women do,' said Tim. 'I always thought I'd do my best, after the war, to get you married to me. I had in mind there'd be more of a future for us after the war, when we'd be more mature, and not so brash. But circumstances have changed my mind. We'll get married as soon as you've finished convalescing and can stop walking into furniture.'

'Married?' said Felicity. 'Tim, you're mad.'

'Well, I love you, and there's nothing mad about that,' said Tim. 'It's a plain fact. As soon as you're fit and know how to cope with the basics, I'll come down and take you back to Troon with me, to 4 Commando's base, and we'll live at Maggie's. I've spoken to her, and she can't wait to be a landlady and a godsend to both of us. My mother was a godsend to my father when he was blind. We'll have a quiet wedding before we go to Scotland. I'll be commissioned in a week or so, and have an officer's pay and allowances.'

Felicity said, 'For God's sake, have you thought all that through?'

'Yes, all of it,' said Tim, 'and I can't wait for some of it. Well, our bedtimes, for instance, and so on.'

'Tim, is this really what you want or are you simply terribly sorry for me?' she asked.

'I'm sorry you've lost your sight, bloody sorry, of course I am, but I've always been serious about you and me,' said Tim. 'You're the one who's been playing games. You can stop now.'

Felicity, who had spent many days trying to come to terms with what the savage hand of fate had done to her, felt every kind of emotion take hold of her. Among them was the bitterness of knowing Tim was here and that she could not see him, nor ever would again. There was also a giddy feeling at what he was offering. Marriage, care, their own kind of relationship, and a home in Troon under Maggie's roof, close to the Commandos. It amounted to a cherishable lifeline. She could turn it down, she could fight her blindness with the help of her parents, but what would she prefer? The selfish option, the one that might be a drag on Tim, when he had to give most of himself to the Army, to the war? But if 4 Commando remained in Troon he'd always be there, except for when the group made its raids. God, the temptation to be with him in Maggie's house was tearing at her.

'Will you let me think it over?' she asked.

'Fair enough,' said Tim, 'I'll give you five minutes.'

'But I'll need a day at least,' she said.

'You're not getting a day,' said Tim, 'just ten minutes at the most.'

Her smile was faint but visible.

'Still a tiger, are you, Tim?' she said. 'Well, I'm

going to call your bluff, I'm going to say yes, even if it's unfair on you.'

'Unfair? Not on your life,' said Tim. 'Best thing for both of us. Yes, ruddy good show, and it saves a lot more argumentative chat. We're young, of course, but fairly grown up. We'll make a go of it, war or no war.'

Felicity couldn't get further words out for a moment, then she said in an over-bright way, 'God knows how I'll do the ironing.' She made another little face. 'Tim, have you got a hankie?'

'Here we are,' said Tim, and put his handkerchief into her hand. She dabbed her nose. If there were any tears, the bandage hid them.

'Love you, Tim,' she said huskily.

'Seriously?' smiled Tim.

'You can say that again,' said Felicity.

Tim, settled in his mind now that she was going to let him and Maggie take care of her, decided that in a day or so he'd be calm enough to talk to the family about it.

Chapter Twenty-Nine

Sunday, April 7.

'You're taking your officer lady out again today?' said Matthew's sister, Maisie.

'Picking her up at two-thirty for an amble,' said Matt.

'Maybe she expects more from you than riding out in that old dogcart on Sundays,' said Maisie.

'I'm short of being able to give her more,' said Matt. They were out in the garden, Maisie in the chicken run, scattering feed.

'You'll be needing someone when I'm married in June,' said Maisie. 'Mind, Mrs Beale will come in and clean and tidy up for you.'

'You don't suppose, do you,' smiled Matt, 'that I could get Rosie to do it for me?'

'No harm in asking,' said Maisie.

'Asking her to do the housework?' said Matt.

'Asking her to marry you,' said Maisie. 'You can't hide your feelings, Matt, not from me.'

'Feelings for a woman aren't the same as what a man can do for her,' said Matt, 'and I can't do for Rosie what she's entitled to expect, give her a decent standard of living.'

'Nor is what a woman's entitled to expect the

same as what she might want,' said Maisie.

'And what's your idea of what Rosie might want?' asked Matt.

'The chance to make a go of it with you, you great lummox,' said Maisie. 'I don't know why you're hopping about, seeing this cottage is yours and we've hardly been living with one foot in a poorhouse. Of course, I know there's been my pension as well as your earnings, but all the same you'd be able to do better for a wife than dress her in rags from the village jumble sales. Do you want to lose Rosie?'

'A man can't lose a woman who doesn't belong to him,' said Matt.

'You mentioned she might be going overseas,' said Maisie. 'If she does, you'll lose your chance with her. But as a married woman, well, married Servicewomen can resign, can't they?'

'In wartime?' said Matt. 'I doubt it.'

'You'll live with a lot of regret if you let Rosie fade out of your life,' said Maisie, surrounded by pecking chickens.

The dogcart was bowling along the road from Bere Regis to Tolpuddle, Lieutenant Rosie Adams seated beside Matthew, the horse going at a frisky trot. The afternoon was surprisingly warm, and on either side of the road the hedgerows were green with rising sap, the undulating landscapes sunlit, long-standing farmhouses symbolic of solid permanency in a land whose capital had seen bombs turn ancient stone churches into rubble.

'Well, Rosie?' said Matt, hands light on the reins.

'Lovely,' said Rosie.

'This old nag and dogcart?' said Matt.

'Everything,' said Rosie.

'Except the war?' said Matt.

'Except that,' agreed Rosie, glancing at him. He wore cord trousers with a brown sweater over an open-necked shirt, an outfit Grandma Finch would have considered much too casual for a Sunday. Hatless, the breeze was tugging at his hair.

'Matt, you need a haircut,' she said.

He looked at her, his smile good-natured, and she thought what a friendly man he was. That was how he always seemed to look at life and people, in a friendly way. Boots had a similar approach, a whimsical one, except when speaking of Hitler and Nazi Germany. Then his steel showed, putting a hint of blue into his grey eyes. He had a very chilling idea of what was happening to Germany's Jews, as did other members of the Adams family. Information that had crept out of Germany to reach the ears of London's Jewish community had been passed on to them by Rachel Goodman, their old family friend.

'Haircut?' said Matt. 'I think you've mentioned that before.'

'You haven't done anything about it,' said Rosie, blue eyes shaded by her peaked cap, sunlight kissing her lips.

'Maisie's my barber,' said Matt. 'She's been a little busy since becoming engaged to Constable John Rawlings. But I'll ask her if she can find time to give me a trim.'

'Never mind, old thing,' said Rosie lightly, 'I like to see your hair blowing in the wind, I like being out with you in your horse and carriage. It's—'

A sudden noise interrupted her, the noise of a growling engine. She turned her head. A large lorry was charging up behind them. Peacetime Sundays saw very little heavy traffic in Dorset. Wartime Sundays saw the occasional monster.

The lorry's horn blared.

'I call that disturbing the peace,' said Matt, 'and what's the point? He can't pass here.' The road was too winding, and lacked width. The horn blared again. Matt let the horse trot on, although a touch on the reins made the nag move closer to the verge, and the nearside wheel of the dogcart brushed grass. Again the horn blared.

'He's in that kind of hurry on a Sunday?' said Rosie.

'Impatient idiots are idiots every day of the week,' said Matt.

The lorry's loud engine vibrations attacked their ears. Rosie turned her head again. The huge bonnet, glowering and menacing, loomed above the tail of the cart, and once more the horn blared.

'Matt, he'll ride over us,' breathed Rosie.

'Well, damn his thick head,' said Matt, and brought the horse and dogcart onto the verge, the nearside wheel only six inches from the ditch. The horse stopped, placid at all times. The lorry pulled out and thundered by, but in such a way-ward and reckless fashion that it mounted the opposite verge. Its rear offside wheel momentarily sagged inside the lip of the ditch. The driver had

371

his engine roaring as he trod on the accelerator, and the lorry lurched forward and slewed. It came to a stop at an angle, blocking the road, and the driver climbed out. Beneath his flat cap his beefy features were red, his scowl ill-tempered and aggressive. Large-boned, thickset and paunchy, he advanced on the dogcart. He looked up at Matt.

'What's the bleedin' idea, eh?' he asked, his red face mottled.

'I was thinking of asking you the same question,' said Matt.

'Don't come saucy with me, you ponce,' said Redface, 'I've 'ad six like you for breakfast.'

'Six?' said Matt, deceptively mild. 'I call that a mite greedy.'

Rosie liked that. The lorry driver didn't. His scowl turned ugly.

'You lippy sod, what the bleedin' 'ell you doing on the road, anyway, with that piece of match-wood?' he said. 'Gettin' in me way, forcin' me off the road and near ditchin' me, what's yer bloody game? I ain't come all the way from London to 'ave a ponce like you land me in no bloody ditch. Who bleedin' let you out of yer nursery with yer toy cart, yer grandma?'

'In case you haven't noticed,' said Matt, 'I've a lady up here with me. So do me a favour and watch your mouth.'

'Sod 'er,' said Redface, 'she's Army, and I hate the Army and the bleedin' war.'

'Have you had a liquid lunch in some pub?'

asked Matt, and Rosie thought how calm he was.

'Mind yer bloody business,' bawled Redface. His large fat hands gripped the side of the dogcart, and he actually attempted to shake the vehicle. 'Git down, you and yer khaki tart, so's I can shove this toy in the bleedin' ditch. Right?'

'If you insist,' said Matt. 'Stay there, Rosie.' He gave her the reins and climbed down, his lame leg no hindrance to his movements. Rosie, tense, wasn't sure whether to be alarmed or not. She opted to have faith in his self-control. The road was quiet, no other vehicle in sight. She watched as Matt faced up to burly belligerence. 'What was that you said about my lady friend?' he asked.

'Bit of all right, is she?' leered Redface, and Matt caught a whiff of his beer blown breath.

'I'll say this much, her manners are a sight better than yours, you fat fairy,' he said, and anticipating what that was going to provoke, he eluded it, a teeth-breaking blow from a bunched fist. He caught the man's wrist in an iron grip and squeezed. The pain of it brought forth a gasp from the astonished lorry driver. 'Now, before you attempt assault and battery,' said Matt, 'perhaps you'd like to know it's a serious offence to strike a police constable in any way.'

'Don't believe yer,' panted Redface. 'Leggo me wrist or I'll bleedin' do for yer.'

Matt applied more pressure, and Redface hollered.

'This lady will confirm the name, Constable John Rawlings,' said Matt, 'and I'll confirm the fact that being drunk in charge of a vehicle is another serious offence. Are you drunk?'

'Leggo, will yer?' bawled anguished Redface. Matt's left hand was like a band of steel, his right hand around the man's other arm. Rosie watched open-eyed and enthralled. The lorry driver was dancing in agony. He shouted at Matt. 'Leggo— you're breakin' me bleedin' wrist – oh, yer bugger!'

'I think you'd better come along to the police station in Tolpuddle,' said Matt, 'and the duty sergeant there will find out if you're drunk or not. But move your vehicle first, it's blocking the road.'

'Gawd 'elp yer if I don't break you in six bleedin' pieces in a minute,' gasped Redface.

'This lady, by the way, will bear witness to your behaviour,' said Matt, and Rosie was sure then that, like Boots, Matt had his own share of hidden steel. 'Now, move your lorry, and quick. Then I'll take you to Tolpuddle and the station.'

'Sod yer, I'll lay me own complaint,' growled Redface as Matt released him. He lurched back to his lorry, rubbing at his bruised, painful wrist. He clambered clumsily up into the cabin, cursing and swearing. He started the engine, Matt and Rosie watching. The lorry began to move, to straighten up and then it was away, the engine howling in protest at being ill-used.

'I don't think we'll see much more of him,' said Matt. 'Sorry about his manners, Rosie.'

'Fascinating,' said Rosie.

'His manners?' said Matt, looking up at her. He received a delighted smile, and wondered, not for the first time, what a man with uncertain prospects could do about being in love with such an entrancing woman. 'His manners, Rosie?'

'No, your mastery of the situation,' said Rosie. 'Well, I ask you, think about it. Fair maiden – me – about to be in distress and all that, fearful for her life, and suddenly King Arthur's in fantastic action, turning Sir Mordred Blackheart into a wet rag. Believe me, I thought you were going to wring him out and toss him over the hedge. Utterly thrilling, you lovely man.'

Matt laughed.

'Read me the next chapter,' he said.

'It hasn't been written yet,' said Rosie, adrenalin running high. Matt's way of dealing with an ugly bruiser had her pulses racing. A university graduate, a well-loved member of a family of extroverts, Rosie had seen many of life's different facets and known a number of its dramatic moments. Action in a crisis could exhilarate her. She felt charged with electricity now, much like Uncle Sammy in his inspired moments. 'Come up here,' she said, 'and we'll write it together.'

'Let me know how it should start,' said Matt, and climbed back into his seat. The horse was cropping grass. An Army car, passing at speed, was a relatively minor disturbance for a few seconds, and then the road was quiet again.

'Oh, the start is important, of course,' said Rosie.

'How important?' asked Matt.

'Well, would you like to propose to me?' asked Rosie.

'Come again?' said Matt, looking stunned.

'I'm sure you heard,' said Rosie.

'Hearing isn't always believing,' said Matt.

'Now's a very good time for believing,' said Rosie.

'Rosie—'

'I don't want you to find reasons why you can't,' said Rosie.

'I've got a hundred reasons,' said Matt.

'Well, rats to all of them,' said Rosie.

Matt came up for air, steadied himself and said, 'If you were married, would you still have to go overseas?'

'I'd ask for a discussion,' said Rosie.

'On staying instead of going?' said Matt.

'If I were married,' said Rosie, 'I'd want to be near my husband, not on a troopship, especially if my husband happened to be in love with me.'

'He'd be a dull old carrot-top if he weren't,' said Matt. 'Well, supposing—' He stopped. 'That is, if I could keep the garage going and if you—'

'Matt, stop coming up with ifs and buts, or I'll bite,' said Rosie. 'There's no need for any ifs and buts. Of course I'll marry you, if that's what you're trying to ask – heavens – now look what you've done, you've made me say "if". Oh, well, since we're a couple of "ifs" together, we should get married. I'm very much in favour of that myself. Are you, Matt?'

'Damn all, Rosie, if you aren't the most adorable woman God ever made,' said Matt.

'If that means you love me madly, some old troopship can definitely sail without me,' said Rosie.

Matt brought the dogcart to a stop. There were

other things to do then that had the edge over trotting. Rosie slid closer on the seat. Matt turned and she went into his arms, knowing she had at last found someone who meant as much to her as Boots, and in a way that was not only different but deliciously exciting.

In a little while, and in the uninterrupted quietness of the day, she said, 'Matt, look.' She drew back her skirt and slip. Around the tops of her regulation stockings were frilly pink garters.

'Well, I'll jump over the moon,' said Matt, delighted.

Rosie laughed, sharing his delight.

'I had an impulse and put them on for luck,' she said.

'What kind of luck?' smiled Matt.

'Why, you old carrot-top, the luck of being asked to be married, even if I did have to push you a little,' said Rosie, 'and I'll wear them on our wedding day. What d'you think, you dear man?'

'I think,' said Matt, 'I think I'm in luck too and that we'll win the war, you darling woman.'

'What a lovely thought,' said Rosie.

On the morning of April 10, the wireless set in Chinese Lady's kitchen gave forth the news the whole country and its sorely tried people had been hoping to hear.

The biter had been bitten, savagely.

The RAF had launched a massive air attack on Berlin during the night, inflicting heavy damage on the centre of the city and reducing Government buildings to ruins. Fires roared and flamed, the State Opera House spewing great tongues of yellow light. The New Palace at Potsdam was badly hit and other landmarks destroyed. Casualties were fearsome.

Goering was in disgrace, for in his bombastic way he had sworn that not one British bomber would ever reach Berlin.

'. . . a number of our aircraft failed to return,' concluded the BBC announcer.

Chinese Lady sighed. War not only brought death to people, it brought hatred into the lives of friend and foe alike. She herself had wanted the Germans to be given some of their own medicine, and in no uncertain fashion.

It was wicked what their bombs had done to towns and cities, and to people. Yes, and to families too. Her own family was scattered. It was true that Lizzy and Ned, Tommy and Vi, and Sammy and Susie were still close by, but Boots was away, and no-one knew just how much she missed her eldest son, always the one who held the family together in times of crisis. Emily, poor Emily, had gone, killed by the Germans. Chinese Lady sighed again, and thought of her new daughter-in-law, Polly. Polly was away as well, living with Boots in a cottage close to his headquarters.

Grandsons, granddaughters and great-grandchildren, they were all far from home too. Emma was the exception, along with little Paula, Sammy's youngest. Emma was happy just now, because her fiancé, Jonathan Hardy, was at last going to enjoy a long enough leave to enable them to marry. Against this, however, was the fact that Jonathan had confided to Lizzy and Ned the news that his unit was preparing to go overseas. He didn't want Emma to know this yet.

Lord, so many of the family were in the Forces along with Jonathan. Boots, Polly, Tim, Bobby, Rosie and Eloise, as well as Annabelle's husband Nick Harrison, Susie's brother Freddy and her brother-in-law, Horace Cooper. Where they would all end up, only the Lord knew.

Chinese Lady sighed once more and switched off the wireless that had told of the RAF's bombing raid on Berlin. As she did so, her husband came down to join her for breakfast. They had this large house to themselves again, for Rachel had moved to her new home, and Mr Goodman, discharged from hospital, was with her.

'Any good news, Maisie?' asked Mr Finch, and she looked at him, the man she had been married to for twenty years, a husband of kindness and understanding. He had secrets, she knew that, but she had never wanted to know about them. They were locked away, like forgotten memories, and she did not want to turn the key. Edwin was of all things a gentleman, and what lay in his past would never alter that. Nor would it alter the respect and affection she had for him. It was a wife's duty to honour her husband, not to judge him, just as it was a husband's duty to provide and protect. It was what God had ordered, and she would stand on that to her dying day.

'Sit down, love,' she said softly, and as he did so she lightly patted his shoulder.

'No good news, Maisie?' he asked.

'Oh, that old wireless,' she said, 'no, no good news, Edwin.'

THE END

THE CAMBERWELL RAID
by Mary Jane Staples

There was a double wedding planned in Walworth. Sally Brown was marrying Horace Cooper, and her brother, Freddy, was at last getting hitched to his childhood sweetheart, Cassie Ford. But the wedding wasn't the only thing being planned, for Ginger Carstairs and Dusty Miller were working out a bank robbery and, unbeknown to the inhabitants of Walworth and Denmark Hill, both Freddy Brown and the Adams family were to be deeply involved and put in considerable danger.

It took much ingenuity on Boots's part to come up with a scheme that would foil the plans of the raiders. And all this was happening at a time when Boots had other worries in his life, and when the unity of his own little family was being threatened.

Here again is the Adams family from *Down Lambeth Way, Our Emily, King of Camberwell, On Mother Brown's Doorstep, A Family Affair, Missing Person, Pride of Walworth* and *Echoes of Yesterday*.

0 552 14469 X

THE LAST SUMMER
by Mary Jane Staples

Job and Jemima Hardy weren't Londoners by birth. They had both lived in a Sussex village until lack of work had sent Job and the family to Walworth – to a house in Stead Street. They got it cheap because of the poltergeist but they were sensible folk and decided that eight shillings a week rent was a bargain and – well – if the floors and doors sometimes moved a bit, they could live with it. They settled quickly into London life – particularly Jonathan, the eldest. Jonathan got a job at Camberwell Green and it was there, in Lyons teashop, thet he met Emma Somers, neice of Boots Adams. Over a long and hazy summer – the summer of 1939 – the two young people met, always at lunchtime, and never allowing their friendship to progress too far.

Then, as the clouds of war gathered over Europe, Jonathan got his call-up papers. And the first alarms of conflict began to affect the Adams family in other ways. Boots, on the Officer's Reserve list, was called onto the staff of General Sir Henry Sims, and Polly Sims herself joined the Auxiliaries. Suddenly there was only a little time left for people to lead ordinary lives – and Jonathan Hardy and Emma Somers had to make decisions about their future.

Here again is the Adams family from *Down Lambeth Way, Our Emily, King of Camberwell, On Mother Brown's Doorstep, A Family Affair, Missing Person, Pride of Walworth, Echoes of Yesterday* and *The Camberwell Raid*.

0 552 14513 0

THE FAMILY AT WAR
by Mary Jane Staples

It was 1940, and many of the younger members of the Adams family were caught up in the war in France. Boots, now a Major and on the staff of General Sir Henry Simms, was one of the thousands of British troops trying to escape in the armada of little boats from Dunkirk. His son Tim and nephew Bobby were also struggling to reach the coast and safety, while Eloise was with the ATS awaiting the home-coming soldiers at Portsmouth with a comforting cup of tea and a ticket home. Boots and Tim both made it safely back, but of Bobby there was no sign, and the family all feared the worst.

In a farm some miles from Dunkirk, however, Bobby was alive but injured, and trapped by the advancing Germans. The farmer and his wife offered him refuge but Helene, the farmer's independent-minded daughter, was scathing about the retreating British army and gave the brave, joking young sergeant a hard time. Working in the fields, dodging the German soldiers, Bobby was desperately looking for a way to escape and Helene, despite her hostility, found herself increasingly anxious to help the Englishman to get back home.

Here again is the Adams family from *Down Lambeth Way, Our Emily, King of Camberwell, On Mother Brown's Doorstep, A Family Affair, Missing Person, Pride of Walworth, Echoes of Yesterday, The Camberwell Raid* and *The Last Summer.*

0 552 14554 8

A SELECTED LIST OF FINE NOVELS
AVAILABLE FROM CORGI BOOKS

THE PRICES SHOWN BELOW WERE CORRECT AT THE TIME OF GOING TO PRESS.
HOWEVER TRANSWORLD PUBLISHERS RESERVE THE RIGHT TO SHOW NEW
RETAIL PRICES ON COVERS WHICH MAY DIFFER FROM THOSE PREVIOUSLY
ADVERTISED IN THE TEXT OR ELSEWHERE.

14453 3	THE DARK ARCHES	*Aileen Armitage*	£5.99
14096 1	THE WILD SEED	*Iris Gower*	£5.99
14537 8	APPLE BLOSSOM TIME	*Kathryn Haig*	£5.99
14385 5	THE BELLS OF SCOTLAND ROAD	*Ruth Hamilton*	£5.99
14220 4	CAPEL BELLS	*Joan Hessayon*	£4.99
14333 2	SOME OLD LOVER'S GHOST	*Judith Lennox*	£5.99
13910 6	BLUEBIRDS	*Margaret Mayhew*	£5.99
14498 3	MORE INNOCENT TIMES	*Imogen Parker*	£5.99
10375 6	CSARDAS	*Diane Pearson*	£5.99
14125 9	CORONATION SUMMER	*Margaret Pemberton*	£5.99
14400 2	THE MOUNTAIN	*Elvi Rhodes*	£5.99
14549 1	CHOICES	*Susan Sallis*	£5.99
13951 3	SERGEANT JOE	*Mary Jane Staples*	£3.99
13845 2	RISING SUMMER	*Mary Jane Staples*	£3.99
13299 3	DOWN LAMBETH WAY	*Mary Jane Staples*	£5.99
13573 9	KING OF CAMBERWELL	*Mary Jane Staples*	£4.99
13444 9	OUR EMILY	*Mary Jane Staples*	£5.99
13856 8	THE PEARLY QUEEN	*Mary Jane Staples*	£3.99
13975 0	ON MOTHER BROWN'S DOORSTEP	*Mary Jane Staples*	£3.99
14106 2	THE TRAP	*Mary Jane Staples*	£4.99
14154 2	A FAMILY AFFAIR	*Mary Jane Staples*	£4.99
14230 1	MISSING PERSON	*Mary Jane Staples*	£4.99
14291 3	PRIDE OF WALWORTH	*Mary Jane Staples*	£4.99
14375 8	ECHOES OF YESTERDAY	*Mary Jane Staples*	£4.99
14418 5	THE YOUNG ONES	*Mary Jane Staples*	£4.99
14469 X	THE CAMBERWELL RAID	*Mary Jane Staples*	£4.99
14513 0	THE LAST SUMMER	*Mary Jane Staples*	£4.99
14548 3	THE GHOST OF WHITECHAPEL	*Mary Jane Staples*	£5.99
14554 8	THE FAMILY AT WAR	*Mary Jane Staples*	£5.99
14118 6	THE HUNGRY TIDE	*Valerie Wood*	£4.99

Transworld titles are available by post from:

Book Service By Post, PO Box 29, Douglas, Isle of Man, IM99 1BQ

Credit cards accepted. Please telephone 01624 675137
fax 01624 670923, Internet http://www.bookpost.co.uk
or e-mail: bookshop@enterprise.net for details

Free postage and packing in the UK. Overseas customers: allow £1 per
book (paperbacks) and £3 per book (hardbacks).